"L. Marie Wood continues to be a force in the world of horror with her unique writing style and her ability to spin a tale that will stay with you long after you have read the last sentence."

- Midwest Book Review

"[CALIGINY] IS CHOCK-FULL OF THE MOST DELIGHTFULLY DARK SHORTS I HAVE SEEN GATHERED IN ONE PLACE."

"Writing a short story that is both, full and entertaining is quite an art and one that L. Marie Wood has totally mastered. This collection is filled with story after story of dark delightful prose dredging up emotions that toggle between fright, disgust, humor and even erotic tension. The author has shown here that she can stretch her writing vocal chords to many different ranges with ease."

- Midwest Book Review

"[THE] STORIES ARE SO LYRICAL AND INTERESTINGLY STRUCTURED."

"[Caliginy] is an absolutely stunning collection."

- Creature Feature Tomb

"L. MARIE WOOD IS A WRITER WHO FEELS COMFORTABLE AND CONFIDENT WITH HER CRAFT."

"Her work gives one the feel of traditional storytelling with a touch of poignancy, believable settings, and a persistent sense of the uncanny. Her characters emerge from the written script, and you find yourself with a genuine enjoyable read."

- Paul Melniczek Author of Restless Shades,
Frightful October, and A Halloween Harvest

"L. MARIE [WOOD] IS A TOP-NOTCH WRITER!"

- Stephanie Simpson-Woods, Castle Dracula

"THIS IS AN AUTHOR WHO HAS FULLY GRASPED WHAT IT MEANS TO DISTURB HER READERS."

"She knows the fine balance of detail versus story making her pacing superb."

- Midwest Book Review

The Unholy Trinity

L. Marie Wood

Mocha Memoirs Press

Rock Hill, SC

Copyright Notice

Other L. Marie Wood titles

<u>The Realm Trilogy</u>

The Realm
Cacophony-The Realm, Book 2
Accursed-The Realm, Book 3

<u>Other Titles</u>

12 Hours

Mars, The Band Man, and Sara Sue

Crescendo

Telecommuting

The Black Hole

The Open Book

Tales of Time

The Promise Keeper

About Horror: The Study and Craft

Aknowledgements

Thank you, Sean, Bree, and Mike, for helping me find pockets of time to do this thing I love.

Thank you, Laura Fasching and MaryAnn David, for your keen eyes along this journey.

Thank you, readers, for travelling along this road with me.

Dedication

For SAW, BKW, and MDW – always.

Table of Contents

Foreword..1
Caliginy..3
A Bat Out of Hell...7
The House on the Corner..13
Flowers..17
The Message..18
The Dance..23
The Inn by the Cemetery..31
Q & A..48
A Nice, Sunny Day...52
Betrayal...54
The Salacity of Death...55
Dead and Gone..60
The Black Hole..62
What the Mirror Sees..86
Reflection..92
My House...93
The Woman in the Sepia Picture..97
The Interview..98
The Properties of Blood...107
One...111
The Keeper of Souls...113
Ole Hallows Eve...116
Section F..118
Dear Monique..120
The Awakening...131
Of Body and Blood...132
Moonlighting..134
Love Nest..137
Carrion..142
Baie Rouge..146
The Last Port...152
Room 3708...158
Island Girls...164
To Die A Fool..165
The Visitor...169

Table of Contents (cont'd.)

Phantasma..177
    Last Request..172
    Everything She Wants...180
    Nigh...183
    Blue Sally...186
    Verity..188
    One Night Stand..198
    The Shower..199
    Issue..200
    Things That Lovers Do..216
    Congratulations on your Wedding.....................218
    Malady..223
    Jezebel..225
    The Bathroom Door...226
    Office Visit...229
    Shadows...232
    The Coming...233
    Noon...236
    Patty...240
    The Blackout...254
    'Tis the Season..256
    Hell..257
    Idol..258
    Day By Day..260
    Another...262
    Maybe..263
    Old Friends..264
    The Gift..268
    Word of Mouth..269
    Cerulean Blue..271
    Bored..274
    Moonlight Kisses..275
    3rd floor window..276
    Voices...277
    Abstract..278
Anathema..**281**
    Green in Brown...284
    Skin...285
    Spinning...291

Table of Contents (cont'd.)

Inheritance..294
Worthington Court...298
Vices..302
The Color of the Day..305
In the Morning Light...306
Somewhere There's a Love Just For Me.........................307
Forever...309
The Experiment...311
Detour..312
The Proposition...316
Hidden...317
The Moment Between...318
By Prescription Only..319
Hindsight..322
Eternally Yours...323
Her...324
Sweet Tooth..325
Aftermath...326
The Joy of Gardening...327
A Moment in Time..328
The Morning After...329
Hangover..330
Peculiar..332
All in a Day's Work...333
A Glimpse...334
Soulmates...335
Afterword..336
About the Author..338
More from L. Marie Wood...339
About Mocha Memoirs Press.......................................342

Foreword

by Linda D. Addison

Some people think that writing a short story is easier than writing a novel. The fact is that it's not just a matter of how many words are written, it's about holding a reader's attention from the beginning to the end. L. Marie Wood has published novels, short stories, as well as other forms of the written word (screenplays, essays, poetry, etc.). This collection reveals the many ways that she can write short stories, and not just with one style/voice. I had to remind myself this was written by one author.

One incredibly skillful storyteller!

Well-written stories grab the reader from the very beginning, those first lines pull you in, no matter how long the tale. Wood's first line in these stories hooked me immediately, made me need to know more about what was going to happen next, whether they were 50 words, or pages long.

"The Wind", a poem, opens the collection, and sets the mood for the upcoming journey.

There is wind, dancing and blood!

As the title of the collection hints, there are monsters (human/supernatural), ghosts (friendly/loving/vicious/wrathful), vampires (sensual/familial), and other collectors of souls.

Some character motivations are bred from love (scorned/found/imagined), like the story "Love Nest", where intense jealousy has monstrous results. In "The Dance" a provocative dancer at a night club inspires desire in one who watches; the dangerous seduction and surrender that follows births a transformative kind of love.

The settings authentically varied from city to small town. Various facets of life are twisted by Wood until unexpected shadows leak out: church, funeral homes, day/night adventures, old/new houses, range of ages, racism and religion.

The story, "A Bat Out of Hell", begins with Carly excited that Trent invited her to an amusement park in the middle of the night, not for the phantom roller coaster, but for the ultimate romantic moment. Needless to say, romance isn't what they and others on the ride experience that night. Note to self: no riding roller coasters at midnight.

Some stories shift and slide reality, like "What the Mirror Sees", where Janice intends on spending a sick day home alone, watching television, but her plans break down when she sees something startling reflected in glass that ultimately changes her belief of the real world. My kind of trippy!

Wood expertly changes point of view, creating fascinating storylines. In "A Nice, Sunny Day" a woman drives home from work, enjoying the weather after a week of rain when she sees a creature in her car that quickly ends any joy and niceness the sunny day promised.

Outside of the usual fiction form, Wood has tales told as letters, interview Q&A,

answering machine messages. Some of her stories used dialect wonderfully transporting me to other cultures.

I took my time reading this collection because each piece left me with a different flavor of unsettling chills, from the very short flash fiction that created bold images to the longer stories that spanned generations.

Now it's your turn.

— Linda D. Addison, award-winning author, HWA Lifetime Achievement Award recipient and SFPA Grand Master.

Caliginy

Watch the wind blow

whirling 'round her ankles like a gypsy's patchwork skirt.

She spins so gaily

as though basking in the sun

even when night falls around her

and the moon hides out on the other side of the world

Watch the wind blow the hem of her skirt

as she spins in the dark

The blood from her wrists

coloring it black under the stars

- The Wind by elle wood

A Bat Out of Hell

"Tonight?" Carly couldn't hide the excitement in her voice. It wasn't the idea of going to an amusement park in the middle of the night—the County Fair had been in her town before. She used to go with her father. They would eat cotton candy and candy apples until her stomach felt queasy. They rode all the rides, even the Rotor which made her father's face turn a sickly green. They raced plastic horses powered by water shot precisely into a hole from the guns they held, tossed rings on top of bottles, dumped clowns into the drink. Her dad was pretty good at that game, the clown dunk. He always won her a stuffed animal. It was always just the two of them. Carly's sisters didn't enjoy the rides as much, didn't like the electric atmosphere of an amusement park and her mother never stepped foot into one. So they went together, the two daredevils in the family. They turned it into a game. Their summer jaunts became special missions, ones that only they knew about and only they could complete. Carly and her dad went to every Fair and amusement park within a fifty-mile radius each year until she was sixteen. Until her father died in a car accident on his way home from work. She hadn't been to a Fair or amusement park since then. The rides, the games the atmosphere had lost their luster.

But she was going that night. Trent had just told her about a Fair two counties over that had a phantom roller coaster, one that started off outside at the top of a huge drop. Then, it ducked inside a haunted house, hitting loops and splashing into water. Neat, but that wasn't what excited her. Trent was finally going to ask her to marry him! She could feel it in her bones! Trent was the kind of guy who did everything as a surprise. On their first date he had blindfolded her and taken her to dinner on City Island, bypassing the regular places that lined Rte. 59 and driving 45 minutes away. Flowers made their way to her office for no other reason than to brighten her day. Going to a Fair in the middle of the week was a surprise that seemed right up his alley. Carly was ready. After three years of dating, she was ready to ink the deal. Her mind drifted, fantasizing about a proposal on a Ferris Wheel, underneath the stars.

"This ride sounds awesome. I thought it might be a nice night out," Trent said, trying to coax Carly into going. He knew how she felt about amusement parks and Fairs, but that night would be different. He was going to ask her to marry him after they got off the roller coaster. He had it all planned. He would win her a stuffed animal at one of the games, plant the ring on the toy, and trick her into finding it. He wanted to make the night special, different than anything she had ever experienced. The news that a Fair was in town couldn't have come at a better time.

"So, what do you say?" Trent gave her his best puppy dog face, hoping it would work.

It did.

"Sure. Let's check it out."

The parking lot was full of cars with license plates from as far away as Maryland. Carly turned to look at Trent, trying to get a hint of what was to come. He was suppressing a smile; she could see that much. What she didn't know was whether the smile was because of what he was planning or from excitement.

The phantom coaster was off in the distance, the stairwell leading to the top visible over the trees. The frame, unpainted metal with a winding staircase, reminded Carly of a ride she and her father used to love. Every year they would drive to the amusement park up the turnpike, talking about the drop the ride possessed for the three hours it took them to get there. They would walk around the park, sampling the other rides until dark. Then they would get in line for the ride they had been waiting for, a monster coaster with dueling cars. A steep drop on either side led to one mammoth loop in the center. The car would stop at the top of the hill opposite where they started, the loop behind them. A red light was mounted at the top of the stairs. Carly could remember staring at that light, watching it, knowing that when it flashed, she would be in for a treat. The night wind would tousle her hair while she waited in her car at the top of the hill, waited for the red light to flicker. She could see the black tops of the trees from that height, could see the span of the park and the rolling hills behind it. The darkness of the night before her was impenetrable, save for that red light. She felt as if no one else was around. The heavy breathing, the whimpering, the pleas to be let off the ride around her fell on deaf ears. It was just her and the light – not even her father existed. The light was her beacon, her only connection to earth in those moments. The feeling of solitude was immense. And Carly liked it.

But it was always short lived. The red light would flicker and the ride would take off fast – faster than any other coaster in those days. The car would descend the hill at top speed, heading toward the loop backwards, sending people's frantic screams into the wind and lifting their stomachs into their throats. Carly screamed along with everyone else, but something was empty about it. She had the distinct feeling that she had left something up there at the top of the hill. Something that had been a part of her for a time.

Seeing the ride peeking out above the trees made her heart leap. She urged Trent on to find a space so that they could hurry up and go into the fair. She was sure she would find what had been missing up there, although she didn't say it. She wanted to see the red light flicker again.

Trent and Carly entered the Fair and zigzagged around people toward the coaster. She was a step ahead of Trent, her excitement taking over. Trent smiled as they hurried along, happy that his soon-to-be fiancé was loosening up.

The coaster was at the back of the park, a good distance away from the other rides. The attendants were dressed in black robes, adding to the mystique of the ride's name: A Bat Out Of Hell. Huge wings shot out of both sides of the building that housed the bulk of the ride. Red eyes that seemed to glow as though a fire raged behind them looked out at them from within a large replica bat head.

"Spooky," Trent said, looking over at Carly. She was grinning from ear to ear. She loved it! Horror movies, Halloween, anything scary, she ate it up. The ride was right up her alley.

"Let's get in line," Carly said and started walking toward the tall stairwell before she finished her sentence.

"There *is* no line," Trent said, picking up the pace to catch up to her. The line for the ride was almost nonexistent. There were six people waiting at the top of the stairwell and they were the only people around. No one milled around to look at the ride or to wait for friends and family to get off, no people from the last car stood around talking excitedly about the ride.

There was no one else out there.

A hooded attendant wordlessly ushered Carly and Trent toward the stairs, urging them up. Carly turned to Trent, shrugged her shoulders, and started up the stairs.

Once at the top, Carly and Trent caught their breath from the steep climb. Carly was fidgeting, eager to get in the car and ride. The people in front of them were acting the same way, excitement etched all over their faces. Trent was excited too; he just didn't feel completely right about the ride. He didn't know what it was. There was something just below the surface that seemed off. He didn't say anything, didn't want to bother Carly with it. She obviously didn't feel the same way he did, and he didn't want to ruin it for her. It was probably just pre-roller coaster jitters. He got those sometimes, especially when a coaster was his first ride of the day.

The car came out of nowhere from the darkness on their right. It was moving fast, like the bat out of hell it was named for. It stopped on a dime though, right in front of the platform. Carly sucked in her breath as she looked at the ride. Gargoyles headed each car, linked together with serpentine tales. Each seat was crested with a skull patterned from metal. The seat cushions were blood red and the shoulder harnesses were fashioned from chains with padding affixed to them. Scentless smoke emitted from the sides, another part of the illusion. It was better than she had ever imagined a ride could be. She and her father used to construct their dream roller coaster while waiting in the long lines customary to every good amusement park ride. Their coaster had a horror theme with ghosts painted along the sides and chains rattling somewhere off in the distance. If ever there was an embodiment of a dream, the Bat Out of Hell was it for her. She just wished her father were there to see it.

Trent had to admit, the car was cool. Roller coasters usually weren't his thing. He liked them all right, but there were other things at an amusement park that tickled his fancy. He was a fan of the Spider and the Battering Ram. He even liked the bungee cord drop better than coasters. But this one was different, had a distinct personality. He started to think the ride would be all right after all.

Carly turned to Trent and squeaked, "This is awesome!" before taking her seat. Trent laughed and got in after her. The chain harnesses lowered over their heads and they looked at each other one last time before the ride began. Carly's smile was brilliant. Trent thought to himself that it was all worth it, everything was, if he could see her smile at him that way.

Carly looked around for the red light. The feeling she had on the coaster with her father so many years before was back, and she knew the light had to be there somewhere. The night was silent. Even the chatter of the excited riders had ceased since stepping off the platform. Only the trudging feet of the hooded attendants could be heard as they locked this and checked that. Carly's heart was in her throat. She was excited and a little frightened – she hadn't been on a roller coaster, or a ride of any kind in years. But there was something else. Something else that frightened her. She couldn't put her finger on it in the beginning, but as they sat waiting for the ride to begin, as they waited on tracks suspended high in the air over the trees and houses below, it came to her. Carly was starting to fear the light. What she had wanted most she was becoming afraid of. The light was not a beacon anymore. It was something more, something evil. Her hands felt clammy in her lap.

The trudging feet stilled, leaving the night soundless. No leaves rustled in the wind, no voices muttered, the sounds of the Fair below them so quiet, she wondered if there had ever been any at all. It was though no one dared speak. Carly wanted to break the silence just because, but she couldn't come up with anything to say. She sat, staring ahead, in silence like everyone else.

And then the red light flickered.

The eyes of a skull on the outside of the building below flickered red. Panicked, Carly turned to her right and saw a hooded attendant standing on the access stairs. His face was partially exposed, revealing blistered skin, darkened by fire. The one visible eye socket was devoid of an eye. Instead, a black forked tongue licked out from the orifice, tasting the air and her fear upon it. Before she could scream, the coaster took off with a roar, pushing into the night with incalculable speed.

The drop was steep, as though they plummeted into hell itself. Carly couldn't catch her breath. Her stomach had dropped and her heart beat dangerously fast in her chest. She turned her head to see Trent, to connect with him. She was frightened, more scared than she had ever been, and she needed to touch Trent, to know that he was beside her.

Trent's head was turned away from her, lolling to the side at an odd angle. Carly forced her hand over to him, fighting against the pressure from the velocity of the coaster and touched him. The coaster hitched as they entered the haunted house and Trent's head bobbed in her direction, limp on his neck. His open eyes were lifeless. His mouth hung open, as if he had tried to scream at his end.

Carly's wild eyes scanned the front of the coaster to find the heads of the other riders at impossible angles. At least, the ones she could see. Some were perpendicular to their necks, others were pressed so tightly against the headrest, they had destroyed the skin and bone. All of them were dead.

A moan from behind her, made Carly wrench her eyes away from Trent, his head bouncing on his neck as though it was elastic. The man behind her had been cut across his face with a sharp object, his countenance nothing more than a mass of open, bloody wounds. One of his eyes laid on his cheek, the iris already smeared with blood.

The coaster rose into a loop like the one in the roller coaster in Carly's memory. It crested and fell… and crested and fell, and crested and fell, caught in a cycle of going up and coming down, going round and round.

The man behind Carly dislodged himself from the chain harness to reach out to her as her mouth opened into a soundless scream. With a bloody hand, he touched her hair, used it to pull himself closer to her. Carly recognized him by his good eye. It seemed to speak to her from his soul, showing her love and loss, and worse: excitement. She looked into her father's soul and saw glee. They were together once again on the coaster built from their dreams, the roller coaster from hell. And it was as it should be. It was just the two of them.

Carly's father's breath was thick with rot, the stench wafting to her nose in torrents. He spoke using damaged vocal cords, the sound produced more scratchy than tuned. Even as his discolored lips formed the words, Carly knew that she was dead. With a smile that ripped the paper-thin skin of his checks and jaw, her father asked,

"Enjoying the ride, baby?"

The House on the Corner

The house had always been there, standing on the corner of our street, its windows still adorned with the handmade drapes fussed over by a woman who had long since passed away. When I was little, it was the point where I had to turn my Big Wheel around and head back home. When I was nine, I rode my bicycle by it, cresting the hill on the property, perfecting my jump. When I was sixteen, I made sure I had passed the house before I roared off into the night in my new car. And now, at age thirty, I'm driving by it for what seems to be the last time.

My mother still lives in our house, the same one I grew up in, the same one I was born in. She had lived there for at least ten years before I came along, moving in just after she and my father were married. She remembered the woman who lived in the house on the corner well, often musing about her sitting in her rocking chair and looking out of the window while she knitted. I had memories of my own, though by the time I was old enough to know, she had been dead for six years.

"What's happening with the house on the corner?" I asked Mom when I came in. My interested was piqued, so much so that the back of my neck was hot. My subconscious had seen it again, but my conscious mind fought it back, not allowing the visage to form in my mind.

"Hello to you too, Charlie," Mom said as she lifted her head to kiss me on the cheek. I returned the kiss and waited a beat. I was too preoccupied with the house to indulge in pleasantries.

"Sorry Mom. So, do you know what's going on with it?" I took a can of soda out of the refrigerator and sat down at the table in the kitchen nook.

Mom sighed under her breath and sat down with me. I didn't know if the sigh was because I came in and didn't say hello first or because I insisted upon talking about the house. The question stuck in my mind long after I left and made my way up the street, long after I laid eyes on the house again.

"I don't know. I guess they're taking it away. Why do you care so much about that house anyway?"

"What do you mean? I'm just asking about it. The street will seem weird without it. It's always been there."

"Longer than we thought. I found out the house is more than one hundred years old."

"No way!"

"Yes," she said as she got up to get some coffee. Pouring it into her mug, she continued, "Alma's father built it. You wouldn't remember Alma, though, would you? You were just a little boy when she died."

I just nodded, keeping my face noncommittal. I only had one memory of Alma Vincent, one that I had never shared with anyone.

"They moved here from Maryland and bought the land. Apparently, her father built the house with the help of his brother and a small crew. He moved his wife in and soon they had a little girl. Alma. Her mother died in childbirth, and her father never remarried. Alma never married nor had any children. So, the house has been empty ever since she passed away." Mom stirred sugar into her coffee and shook her head. "She was a sweet old woman, at least when we moved in. She was the first one to come by and bring us a cake. They used to do that in the old days, come by and welcome new neighbors. Now people move in and out without ever knowing the people that live around them. It's a shame, how impersonal people are now."

"I know my neighbors." I said it just to keep the flow going. I figured that she'd have to get back to the house at some point.

"Sure, that's because they're all women. There's an ulterior motive there, I'm sure." My eyes urged her to continue through her chuckle. There was something uneasy in her face. I couldn't put my finger on what it was, but something had changed from when I had come in the house.

"Then Alma withdrew. She stayed in the house most of the day, only coming out to get her mail or to tend to her garden. What little visiting she did stopped. We never went to the house to see her, of course. She was much older than us. You know what I mean." I nodded, waiting. Mom fell silent then, seeming to drift away, caught in the swirl of the stirred coffee. "And then she died," she finished, her voice cutting through the silence suddenly.

"So, what are they going to do with the house now?" I tried to sound casual, unconcerned. But I wasn't. I needed to know.

"I don't know," Mom said as she sat down across from me, smoke rising from the coffee mug. "Demolish it, I guess."

"They don't have to take it anywhere to do that. They could bulldoze it where it stands."

"True. I don't know." She sipped her coffee loudly. "So, what have you been up to Charlie? How's that new girl you've been seeing?"

The rest of the conversation was muted. I participated, answering her questions as they came void of enthusiasm or conviction. I was too busy thinking about the house. Thinking about Alma.

I left my mother's house a half hour after having gotten there, begging out of the visit early. I drove up the street and pulled in front of Alma's house, just out of my mother's sight.

Alma's house was off the ground, sitting on the bed of a house mover truck, its big tires tattooing grooves in the Virginia clay. I got out of the car and stood before it, looking at the relic from my past, the thing that haunted my childhood dreams. What Mom didn't mention was that Alma's body was found in the house days after she died, sitting in her rocking chair facing the window. She had gouged out her eyes with her knitting needles. All the kids in the neighborhood talked about crazy old Alma and how she'd pluck your eyes out if you trespassed on her property for years after that. She was our very own ghost. It made our neighborhood popular in school.

No one really believed the stories they told, pieced together with slivers of truth over time. Like the one about the kid who went into the house and walked upstairs to Alma's bedroom. He was goofing around, looking for something cool to take out of the house to prove that he'd been inside. He was fiddling with a hairbrush on her dresser when the room fell cold. It was mid-summer and the heat was raging outside. When the boy entered the house, it was hot and stuffy, stale from stagnant air. But as he stood in front of the oval mirror attached to the dresser, it felt as if someone had turned on the air conditioning.

The boy's grip on the brush loosened and it fell to the floor. The sound of it hitting should have been muted by the carpet that covered the hardwood, but instead the brush crashed against it loudly, splintering into pieces. The boy turned to run out of the room, but found the door was blocked by a woman. She was staring at him from the doorway, her countenance more transparent than solid. A smile spread across her lips as she regarded the boy. She walked toward him, her feet never touching the ground, her footfalls not making any sound. The boy tried to back away but found himself pinned in place, unable to move a muscle. As the woman approached him, he could see that her eyes were missing, gone. Empty sockets stared back at him as she leaned forward, bringing her ghostly face closer to his. She reached a hand gnarled with arthritis toward him while her other hand remained behind her back. She caressed his face, the sensation of tiny pin pricks cascading beneath his skin.

With a voice that seemed to come from all around him, she said, "Such a pretty boy. I have a surprise for you. Do you want to see it?"

The boy could do nothing but whimper under the sightless gaze of the woman, his entire body in the grasp of some unseen force. Smiling grotesquely, her teeth long gone and her gums blackened by death itself, the woman brought her hand from behind her back. In it were knitting needles, their points filed and sharpened.

No one believed that story nor the countless others spun over the years about the house and the crazy old lady who had lived there long before they were born. Stories like that were made up all the time about eccentric people and abandoned houses. But I believed. I knew the stories were true because I was that boy who ventured into the crazy old lady's house.

I was the boy she touched from the dead.

Standing in front of the house, lifted off its foundation to be taken away, I could feel the tingle of her touch on my skin as I had every day since our first encounter. Taking a deep breath, I walked toward the house, red clay mussing my shoes as I went. I climbed the mammoth tire to take a look into the window of the house.

Alma sat in her rocking chair staring out at me with a smile on her face and knitting needles in her hands.

Flowers

"Why not?" Danny asked, picking up the flowers that adorned his Aunt's casket. "They'll just die anyway."

He tossed them in the trunk and got in. Tracey didn't.

"What?"

"We shouldn't take them," she said timidly. "They're Aunt Christine's flowers."

"She had a lot of flowers. She won't miss these, promise. C'mon."

Tracey reluctantly approached the car. Danny put the key in the ignition and turned… nothing. He turned again… nothing, not even a cough.

"What happened?" Tracey asked.

"The damned thing won't start." Danny felt anxious. "It worked fine all the way here," he said under his breath.

Tracey backed away. Danny took the flowers out and put them back on Aunt Christine's grave. He got back in and looked at the key in the ignition for a long time before turning it again.

The hum of the car's engine made his blood run cold.

The Message

Carrie looked at the answering machine in horror. The message being played was garbled, distorted. But the voice sounded familiar. Carrie's hand rested on her chest, her rapidly beating heart pounding against it. She was disturbed by the sound of the voice that spoke, the sheer terror in it. The woman seemed to be screaming, begging for someone to stop, calling out in the midst of static and road noise. Then the message stopped abruptly. The answering machine beeped. It was the last message on the tape.

Carrie replayed the message two more times, trying to decipher the voice, needing to know who had called. The message was so disturbing, she couldn't ignore it. It was even more frightening than the one left two nights before.

When she got the message two nights ago—a woman's voice muffled by the noise of cars and trucks on a busy street—Carrie had called her daughter who lived five hours away. Trisha worked in the city, so the background noise made sense. Trisha rarely called Carrie during work hours though, and never from a pay or cell phone outside of the office. She enjoyed her walk to and from the train with a cup of coffee and her ride with a good book. The commute was her downtime and she liked to enjoy it in silence. Even so, Carrie wondered if maybe Trisha had called to tell her about something at work. Something horrible, like maybe she was getting fired. Or maybe it was something else. Something about her and Mark. Maybe they were having problems or getting a divorce, even. Or maybe Trisha was calling to tell her that she was sick, deathly ill, feeling weak as she walked along the street to the train. Carrie's mind always leaned to the negative spectrum of possibilities when it came to Trisha, even in the face of positivity. She was almost always sure that something was going on, something terrible that she could fix if only she knew about it.

So, she checked in on her.

If Carrie called and Trisha didn't answer her office phone, she would call her cell phone. If she didn't answer that, she would call her home phone. If neither Trisha nor Mark answered that, Carrie would call Mark's office phone, then his cell phone if he didn't answer. God help her, if Mark didn't answer that, she would call Mark's mother's phone. Seeing as his mother lived closer to Trisha and Mark, Carrie was sure that she would know their whereabouts. Hell, they were probably with her, Carrie's mind often thought, wandering into the pool of her insecurity every time. She never thought that maybe Trisha hadn't answered her phone because she might have been in a meeting, or at lunch, or offsite. Instead, her mind jumped to the idea that something was wrong. Just what, she could never put her finger on. But something was wrong, all right. Very wrong.

Trisha had tried to talk to her mother about the calls. She told her she didn't need to be tracked down like a child. All of this went in one ear and out of the other. Carrie just let her rant, knowing already that it didn't matter how hard Trisha protested, she was still going to do it. Trisha didn't understand what it was like to be a mother. She didn't know how it felt to live so far from her only child. Carrie would do what she wanted to do, she decided. If she wanted to ask her daughter if she was all right when she sounded different than her usual bubbly self, then she would. If she wanted to know where her daughter was all the time, spot checking her by looking to see if she was on her Instant Messenger, or surprising her with a call during the workday, she would do that too. Trisha was her daughter and she cared about her very much. It was a mother's right to be sure that her child was ok, especially one that chose to live so far away. Most parents did that and more to their kids, at least that's what Carrie told herself after a scolding. The way Carrie saw it, Trisha had it easy.

She never stopped to think that maybe Trisha didn't sound like her usual bubbly self with her anymore because Carrie was aggravating her with her constant questioning.

Carrie took a deep breath and picked up the receiver. The voice on her answering machine sounded familiar, like one she had known forever. She had to check with Trisha to see if it was her, even though it hadn't been her two days ago, nor the times before that. In fact, in the six or so times that she had received cryptic messages, it hadn't been Trisha. Or so she said. Trisha had, at first, blown off the question, but was starting to get annoyed with it. It carried the same intonation that 'Are you okay?' did. It was a meddlesome, paranoid utterance that she was tired of answering. She knew how Trisha felt but, still, she had to call. She steeled herself against the verbal attack she expected from her daughter and dialed her number.

"Hello?" Trisha's voice was curt. She was in the middle of a project and would have let the answering machine pick up the call, but, having seen her mother's number appear on the caller ID, she answered it. Not answering it would have prompted a call to her cell phone. Answering that would have meant a question as to where she was. Answering that honestly, as she was prone to do (she was 32 years old, after all. Why should she feel the need to lie?), would start an argument, one that she didn't have the desire nor the time to entertain. So, she answered the phone, feeling the receiver burn in her hand as she raised it to her ear.

"Trisha?" Carrie started. She sounded strange. Carrie's mind began to fill with all sorts of things that could be wrong: an argument with Mark, getting laid off, etc. Her tongue itched with the possibilities.

"Yes, Mom."

"How are you?" She waited a beat. "Are you all right?"

The questions enraged Trisha. She was so tired of answering them on every single call. What in the world did her mother think was wrong, anyway? She thought, not for the first time, that she should make something up, concoct a rich story about some problem that she couldn't solve, get her mother's gander up. The fantasy was enticing, but she knew that all it would do would be to get her mother to take a trip out to her house to chase the made-up demon away. Trisha didn't want that. The thought of a visit given their interactions of late made Trisha tired.

"I'm fine," Trisha answered, the hint of sarcasm covering her words like a veil.

"It's just that you sound worn out."

"I'm busy. I'm working on a project."

"So late? Why would you be working so late?"

Here we go again, Trisha thought. *Twenty questions. If I want to fly to the moon and dance a jig at this hour or any other, that is my prerogative.* It wasn't that the questions were intrusive, even though they were. It was that the answers were stored for later, applied to some imaginary problem that her mother was sure was brewing in Trisha's life, to be brought out at a later date. Trisha sucked her teeth as she felt the familiar disdain for the situation growing within her.

"It's not that late for me. So, what's up?"

Carrie paused. There was something Trisha wasn't telling her. She could hear it in her voice. She decided to press her.

"Are you sure you're okay?"

Trisha lost her grip on her temper before she realized it. "Dear God, Mother, what do you think is wrong? How many times do I have to tell you that everything is fine in my life?"

"You don't have to get upset," Carrie said.

Jack, her longtime beau, had just walked into the room. He always seemed to catch Carrie when she was backpedaling out of something, he thought to himself, wondering if sometimes it was set up that way.

"Everything I do seems to upset you," Carrie finished.

"Oh God. I just don't understand what is up with you. Why do you keep asking me if there is something wrong?"

"You sound so detached."

"I sound busy. I've got a lot to do tonight." Trisha sighed, trying to regain her composure. *It's not worth it. It's not worth it,* her mind pushed the mantra through the red-hot anger, dissipating it slowly. "So, what's up?" Trisha said once she unclenched her teeth and loosened her jaw.

"I don't know. You are so unapproachable, I'm not sure—."

Trisha didn't hear the rest of her mother's sentence. She pulled the phone away from her ear, just far enough to miss the words, but close enough to hear the sound of her voice. Her mother's voice, a thing she used to love hearing. When she was a child, she loved to hear her mother sing. They would sing songs from her mother's youth—Trisha learned all the words to her favorites. Her mother had a beautiful alto voice that, if it had been trained, could have been a lead for a girl group. Trisha loved to join in with her squeaky soprano, as off key as she was. She still did. But of late, there was more yelling than singing going on between them. The loss of the connection made her want to cry. Or punch her fist through a wall.

"Mom, just—What is it that you called about? Surely you couldn't have been calling to ask me if I was okay again." Trisha's hand clenched and unclenched unconsciously as she waited for the response.

Carrie paused, trying to decide whether she was going to go through with asking her. Trisha was so upset, always seemed so upset when they talked, that Carrie didn't know if she should. She gritted her teeth and did it, though. Might as well, after all that had already transpired.

"Did you call me today and leave a message on the machine?"

"No."

"Not while you were at work?"

"No. Why?"

Carrie hesitated. Was Trisha lying?

"I got a message from someone. She sounded like she was screaming, asking someone to stop. It sounded like you."

"It wasn't me." *What is this, now?* Trisha wondered.

Her mother had called her a couple of days before with the same question, and a couple of days before that about the same thing. At first Trisha took her seriously, but then, she realized, the calls always came after she and her mother had some sort of run in. Two days before, they had argued over why she and Mark wanted to vacation by themselves. Before that, they argued about where Trisha had been for four hours during her workday. That night's call might be coming off their conversation about boundaries and how Trisha was a grown woman and deserved to be treated as such. Her mother hadn't liked that conversation, had lashed out. And then, mysteriously, she got another call.

"Delete it," Trisha said more harshly than she meant to.

"Okay…" Carrie stretched the word, giving Trisha time to come clean. "You're sure it wasn't you?" she asked finally.

"Yes, I'm sure! Why would I call you screaming? That would mean that something was wrong and I have already told you that nothing is wrong. What is the deal with you?"

"Okay, just forget it."

They were silent for a moment before Carrie asked, "So, what are you working on?"

The question itself wasn't an issue. Trisha just didn't feel like having a conversation with her mother anymore. And she was busy.

"Just something for work. Can I call you later in the week? I've really got to get this done."

Carrie whispered an almost inaudible, "Okay," her feelings hurt yet again. They hung up without an apology.

Jack sat in a chair behind Carrie, looking at her. He made it a practice not to comment on her calls with her daughter. Why get himself in a discussion he could never win? Winking and softening his face, he reached his arm toward her. She curled into it as she always did, but this time his warmth didn't make her emotions calm. She couldn't get the feeling that something was wrong out of her mind. As Jack rubbed her back with his massive hands, she cried.

Carrie received three more calls over the next week, each one more disturbing than the last. She braved the calls to Trisha to ask if it was her. She said it wasn't. Carrie wasn't so sure.

That Saturday Carrie went into town to get her hair done. Afterwards, she went to the mall to window shop. After about an hour, she decided to make her way home. A delivery truck drove in the lane next to the one in which she was walking, moving faster than it should have been. At midday, the mall was crowded and cars drove up and down the aisles looking for spaces to park. It was a sunny day, only about 80 degrees. Carrie inhaled deeply and breathed in the light air. The weather had been rainy and cloudy for so long, it felt nice to get a day that was almost humidity free and sunny. It would be a shame to waste it.

Carrie reached into her purse and took out her cell phone. Maybe she and Jack would go to the island and get some seafood. Yes, she decided that was exactly what they would do.

Carrie never heard the answering machine pick up. The sound of the truck barreling down on her, out of control because of its excessive speed, and her own screaming drowned out everything else.

The Dance

I stood in the doorway, watching her. I couldn't take my eyes off her body, the way she moved. Her hair danced in the middle of her back as she swayed. Her hips rolled rhythmically to the beat of the music. Her gyrations were slow and hypnotic, at one with the bass. Her breasts rose and fell delicately, almost still. I could look at her forever. She turned and saw me watching. Her lips parted in a sensual smile that confused me more than any of the feelings stirring within me. Did she like me looking at her? Did she, with her engaging eyes and coy smile, want me to blanket her body with my eyes? To stare at her as I had been? My own lips parted with the thought, glistening with the moistness flooding my mouth. My eyes trained on her until there was nothing else. Some part of me, some distant civility was embarrassed by my behavior, my staring, my disregard for the manners I had been taught as a child. That same part of me turned its back as warmth crept its way up from my stomach to my chest and then to my lips, lips that longed to feel hers against them. My God! I shook my head against my feelings, against her, but she stared back at me still, her gaze unwavering. Could she know what I was thinking?

Did she?

I didn't know what I was thinking. I didn't know much of anything except the sensual curve of her hips as they pressed against her dress. I didn't care to know anything else. With a smile that induced my tongue to flick out of my mouth and lick my pulsing lips, she broke her gaze with me and spun to the music. Her hair took flight and whirled about, seeming to float on the very air that whipped it. Her eyes were closed as she twirled, her mouth open in satisfaction. It seemed to me that the music had grown louder, sharper, the bass thumping into my soul now instead titillating my ears. I felt it. I felt her. As though she moved in my arms, grinding against me, pressing her bosom to mine, I felt her. A film of perspiration leapt onto my brow as I imagined touching her skin. I knew it wasn't real, even as I traced the round of her breast beneath my sweaty palm, almost feeling the warmth from her body on my fingertips. The nagging question was why. Why was I thinking this way? Why did she, this woman I did not know, rouse such feelings in me?

The woman stopped to face me once more, her hair settling on her shoulders. Wisps of light brown strands webbed her face, covering her eyes like a veil. She peered at me from between them, a knowing look standing in her eyes. She knew me, knew the thoughts that were ruling me at that instant, my turmoil. And she liked it.

She flipped her hair away from her face gently. Her copper skin looked like smooth cream in the dim light. I wanted to reach out and touch her hair, run my fingers through it. I wanted to run my hands down her spine, feel her moving against my skin as I had in the beautiful illusion that played in my head moments before.

I felt that increasingly familiar tingling sensation in my stomach as she resumed the dance. She had pulled a man from the wall, beckoning him with her eyes alone. He joined her, swaying to the music with her, pressing himself closer, deeper. My face and hands were hot and my breath was quick. I watched as they moved seamless to an old reggae song, the music pouring over them like warm water. As the beat slowed down to a pulse, she pressed her body closer still, rolling her hips from side to side, backwards and forwards. I began to sweat.

He held her by the small of her back as she bent backwards to touch the floor with her outstretched hand. Her breasts perked toward the sky and I could almost see the supple flesh. She looked at me as she shifted with her partner, turning around to rub her buttocks against his genitals. I nervously met her stare. Her beautiful oval eyes engulfed me, took me on a journey to a place I had never thought I'd go. And I didn't want to come back.

She began to touch herself as she danced, pulling her hair away from her face and rubbing the moist skin on her neck. Her hands found their way to her breasts and she provocatively traced the shape of them. I watched her playing. I wanted to play too. Her partner's arm tightened around her waist as the line of his jaw imprinted itself on his brown skin. She smiled at me conveying her pleasure as her partner enjoyed himself behind her. She turned towards him then, resuming the dance, and breaking eye contact with me. But still I watched.

I sighed heavily watching them tease each other on the dance floor. She didn't resume eye contact with me after that, preferring to dance with her partner for the rest of the song. My throat was unbelievably parched and my breathing was erratic. She had gotten to me. I shivered unconsciously, feeling the air on my damp skin as I hadn't before. I was coming out of her spell at last. I didn't know if that was good or bad.

I walked over to the bar and ordered a drink. With my back to the club and my eyes on the glass in front of me, I tried to forget the woman's face, her body, her eyes. I tried to forget the feelings that arose within me when I watched her move. I discounted them as the hallucinations of a drunk and an indication of when it was time to be cut off. I suppressed the fact that I had only had one drink, a mild one at that. I ignored it because I wasn't ready to face the truth. The woman had awakened feelings in me that I didn't know I had, didn't know I was capable of having. It was frightening. It was incredible, unbelievable; it was all of those things. But the emotion that bothered me most, the one that I couldn't seem to understand was how much I wanted it to be so. I wanted to look at her, to watch her body move. I wanted to touch her, to feel her, to taste her. My confusion was paralyzing.

As I swirled the swizzle stick in my glass I tried to push her out of my mind. The clank of the ice cubes hitting the sides became distant as she took over, commanding my thoughts. Her body moved seductively in my mind, swaying to and fro, calling to me. I had to see her one more time.

When I turned back to the dance floor they were gone. Another reggae song, this one with an even slower beat than the first, began and people filled the dance floor, capitalizing on the opportunity to feel their partner's bodies against their own. I scanned the room looking for her, wanting, needing to see her again. I saw the man she had been dancing with standing in the hallway talking to someone. I couldn't see the person he was with. Slumping, I resigned myself to the fact he was talking to her and that he was getting her phone number. But why did that bother me?

"Anything good mixed with that soda?"

I turned to see her standing next to me. At 5'7", I was more than two inches taller than her. Her head tilted a little to look at me. I liked that for some reason. Her hair was stuck to her damp forehead and she was slightly winded. She was breathtaking.

"Just plain old soda," I said, unsure of the timbre of my voice.

"Oh," she said as she watched the flush of blood rise in my face. She pretended not to see it, but I knew she had. A provocative smile curled the corners of her lips. I could almost taste the sweetness of it.

"Can I buy you something with a little more kick?" she asked, her body swaying to the hypnotic beat.

I smiled.

"No. This is all I can handle right now. But thank you."

She smiled again, her lips curling seductively. I envisioned my mouth on hers, kissing her passionately. The thought both frightened and intrigued me.

"Do you like reggae music?" she asked, catching me off guard. She dabbed her head with a paper towel looking at me all the while, waiting for me to respond.

"Yeah. Why do you ask?"

"Because I saw you looking at me while I danced."

I blushed. Was I that obvious? That part of me, the part that had admonished me before, laughed bitterly at my surprise.

"I like the way you move." I couldn't believe I said it.

"Thank you." Her words carried the faintest of accents on them. The sound was bewitching.

She looked at me knowing that I admired more than her dance steps. A man came over to order a beer from the bartender. To move out of his way, she stepped closer to me. I could feel the heat coming from her body as she pressed closer still, closer than I thought possible. I stood rigid, not knowing what to do.

"Would you like to dance with me?" she asked, her voice no more than a whisper.

I looked at her, amazed. Is she coming on to me?

"To reggae music? I think people would look at us a little strangely, don't you think?"

"Why? I'll teach you a few steps."

She was dangerously close.

"I don't know —."

"Well, if you don't want to —."

She started to walk away. I felt panic rising within me.

"I didn't say that. I just don't know about dancing… here." What was I doing? My mind reeled as the sound of my last sentence echoed in my head. It went against everything I thought I knew about myself. Everything I thought I was. But the truth of my feelings was undeniable. Had I said it aloud? Had I tossed out the past ten years of my life for naught with the utterance of that one simple question? Was I coming on to her?

She smiled at me and picked up a napkin. She took a pen from the bartender and wrote down her number.

"Give me a call when you want to dance with me."

She put the napkin in my hand and walked out to the dance floor, never casting me a backwards glance. The sway of her hips tantalized me as she walked away. I felt my stomach drop as though I had been on a roller coaster at the top of a hill and ridden down to the bottom. She was merging into the crowd, moving her body to the reggae beat that filled the room.

The bass was heavy; the throbbing seeped into my soul, thump, thump, thumping as did my loins. She rolled her hips, ticking top, right, back, left to the constant beat. The sensation was exquisite. She turned to look at me and parted her lips in a smile. Her rosy mouth, seductively wet, was drawing me close. I found myself wanting to kiss her again, to lick the moisture from her lips and drink it like the sweet nectar elixir it was. I breathed deeply and my hand fluttered up to my chest. I had never felt that way before.

My legs moved of their own volition, following her as she moved deeper and deeper into the crowd. The bass, the slow grind of the music, entranced me and I felt my hips swaying, rolling, gyrating to each beat. She faced me as I approached her, her eyes gliding up and down my body, watching me move. I felt self-conscious under her stare but I kept moving towards her anyway. I slid between couples on the dance floor, still standing apart from each other, one tempting the other with a twist of the hips, a shake in the shoulders. 'You can look but you can't touch', their eyes said; two strangers circling each other in a mating ritual. I saw them but didn't. They made up the clutter that was my peripheral vision. My eyes were honed in on her. And hers on me.

As the reggae beat moved me, covering ground I didn't feel beneath my feet, I navigated the dance floor to find myself standing right in front of her. Her lips were parted still, and I could see her white teeth below her upper lip. Her face and chest were dotted with perspiration; the ends of her hair were wet with it. The glistening line of her cleavage shined in the light of the strobe, the tops of her round breasts peeking through, pushed up by the under wire of her bra. I followed the scoop neck of her dress from the sides of her breasts and over the tops, fancying I could make out the nipple, slightly erect, beneath the material of her dress. My own nipples hardened at the thought. I took a deep breath to clear my mind.

We stood inches apart, our breath mingling, blowing wisps of hair from each other's faces. She tilted her head the slightest bit upward, toward mine. Her hair fell from her shoulders and cascaded down her back. I wanted to put my hand in it, to smooth it against her skin, to feel its silkiness between my fingers. Instead I stood still, unable to move, staring into her spellbinding eyes.

She said nothing as she moved closer to me. I backed away on contact, suddenly aware of my surroundings. 'People are staring at us', my mind screamed. My face flashed hot as I thought of them watching. What must we look like? Two women undressing each other with their eyes in the middle of the dance floor. I imagined them pointing and snickering at our public display of affection, certainly deemed gratuitous by the straight couples in the room. I would think as much if the shoe were on the other foot, I admitted to myself. Homosexuality still made me feel uneasy. Especially women. Even a casual touch, a knowing glance from one partner to another was enough to make me leave the room, remove myself from their presence. Was it that I felt threatened by the intensity of the relationship? No. I'd had my share of boyfriends and didn't long for companionship. Did I feel some sort of kinship with them? Did some longing awaken within me when I saw the affection in a lover's eyes for her girlfriend? No. No?

She moved closer to me, until our bodies touched through our clothes. Her hands rested on my hips as hers rolled to the beat, the slow grind growing salacious. She caressed the line of my hips, her hands patterning from waist to thigh, from outer to inner, as she danced. I soon forgot my concerns and fell into her control, moving my body against hers, and feeling pleasure in the contact. Her breasts rubbed against me, just underneath my own, her nipples as aroused as mine as they pressed against me. She smiled as she touched me, enjoying my reaction as the façade I had lived under all my life melted away under the touch of her hand. I danced with her, pressing my pelvis into her form. She touched her hands to mine and guided them over her body. She moved them over her hips, the tops of her thighs, up and down her ribcage, each time teasing me with a fleeting touch of her bosom. I was throbbing with desire, my heartbeat rising in my throat. She brought my hands around to her buttocks and pressed them there, spreading my fingers so that both of my index fingers danced along the edge of her cheeks before the round. I felt her move beneath my hands as she danced. I pressed myself closer still to her warmth, longing to taste her skin.

After a while of this, my revelation and satisfaction, she had me raise my face from the divine nook formed by her shoulder and neck where I had taken residence, and regard her. She looked at me then with eyes that were the most endearing brown I had ever seen. The smile that played on her lips was amative, so seductive I almost couldn't look. But I wanted to. More than anything, I wanted to kiss her lips, to give her what she seemed to be asking for, begging for. The realization floored me, but I set it aside. This woman had turned me on.

The music, the smell of her sweat, the heat of her breath captivated me. I no longer felt the prying eyes staring at me, no longer heard the chattering voices around me. It was just she and I standing there, on the brink of coition, moving to the rhythm of the music. It was intoxicating.

Her hands had found their way to my breasts and were kneading my nipples gently. I closed my eyes, surrendering myself to the feeling as she circled my areolas, her hands masterful at manipulating my flesh. A moan escaped my lips as she caressed me so intensely I thought I could feel her fingers against my skin instead of through my shirt. My head tilted back in ecstasy.

I felt her hands on my neck pulling me toward her gently, and at the same time, I could feel her pushing herself closer to me. Her lips grazed my neck and sent shivers down my spine. My sex pulsed against my underwear as her tongue licked the hollow of my neck. My mouth opened, slack from excitement. I leaned into her, wanting more. She kissed my neck, sucked it, licked it, devoured it as though consuming a delicacy. I stood allowing her to do as she would, willing to experience anything she wanted me to. The throbbing in my sex became rapid long before she placed her finger upon it, urging it out, making it crave her. I was delirious with want for her.

She spoke in the softest of voices at the base of my neck, her voice so quiet, I didn't hear her words.

"What did you say?" I breathed airily, inebriated by her touch.

"I asked if you remembered my name. Do you?"

My mind grasped for an image of the napkin upon which she had written her name and number. In the fog of arousal, I couldn't remember the letters, whether they were cursive or printed, or the color of the ink. All I could see was her. All I could feel was her touch.

"Do you?" she asked again, more insistently this time, her mouth hovering over my neck as she spoke.

I squinted my closed eyelids, bidding my mind to clear itself, if only for a moment. To think for fear that she would take this feeling away from me if I couldn't answer her. My mind swirled, frenzied. And then it came to me. I saw the napkin she had given me as clear as if I were holding it in my hand then. In flowery, calligraphic handwriting she had written the name Vanessa.

The name tasted sweet on my lips, like a sip of fruity wine. I opened my mouth to say it, to mouth the syllables of the name belonging to the woman whose touch made me a different person when I felt her lips upon my skin again.

"Van—," I started. Before I could finish, I felt something sharp pierce my neck. My eyes flew open as I gasped. My hands reached out for Vanessa and found her shoulder, taut now as she held me in place. Muted shrieks emanated from me, like the dying cries of an animal in the wild. My neck was hot. My hands grew cold. I could hear my blood rushing in my ears as she sucked noisily, wildly on my life's blood. My eyes fell upon the people around me, my subconscious beckoning me to look. The men and woman who, only minutes before, were dancing to the music, sipping their drinks, and talking, were now staring at us, their faces beastly in their vampiric state. Some of them laughed, saliva dripping generously from their fangs. Others stared proudly, watching the display with nobility. All of them had a frighteningly greedy edge; it was a look in the eye for some, a gaping maw for others. All of them were hungry. All of them wanted to feed.

Vanessa drank her fill of me and pushed me away when she was done. Her rich laughter filled the air, the sound reverberating in my head. I looked at her, at the blood—my blood—that coated the front of her dress as well as the exposed skin above the scooped neck. Even then, her bloody fangs protruding over her bottom lip, her yellow cat's eyes glowing in the dim light, she was gorgeous.

As if in slow motion, I raised my hand to my neck. My fingers touched the puncture wounds tentatively; I cringed from the touch. My vision clouded over as I stood among the undead, before the woman who would be the one to take my mortal life. My legs weakened and I sank to the floor, hitting it with a dull thud. I sat looking up at her, at Vanessa. Tears blurred my vision of her as I faltered, what was left of my blood flowing out of my wound and down my shirt. I saw her walk toward me as I laid my head on the dance floor. She knelt before me and brushed my sweaty hair out of my face, smoothing it with her delicate fingers. Her eyes held a profound sadness as she watched me die. The warmth of her hand burned my face as she touched me, growing hotter and hotter against my chilled skin. She entered my open mouth with a probing finger, aggravating it, inducing me to swallow. Once done, she removed her hand and closed my mouth gently, caressing my chin as a lover would. Again, Vanessa spoke, her voice tender and sweet,

"Do you love me, Gillian?"

With my last breath, I moaned. I died with the face of Vanessa in my eyes and the smell of my blood wafting from her lips.

I blinked my drying eyes and swallowed with my parched mouth. Pushing my torso up with my arms, using muscles that felt invigorated and strong in a way they had never felt before, I raised myself from the floor and stood. Vanessa stood with me, her face concupiscent and alight. I looked at the faces of my family then and saw respect and rivalry toiling within them, just beneath their fragile skin, as I stood in front of their one true love. With hubristic poise unknown to me before my mortal death, I smiled and said,

"Yes, I do."

The Inn by the Cemetery

1

"What do you think it is?" Sharon asked, her eyes squinting at the indiscernible snake-like thing covered in the red Virginia clay that passed for dirt in that part of town. Its sections coiled beneath the caked soil, stilled seemingly from the sheer weight of the reddish-brown clumps that buried it.

"I don't know," Mitch said, his voice airy, almost a whisper.

The thing looked like it could be a piece of jewelry, yet it was different from anything he had ever seen. His wife was a fan of bracelets and necklaces, rings and earrings. Almost anything gold caught her eye, and if it contained a diamond, she was enamored with it. He couldn't care less about jewelry, at least for himself. He wore his wedding band and his wedding band alone. That was enough jewelry for him. Still, he indulged his wife as best he could, buying her a piece every now and then because she liked it. And if it made her happy, he was happy. The problem was that now had become then and the gifts were becoming few and far between. Sharon never complained. She just window-shopped silently, adding things to her mental wish list.

But that thing, the piece laying beneath the clumps of dirt and grass, was suddenly more stunning to him than anything he had ever laid eyes on before. He realized he was as enthralled with it as Sharon seemed to be. Maybe more. The grit covering it couldn't conceal its beauty. It was a gold bracelet adorned with garnets. Its construction was early, maybe early1800s antique. The detail was meticulous; someone took care in crafting the perfect setting for the pure stones, making sure each sat nicely in the gold and would hug the delicate wrist of the woman who wore it. The bezel cut garnets were arranged in the shape of roses. They sat in a base of vermeil, each rose connected to the next by a sliver of gold. He could see the bracelet as though it were clean, its stones gleaming under the chandelier's light. It was exquisite.

Mitch's mind filled with the aura of the bracelet, setting the scene of a grand ballroom with men dressed in tails and women dressed in their finest gowns, their bodies accentuated with corsets and bustles covered with stripped cut velvet. He heard laughter and the sound of music in the background. Sharon reached down to touch the undecipherable thing on the ground. Mitch saw her just as she was about to pick it up. The daydream of times past dissolved as he watched her lean closer to the dirt-covered bracelet.

"Don't touch it!" he said a little louder than he meant to. "It could be anything."

"Like what?" Sharon asked as she knelt down, leaning closer to the coiled thing on the ground. "It looks like a bracelet," she said, her voice rising in the excitement of the find. She got even closer to it, getting down on all fours. "Mitch, you gotta see this. It's beautiful! It's a bracelet with some sort of red stone…"

Sharon kept talking but her voice sounded further and further away. Mitch's mind drifted back in time to a place where he was dressed to the nines and a regal looking woman hung on his arm. They entered a room, a large expanse in a private home with hardwood floors and ornate molding framing a high ceiling. A crystal chandelier hung from the center of the ceiling, the colors from the light dancing on the wall.

The room was full of people. A band was perched on the step that led to the sunken ballroom, attired in the obligatory tails and white gloves. Negro servants stood in the shadows waiting to pick up discarded plates or to refill empty glasses. As he looked on, a man servant named Sammy…

How do I know his name?

She smiled and nodded at him. A chill came over Mitch and suddenly he could hear Sharon's voice talking at him again.

"… Don't you think? I mean, whoever dropped it is long gone. This thing looks like it was buried in the ground."

Sharon reached her arm out to pick the bracelet up, but Mitch grabbed her arm.

"What?" Sharon said, her voice sounding as exasperated as her face looked. "What's the big deal? It's just an old bracelet. Nobody even cares about it."

"How can you be so sure," Mitch said, his mind still clouded in a haze of roses and wine.

"Mitch, what are you talking about? Whoever left it is long gone. Look around you. Nobody even comes here anymore. It's just some old, forgotten cemetery."

Her words brought him back to reality and away from the fantasy world his mind had concocted starring him as the dashing escort at a century old party. He blinked twice to clear his eyes and ground himself. His gaze tumbled over the tombstones, some crumbling, some sunken. The cemetery was falling apart and indeed looked as if it hadn't been visited by friend or family in decades. An old church sat at the far end of the land behind the tombstones. Reedy vines crawled up the building's façade. The constant beating of wind and rain had weathered the structure, soiling the exterior and eroding the carvings. The place looked as though it had been standing for centuries. It was sturdy, like the relics in Europe.

The church was the reason they were standing there among the graves. A spontaneous weekend trip brought them to town and to an inn that had opened in 1909. Mitch never wanted to stay at an inn or a bed and breakfast, for that matter, but it was on Sharon's list of "life experiences." Mitch thought he was ingenious when he picked the place. She wanted to experience staying at an inn? She's got it. She wanted to experience staying at a bed and breakfast? She's got that too. The inn they were staying in was originally opened as a bed and breakfast until converting to an inn five years prior. There you have it. Two "life experiences" down. God knew how many more of those she had left to put him through.

Sharon noticed the cemetery as soon as they got to the inn. The large slabs of stone, the mini George Washington monuments, the statues of Mary looking mournfully down at the ground, presumably put there to console the sorrowful loved ones left behind. All those things were lost on him.

Cemeteries were places for the dead and no place for the living to hang out in, or even look at too long. He had felt that way for years. Ever since he was a kid. When Mitch was seven his grandfather died of a heart attack. He had been close to his grandpa so he wanted to be a big boy and say goodbye like everyone else did. He sat through the open casket funeral with the body displayed full couch, managing not to get up and run out of the room even though he wanted to — every time he looked at his grandfather lying in the casket it was like the world zoned out, faded into a static kaleidoscope, and all Mitch could see was his profile. He didn't hear the minister talking about the reward in Heaven, didn't hear the sniffles and sobs coming from the people in the congregation. He only saw the side of his grandfather's face. Even from his seat Mitch could tell that his grandfather's face was as hard as stone. It didn't look natural. The lines he'd had around his mouth when he smiled were pulled taut, the hair in his beard seemed to lack its usual luster. In fact, it seemed that he could see each individual hair reaching out from the bulb embedded in his chin. His eyes were probably the most troubling of all. The top eyelid was pulled to his bottom lid tightly and, between the gray lashes, Mitch could see a glint of the glue picked up by the light. It looked like his grandfather's eyes were tearing, but Mitch knew better. But still, it looked that way.

The rest of the congregation mourned the loss of Carlton J. Richards, lamenting over him with exclamations of 'Lord Jesus' and 'Help, Lord' peppering the ceremony, but Mitch was far away from them. The body of his grandfather intrigued him, possessed him somehow. Mitch was stuck there, staring at his lifeless face, powerless to turn away until the force field was broken. He did this for a while, staring without blinking for what seemed like minutes before finally looking away, released by the same unseen force that held him in place a second before. And then his grandfather turned toward him.

Mitch could hear the sound of his grandfather's bones creaking, snapping, breaking as he turned his neck to face him. His eyes and mouth were still closed, but Mitch could see his lips working to open into a smile. Finally, his grandfather snapped the threading that had been sewn into his lips to keep his mouth closed. It hung from his lips like disturbed cobwebs. He arched his eyebrows and rolled his dry eyes in their sockets until the glue that held his eyes closed cracked. Mitch watched as his grandfather blinked once, twice, three times as though he was trying to clear his eyes. Mitch's eyes cascaded to his grandfather's chest and saw that it was still. In that same moment, his grandfather unfolded his hands with some effort and put his right one on the edge of the bronze-colored casket within which he laid. He sat up, a deep, guttural groan emitting from his chest as he did it, and scanned the room with his withering eyes.

Then he swung his right leg over the side of the casket.

Mitch screamed out loud then and stood up from his chair. His mother put her hand on his back, rubbing in smooth gentle circles the way she always did when he was upset. She was saying something, but Mitch didn't hear her. His eyes were focused on the body of his grandfather again, lying in the casket as though nothing had happened. His hands were folded across his lap in the unnatural way undertakers like to position the dead. His eyes and mouth were closed. Mitch sat down more out of shock than embarrassment. No one really paid attention to his outburst other than his parents. Everyone else was wrapped up in their own grief display. His was just a number in the act, and a relatively weak performance at that. Mitch never looked at his grandfather's face again after the funeral. Not even in pictures. He was afraid of what he might see playing at the edges.

When Sharon mentioned the tombstones, her enthusiasm was met with a dull mumble. She didn't let it bother her. She studied history in college and had worked on her family's genealogy, tracing her mother's line all the way back to the mid-1500s. She discovered while she was looking for family tree connections at a cemetery bearing her family's surname, that the old dates on the tombstones fascinated her. She had a tendency to view the world as if things just happened recently, certainly no more than one hundred years prior to her birth. It wasn't something she was conscious of, initially, not until that day in the cemetery. She was amazed one day, when surfing the internet, to find out that homosexuals had been persecuted in Germany in the early 1900s, and that that ancient civilizations had been advanced enough to create what are now the ruins at Chichen Itza—whole cities with homes, religious buildings, centers, and even out of the home eating areas. In her mind, people who lived that long ago didn't—couldn't—have had the same struggles, stresses, or issues that people experienced in the present. Not that she found earlier generations lacking in capability, it wasn't that at all. She just didn't see far past her scope of things. What was prevalent in her generation just couldn't have been an issue way back when. Her mind couldn't grasp it.

The same went for lifespan. Everything she had been taught in history books showed that people that lived in the 1700 and 1800s didn't live long. They typically died in their mid to late forties. The first time she saw the tombstone of a person who was born in 1789 and died in 1882, she was floored! She stood in front of the woman's chipped tombstone and read the dates over and over. She started to imagine the life she might have had. Sharon's mind replayed the historical events that took place while the woman, Mrs. Eleanor Patterson according to the stone that marked her grave, was alive and wondered how they might have affected her. Before she knew it, she had spent a half an hour standing in front of the grave of a woman to whom she was not related.

From then on, she was hooked. Whenever her genealogical research took her to a cemetery, she went early in the morning, excited about the dates she might find, the lives she might envision. One leg of her family line brought her to the property of a renowned slave owner in North Carolina. She drove three hours from Washington DC to Henderson, North Carolina wondering all the while what she might find there aside from her relative's tombstone. After about an hour of rubbing the tombstones, she needed and taking pictures of the plots themselves, she happened upon a wooded, unkempt area with large rocks scattered about. Some of them had sunken into the ground. Almost of all of them were covered with childlike handwriting that was all but worn away.

A slave cemetery.

2

Running in tandem with her genealogy research, Sharon looked into the slaves and the North Carolinian owners, trying to pinpoint whose graves she had found interred on the land. After long hours and a year of solid research, she found the name of one of the slaves buried there. Priscilla. Sharon spent days dreaming up a life for Priscilla. She wondered if she worked in the fields or in the main house, if she was dark or light skinned, if she longed for freedom or carried her burden in silence. Priscilla consumed Sharon's thoughts, so much so that she decided to write a book about her. Sharon's novel, *Of Life and Death*, was due out the following February. To say that traipsing along in a cemetery was right up her alley was an understatement.

They checked into the quaint inn, its décor done in antique rustic, an interesting combination that somehow worked. They took the stairs up two flights to their spacious room, opened the tall wooden door, and breathed in the soothing smell of cedar.

The door opened to a large sitting room with a window running the length of the back wall. A carved walnut settee with a rose embroidered cushion sat beneath the window with reading lamps on either side atop end tables. A pair of striped high-backed chairs sat opposite the settee. The floors were a deep brown hardwood. A sectional rug covered some of the space in the sitting room. The bedroom was to the right of the sitting room, at the end of a long, narrow hallway. A writing table stood flush against the closest wall to the doorway. A cherry wood armoire stood opposite the writing table, its scalloped carvings and pierced apron prominent in the light of the setting sun that trickled in from the window opposite it. A queen-sized, Spanish iron-framed bed took up most of the room with its tall mattress and assortment of throw pillows. The room was incredible.

"Isn't this great?" Sharon asked, unable to conceal her excitement as she flopped onto the bed. Mitch looked at her, at the smile on her face as she scanned the room. God, he loved her, her love of life, her exuberance. She was like a breath of fresh air. And her excitement was contagious.

"Yeah, it is kind of neat, that is if you like bed and breakfasts."

Sharon shoved him playfully and said, "I already know your game. You think because this used to be a bed and breakfast you're killing two birds with one stone. Not a chance."

"Why not?" He pointed to the bed and said, "Here's the bed." He picked up the room service menu and found the breakfast section. "And here's breakfast. Get it? Bed," he pointed again, "and breakfast. And the name of this former bed and breakfast is now The Dandelion Inn, so that covers the inn part. I don't see the problem."

Sharon smiled even wider as he tried to combine the two experiences. He talked a good game, but she knew he enjoyed their little escapades as much as she did. She picked up one of the throw pillows from the bed and threw it at him.

"Sorry Charlie. No dice on this one."

Mitch walked toward the bed and leaned over her. He could smell her perfume. It was just the slightest bit sour, mixed with her sweat. It drove him crazy. He licked his lips as he let his eyes linger on hers, full and moist, ready to kiss.

"I can think of other ways to get the pillows off this bed."

"Really," Sharon said, her voice catching in her throat. "Why don't you show me?"

3

Mitch woke up to find himself alone in bed. The sound of the shower was muffled — the bathroom was all the way at the other end of the hallway near the front door. The sheet was bunched between his legs the way it was when he fell asleep. He had a tendency to stay still while he slept. Sharon, on the other hand, was restless. She would kick the covers off and knock her pillow to the floor. But he stayed in the same position he drifted off in. He smiled at the memory of Sharon that flooded his mind. In the beginning of their relationship, she thought he was pulling her leg about his sedentary sleep. She would watch him fall asleep, staying up as long as she could keep her eyes open to try and catch him moving. She even went as far as to set up a camera to tape him while he slept. She played the video the next morning when they ate breakfast, sure she was going to prove him wrong and expose his little trick. She watched all six hours of the tape that day to try and catch him, but she couldn't. There was no movement other than the rise and fall of his chest when he breathed. She called him a freak when the tape was over.

Who knows? Maybe she's right, he thought.

Mitch got out of bed and walked toward the window. He contemplated joining Sharon in the shower to start round two. In their four years of marriage, they had never done it in the shower of a bed and breakfast/inn. They could add it to their list of "life experiences."

Mitch was about to turn down the hallway and jump in with Sharon when the small window in their bedroom caught his eye. He turned and walked over to it without realizing what he was doing. It was dark, with a light fog hovering over the street, but that wasn't what had caught his eye. The cemetery they passed when they turned into the inn's parking lot was right across the street. Seeing the tombstones reaching toward the night sky, their shapes accented by the dull yellow light from the streetlamp on the corner, made him feel uneasy. His skin felt clammy, chilly, as though a draft had just swept through the room. He touched his forehead and felt a film of sweat at his hairline. There were so many of them, markers of the dead. His mind lurched toward images of decaying skin and tattered rags; horror movie depictions flooded his head. He could feel them, the weight of their death pressing down on him. He could see their hands clawing furiously at the dirt, could hear their bones cracking as they strained to pull themselves up, could hear, their moans of discontent. His chin trembled as he watched them moving, milling, haunting their burial place.

Then he saw her.

She stood in the center of the fray of ghostly figures, her countenance clearer than the others. Almost solid. She wore a dress in the deep shade of wine, almost indecipherable against the backdrop of the night, with a plunging neckline that showed her ample cleavage. The folds of the dress were full and the length was long, but he knew somehow that the legs beneath were slender and smooth. Her hair was pulled up with ringlets of dark brown cresting the top. Her delicate neck was adorned with a beautiful necklace of intricate design, garnet and gold, the stones shaped like roses, the gold so thin as to not be seen.

He could see her, her face, her body, clearly, as though she were standing in front of him in the room rather than through the glass, two stories down, and across the street. Her features intensified the longer he looked. Fear lingered around the edge of his consciousness.

She smiled at him as he watched her, at home among the dead, yet appearing different than them. Her lips were painted with the sultriest of reds, pouting ever so lightly around the edges. She ran a hand from the hollow of her throat, between her breasts, down to where her belly button would be, all the while looking at him, calling to him with her eyes. Mitch could feel himself rising as he watched her. The thought frightened him at first, but arousal wiped the fear away. He didn't hear the water in the shower stop running, nor did he hear the sound of Sharon's feet on the hardwood floor as she approached him from behind.

Sharon slapped Mitch on the right buttock, his bare cheeks too hard to resist. The smack jolted Mitch's attention from the woman in the cemetery to Sharon. He turned to her, his eyes wide and wild looking. The smile on Sharon's face quickly dissipated when she saw him.

"My God Mitch, you look like you just saw a ghost! Are you ok?"

Mitch released the air he had been holding in his lungs and realized he hadn't taken a breath since walking over to the window. He looked back and saw the other ghosts had disappeared, leaving her alone in the cemetery. Her mouth was open slightly as she darted her tongue over her lips, moistening them. Mitch felt Sharon move from behind him to his side. He thought about blocking her view of the cemetery but moved too late.

"Oh yeah, the cemetery is right across the street. I saw that when I got up."

Mitch looked at Sharon incredulously. Couldn't she see the woman in the cemetery? She was staring right at them!

The woman looked at Sharon with eyes that blazed red. She cast one last glance at Mitch before turning her back and walking deeper into the cemetery, among the graves. She seemed to fade as she walked, disappearing all together within seconds.

Mitch looked at Sharon again and realized she hadn't seen anything at all. The woman had only shown herself to him for some reason. He shivered.

"You ok?" Sharon asked, walking away from the window. "It doesn't bother you, does it? The cemetery."

Mitch swallowed and tried to find his voice. "I'm ok."

"I mean, I know you don't like them and all, but they're harmless," she said as she squeezed lotion from the bottle and applied it to her leg. "It's not like ghosts come out of their graves at night to prey upon the people who stay in this Inn or anything," she continued, "although that might make an awesome movie."

She laughed.

Mitch could barely force out a chuckle.

"There's no boogeyman or anything like that. It's just a place where people put their loved ones after they die. A resting place. Nothing more, nothing less," she finished.

"I know," he offered weakly. He knew what he had just seen and it haunted his thoughts. As his memories returned to his grandfather's funeral, he couldn't help but wonder if maybe the dead never truly rested.

"I'm going to take a shower," Mitch said over his shoulder as he started towards the bathroom.

"Good. Maybe when you're done we can have another go in the sack." She smiled playfully at him, her naked body lying on top of the beautiful bed, positioned seductively. All he could do was smile at her. He didn't much feel like having sex anymore

at least, not with her

his mind echoed.

At least, not with her.

4

After he got out of the shower, he and Sharon made love again. He could tell that she wasn't as satisfied with their second romp as she had been with their first, but he was able to cry fatigue and leave it at that. It was one of the joys of marriage. Occasional sexual inadequacy was accepted and ignored; passed off as nothing. There was no more trying to prove yourself, trying to make it perfect every time. Marriage gives you the do over option.

After sex, they ordered dinner in. Sharon fell asleep about an hour after dinner and was still sleeping when he opened his eyes to the dark room. He stared at her while she drifted to sleep, watched her eyelids flutter when she started to dream, watched the rise and fall of her chest as she breathed. He would never let anything happen to her, he knew that then with clarity so sharp, it was painful. Nothing would ever touch her if he had anything to do with it. Not man nor animal. Or spirit.

Mitch woke up again at 2:00 o'clock in the morning. The quaint little room they'd rented at the inn had lost its appeal in the dark shadows of early morning. Mitch heard the floorboards creaking in the room above them. Apparently, some lucky couple was making good on their weekend escape instead of sleeping the night away.

"Good for them," he said under his breath.

At least somebody was having a good time. The neighbors in the room next to theirs weren't faring quite as well. Mitch could hear the woman sobbing as her husband/boyfriend/date spoke demeaning, cutting words in the most angry, stentorian voice he could muster. Mitch felt sorry for the woman. He was happy Sharon was sleeping soundly next time him, unaware of the argument in the next room. She would have felt terrible for the woman and would dread going into the hallway or lobby the next day on the off chance they would meet. She'd be afraid the woman would show her embarrassment on her face, would know somehow that his wife was in the next room and had overheard everything. Sharon would then feel uncomfortable knowing that she had heard it, and so the cycle would go until they left the Inn for home. Mitch was glad that Sharon slept like a log, for once.

The darkness in the room seemed impenetrable, palpable almost, like it could swallow him whole if he stepped into it. His eyes struggled to see, to get used to the darkness and make out the furniture, their clothes strewn on the floor, anything. After what seemed like forever, his eyes cleared. He could see the chair and lamp that sat by the window, the dresser, the edge of the rug. He started to feel a little better when his vision opened up, unconsciously unfurrowing his brow and relaxing back into the pillows. He hadn't realized he had sat up in the bed to scan the room, looking for something, anything decipherable in the dark. It wasn't the same, the dark at the inn. It was different than the dark in his bedroom back in Herndon, VA, even with a wooded lot surrounding the house. The dark didn't seem as heavy, as tangible, at home. It didn't feel as if it were teeming with unseen creatures that were lurking there, just beyond his view, waiting for him to step off the bed and into their world. Mitch chuckled to himself, but his laughter sounded on edge. *This is silly*, he told himself. *You're a grown man! You can't be afraid of the dark!*

But the dark at The Dandelion Inn was different. It was alive.

Mitch could see the floor plant standing in the corner of the room, engulfed in the shadows of the night, its shape resembling that of a voluptuous woman. The vision beyond the window came back to him then, the woman who stood in the cemetery earlier that night. The memory of her didn't frighten or startle him, instead it warmed him, made him stir. She was beautiful, a sight to behold. He remembered her eyes, her lips so full and inviting. His mind allowed him to forget the ghosts that danced around her and the fact that he saw her appear out of thin air. Instead, it reminded him that it was her that he wanted to see that evening. And he couldn't deny it.

He indulged in the fantasy, shutting his eyes to the odd room, and stepping into a white-walled space with a bed and soft music playing. It existed only in his mind. She came to him there, dressed not in the wine dress she wore in the cemetery, but in a short black silk gown with spaghetti straps and lace. Her hair was down, loosened from the bun, and resting lightly on her shoulders. The soft curls caressed her cheeks and forehead. Her eyes, the same rich brown as her hair, looked seductively at him from behind thick eyelashes. Her lips were colored with the same luscious red.

She stood in the doorway of the room watching him as he laid on the bed. He was erect from the very sight of her, wanting to go to her, but knowing he couldn't. This was her game and it would be played by the rules she set forth, and none other. He looked at himself, at the veins that stood out as if they had been carved into stone. He was hard, almost painfully so. Mitch could almost see his member pulsating, throbbing as hot blood coursed through it.

She took leisurely steps toward him, rolling her hips as her weight shifted, drawing out her approach. She enjoyed his look of desire, his impatience; she could smell his lust on his skin.

She crawled onto the bed on all fours, giving him a view of her cleavage as she did. Mitch reached for her and his hand met with the softest skin he had ever touched. He kissed her hungrily, pressing his mouth to hers, and darting his tongue inside her mouth. He couldn't control himself. He needed to touch her. She returned the kiss with passion, slowing him down, controlling their rhythm. Her mouth satisfied him more than any other kiss had ever done. Her hands upon his chest gave him chills. He moaned under his breath.

The woman pushed him away abruptly, catching him off guard and leaving him longing for her touch. She kneeled in front of him with her back slightly arched, pointing her pert nipples toward the ceiling. She ran her hand over her left breast slowly, caressing herself, seeming to savor the curve, the feel of the satin that covered her skin.

Her hand moved slowly, sensually, up to her neck. It was smooth with only a small blemish on otherwise clear skin: a perfectly round mole. Her brown hair fell in wisps around her neck, blowing in the faint breeze that encircled them where they lay, a breeze he couldn't feel. He thought his sensibilities might be swirling in the breeze also, funneling like a tornado, whipping like the winds of a hurricane.

A gleaming red suddenly took his attention away from the travels of her hand, making him focus on the base of her neck. A choker of garnets and gold rested just above her collarbones. The necklace was intricately designed with little clusters of garnets bound together in rows of three. The rich color of the gemstones seemed to pulse, in time with the beating of his heart. He watched as the flash of light intensified as his own heart rate sped up with desire.

Her wrist bore the complement to the necklace; strung garnets clustered and bound to a sister set with the thinnest of gold. It too pulsed with the beat of his heart, hypnotizing him. A smile formed on her lips as he was drawn into her spell. She pulled gently at the spaghetti straps on her shoulders, letting them drop just above the elbow. The gown slid effortlessly from her body. Her nakedness was mind-blowing; her body the most perfect one he had ever laid eyes on. Her breasts were round and firm, her stomach was flat, her hips were wide, and her legs were slender. She had the most perfect hourglass shape he had ever seen. He couldn't help but put his hands on her waist, her shoulders, her thighs, anywhere and everywhere he could. He needed to feel her curves beneath his palm.

She crawled over him leaving his skin feeling tingly from the touch of her skin on his. She pressed her lips to his and his mouth felt refreshed and cool. He put his hands on her hips, just above her buttocks, and moved her body back and forth. She didn't resist. Another moan escaped his lips and died in her kiss.

He sat up, turned, and pulled her body beneath his. Her hair splayed across the pillow, framing her face angelically. She smiled sensually, closing her eyes in anticipation of his lips on hers, pulling him to her through some unseen force. He was happy to oblige and kissed her once more, running his fingers through her soft hair.

His hips gyrated slower as he prepared to enter her. He wanted to feel her, all of her. The shifting of the mattress was not what turned his attention, but the cough neither he nor the woman beneath him had issued.

Mitch looked to his left and saw Sharon's blanket covered body shifting in her sleep. Her hand rubbed her nose, making a squishing sound — a telltale sign that she would wake up in the morning with the beginnings of a cold. He remembered that she had complained of a draft earlier in the day. It was then that he felt the air he knew to be swirling around him. Around them. A cool wind with such a crisp edge as to raise goosebumps on the flesh. He felt them rising on his skin as he watched his wife rub her nose in her sleep. Sharon sniffled once and then drifted back into her dream state, never having opened her eyes.

Mitch turned back to the woman beneath him only to find that she was gone. His eyes took in the inn as it had been before the dream: a dark, shadowy room. The white-walled room of his daydream disappeared the moment he heard Sharon's cough. He looked for the woman anyway, peering into the darkness, trying to make out her shape. He caught a glimpse of his reflection in the mirror. He was on his knees with his right arm extended and leaning into the bed. He held his penis in his left hand, still erect. The space beneath him was empty except for rumpled sheets and a pillow.

He eased himself back into his place on the bed being careful not to bounce the mattress and wake Sharon. He controlled his breathing and the beating of his heart. He felt himself relax. The pulsating desire he had in his loins dissipated with elapsed time. He looked over at Sharon's back; her nightshirt was bunched up and wrinkled, her hair a tangle around her head.

The wind was gone.

The stillness of the room was like static electricity to him. His eyes darted around the room more in fear than confusion. But fear of what? Of a woman who seduced him in his dreams?

His eyes glanced at the window at the other end of the room. It was smaller than the one in the living room, but he could still see the tops of some of the taller monuments in the cemetery. He could almost hear a voice calling him, moaning seductively in the night. He turned his eyes away with great effort. A chill covered his skin. He shivered as he settled deeper into the bed, pulling the covers over his shoulders.

Mitch stared at the end of the bed, looking at the hump his feet made under the covers for a long time. He was afraid to look anywhere else in the room and afraid to close his eyes. After a while of cowering in bed like a child after a nightmare, a chiding chuckle rose in his throat and spilled out into the darkened room. He admonished himself again for being such a 'fraidy cat. His voice was the only sound; the neighbors upstairs had apparently turned in for the night and the ones next door had quieted down. The sound of his voice bounced off the floors and walls. There was something wrong with it, though. On the surface it was jovial, like the laughter behind a good joke. But at its core, it was edgy and ragged.

"What's so funny?" Sharon asked in a sleepy voice, her eyes still closed as she turned toward him and nuzzled his arm.

"Nothing baby. I'm sorry I woke you," he said, bringing his voice down to a whisper. He ran his hand through her hair and said, "Go back to sleep."

Sharon nodded and drifted back to a full sleep with ease. Mitch kept touching her hair, feeling the texture, and remembering the woman in his dream. *That's what it had to be*, he told himself, *the best damned wet dream I ever had.* He laughed again, but this time it held no humor.

5

The next morning, Mitch woke up to find Sharon already out of bed. He called to her, feeling uncomfortable in the bed by himself, feeling uncomfortable in the room itself.

"I'm out here," she replied from the living room. He knew why she was there. She was looking over at the cemetery. She would want to go there before they left to walk among the graves and concoct fantasy lives for the people in them. He'd have to oblige her, after all, her imagination thrived on things like that. A half an hour in the cemetery could be fodder for her next book. He only hoped she wouldn't make him stay any longer than that.

He got out of bed and met her in the living room. Her face was awash in sunlight as she looked out at the cemetery across the street. He couldn't resist kissing her on the cheek; she looked so gorgeous in the morning. He forced the memory of his dream girl, lips parted, waiting for him to kiss her out of his mind.

"Whatcha lookin' at?" he asked, trying to affect a light tone. He kissed her cheek and the side of her neck playfully.

"See that cemetery over there? Right across the street?"

How could I miss it, he replied in his mind, but managed to keep his response to Sharon even. "Yeah."

"There's a neat old church back there behind the graves. I've been thinking of a plot for a short story the whole time I've been standing here. You know, nineteenth century demon possession, haunted land, pre-*Night of the Living Dead* kind of story. I thought it might be neat to check it out. Go in, walk around. It doesn't look like anyone has been there in years, at least from here. It might be kind of spooky. It could give me some great ideas. You up for a good scare?" She poked playfully at is ribs, giggling at the idea of Mitch in a creepy church surrounded by a cemetery.

"What? You don't think I can handle it?" he said with his best try at machismo. He puffed out his chest and said, "I can take anything. It's you I'm worried about."

"Great. Let's get dressed. I really want to check the place out. I feel an evening of writing coming on!"

Sharon bounded into the bathroom and within seconds, Mitch heard the shower running.

Damn, he thought to himself, and looked over at the cemetery grounds, its tombstones gleaming in the morning light.

6

They found the church door closed, welded shut. All of the windows were boarded up, and the stained-glass murals were broken. The stone was cold, uninviting. Mitch found himself wanting to leave the place because of the church as much as for the cemetery. But Sharon oohed and ahhed, genuinely enjoying the "life experience."

"Look at the doors, Mitch. They must be hundreds of years old!" She stood looking up at them, with their high arches and ornate hinges. They looked creepy to him.

"I wonder what the stained glass might have looked like." Sharon strolled the length of the church talking about what could be inside, what services might have been held there. By the time she came back to the front where Mitch had remained, she was wondering about the congregation. "What did they look like? What might they have worn to church? What was happening in their lives when they belonged to this church? You know?"

She was rattling on by then, and Mitch knew better than to answer her rhetorical questions. She really wasn't looking for his input. She was just talking. It was interesting to see because this was her way of creating an outline. She was organizing her thoughts for her next piece, rounding it out without pen or paper.

Sharon started walking away from the church and toward the graves. It was just like Mitch thought it would be. He knew they would end up looking at tombstones after a while. It was inevitable.

"Who is buried here? Members of the congregation? People in town? Fallen soldiers? Maybe the town rogue whose family owned a plot here? Maybe the harlot who no one ever looked in the eye?" Her voice sounded farther and farther away as she walked up and down the rows of tombs, stepping over broken monuments, walking around sunken plots.

Mitch stood where he was, at the end of the footpath to the church, ready to leave. There was a chill in the air and goose bumps rose on his skin. The bumps made him think of the previous night and he glanced quickly at the inn, seeing what he thought might be the window in their bedroom.

Standing in front of an old church, in the middle of a graveyard, Mitch wished he had never picked that particular Inn, the inn by the cemetery, with an unobstructed view. He wanted to leave, to forget the place existed.

"Mitch," Sharon called from up ahead. "Mitch, come here!"

His heart sank when he heard her voice. His mind called up the images of the night before, the ghosts that crawled out of their graves to walk the cemetery, the woman who stood looking at them in their room. The woman who visited him in the wee hours of the morning. He remembered the look on the woman's face when Sharon peered out of the window in her direction, standing next to Mitch. The look of anger was indescribable. Her eyes had burned with a fury unknown to humans. But there was something more, wasn't there? Something else behind the anger, the jealousy that shot from the woman's eyes. It was a look of possession.

Mitch ran through the cemetery toward the sound of Sharon's voice, imagining the ghosts on either side of him cheering, laughing as he went. He finally found her around the side of the church, bent over a tombstone. There were no ghosts, no swirling beings surrounded her as she read the writing on the tombstone. There was no woman standing over her with vengeance etched on her transparent face.

Mitch felt the pressure lift from his shoulders and he looked at Sharon's body, bent at the waist, engrossed in the etching on the tombstone in front of her. It was all in his head. His mind had been playing tricks on him since they started the trip. He decided then that he wouldn't visit another cemetery with Sharon, except for funerals. His imagination ran wild when he did, and for him, that wasn't a good thing. He decided he had to tell her that visiting the cemetery could be checked off his, "life experiences" list. Been there, done that.

As he walked toward her, he realized that his argument might actually work.

Sharon turned to him with excited eyes and said, "Look at this Mitch! Elizabeth Mabry, born March 31, 1717, died March 17, 1817." She paused for a moment, waiting for a reaction. Mitch stood silent, a feeling of dread coming over him again. His eyes caught sight of something that his mind couldn't believe, couldn't fathom.

Sharon didn't notice. "This woman almost lived for 100 years! Only two weeks more and she would have been 100 years old! That is incredible! I mean, we're talking about the 1700s! The life expectancy couldn't have been more than 45!"

Mitch tried to smile while Sharon looked at him, but he wasn't sure if he had pulled it off. Sharon didn't care, she was off in a world of what ifs and how dids, imaging a life for the woman whose grave they stood over, romanticizing a death that happened two hundred fifty years before they were born.

The story she designed made Elizabeth Mabry the wife of a rich landowner, an affluent developer of his time. She socialized with all of the right people and went to all of the important balls and parties. She wore beautiful gowns and stunning jewelry, setting the pace for the socialites of the era to follow. Mitch's head reeled as Sharon described her life, a life he saw with vivid clarity, as if he were recalling a memory of his own.

"Look at this," Sharon said, cutting her description of the life of Elizabeth Mabry short. "What do you think it is?"

The bracelet t the woman in his dream wore on her wrist laid at the base of Elizabeth Mabry's tombstone, its pure garnet stones pulsing bright red through the Virginia clay, in time with the beat of his heart.

Q & A

Click

Tony: OK. Why don't we get started?

Crystal: OK.

Tony: I'm Tony and I'm doing interviews for a book I'm writing about relationships. You, Crystal Pete, have agreed to sit and talk with me about relationships and stuff like that and I have supplied the sodas and the lovely ambiance that is my apartment.

(Chuckling)

Tony: I'm going to tape our talk and I'll take a couple of notes as we go along. OK?

Crystal: OK.

Tony: OK, now that all of that stuff is out of the way, let's talk about relationships.

Crystal: OK.

Tony: How many have you had?

Crystal: What, like ever?

Tony: Yeah. How many have you had in your life?

Crystal: I guess about ten or twelve.

Tony: And you're a 28-year-old woman, right?

Crystal: Yes.

Tony: Do you think that's a lot or a little?

Crystal: I don't know. What do you think?

Tony: Well, I guess it depends. Of those 10 or 12 people, how many of them have you had sex with?

Crystal: I guess about 5 of them.

Tony: Have you had sex with people that you haven't been in a relationship with?

Crystal: Yeah.

Tony: So how many sexual partners have you had?

Crystal: 30. Maybe more.

Tony: Do you find that sex is better with someone that you aren't committed to?

Crystal: Yes.

Tony: Why is that?

Crystal: For one, you don't have to deal with all the bullshit, know what I mean?

Tony: Like what?

Crystal: Like jealousy, arguing over the smallest things, petty stuff.

Tony: Were any of those people you had sex with one-night stands?

Crystal: Oh yeah, most of them were. Those are the best kind. That way you don't have to deal with that person again if you don't want to. It's great.

Tony: What is the dirtiest thing you've ever done in bed?

Crystal: (Hesitates) What do you mean?

Tony: You know, what's the wildest thing you've ever done with a partner? Nipple pinching, hot wax, what?

Crystal: (Laughing) It's worse than that. That stuff is pretty tame.

Tony: So what is it?

Crystal: I don't know. (Deep breath) It's not what you're thinking.

Tony: I'm not thinking of anything in particular. You tell me.

Crystal: Well, it's not what I've done; it's who I've done it with.

Tony: (Hesitates) You're not going to tell me that you've had sex with a family member or anything like that, are you?

Crystal: No! Nothing that far out! But it is different.

Tony: Spill! I can't take the suspense!

Crystal: I love to have sex with a male body.

Tony: Ok…. What's so strange about that?

Crystal: No, you don't get it.

Tony: Help me out here.

Crystal: I like to have sex with male bodies. Dead men. Corpses.

Tony: (Hesitates) Dead men?

Crystal: Yup.

Tony: You're kidding, right?

Crystal: I told you it wasn't what you were expecting.

Tony: What? I mean, they're dead. What can you possibly like about doing it with a dead guy? How can he satisfy you?

Crystal: There's something about their faces. I can see their soul lurking just under the skin, staring back at me. It's like they're alive again.

Tony: Wouldn't you get the same effect from a living man? I mean, he would actually be alive.

Crystal: When I look at a living man, when I stare right into their faces, for all of their gyrating and contorting, their souls are still. There is no life in them, even when they climax.

(Pause)

Tony: So what do you do, sneak into a funeral home and jump a guy in the casket?

Crystal: I've done that, but by the time they get in the casket, they've been dead for too long. They feel different.

Tony: Yeah, they're as hard as a rock, I bet. But then, that could be a plus.

Crystal: It's not just that. They're cold. So cold, you can almost feel it in your bones when you touch them. It's like having sex with cement. No, I like them a little fresher.

Tony: So I guess you raid the morgue?

Crystal: Sometimes, but if they've already made it into the freezer, it's the same problem.

Tony: Then how do you get them fresh? Sneak onto a crime scene or something?

Crystal: That's one way to do it. Sometimes I just make my own.

Tony: What?

Crystal: It's better that way. Then they are as fresh as they can be. Their flesh is still warm.

Tony: What?

Click

A Nice, Sunny Day

It came in through the window and crawled over the leather interior, its hairy, black legs just a step away from her hand. She didn't see it at first as it made its way into the car. It was a nice, sunny day, the first one after almost a week of rain. The radio was on, she was done with work for the day, and she was in a great mood. She was thinking of stopping at the mall when she saw it, trying to decide which store to go to first. Sundresses, she thought. Can't ever have too many of those.

She was making a left into the parking lot of the mall when she saw it. The sunlight caught its iridescent eyes, reflecting brilliant magenta and cobalt atop beady blackness. It was looking back at her, both of them temporarily paralyzed by the other's presence.

She almost lost control of the car as she stared at it. Her hands were suddenly clammy and a light film of sweat coated her brow. Her breathing grew more rapid and her mouth hung open. She was terrified. She pulled the car into the first spot she could find, being careful not to make any sudden moves that might startle the hideous creature. The car was parked haphazardly, filling two lanes, but she didn't care. She was just happy she had been able to control herself before having an accident.

When the car stopped, the mini monster crawled into the air vent with disconcerting grace. The woman saw its color in a blinding flash, white against black that she might have considered pretty under different circumstances. The creature turned to face the woman again, looking out at her from the safe haven the vent provided. The woman's breathing was shallow, almost a gasp.

She hit the base of the air vent one, two, three times. The creature moved, drew deeper into the vent. It lifted its body higher on the final hit, rising as though on its toes, feeling it might have to protect itself from the giant looking in on it.

The woman's breathing was rapid yet hollow, growing thinner with every inhalation. Sweat poured from her face, dampening the collar of her shirt. She wanted to open the door and get out of the car, but to disengage the lock she would have to put her hand near the air vent. The thought of the repugnant creature jumping on her then, abandoning its hiding place, and perching on her hand sent shivers down her spine. Her body tingled with fear. Tears sprung from her eyes as she sat and stared at the creature in the air vent. It stared back, matching her intensity.

She rested her head on the headrest, trying to get more air into her lungs. Her throat closed and her chest cavity felt cramped and constricted. She clutched at her throat, massaging her neck, pleading with her body to open up, to breathe the air.

The creature sat in the air vent, its body rigid and still. It watched as the woman gasped for air, her hands fluttering about, her movements no longer restricted. It could have gotten out then, if it had wanted to, but still it sat; the giant was still awake and could be a threat.

The woman pressed the horn on her car in her last movement, her hand falling away from the steering wheel almost as soon as she had touched it. The sun shone in on her as she died, caressing her face with its yellow glow, bidding her goodbye.

The creature stared at the woman from the air vent as the sun set and nightfall crept in. She hadn't moved for hours. The swirling air that had emitted from her mouth before was stilled. It gained courage and ventured out of the air vent to inspect the dark, cavernous openings on the giant's face.

Betrayal

54

She died.

The breeze tousled her hair gently as she hid behind the bushes. Watching. Waiting. Dying. The sun blessed her by blinding her with its rays, obscuring her vision as he stepped out of the doorway. His shoulders were hunched in humiliation, the agile stride gone from his step. He was beaten. As he got into the car, she cowered lower, hiding her face from view. The car drove solemnly past as she shuddered, the game finally over for her. For him.

He didn't cry when she died.

He laughed.

The Salacity of Death

The day was bright and clear, the humidity was low. Earlier that morning he had mown the lawn, taking care to trim around the stones and the bases of the trees. He wanted everything to be neat for them, even though they would only see the fruits of his labor as an afterthought. He knew that if he left the place the way it was that morning, the day after a week-long span of spring storms, they would see the weed-choked grass and the sprouts of dandelions. The disorderliness would stand out like a bright pink pimple on the end of a young girl's nose. And they would complain. He couldn't bear the tone they would use, that 'How dare you? What are you, some kind of moron?' expression they would hold on their faces. So he tidied up before they came. Made everything nice and neat.

The cemetery was small and old, much like the town it serviced. The grounds held the town's only claim to fame, a football player whose first and only pro season ended with him paralyzed from the waist down. He withered away when he got home, becoming a shut-in from the moment he wheeled himself through the door of the house he grew up in. His mother tried to get him to go out, to use his celebrity to build a new life for himself in the town that loved him. She tried to get him to address schools and charity functions. She even set up a speaking engagement for him at her women's club to discuss college team recruiting methods 101. She thought he would have been perfect to address the mothers in her group who had kids on sports teams in high school. She wanted him to do something, anything to recharge himself, to have a life after the injury. But he had slipped into a world of self-pity and anger. He barely spoke to her, let alone entertained any of her ideas.

His mother died one day while she was making his breakfast. The cops thought he found her dead on the floor of the kitchen, right under the stove. He picked her up, put her on his lap, wheeled her into her bedroom, and put her body on the bed. Then he visited her. He would bring her the old magazines that sat on the coffee table in the living room to read. He would prepare coffee for her and even full meals. He would dress her every day, changing her clothes from casual to evening wear as if he meant to take her out for a night on the town. This went on for weeks.

When she missed her club meeting, a friend of hers called to tell her about the goings on. When she didn't pick up and the answering machine stopped taking messages because it was full, she went over to see about her friend. The story around town was Joan went to the house to find it in disarray. It wasn't the house itself that bothered her. It was the lawn. It had grown up to the point of being wild. All manner of bug life could be heard buzzing and slithering in it. The bushes had lost their form. The flowers were overrun by weeds, their bright colored petals littering dry dirt. The unkempt lawn made the house itself look abandoned. Haunted. Joan knew something was wrong right then and there. Margaret always prided herself on her flowers. She was always outside watering or pruning; she had the only true green thumb on the street. The sight of the ruined lawn sprang anxiety in Joan's heart. She rushed up the front steps and knocked on the door. She noticed a stench coming from the house, one so repugnant it could have knocked your socks off. "Indescribable," Joan told some of the town folks. "Like something out of a horrible dream."

Joan knocked and knocked, calling Margaret's name louder and louder each time. But nobody came to the door. She started to call the boy's name out, hoping he would hear the desperation in her voice and come to the door. Joan hadn't been able to get more than two words out of John since the accident, so she didn't expect him to answer her then. And he didn't. She listened for movement on the other side of the door, for the squeak of his wheelchair wheels over the hardwood floor. Nothing. The complete silence, the absence of every sound except her knuckles rapping against the door, made her blood run cold. She cast a glance over at the driveway and saw that Margaret's car was still there. She had noticed it before, but felt the need to do it again, just to be sure. Sweat dotted her forehead.

Joan went around back to the kitchen entrance and knocked. Still nothing. She peeked in through the shear curtains and saw the kitchen table set for a meal. A milk carton sat on the table next to a filled glass. The liquid inside was a putrid green. Joan's heart beat loudly in her chest as she called Margaret and John, her voice cracking with adrenaline. She started to rattle the doorknob, shaking it fiercely. It wouldn't budge. Her eyes scoured the back yard until she found a sizeable rock. She threw it through the glass in the kitchen door. She took off the sweater her granddaughter had given her for Christmas, wrapped it around her hand, and cleared the jagged glass. Joan took a deep breath before reaching her hand through the window to turn the lock on the other side.

She walked in and was met with the smell, more pungent than ever. Her knees almost buckled as she staggered forward, covering her mouth with her sweater. Tears streamed out of her eyes as she searched the house looking for Margaret. John was nowhere to be found.

Joan went to Margaret's bedroom last. It was the only closed door in the hall. The smell seemed tangible there, like a wall erected in front of her. Summoning all of her courage, Joan reached for the doorknob and flung the door open.

Margaret was sitting on top of the bed, dressed in an evening gown she hadn't worn since her husband Walter was alive. Her face was waxen, her jaw slack. The skin at her hairline was greenish-black and pulled away from the scalp. Her limp, lackluster hair was splayed over the pillows.

Sitting next to her, in his wheelchair, was John. Having disconnected his catheter after his mother's death, John's body had poisoned him. He sat in a pile of his own feces and urine expelled after death. His eyes were open, staring adoringly at his mother.

Years later Joan killed herself in her bathroom. No note. She had been the only one who visited John's grave. Now, no one did.

The cemetery's caretaker, Wally, had been there for forty years. His grandparents were buried there, as well as his parents. He had never married and that fact was a great disappointment to his father. "You're killing us," he had been fond of saying, "destroying our family line. After you, there will be no one else." That was a good thing, Wally thought. No child should have to endure the thoughts and desires he had. No child should do the things he has done.

Wally lived at the cemetery in a small house at the edge of the property. He never mingled with the people in town until they came to the cemetery to bury their dead. That was few and far between now. There weren't any new plots left, and only a few waiting for their owners to die and take up residence. A bigger cemetery had been built twenty years prior across town. All the "new blood" in town buried their dead there. The people in the old cemetery were all but forgotten. The relatives who knew them in life were dead, for the most part, and the generations after either moved away or bought huge mausoleums in the new cemetery. Burials were rare and visitors even rarer. It made Wally's work all the more easy.

The mourners trickled out of the cemetery, some stopping to visit long dead relatives, other racing to their cars to leave. An hour after they arrived, though, the cemetery was barren once again. Wally eyed the mound of dirt piled next to the open grave and thought of the work ahead. It could wait until later. First, he had to see about the dearly departed.

The casket sat on blocks covered with Astroturf and adorned with silk flowers. Wally sat down on one of the chairs he had set up for the funeral party and thought about the woman inside the box.

Ellen Ramsey had been a beautiful girl when they were growing up. She had been popular among the boys in town. A real looker. After high school, she married an older man, a friend of her family. He was a doctor in the next town over. Together they had three children, all boys. Their life was picture perfect with him as the ambitious breadwinner and her as the beautiful housewife.

Wally knew her in high school. He sat behind her in English class and had Phys. Ed. With her in their freshman year. Her family lived two blocks past his, so he would race home to watch her walk by. He loved to watch her hips sway under the material of her skirt, or to watch her lips move while she chewed her food. But the day she got her period was the first time he had ever been aroused by her. They were in gym class stretching for track and field trials. She was sitting on the floor, her legs spread, stretching her head to her right knee. Wally sat down too, faking a stretch so he could have a better look at her crotch. He fancied that he could see the split of her lips, and his mouth spread into a satisfied grin at the thought of it. While he was imagining the shape of her vagina, her white gym shorts turned crimson. It started as nothing more than a dot, a dime-sized spot on her shorts. His mouth watered as the stain spread, feeling himself rise with every passing second.

She realized that she was bleeding and jumped up from the floor with a shriek. She was out of the gymnasium within seconds. Wally excused himself and went straight to the boy's locker room. He shut himself up in a stall. He had never been as excited as he was then, and he began to satisfy himself as soon as he closed the door. The sight of the blood made him feel arousal more intense than he had ever experienced from magazines or peeping in the girl's locker room. The guilt of it only fueled his desire.

As night shrouded the graveyard like a black cloak, Wally sat staring at Ellen Ramsey's casket. She had been waiting there all day to be buried on top of her husband, who had died ten years earlier, and next to her parents, who bought the family plot. There were two other graves available in their section: one for Ellen's brother and one for his wife. Wally would visit with them when they came in as well, would reminisce of times past.

Wally stood after hours of sitting, and turned on his flashlight. Clinching it in his teeth, he pried the casket open with the crowbar he had brought with him. There Ellen laid, her face and body rigid and still. Wally marveled at how she had changed over time. He had only seen her twice over the years: at her husband's burial, and once while visiting his grave. They never spoke. He doubted she ever knew who he was, at the cemetery or in high school. It didn't matter anyway. He preferred to admire her from afar.

Her hair was gray, her face wrinkled and haggard. The last couple of years of her life had been hard. Fraught with illness, she was in and out of the hospital before succumbing to death in her home. He could see the strain of it on her slightly down-turned lips, her paper-thin eyelids. Wally touched her cheek with his hand and was met with cold, unmoving flesh. He felt himself stir as the chill permeated his skin down to the bone. As he carefully lifted Ellen Ramsey's body, clad in a beige spring suit, out of the casket and onto the Astroturf-covered land as he had done with so many others he buried, his mind drifted back to the dime-sized dot of crimson on her shorts and he felt his heart pound in his chest.

Dead and Gone

And then I was here. I remember being in the hospital room with its pastel yellow walls and medicinal smell lingering in the air. Funny that I would be conscious of that then, during my final moments, but I was. The place just smelled so… sterile. So clean, so neutral. Like it could ward off illness and death with a quick swipe of the mop against the floor. It was laughable, after all, the notion. Nothing could have saved me then, least of all that clean, sterile smell.

What was wrong with me? Did it matter? What was wrong with all of the other poor saps holed up in this hospital? Or the ones dying in the streets? It doesn't matter anymore what ailed me. The fact that it killed me says enough.

One minute I was lying in bed smelling that smell and contemplating my next visit from the handsome GP doing his rounds. It had been the highlight of my days in the hospital, watching him lean over my prone body, checking this, touching that. Oh, the things I would have done to him if only I could move. I thought about leaning into him, pressing myself into his neck, smelling his cologne mixed with the sweat of a hard day's work. Sometimes the daydreams were so vivid I actually thought I felt myself stir. When I imagined he and I kissing, him lifting me from that prison of a bed and taking me on the floor, I didn't see my body as it was then, frail and thin, ravaged by disease. Instead, I saw myself as a healthy woman. My skin was firm, my breasts full. My hips and thighs were as enticing as they were in my youth. That was me. The me I wanted to be. The me that I still was inside.

The next minute I was here. It wasn't quite that fast, my transition from there to here, but everything moved so quickly that it was hard to time. I was lying there with my eyes closed. Chatter had entered my room. My family had come to see me again, as they had been doing for the past couple of days. They fussed over me, combing my hair, oiling my lips, lotioning my hands. They read to me, talked to me about current events, and what happened in their day. Their visits troubled me, left me cold.

They went on chattering, their conversation moving away from me and into each other. They talked among themselves about their lives and the people in them. The chatter, the sound of their voices so giddy and consumed, grated on me. I couldn't help but feel envious. They could get up and walk out of the hospital. They could leave the sterility and breathe fresh air into their lungs. But I couldn't. I would never be able to again.

I opened my mouth to tell them as much. I wanted to scream, 'Get out of here! Go back to your world and leave me in peace!' Maybe then they would see that their good intentions did nothing more than make real the situation I was in. I was dying and I knew it.

They kept chitchatting and I kept trying to lash out. I extended my arm, grabbed the metal guard on the side of the bed (you know, the one to keep invalids like me from falling onto the floor), and lifted myself to a sitting position. I hadn't used my arms in weeks, months maybe, and the stretch was excruciating. But good. God, it was so good to move again, to feel my body work again. I smiled in spite of myself.

I heard a shriek of surprise emit from my niece's mouth. She had been so preoccupied with the details of the dance she was going to that night—the wiry, braces-wearing boy that was taking her, the dress she was going to wear, who was going with who—that she didn't see me get up. Her mother, my sister, turned to see what was going on. Our eyes met. The smile on my face seemed wicked to me then, callous somehow, as I watched my sister's mouth contort into the beginnings of a good cry. Her eyes watered as my own dried, her cheeks flushed as my own grew cold. Her hand fluttered up to her mouth just as mine lost its grip on the guard. I drew in my last breath as she let out her first of many sobs.

And now I'm here. Not in hell, not in heaven, not in purgatory or in any other waiting area deemed appropriate by some religion. I'm on Earth again, seeing the sights anew. It seems that I only closed my eyes to blink and I left the life of pain and suffering that was mine for fifty-nine years and awoke as a spirit, light and airy, floating among the dead and the living with ease.

I couldn't sit still the night of my death. I tried to remain with my body, not knowing what else to do. A bunch of us did, in fact. The morgue was hopping. It didn't take us long to realize that we could leave our bodies where they were, could travel anywhere we wanted to, could visit anyone we wanted to. Everyone else left before I did, some going to visit their spouses one last time, others off to see who they could spook. I thought long and hard about what I wanted to do. I left just as they were uncovering my body, removing the white, sterile sheet from the shell I no longer inhabited to perform an autopsy.

The lights were off at his house.

The Black Hole

1

"Damn man, gotta bring a nigga out to the boonies to play souped-up tag," Shaun said in his best thug impersonation as he looked through the fogged window of Martin's black Cherokee Limited Edition. It was cold that morning and he could see his breath in the air when he rolled down the window to get a better look outside.

"Shaun, what's up with the window? It's not like it's summer up in here," Martin said.

Shaun was too busy making faces and hand gestures at Gary, Kevin, and Robert in the forest green Jetta following behind them to pay attention to what Martin was saying. He was pointing out the horses grazing in the field on the right side of the car and shaking his head.

"Are you sure we're going the right way, Martin? I don't see any street signs," Craig asked as he looked curiously at the bales of hay neatly stacked on the driven land to the left of the car. He poked Shaun and said, "Are you seeing this shit? It's like we drove out of Maryland and into the backwoods of North Carolina!"

"I've followed the directions to the letter. They told me there wouldn't be any street signs. Nothing but farmland in sight for miles, they said," Martin picked up the crumpled piece of paper that had the directions on it and double-checked his steps. He had been invited to play 'Capture the Flag' by a guy he worked with. It was a dare, really. Martin had heard about the paintball craze before. A lot of the kids in his area seemed to like to do it on Friday nights with flashlights on their face masks. They would go into the woods and shoot at each other like crazy, until one of the teams surrendered. It was nothing but a little fad that the kids would soon be tired of, he thought. Nothing but a fad.

His co-worker, Jeremy, issued the paintball challenge to him one day during lunch. He said that he and a couple of his buddies go out every once in a while and horse around after work to shake the stress off. He said it was a lot of fun and a damned good release. *Lord knows I could use that,* Martin thought while Jeremy explained the rules to him. What Jeremy told him seemed to be a lot different than what he had heard before about paintball. He thought that playing paintball, or going paintballing, or whatever you called it, was nothing more than a kid's game. It certainly wasn't anything that he and his boys would want to do with their Saturday afternoons. Hoops was more like their speed - not pseudo-military combat with pretty little pink paint balls that splatter all over you on impact and color your clothes with water-solvent fluorescent paint. No, a real challenge was to take it to the hoop and slam it down somebody's throat. That's a game. That's sport. That's relaxing. It's what he and his boys did to shake the stress off.

Martin tried to explain the differences, both physical and mental, to Jeremy at lunch. For every point he brought up, Jeremy countered with another. It went on for almost the entire hour, both of their sandwiches going completely untouched. Finally, he said it. Jeremy issued the challenge.

"You want to try it? Your men against mine in the brush? I mean, that's if you can handle it," Jeremy said with a taunting smirk on his face. He sat back dramatically in his chair, satisfied with his lead. Jack, the controller who was sitting at another table, inched forward on Martin's pause. His forehead was peppered with sweat and his skin was furrowed with anticipation. Martin glanced over at Jack, and he looked away quickly, trying to act nonchalant. He began eating his sandwich slowly, his eyes darting towards Martin's table. Martin shook his head in amusement and turned back to Jeremy. Jack looked up from his sandwich and turned his attention to Jeremy and Martin's conversation again. He was listening, eagerly awaiting Martin's response. Martin was amazed at Jack's intrusion and tried to ignore it.

"You don't think I'll play, do you?"

Jeremy shrugged his shoulders theatrically.

"Would you come out to the court and sweat it up with the big boys," Martin asked. He didn't think that Jeremy would bring his lily-white, country-club friends down to the gym to play b-ball with a bunch of Black guys. Not that he and his boys played ball in Southeast, DC, but anywhere in Chocolate City would scare the pants off the likes of Jeremy and his boys. It's a wonder Jeremy made it to work in Northwest without hyperventilating in his car.

Martin had met some of Jeremy's friends before. One day after work he and Jeremy met up with them in Georgetown for happy hour. They were in some hoity-toity bar where the drinks were extremely expensive and watered down. Places like that were always full of loose girls who were willing and able if you bought them enough drinks and patted them on the ass real nice. They flaunted their plastic surgeon's sculpted breasts in increments, teasing you with what could happen later, as long as the car you had parked outside was a BMW or a Porsche. Yeah, it was that kind of place.

Jeremy's friends Kurt, Chuck, and Brad came to the bar fifteen minutes after Martin and Jeremy arrived. Jeremy and his friends graduated from Georgetown University. Martin came out of Howard University. Even with four against one odds, a pretty heated discussion ensued about the two Alma Maters. They bickered over curriculum, campus structure, student government, et cetera, but the real conversation, the underlying jab, was about the competence of historically black universities versus white universities.

Kevin, Martin's friend and fellow alumnus met up with them about an hour into the discussion. He sat down and loosened his tie, listening to the back and forth, and shook his head. It was the same ole thing. It seemed that every time he and Martin went out with White boys, they always wanted to talk about who is better. Inadvertently and undercover, for sure. But it was always the same discussion. Don't they ever get tired of it?

While he sipped on a Kahlua and Cream, the old white magic went to work. His friends called it white magic because Kevin had a knack for picking up women without even trying to. White women. He was like a magnet. They flocked to him like he was the best thing since hot cakes. The first one that came over was blonde. She was tall and slender with breasts as big and round as the water balloons that kids used to throw off the roof to hit the mailman. Martin had a fleeting daydream about touching them. He wondered if they would pop if he squeezed too hard. He chuckled at the mental image and caught a glimpse at Jeremy and his friends. Jeremy was looking distractedly around the table and the bar. It was so deliberate, the way he looked past Kevin and the girl. He looked as if he wished that no one could see him sitting there. He creatively dodged the courting going on in front of him, if that's what you called it, by pretending to be intensely interested in the busy crowd funneling into the tiny bar. He watched as men checked women out and women coyly lured men in with no interest. He just needed something to avert his eyes from the scene unraveling before him. Brad had a sour look on his face. He kept staring at the girl, trying desperately to make eye contact. Chuck looked like he was going to be sick. His skin had taken on a strange green tone and his eyes were watery. The murmur of the crowd around them seemed far away.

Martin looked at Kevin and his lady du jour. He was working it, throwing every line he could at her. She was sitting on the stool closest to him. So close she could probably feel his breath on her face. She was fine. Martin was sure that's why Jeremy and his friends were reacting the way they were. Jealousy, pure and simple. He applauded Kevin inside.

Kevin got the girl's number and kissed her lightly before she left. When she walked away, he shot Martin a look that said, 'No sweat, man. It's as easy as pie.' Martin shook his head and laughed as he patted him on the back. That was his boy. Martin never had a problem getting girls either. He had been told time and time again that his soft hazel brown eyes were capable of hypnotizing women. That's what they said after the fact. Martin hadn't figured out the trick to make women come after *him*. Sure, he could close the deal when he went to them, but they hardly ever made that uncertain, 'everyone's looking at me' walk across a crowded room to go and talk to him like they did for Kevin. None of them. Black, White, Asian, Spanish, Indian, none of them. Not for Martin.

Kevin had to work at getting play with his own, though. Black women were used to his chocolate brown skin being silky-smooth. They were used to his naturally curly hair having a little wave to it. Black women didn't bug out on that kind of stuff. It didn't float them as easily as it floated White women. White women just loved Kevin's 'deep' skin. It was enough to make a light-skinned brother like Martin mad. Not that he wanted attention from White women so much; he was quite content with his Black Queens. But it was an ego thing. Play seemed to fall into Kevin's lap and Martin had to work for his. That kind of thing messes with a man's head.

The six of them started talking again. The conversation seemed so normal, and everyone seemed to be having such a good time that Martin shook off what he thought he saw when Kevin was talking to the woman. Not ten minutes after the blonde-haired woman left did a brown-haired woman stare in Kevin's direction. He saw her and motioned for her to come over to the table. White magic. Kevin was player-elite again. Just like that.

As Kevin turned his back to the guys, Martin got ready to comment on his 'flow' in jest. But he didn't. When he looked at Jeremy and his friends, their expressions were indescribable. There was an evil look mirrored on all four of their faces. Mutual disgust. It was only there for a second, just one split second, but Martin saw it. He saw it, and it made him uneasy. It made him angry. That was the last time they all hung out.

But there, in the lunch area at work, Martin couldn't ignore the challenge. Even though he didn't particularly care for Jeremy and his friends, he couldn't make himself pass it up. He knew that he and his boys could beat any bunch of White men at any sport, except maybe hockey. He knew that like he knew his own name. He relished the idea of being able to beat Jeremy and his boys at their own game. Martin wanted to beat them for the look they gave Kevin at the bar, or at least, the look he *thought* they gave Kevin. He had never told anyone about that because he wasn't one hundred percent sure he saw it. He had been drinking, after all. He wanted to beat them for what that look really meant.

Martin got himself so riled up that he fantasized about the game. The night before the event, Martin, Kevin, Shaun, Gary, Craig, and Robert went out for drinks. After about three beers and a lot of trash talking Martin slipped into an alcohol-induced daydream. He envisioned a plantation on which he and his friends were slaves. They had been taken from Africa to work for Jeremy and his kind. Martin imagined a great uprising where he and his friends broke their shackles and ran for the woods, determined to gain their freedom. The slave owners, led by Jeremy, advanced upon them with fire lighting their way, but he and his friends fought them off and made them retreat. Chuckling himself back to reality, Martin raised his fourth beer in a toast.

"Let's show Jeremy and his boys who's runnin' shit up in here. Paintball, basketball, baseball, racquetball, any kind of ball game they want. There's no stoppin' us."

They all raised their bottles and toasted declaration. They were ready for paintball.

That was the last time they drank together.

2

"Man, I don't think we're going the right way," Shaun muttered as they passed through the farmland. It was a gray and cool day. Something about how the sky looked bothered him. He wasn't up for this, not like the others were. He glanced warily out of the window.

"Look, Martin. There's a sign." Craig pointed at a little card stock sign flopping around on its stick. It was colored with what must have been fluorescent paint a long time ago. Now it just looked like faded orange and yellow.

Pete's Paintball.
Play with a group.
Next Left.

"I'm guessing that's it," Craig said playfully.

"No shit, Sherlock," Martin retorted. He made a left turn into a makeshift driveway. There had been a lot of rain in the area over the past couple of days and *the land was nothing but a muddy mess. Martin drove slowly, being careful not to get stuck. He didn't know how far the paintball field was from where they were, which was out in the middle of nowhere. It was certainly not the right time to get stuck, if there ever was a right time. Gary pulled off the driveway and onto the grass. The Jetta couldn't handle the mud. Martin decided to do the same and he followed Gary up a winding driveway that led onto a private street.*

In the overcast lighting of the Saturday morning, the tree-lined street looked ominous. There were towering oak and maple trees growing haphazardly in the thick of the woods. The leaves had been falling for the past couple of weeks and the ground was covered with what looked like two inches of red and orange foliage. Evergreens and cedar trees stood tall and thick. They were sinister looking on that cold November day. The trees were unyielding. Their appearance was upstaged by the leafless, contorted branches of the dogwood and magnolia trees that lurked in the thick. They deflected one's sight from the pine trees and the tangled brush. The trunks looked like horribly distorted torsos in the light of that overcast day. They likened themselves to a visual of tortured souls. The branches seemed to be reaching towards the cars, trying to suck them into the thick underbrush that lay below their massive bases. Shaun recoiled in his seat at the sight of them.

"Y'all ready to kick some ass?" Martin shouted in the truck. He was trying to rile them up; trying to get them motivated for the excursion. He too felt a little funny about the woods they were driving deeper into. He didn't like the sight of it one bit. But what the hell? It was just a stupid paintball game for kids. Right?

"Yeah, man. Yeah! I can feel the gun in my hands already." Craig held an imaginary gun in the shape of a rifle and aimed out of the window. With one eye squeezed shut, he cocked it and shot. He looked out at the trees. It seemed like the leaves rustled just as he shot the fake plug into the woods. He shivered unconsciously.

3

He saw a Cherokee and a Jetta make the turn onto the road leading to the paintball site through his binoculars. He zoomed in and saw one of the boys in the car looking around his woods nervously. He chuckled to himself. 'Be nervous, boy. Should be. Ain't got no kinda idea what you got comin' do ya? Soon enough, though. Soon enough,' the old man said to the empty room and let out a cackling laugh that shook his entire body. He put down the binoculars and called to his son.

4

Martin jumped out of the truck onto the moist, leaf-covered ground and looked around slowly. He tossed his keys back to Craig, like usual. Martin had been prone to losing his keys. Since he was eighteen or so he had passed his keys to Craig for safekeeping. Craig picked on him when he did it. He would make a big deal about it, laughing and calling him absent-minded. This time he didn't say a word.

It was quiet. He could hear the leaves crunching under his feet as he walked. Tall, threatening trees stood around them, encasing them in a wooden heaven… or hell. Shaun was the first one to break the silence.

"I don't think I've ever been out in woods like these. I mean, my grandmother's house has a little patch of trees in the back, but nothing like this. It's so…"

"Dark," Gary cut in. He put the steering wheel lock on his Jetta out of habit and got out of the car. His face looked concerned; worried. So did Kevin's.

"Hey y'all! C'mon back this way. The paintball field is way in the back, down here." A short man came out from behind the bushes and called out to them. It was like he came out of nowhere. He was wearing dingy overalls and an old baseball cap that had seen better days. With a grin, he motioned for them to follow him deeper into the woods on foot. Martin went first. He thought that if he didn't no one would. As he followed the old man and heard his friends falling in behind him, he thought about the last five minutes. They got out of the car in what seemed like a barren patch of land in the woods. There was no sound. There was no movement other than their own. Suddenly there was a guy talking at them. Giddy like. It looked as though he was excited to see them. Exceedingly excited. Something was wrong with that. Martin was uneasy, but he didn't want to let his friends know that. They already seemed a little apprehensive about the situation. He walked behind the old man with caution.

They went down a steep hill that led deeper into the woods. Robert looked back and couldn't see the car. He whispered to Martin, "I can't even see the car anymore. We're really going deep in here, huh?"

"Good," Martin said without turning around, "This way we won't hit the cars with any paint. You know I'd be pissed off if I messed up my truck."

He chuckled and picked up the pace behind the man. Robert looked back towards the car and shook his head, disturbed.

The man stopped in front of a dilapidated wooden shed and said, "Right here's where y'all will meet up wit' the other team. Go'n be a good game today, yup. Imma go an' get 'em right now. Y'all stay put." He walked around the corner and disappeared as quickly as he had appeared by the cars. They and looked at each other in silence. Kevin said, "So, what do we do now," Gary asked.

"I guess we wait. Jeremy will be here soon enough," Martin said. After about 15 minutes Martin saw them coming down the hill, eight strong. They were dressed in fatigues and seemed in unison with their stride. Looking at them was like watching a platoon prepare for battle. They were focused and serious. Martin's stomach dropped.

Jeremy was ahead of the pack. He looked confident and determined. He walked up to Martin and said with a straight face, "I'm really glad you came. You and your…friends."

He glanced through them, committing their innuendoes to memory. He looked back at Martin with soft venom in his eyes. Martin saw the change in Jeremy, but only for a second. He wasn't sure what it meant but he didn't like it. He was starting not to like much about the set up for this game.

Jeremy's face lightened and he offered a chuckle, but his eyes remained cold. He said, "You remember Chuck, Kurt, and Brad, don't you? Eddie, Doug, Wally, and Steve came along too. This should be a real good game."

"You've met Kevin. This is Shaun, Gary, Craig, and Robert." Martin pointed them out one by one to Jeremy and his friends. It was a stare down, but no one acknowledged it as such. It became clear to Martin that they weren't there just to play tag in the woods.

"Looks like we've got two more guys than you do. Tell you what, why don't we even it up? Make it seven on seven. Take your pick of one of our men," Jeremy said to Martin. He was smiling, but there was no warmth coming from it. He was cold. There was something glistening maliciously in his eyes. Hate, fear, jealousy, Martin wasn't sure. But he saw it… again. And Jeremy knew it.

Martin looked at the guys Jeremy brought with him. They were all of average build, nothing spectacular. *Nothing me and my boys can't handle,* the little voice in his head chimed in. They all had a certain confidence about them. Not inherent, he didn't think. No, it was more like they had set something up, some prime situation that they had complete control over. They were ready to play. They were sure to win. He glanced tentatively at his friends. They were all strong, all athletic. Physically, Jeremy and his friends were no match for them. But something in the back of his mind told him that this was not going to be a challenge of will and stamina. This would be something worse than that… something much more important than that.

Craig spoke up and said, "OK, since we get to pick. How about you?"

Craig pointed at Chuck. He was the bulkiest guy on Jeremy's team. He looked like he worked out more than the others, and that would make him able to handle the challenge ahead. He thought.

"What's your name, partner?"

"Chuck," he said as he snickered and looked back at his friends. He walked towards Martin's team and said, "Sure, I'm game."

"Looks like we've got a game, then! Let's head up so we can get this started," Jeremy announced as he led the way to the ammo station. They followed in single file, silently, contemplating the situation. Shaun looked over at Martin as if to ask a question but shook his head instead. Martin shrugged and slapped Shaun on the back in an effort to reassure him that things were cool. It was just a game, after all. Shaun looked away; his face grimaced slightly with worry.

5

Both teams got their ammo and bought extra just in case they ran out in the heat of battle. While they loaded their guns, Martin and his team had a strategy huddle. "We have to be ready for them to come out of a bag on us. Jeremy knows this is our first time playing. We're not going to let them take us though, right?" he questioned.

"Naw man, no. This'll be a piece of cake. We just have to stick to the plan. Get the flag and cover each other," Kevin offered.

"We should make sure that we have one person at the fort protecting the flag at all times, just in case they infiltrate somehow," Chuck added.

"Yeah, yeah. I don't know about you, but I want to be out in the middle of things. I want to go for the flag and bring it home," Robert said uncharacteristically. Robert was usually the one who waited for other people to take control of things before he jumped in. He'd been that way for as long as Martin had known him, and that was about 10 years. In high school he wouldn't go out for basketball unless at least one of his boys was going out for it too. He wouldn't go to a party unless one of his boys was going, even when a girl asked him to go. He even went to Howard University because Martin and Kevin were going. So, when he stepped up to the plate, wanting to be the one to go for the flag, everyone looked at him in shock.

Robert looked at their surprised eyes and said, "What? A brother can't want his 15 minutes of fame? Step off, y'all."

They laughed as he rolled his eyes. Shaun looked over at the other group while his laughter subsided. They weren't in a huddle like his team was, strategizing and planning. They weren't talking to each other at all. Jeremy and his team were staring at them. One of them was looking right into his eyes. Shaun looked back, unwilling to tear his eyes away. Unwilling or unable. Everything else became dark around him. Tunnel vision blocked everyone else out. The shirt the guy was wearing was completely out of focus and the features of his face were blurry. The only things Shaun could see clearly were his eyes. They were a light shade of green, but to Shaun, they looked as black as ebony. Dark and small. They were so hot they could bore holes into his head, he thought. He looked away to shake himself from the grip.

"You OK, man?" Craig asked him. He looked like he had just seen a ghost. Craig looked in the direction that Shaun had been staring and saw nothing out of the ordinary. Just the other team going over their plans, just like they had been doing. He put his hand on Shaun's back and said, "Man, what's the deal?"

"I don't know, I thought I saw something. I thought-" He stopped short and looked at Chuck. He was staring at him with dark eyes…for one second. When he blinked Chuck looked normal. He looked like a regular guy, concerned for his teammate. Not like a ghoul or a man with something up his sleeve. Just a regular guy.

"Nothing. I'm cool. I'm cool," Shaun said. He glanced tentatively back at Chuck who still looked …normal. A shiver crept up his spine.

"OK, since Robert's layin' down the law, we go with that plan," Kevin continued. "Me and Rob'll go up the middle for the flag. We'll need two to stay with our flag and everyone else needs to disperse and take care of things as they come. Sound like a plan?"

"Yeah, that'll work," Shaun offered. He sounded more like he was trying to convince himself than just agreeing with the plan.

They broke the huddle and prepared for the referee's word. A beefy man dressed in fatigues with a fluorescent orange pull over vest stretched tightly across his torso stood between the two teams. Martin looked at him and nodded hello. The man returned a smirk and glanced over to Jeremy's team with a knowing glance. Confused, Martin looked at Kevin who was standing next to him, and said, "Did you see that Ref? What's up with that?"

"I don't know, man," he said as he looked at Jeremy and his friends. They were ready. Mentally and physically. They had all the extras also. They had smoke bombs, side arms, grenades, you name it. He didn't even know they made those kinds of accessories for paintball. Something about that made him nervous. Martin shook his head lightly. "Don't sweat it," he finished.

The referee spoke loudly into the bullhorn. In a muffled voice he yelled, "The idea is to get the flag and take it to your fort. If you get hit three times, you out the game fer good. Do y'all get that? The game is over when one team has taken the other team's flag, or when there's only one man standing. Got that? Play to the end, boys. This is war." He held up two bandannas – one yellow and one red. "These is yo' flags. Jeremy's boys got the yellow one and you boys got the red one." He tossed the flag lackadaisically to Martin. "If there ain't no questions, I say let's get this goin'. Any questions?" No one said anything.

"When I blow this whistle, it means y'all got 'bout one minute to get to yo' places. When I blow it again the game starts. Here she goes."

He licked the perspiration off his upper lip and blew into the whistle. The two teams dispersed, hanging their flags in equidistant forts on low branches, and securing their hiding places. They moved without a sound. Martin and Shaun were protecting the flag, Robert and Kevin were the flag runners going up the middle on opposite sides of the path, and Craig, Chuck and Gary were on the outskirts protecting the flag runners like line backers.

When Kevin got to his hiding place, he could hear Shaun behind him breathing heavily.

"What is it, man? You ok?"

"Yeah man. I-I'm fine," Shaun responded. But he was far from fine.

The whistle sounded for the second time.

The game had begun.

6

They sat in complete silence for an eternity. Their hearts beat loudly and rapidly in their chests. Martin looked between the bushes at his friends. They were tense and uptight. There was something brewing in the woods that was more than competitiveness. It was more like fear. Genuine, uncontested fear. And they all felt it. Even him.

Kevin knelt hidden in the brush, covered by leaves and twigs as camouflage. Beads of sweat fell into his eyes underneath the protective goggles, stinging them, but he dared not wipe his forehead. He didn't want to move at all. Something was going on and he knew it. *Something is wrong with this set up*, he thought. *I mean, those guys came down looking serious about…something.* This wasn't just an ordinary game of paintball. He knew it the moment he saw the other team. He could tell by the way Jeremy and his friends were looking at them. Jeremy and his friends were looking at them like they were fresh meat, a succulent cut at that. It made him nervous.

He looked beyond the tree at Jeremy's fort. He could barely see their flag above the bushes and tall grass. He couldn't see any of Jeremy's team either. Not one person. He adjusted his footing and raised up slightly to get a better look. He thought he saw movement, so he shot off a round of pink paint. The paintball shot out of the gun propelled by the CO2 tank connected to its base and splattered against a tree. When there was no retaliation, Kevin relaxed back into his hiding place. He didn't see the gunman in the bushes picking him out. He didn't hear the barrel cock as the gunman took aim. He didn't see the barrel squared off at his head. He didn't hear the bullet cut the air. He didn't see or hear anything at all.

7

"Did you hear that," Shaun shrieked in a low, raspy, panicked voice. They all hit the dirt as soon as the pop of the bullet broke the uncomfortable silence. "It sounded like gun fire. Real gunfire, man! What the fuck is going on?"

Martin was crouched in the thick of kikuyu grass, his eyes searching frantically. The shot rang in his ears loudly, incessantly. He looked nervously around for his friends. Robert was standing now, looking around himself in fear. Martin wanted to yell out to Robert and tell him to sit down, to take cover, to run damnit, but when he opened his mouth, nothing came out. Nothing. He tried to inch towards Shaun who was across the weathered path from him, lying in a makeshift bunker. He wanted to go to him so that he wouldn't be alone. So that neither one of them would be alone… but he couldn't move.

A second shot was fired, and a gargled scream permeated the air thick with tension and fear. Martin looked up just in time to see Robert grab at his throat. Blood shot out in spurts between his fingers, mimicking his racing heartbeat. Robert gagged and coughed, trying desperately to catch his breath. His bulging eyes were glazed over with pain. He fell to his knees and sprayed the mallow with his dying blood.

Oh Shit! Oh, Holy shit, Martin thought to himself. He peered over the tangle weed he had buried himself under and saw Chuck retracting into his hiding place. Chuck! The big guy on *their* team, courtesy of Jeremy. *He led them right to us,* Martin thought fleetingly. Chuck had a hideous smirk on his face. He was laughing. They were all laughing. The low roar of their impervious glee seared his eardrums.

"Got that, boys? We fixin' to play us a good ole game of paintball today," someone shouted into the thick air. It was Jeremy's voice.

"Yeah, your blood will do nicely in place of paint. Those balls don't quite splatter the way blood does, you know. It's just not the same. So we go'n make sure we do this right. Why, we wouldn't want to bring you all the way out here to play a half-assed game. We want to make sure your first game of paintball is the real thing. Your first and your last, that is." He heard Jeremy chuckle and walk away. The crunching of the leaves under his feet became distant, and it sounded like he was walking back towards the common ground. Jeremy might have left, but the others hadn't moved. They were lying in wait, ready to pounce. Waiting...

8

He could hear the laughter emanating from the bushes. He could hear the distant gait of Jeremy's smooth, calm step. He could hear his heart thumping wildly in his chest; he could hear all of these things. He could also hear, underneath all of the peripheral noise, he could hear Shaun panting heavily, trying desperately to get a handle on himself and the situation. He could hear Craig shaking against the dead leaves. He could hear Gary's soft cries of confusion. Martin heard it all. He covered his ears and sank his head. A deep, guttural yell rose from his diaphragm, shaking his body in anger and dread.

9

It seemed like hours before he moved. He could see Martin's shoulders heaving massively as he sobbed loudly. God, he wanted to get up and run. He wanted to run for his life. Instead, all he could do was stare at Martin's back as hot tears streamed down his face.

"Shaun? Shaun??" He heard his name whispered in the cool of the unfolding day and it woke him from the trance he slipped into.

"Shaun," Gary pled.

"Yeah man, yeah. I'm here, man."

Gary inched close to the ground trying not to make a sound. He crawled over to Martin first and put his arm around him. Martin hadn't moved. His mouth was still open, shaped in the grimace left from his painful shout. Tears had dried on his cheeks and he dry-heaved sporadically and rapidly. Gary made his way through the fallen leaves to Shaun and said,

"D-D-Did that sh-sh-shit really ha-p-p-p-pen, man? Did you see that sh-sh-shit-t?"

Shaun looked at him vapidly and nodded. Gary was stammering badly. In the seventeen years that they had known each other, Shaun hadn't heard Gary stammer or stutter or trip once. Not once. He grabbed Gary by the shoulders as he shook and said,

"I saw it man. Good God, I saw Robert go down."

"Where is everybody? Where are they man? Kevin? Craig? Where-"

"Kevin's dead, G. Kevin's gone, man," Craig said from behind them. Martin looked up slowly from the ball he had rolled his body into. His eyes searched Craig's face, laden with mud and leaves and blood. There was blood on his jacket; it glistened in the dull light that the trees let through.

"Are you hit, C.? You alright, man," Gary asked him in a shaky, high-pitched tenor, far from his usual baritone rumble.

Craig looked down at his jacket and said,

"No, it's not my blood. I'm not hit. I was next to Kevin when he went down. I guess I wasn't as far out on the perimeter as I was supposed to be. The shot was so loud, I thought I would never stop hearing the echo. They came from somewhere behind us. They were hiding in the bushes, but there's no way they could have gotten to that position so quick. It was like he got shot seconds after the game started. It wasn't even a minute after the second whistle blew before they gunned him down."

They looked at each other in silence. Craig touched the blood on his jacket and began to sob.

10

"Where are they now," the old man asked Jeremy. He looked pleased but on guard. He paced the room, his toeless foot thumping on the floor hard in unison with his wooden cane with each step. A glaze of sweat was forming on his forehead. He laughed heartily before Jeremy could answer and shook his fist towards the window in defiance.

"Who says we don't own this land, huh," he shouted. "Them niggers think they runnin' us - they think they runnin' everything! They think they such hot shit. We showin' them different, ain't we boys? We finally putting them in they fuckin' places, yup. This is where they belong. In the jungle running scared like animals and hiding like cowards and then dying at the hand of a righteous man. A White man. It's how it always should have been, and would have, if it hadn't been for those bleeding-heart bastards and uppity niggers like King and Evers. Fuckin' coons. Too weak to be a buck so they got book smart. But that book smart shit don't work out here in our place, do it boys? These fuckin' coon bastards go'n suffer today. And pretty soon our mission will take out all of 'em. All of 'em!"

He raised his hands in the air in triumph and Jeremy's hands raised to meet them. "There are four left, Dad. We shot two of those fuckers down already. One of 'em spurted his blood all over the leaves out there. Big fuckin' mess."

"Don't worry about it, boy. Nigger blood is better than rain."

Jeremy smiled and patted his dad on the back. He turned to the door and walked into the hallway. He stuck his head out and said,

"Eddie, you ready for part two?"

"Jerry, I don't think we even have to do it. They're easy pickins out there. They ain't got shit for bullets and we got them outnumbered."

"I know, but it'll be that much sweeter to see them fall for our trick. Trust me on this one. You'll see."

11

The four of them sat together in a huddle. The wind was whipping up and the air was getting cold. How long had they been out there? An hour, maybe two? In that short time their lives had changed forever.

In the bushes to their front right they could hear bugs chirping and buzzing loudly over Robert's body. The hot, pungent smell of fresh blood saturated the air and made it hard to breathe. It was their friends' blood. Robert's and Kevin's.

Craig spoke first, "Look, we don't have anything but paintballs in here. No bullets. We are sitting ducks if we don't run for it. There's no other way." He looked into the clear plastic cover and saw fluorescent pink and yellow paint balls in the hopper. He shook his head. "We've got to go for it."

"What and give them free target practice?" Shaun exclaimed. His face was covered with sweat and tears. His lips quivered as he spoke, "We can't just run out there and book to the cars hoping to hell none of us gets our asses blown off! Who knows where they are now, just waiting for us to make a fool move like that so they can cut us down?"

"He's right," Martin said. He had been silent since Robert's death, unable to speak, unable to think. "We can't just *run* out of here. We need a plan."

They put their heads together to come up with a way out. Splitting up was the only option. They dumped their worthless guns and facemasks and moved within the bushes as quietly as possible, veering off gradually in different directions. The plan was to get to the cars and wait for each other. The first ones to the car were supposed to hide on the floor until all four of them got in. They were going to put the cars in neutral and let it roll down the incline they were parked on. When the cars rolled far enough away from the woods they would start the engines and Jeremy and his friends would have to run to catch them. They could escape if they stuck to the plan. They could get out.

<h2 style="text-align:center">12</h2>

They moved with very little sound and found themselves alone quickly. Shaun crouched and crawled through prickly tangle weed, wincing from the pain, but not uttering a sound. Then he heard something. He kept going; afraid to stop now…and then he heard it again. A low, jumbled sound was coming from the bushes off to his right. It sounded like moaning. His mind flooded with thoughts of Kevin or Robert lying in the cold mud, colored red by their blood. He thought of one of them gasping for air and mouthing his or one of the other guy's names, begging for help.

He whispered, "Kevin? Kevin man, that you?"

It had to be Kevin if it was anyone at all. He saw Robert get shot with his own eyes. He saw the blood and the distant look in his eyes before he was engulfed by the bushes. He knew Robert couldn't be alive.

No answer. Maybe the wind was playing tricks on him. Maybe he wanted it to be one of his friends so badly that he made himself believe they were calling to him. Maybe… A voice beckoned weakly from the bushes. He moved closer, no longer cognizant of the noise he was making.

"Kevin? You're alive?"

He pulled back a branch and uncovered Eddie, one of Jeremy's friends. He was bleeding from a shot to his left shoulder. His gun was lying on the ground close to his right foot, and his shirt was ripped to shreds. He was propped unsteadily on the menacing tree stump, his back painfully hunched.

Shaun recoiled quickly and started to run. He could almost feel the beam of the gun on his back, targeting his heart through his clothes. He was terrified.

Eddie wheezed, "No! Please help me."

Shaun stopped running and turned his head towards Eddie cautiously. Eddie was injured, the pain on his face was unmistakable. He was reaching for Shaun earnestly, wanting-- needing help.

Shaun stood in place and said, "You didn't see me, man. Keep it that way." He turned to leave, but Eddie whispered, "SHH! Be quiet. They're all around here. They're waiting for you—for us."

Shaun looked around him and saw nothing but the twisted branches of trees and evergreen shrubs. He listened intently and heard nothing but the birds vacating the area, in search of warmer weather. Getting away. Like he wanted to.

Shaun walked towards Eddie. "What do you mean *us*? You're one of *them*. Why would they be looking for you?" He nudged Eddie's gun away from him and brought it to his side. Eddie let him do it.

"See man? I'm safe. I'm not with what the other guys are doing." He sucked in air heavily and with marked difficulty. There was blood all over him. It saturated his shirt. He was sweating profusely and shaking slightly. Shaun didn't hold the gun on him, but he kept it close to his side.

"I'm not with them, I swear it. I don't know what's going on. I've known Jeremy for years—ever since we were kids…I don't know what's happening." He breathed in thickly again and coughed. He trembled violently and turned red.

Shaun watched him convulse. He wanted to believe him, but he had to be sure.

"That's bullshit. How could you not know what 's going on? You're one of them! You're on their team! You planned this with them from the start!"

"No, no. I swear, I didn't have any idea this was going to happen. I came out here from Boston to see Jeremy on Friday. He told me he was going to be playing paintball with a couple of friends and a colleague from work. A friendly game, that's all. I never knew there was going to be anything like this. Dear God, if I had known… do you honestly think I would be in this situation if I knew?"

He shifted his weight and gestured towards his wound.

Shaun sighed, "Why'd they do that to you man? Why'd they shoot you and how did you stop them from killing you?"

"Jeremy -" He stifled a sob. "Jeremy shot me. After he shot the first one, your friend, I asked him what the hell was going on. I thought we were just going to play paintball. I had no idea anything like this was going to happen. I told him I wouldn't be involved in this and that I was going to find you guys and help you get out. I told him that what he was doing wasn't right. That it just wasn't right. He…he shot me with absolutely no remorse. He left me to die. He said that he wanted me to suffer, and that he hoped that one of you guys found me and beat me to death. I crawled down here from up the hill. I was trying to get help, but I…I'm so tired. God man, we've been friends for so long I can't believe…I can't believe what he's doing."

Eddie turned his head away from Shaun and sniffled. He pulled his arm up to his eyes and buried his head in it. Shaun watched him as he went through his pain. He had just lost two of his closest friends, so he understood what Eddie was going through. Eddie's body began to shake. Shaun put his hand on Eddie's shoulder to comfort him. He propped the gun against a tree and covered his own eyes as he let his emotion out.

Eddie continued to cry as he quickly put his hand, clad with open handcuffs that were hidden in the bushes, on Shaun's right wrist. Shaun looked up in surprise. The realization that he had been fooled came over him. Before he could process this betrayal - before he could react at all, the hand that held the tears he shed for his lost friends was locked viciously in the cold iron cuff. Shaun couldn't believe what was happening. Eddie's cries of pain and anguish turned into hearty laughter.

He stood and exclaimed, "Whoa, Jerry! You were right! That trick sure as hell did work!"

Eddie leaned down and whispered into Shaun's ear. "Your nigger friend's blood was still warm when I took some and smeared it on my shirt."

Shaun yelled out loud in fear and anger.

Eddie continued to laugh as Jeremy came from behind a nearby bush. He smiled at Eddie, pleased with his work. "Take 'im back to the shed, Eddie. We'll set up the rest of it. Oh, and gag 'im so he cain't shout."

Eddie nodded and giggled as he led dumbfounded Shaun to the shed. Jeremy shouted at the top of his lungs,

"Boys, we got one of yo' nigger friends now. If you want his tired ass, you'll come get 'im at the shed. If all of you ain't there in, oh say 15 minutes, we'll kill 'im and skin 'im. Ain't that what happened to that stupid nigger Nat Turner?" He chuckled and said, "You niggers are just as dumb and gullible as they say you are. This shit is easy as taking candy from a baby." He strolled towards the shed, shooting the blanks out of Eddie's gun into the air.

13

Martin stopped in his tracks and looked around as Jeremy beckoned for them to come to the shed. They caught someone. Who? How? He sat on the ground and looked at his hands. He didn't know what to do. He knew he had to find the others if they were still in the woods…if they were still alive.

**

Craig turned around quickly at the end of Jeremy's diatribe. The woods seemed to be closing in on him. The trees seemed to be laughing at him. He suddenly felt very small. The claustrophobia that he had once overcome came back viciously and overtook him. He fell to the ground wide-eyed and unable to breathe sufficiently. He was paralyzed by fear.

**

Gary ran down the hill and out of the consuming wilderness, ignoring Jeremy's call to the shed. He could see the cars up ahead. He was so close; he could almost touch them. He kept running, not once looking back, not even when Jeremy reiterated that he had captured one of his friends, not even when he heard the gunfire. With tears in his eyes, he ran to the Jetta. He fumbled with the keys in his pocket, having trouble grabbing them and pulling them out because his hands were shaking so badly.

There were footsteps behind him. They were rapidly approaching. He could hear the heavy breathing and the wheezing, shaky voice uttering what sounded like his name. Elated, he turned around thinking that one of his friends made it out. With a smile he extended his arms, only to see that it was Brad, one of Jeremy's boys. He was holding a double-barrel rifle at his chest. Brad was so close, Gary could feel the edge of the barrel grazing the button on the pocket of his shirt.

"C'mon man. Let me go. You don't have to kill me, OK? You don't have to do this, man."

Brad looked at him gravely, not moving a muscle in his face. With a placid, strong voice he said, "Yes, I do."

He pulled the trigger.

14

Martin clawed through the bushes to find his way back to their fort. With no other safe, as if any place was really *safe*, common ground, he hoped that the others would think to meet there after hearing the announcement.

Martin got to the clearing and fell clumsily to the ground, his body wracked with exhaustion and fear. Frantically he tried to think of who could have been caught. Shaun? Gary? Craig? He didn't know. He tried to be quiet and wait for the others, but his mind was throwing all different kinds of scenarios at him. Could Jeremy have been bluffing and this was a set up? Did Jeremy really have one of them and, if he did, was he still alive? Martin didn't know. He couldn't believe any of this was happening. It seemed like a dream. One that he couldn't wake himself from. It was a horrid nightmare.

Craig came around the corner huffing and puffing. "Where are the others?"

"I don't know. What took you so long to get back?"

"I was out of it, man. The trees, they looked like they were closing in on me. I guess I slipped back into one of those fits I used to have when I was a kid. You know, the ones where I can't move at all, no matter what I do. I snapped out of it a couple of minutes after the gunfire. When I was running back here, I thought I heard more gunfire but it was off in the distance. Did you hear it?"

Martin nodded solemnly. He heard the shot but hadn't processed it until Craig brought it up. *My God, did one of us get shot*, he thought.

"Who do you suppose they have? Gary or Shaun?" Craig continued.

"I don't know, but we only have seven minutes or so to get to that shed they were talking about. I hope whoever's left, Shaun or Gary, will go right to the shed. We can't afford to waste any more time waiting for them."

Martin got up and started to walk into the bushes toward the shed, or in that general direction. Reluctantly, Craig followed behind him, looking back every now and then to see if either Shaun or Gary showed up at their fort. Both Martin and Craig had lost their sense of direction with all the running in circles, and they couldn't recall where the shed was.

They made their way to Jeremy's fort and beyond, still not seeing any sign of the shed. Frustrated and scared with only three minutes left, Martin turned his head up to the sky and shouted, "Where are you, Jeremy? What the hell do you want from us?"

He threw his arms out to his sides in rage. A sarcastic chuckle came from behind them. Slowly Jeremy emerged from the woods. It looked almost like he was arriving from another dimension, the way he seemed to glide out and away from the bushes and trees, floating towards them with unnatural grace. He was unarmed and stripped of the bulky garments they had all worn to keep warm during the game. He was sweating bullets, as though he had been running through the woods, tracking their steps. He was smiling demonically, pleased with the cat and mouse game he had set up.

Hatred welled in Martin's throat, suffocating his rational thoughts. He lunged at Jeremy, throwing all of his weight at him. Jeremy leaned to the side and tripped Martin. He fell flat on his face. Martin turned over onto his back and looked up at him. Jeremy was *smiling*. Craig went over to Martin and helped him to his feet.

"You 'bout done now? I can stand here and fight you 'till the cows come home, but your friend is going to run out of time. Tick, tock. Tick, tock. The seconds keep a' tickin' away." He turned towards the bushes and started to walk away.

The southern drawl Jeremy was displaying was new to Martin. He had never heard it before that day. He didn't think he would ever forget it. Craig nudged him along and they followed Jeremy into the woods.

Jeremy had a streak of blood down the back of his grimy tee-shirt. It was thick and wide with bits and pieces of flesh on it. Craig gagged as they walked, unable to fathom whose blood that might be. He stumbled and tripped over his feet, falling to the ground. He was feeling the same feeling that plagued him before. The trees were starting to close in on him. They mocked him with intangible laughter and pointed their accusatory fingers at him while he writhed on the floor, gasping for air, precious air.

Martin went to him and raised him to a sitting position. Jeremy was drifting out of sight.

"C'mon, C. Get up, man. We've got to go and save our boy. Please Craig. I don't even see Jeremy anymore. We've got to catch up to him."

Craig tried desperately to catch his breath, but he couldn't. He tried to wave Martin on, but his limbs were heavy. His face turned ashy gray from the lack of oxygen, and he started to fade. Faintly now, he could hear Martin begging him not to die. Telling him to hold on. He could see out of the corner of his eye something - someone laying on the ground next to him, hidden away from sight under the bushes. It was Gary. His eyes were upturned, and his face had a tormented grimace forever etched on it. Without fighting he allowed himself to slip into unconsciousness. He couldn't take any more of what was happening.

15

Martin watched his friend drift off helplessly. He couldn't stay with him. It was already too late. Jeremy had completely disappeared in the brush, and Martin only had one minute left to help his friend. He got up slowly, saying a silent goodbye, and ran in the direction Jeremy was headed, casting a solemn look back at his friend Craig who lay partially under the bushes.

Martin caught up to Jeremy quickly and said, "How far are we from it, man?"

"Is that nigger friend of yours dead," Jeremy asked maliciously with his back still turned.

"Yes. He is."

"Bonus. That way I don't have to waste a round on him."

"Is that your plan? To kill us all?" Martin's voice had taken on a shrill quality. It was the sound of panic and disarmament.

Jeremy stopped walking and stood with his back to Martin. He pondered the question for a moment. Suddenly lifted his head to the sky and let out a monstrous laugh that shook Martin to his core. He shook his head and turned to look at Martin. With pity in his voice he said, "Don't you realize that you are already dead?"

He smiled and turned his back to continue deeper into the woods. He pushed the bushes away, clearing Martin's view of the shed, and of Shaun.

16

Shaun's arms and legs were bound by rope to a wooden cross that was wedged into the ground. He was completely naked. His nipples had been cut off and stuffed up his nostrils protruding them grotesquely. The jagged lacerations in his skin were bleeding profusely. Sweat covered his body and he had soiled himself. His head was lowered onto his chest. He had been beaten savagely and his skin was discolored in several places. Martin was certain that his friend was dead.

Martin saw an old man in the doorway of the shed. His eyes were gleaming. He had a look of contentment and anticipation on his face. Next to him stood Jack, the controller of the firm he and Jeremy worked for. His face was red and sweaty. It held a look of mocking satisfaction. Martin could have killed them. All of them.

Before Martin's eyes, Wally and Kurt poured gasoline on Shaun's limp body. Wally lit a match and threw it on Shaun's stomach. It stuck there while the flame ignited.

"Looks like we's fixin' ta have a right ole' Bar-B-Q, ain't we nigger," Steve said jovially. Martin was flabbergasted. Everything that he was seeing, everything he had seen was a blur to him now as he stood incoherently before his friend's burning body.

A bone-chilling scream escaped Shaun's lips and he lifted his head slowly. He shook on the makeshift cross, trying to tip it over and escape perishing in the flames. Quickly though, he was silent.

Martin snapped back to reality and attacked Kurt, pushing him into the flames with Shaun. Kurt lunged away from Shaun's burning body quickly, but he couldn't escape the flames. They clung to his face and shirt, devouring the skin underneath. He screamed deliriously in pain and threw himself on the ground. He groped for something that would extinguish the flames to no avail. Wally threw a blanket over him and tried to beat the flames out, but it was too late.

"You muthafuckin' bitch," Steve said and grabbed Martin's arms. He threw Martin to the ground and put all of his weight on him. Martin shut his eyes; all the fight had drained out of him. He heard all too clearly the cock of the gun. He felt the cool barrel on his temple and welcomed it.

17

The gunshot woke Craig from his unconscious state. He peered through the dead leaves and roots to see if he could detect any signs of movement. He had to get out of there, he knew that now. He didn't think anyone was left from his crew. The gunshot had to be for Martin, he was sure of it. Gary was dead, Kevin was dead, Robert was dead, Shaun had to be dead. He was the only one left.

He got up and moved slowly at first, cautiously. He could hear them talking loudly and cursing about something. They sounded angry. Maybe Martin and Shaun took care of one of them before they were killed. God, he hoped they had gotten at least one of them.

Craig made his way down the hill in virtual silence, blending in with the darkening day and slipping out into oblivion. He made it to the truck and reached for Martin's keys in his pocket. They were warm against his leg. He pulled them out slowly and clenched them tightly in his hand for a moment, unable to stop the memories from flooding back. Unable to say goodbye.

Quietly he got into the truck, taking pains not to slam the door. He checked the back seats to make sure that no one was in there with him. He ducked under the windows as he slid the car into neutral. As the car rolled backwards down the incline and out of the hardened mud onto the dirt road that led to the main drag. He prayed that there was nothing behind him that he could hit and draw attention to himself. He just wanted to get out.

He felt pebbles crunching under the tires and the ride became less smooth. He was out of the mud and on some semblance of a road. He turned the ignition, shifted the truck into first gear, and took off. He kicked up rocks with the back tires as he sped down the dirt road, shifting the gears roughly and abruptly.

Craig made his way through the dense brush on either side of the road, positive that one of Jeremy's friends was waiting there for him, gun in hand, aimed and prepared, but they weren't. He made an uncontested right onto the paved road. He saw the faded paintball sign in the rear-view mirror getting smaller and smaller. Tears rolled silently down his cheeks.

Passing him quickly on his left was a red sports utility truck filled with five guys…Black guys. They made a sharp left turn into the paintball area.

What the Mirror Sees

I was home sick from work the day it happened. I could have gone in, but I really wanted to stay home and watch television. Judge shows and talk shows. The freaks and fools the world is made up of all dolled up to prance in front of countless viewers' eyes in their ill-fitting lace and their mis-sized spandex pants. I liked to watch, I don't mind admitting that. It's entertaining. It's comedy, in a sad way. Anyway, who cared about that fucking job or the brainless, two-faced, self-absorbed, egotistical bastards who worked there? Not me, that was for sure. I cared as much about them as they cared about me and that was zip.

The day I saw her staring back at me, I was enjoying the day off. I loafed around the house in my holey sweatpants and baggy t-shirt. I didn't answer the phone when it rang the one time it did. I didn't care if it was work, the delivery guy, or a telemarketer trying to get me to buy some crappy service or some trendy electronic device. Those were the only people who would call anyway. And they always got my name wrong. 'Hello Ms. Sanchez! Have you heard about the new way to burn fat? Yeah! You can do it in your sleep!' Save it, honey. Ms. Sanchez changed her number five years ago and I don't give a damn if you're selling seats on the next rocket to the moon. I don't want to hear about it. Have a nice day! Of course, I never really said that to any of them, although I've wanted to. The most I could muster was 'Thank you, but I'm not interested'. When they wouldn't accept that answer, I hung up, like a coward. Now I don't answer the phone at all anymore. Classic avoidance. Whatever. It works.

Nope, my phone doesn't ring much. When it does, it's either the telemarketer jerks or a wrong number. Even that doesn't happen much anymore.

I didn't think about inviting a friend over to watch movies or calling some guy over for an afternoon romp in the sack because there was no guy. There were no friends. There wasn't so much as a dog or cat to snuggle up with on the sofa. It was just me, myself, and I. And that was fine. Things were the way I was accustomed to them being. They were the way I liked them.

Anyway, all I wanted to do was relax. To just be. Including anyone or anything else would have just been a hassle. Company is overrated.

The first time she looked back at me was when I was standing in my kitchen. I was in front of the cabinets, about to open the door and take out a glass. I had a nice cold soda waiting for me in the fridge. It was to be my first of many for that day, and I was starting early. At 9:45 a.m., I had to hurry if I wanted to get on the sofa and positioned just right to watch the first barrage of mind-numbing programming. I had to get moving.

She was there then, I know that now. Her visit sticks out in my mind even while I recount the details of today and the days, months, years that I lived before this fateful moment. My mind's eye saw her when my conscious mind didn't. My conscious mind went through the motions: I pulled out a glass from the cabinet, set it on the counter with one hand while the other swung the cabinet door shut. My conscious mind had me walk over to the refrigerator and take out the soda can. It had me retrieve the glass, open the freezer door, get some ice, and drop it into the glass. I remember the clinking of the ice cubes against the glass as they settled. I remember the fizz of the soda as I cracked open the can. My conscious mind had me see, smell, and touch those things, but blocked out the one thing that I should have been looking for. The one thing that, had I seen it, might have changed my life.

But I see her now. I see her as she was then, standing behind me in the kitchen, between the refrigerator and me. I see her standing there now as clearly as I see my own blood trickling onto the floor, staining the tile as it spreads.

She was there, behind me, so close to me I could have felt her breath on my neck had she any to exhale. She was dead, pallid in her complexion as the rot consumed her flesh. Her eyes were drained of color, the whites blending seamlessly with the irises. Her mouth was open and slack, as though she wished to speak but could not. Her face was reflected in the silver knob of the kitchen cabinet for only an instant, but she was there. She had come for me. After all the years of silent torment from her world, she had come for me. It was time for our places in time to sync up, to align and exist in the same space. It was time for the two of us to meet at last.

I went about my day oblivious to her as she toured my rooms. She fingered my things with the most basic of curiosity, her manner that of a person trying to waste time in expectation of an event. Had I seen her then I would have asked her what she wanted, why she was here. Had I known she was coming I would have left the apartment, would have gone to work, to the market, to any place where she wouldn't follow. Had I known I would see her here, in my home, sitting the way she sat, the way I now sit, I would have run.

But I didn't see her and I didn't run. Instead I laughed my empty laughter at the nonsense playing itself out on the television screen, oblivious to the fact that each ticking of the clock, each check point of time passing counted down my own time span, marking it.

I felt different at 3:35 p.m. There was a lull in the afternoon exploitation shows—I was eagerly awaiting their return at 4:00 p.m. Something descended upon me, some sort of veil dulling my senses, making me feel as though something was missing within me. The veil was opaque at first, granting me a hazy view of the room. It surrounded me, closing in just a little, just enough. I tried to shake it, to rid myself of the strange feeling making me feel cold and weighted. I looked at the glass full of the tempting soda I had so enjoyed only moments before and didn't want it. The bowl of popcorn sitting on the edge of the sofa was equally unappetizing and I pushed it away with my foot. The bowl coasted to the edge of the sofa and teetered there for a second, before falling off the side. I watched the popcorn fall to the floor without flinching, without lifting a hand to catch the bowl before it tipped over. I just watched it happen with disinterest so thick I began to wonder if I had seen anything happen at all.

Then the veil darkened. The yellow popcorn changed gradually to tan, then brown, then to black as everything surrounding it did. Suddenly the weight of the veil was so heavy I could barely lift my head. I reached for the edge of the table and got up, thinking my head would clear if I changed my position. My vision returned immediately, the colors of the room returning to their normal hue. The darkness was inside me then, though, no longer hovering in front of me, but filling me up.

I trudged to the bathroom, my feet as heavy as lead and as cold as they would be if I had covered them with snow. I wanted to rub myself, to warm my skin with my hands, but I couldn't raise my arms. I kept walking though, pushing ahead.

I stood in front of the mirror to find myself with dark circles under my eyes. My hair was stringy and sweaty, my eyes looked wild. I brought my hand to my head with much effort and rubbed the clammy skin of my forehead. *I must be coming down with something*, my mind offered weakly. It makes me chuckle now to think of the naiveté my conscious mind desperately displayed then, had displayed all of my life. This was a hell of a cold, if there ever was one.

She appeared to me then, standing behind me like she had been there all the while. The sudden vision would have been enough to make my heart stop right then and there, but that wasn't the way it was supposed to happen. It wasn't the way it happened before. There was an order to things that had to be followed. My case was no different.

She spoke. Her voice sounded ethereal, oddly soothing.

"Janice."

She had only to say my name to send me spiraling towards the edge of my sanity. Who was this? How did she know my name? I looked at her. In death her features were ichorous, seeming to float above her brittle bone structure, beneath her thin skin. Though hard to look at in her state of being, her likeness was uncanny. Her hair, though darkened by the liquid weight of some clear, gel-like substance, was the same color as mine, the same length. Her slender body was the same as mine; the shape of her hips and the lift her breast looked like they could have been traced by an artist's pen to match my own. The woman I was looking at was me in a different time, a different dimension.

My mind had a hard time reconciling that. I remember that I blinked incessantly, trying to clear the ghostly countenance from the mirror. How could this be? A conversation I had been engaged in weeks ago touched upon the idea of people living in other dimensions, in other worlds that ran in tandem with the one that we were conscious of, the one that our minds chose to dwell in. Wendy, a crystal-carrying believer in all things spiritual, made the point that when we dream, we travel over to one of the other dimensions. We mingle with the beings in that world and only come back to this one when our conscious mind summons us, like a mother waking her child for school. When I balked at the idea, she leaned in closer, lowering her voice as if sharing a secret.

"If you don't believe this theory then how do you explain déjà vu? How do you explain the feeling that you've met someone before, even when you know that there isn't a chance in hell that your paths have crossed?"

I didn't have an answer. I sat silently smirking at her outwardly but mulling her words over in my mind. They plugged the holes held open in my head, fitting nicely in their new spaces.

"We are part of a continuum, Janice. What happens today may have already happened in another world or may not have happened yet in another. You could be dying right now, remembering this conversation, this place in time, on your death bed, or it may be a premonition of yours while you lay in your crib, your mind unable to discern the language and emotion we're expressing now. There is a natural order to things. An order that has to be followed no matter what. We are nothing more than players on the board of life, my friend. And there are many different boards from which to choose."

I went home that night thinking about what she said, pondering the validity of it in my mind. I didn't want to believe something so far reaching, so out there, but some of what she said rang true to me. After all, if I believed that there are other life forms in the solar system, the proverbial aliens as we here on Earth seem so comfortable dubbing anything from outer space, why couldn't I believe life existed on multiple layers? Why was it so hard for me to grasp the notion, especially when I have a clairvoyant cousin in New York and an uncle that swears the spirits of his dead brothers and sisters come to him now and again? Why was this so hard to grasp?

Before we parted ways, I asked Wendy why she thought our conscious mind chose one existence over another to live.

"I think it's because this one is more palatable at the time," she offered.

"What do you mean?" I asked, my voice thick with sarcasm as I reclined in the plush leather chair at the corner bookstore within which we debated. I remember picking up my cup of coffee, still warm in the paper cup and bringing it to my lips.

"We're alive now. Happy, healthy, content. Right?"

I nodded, taking another sip of the brew.

"Well, what if our other existences, our lives on other worlds, weren't so happy? What if, on many of them, we were suffering? Dying? What if, on many of them, we were already dead? Let's go even further with this. What if, on some dimensions, we never existed at all? Our minds, operating in self-preservation mode, may choose to dwell in a world where we still have a fighting chance. Maybe because it wants to live, it picks this existence over the others, so it can."

"Yeah, but if we are part of a continuum, death is inevitable. Why would our minds make the decision to step into a world where we haven't met the foreshadowed doom yet, where it still lingered in the shadows waiting for us to happen along?"

I took another sip of my coffee, making a show of blowing at the steam before pulling it into my mouth. I was sure I had won the argument, had shut her up once and for all. But then she said something that never left my mind, not in the weeks between then and now.

"Because maybe, even though we can choose what plane to live on, we can never outrun what has been set forth for us. The death itself, the way that it happens, the suffering will all come to pass no matter what. It's fate. But our minds don't know it. They think they can change it somehow. So they run."

Standing now, Wendy picked up her cup of coffee, finished it off, and picked up her purse.

"But now, in our conscious, enlightened state, we know what our minds hid from themselves. We know the truth."

"And what is that?" The sarcasm was thick in my voice.

"You can never outrun your destiny, Janice. It's yours to keep."

I stood in the mirror looking at myself, at my other worldly countenance come to visit me here on the dimension I inhabited. Her look frightened me. I had seen it before, in my dreams. Her eyes, her skin, the cuts in her wrists gaping open like fleshy mouths. She had come here to visit me not in the form of a child, or that of an old woman, long in the tooth and weathered in life. She came to me as a young woman whose life had already been taken. She was already dead.

"What do you want?" I asked, my voice shrill and shaky.

The me from another world took a step closer, closer, closer still, until she was right behind me. In a voice that was nothing more than air blowing over the death rattle in her throat, she said,

"You."

The room is darkening now; my eyelids are so heavy I'm having trouble keeping them open. My blood is still trickling from my wrists and onto the floor. As I watch it pool around my feet and around the base of the toilet, I wonder who will find me. Who will come into my house and see me sitting here on the toilet seat of my bathroom? Who will see my blood spilt on the floor? My mind is clouding over as I try to focus on a name, a face, anyone who will see me in this state. No one. There isn't anyone that I can think of who might see this, see me as I am here and now. No one. Except, maybe…

My mind rests on the face of my mother, sees the tears on her cheeks glistening like crystals. I think I'd better close my eyes. That way she'll never see.

Reflection

I looked too close at my reflection today. I stared at my eyes, through them, at my soul, and saw Gehenna's strumpet, blood waste at her mouth, the discharge of the dead. I wiped at it, smeared it, rubbed it into my cheeks, loving its tinny taste. And smiled back.

My House

The door was ajar, standing open wide enough to give a glimpse of its dark innards to anyone standing on the steps leading toward it. It had been that way for years, decades even. No one ventured close enough to close it, not even the kids on the street who enjoyed a good scare. People avoided the house, not because of the atrocities committed inside, but because of the house itself. The brick and wood seemed to breathe the same air we did.

I haven't been back here since the day I found my brother's friend dead in the hallway. He laid between my room and Nate's, face down in a pool of his own blood and vomit. I had been out on a date that evening, hanging out with the boy I left behind when I went off to college. I came home late. My parents' car was in the driveway. Nate and Corey's bikes were lying on their sides in the grass. My eye caught sight of them for a second before Robert covered my mouth with his and kissed me again. Mom was usually a stickler about the appearance of the front of the house. No skateboards, no balls, no toys of any kind had ever been allowed to sit on the lawn for more than an hour before she had a fit. Anyway, it was past midnight. What was Corey doing at the house so late? My concerns melted in Robert's mouth.

Fifteen minutes later, after I had gotten out of the car, straightened my clothes, and patted down my hair, I walked by the bikes without another thought. Corey was probably sleeping over, and if he and Nate got home late enough, Mom wouldn't have known the bikes were out there. It was easy enough to believe so I bounded up the steps, forgetting about them by the time I hit the second step. At the top of the stairs, I turned to wave goodbye to Robert. He backed out of the driveway slowly, his headlights blinding me as he turned onto the street and drove past the house. I knew he wanted to get back together, long distance or not. But I couldn't do it. I was having way too much fun at school.

I unlocked the door and walked in. The living room was dark except for the light coming from the television set. An 80s sitcom rerun was on, complete with requisite laughter and quips that aren't really funny. Dad usually sat up at night to watch the old shows, laughing when he was expected to, getting up at commercials to get a glass of soda. Mom slept lightly, so he watched the set in the living room. This way he didn't disturb Mom while she slept, and he had less of a distance to walk for midnight munchies.

I didn't hear his familiar laughter that night when I walked in and I thought he might have fallen asleep in front of the set. I walked up the stairs as quietly as I could, trying not to wake him up. I figured I'd go upstairs, wash up, change into my pajamas, and join him on the couch. A scary movie sounded pretty good to me then, and I hurried up the steps trying to think of what video to watch.

I hit the switch to the hallway light at the top of the stairs, but it didn't turn on. I sucked my teeth, remembering I told my brother to change the bulb before I left that evening. At fourteen, he rarely did anything I asked him to, but I threatened to squeal about him and the neighbor's daughter if he didn't do it. I thought it would have been enough, but obviously not. I felt my way down the hallway, gliding my hand along the wall, until I reached a door opening. Nate's room.

"Hey you jerk," I whispered. I didn't want to wake Mom and make it a bigger deal than it had to be. This was between Nate and me.

Nate didn't answer, so I walked further into his room. I shut his door as quietly as I could and flicked the light switch. Nate's bedroom light didn't come on either.

"You idiot! You won't even change your own light bulb?"

Nate still didn't respond. I walked over to his bed, kicking at the clothes strewn all over the floor.

"Dumb ass, I know you hear me," I said irritably. I couldn't wait to get close enough to him so I could punch him in his scrawny shoulder. I took an unsteady step closer and tripped over something hard. I tumbled forward onto the bed, gasping in shock, expecting to hear my brother and his friend laughing at me in the dark. But there was nothing. I steadied myself on a hollow feeling thing on the bed that was cold to the touch. I know now that it was Nate's body that I was touching, lying dead on his bed. His eyes were open and staring straight ahead. Had the light been on I would have found him staring at me.

I stood up and turned around in place. The darkness was complete. No moonlight, no streetlight rays penetrated the room.

"You know what? Fine. I'll just tell mom about you and Carrie in the morning. We'll see how much you like that."

Still nothing. I opened the door and walked out of the room in silence, my arms outstretched in the dark.

I felt along the wall toward my room. My foot slipped on something about halfway down the hallway. I cursed out loud, almost losing my footing. Those idiots had probably spilled water on the floor and forgotten to wipe it up. Mom and Dad would be pissed in the morning when they saw the watermark. I shook my head and kept walking.

Finally, I reached the molding that framed my door. I turned to walk in, but cast a glance over my shoulder. My parents' bedroom was right across from mine. I couldn't tell if the door was open or closed, but that wasn't what bothered me. I didn't hear anything coming from the room. My Mom wasn't one to fall asleep with the television or radio on, but she did snore. It wasn't one of those loud, obnoxious sounds, but you could certainly hear it if you were standing outside the door. There wasn't any sound coming from the room.

I turned toward their bedroom door and walked toward it. The door was pulled to, partially open. I opened it and took a step inside. I still didn't hear anything.

"Mom," I whispered. I didn't want to wake her by turning on the light if she was sleeping. I felt goose bumps rise on my forearms as I stepped into the dark, silent room.

"Mom?" I called her again, but still there was no answer. I took a couple of steps toward the bed, thinking that maybe this was a night without snoring. I tried to hear her breathing, found myself begging to hear it, but there was no sound coming from anywhere in the room. I walked toward the bed, terrified now, and kneeled next to where her head usually lay. The door to the bedroom slammed shut and I whipped my head toward the sound. Someone stood in front of the closed door, the body nothing more than a shadow.

"Dad?" I called out. "I think there's something wrong with Mom."

The shadow didn't move or say anything.

"Nate, is that you? Seriously, I think there's something wrong with Mom. I can't hear her breathing."

The shadow seemed to grow taller, its pointed head stretching past the inner molding of the door and up to the ceiling of the room.

"Nate, you asshole! I'm not playing a game. Go get Dad. Hurry!"

The shadow seemed to dance along the ceiling, watching me. I reached for the lamp on the nightstand and struck it with my hand, knocking it over. The sound of the crash was deafening in the silence. My mother didn't move.

I put my hand on her arm. Her skin felt cold and rigid. I shrieked and snatched my hand away. I turned toward the door and ran, clipping the leg of the chaise lounge near the bed as I did. I ran through the shadow that stood in front of the door. I turned my head right and left and called out again, "Dad? Nate?" No answer.

My fear tasted tinny, and metallic, like blood. I grabbed for the doorknob and turned it. It didn't budge. I turned it again, yanked at it, pulled as hard as I could. Still it didn't move. My heart was beating fast; I could hear each pump in my ears. The shadow was behind me and drawing closer.

I turned my back to the door to face the shadow. "Who are you," I asked feebly. "Why did you do this to us?"

There was no answer. The shadow seemed to be looking at me with unseen eyes, enjoying my terror, my grief.

"What do you want from me?" I lost myself in my frantic tears; their heat blurred my vision of the shadow and burned my eyes. Once the tears slowed, the room came back into focus and I could see that the shadow had advanced toward me.

I screamed so loudly that I hurt my ears and turned back to the bedroom door. I turned the knob again and it opened with ease. I ran halfway down the hallway toward the stairs before realizing that the light was on. Corey laid face down on the floor. The liquid that I once thought was water was his blood. My bloody footprints led from his body to my bedroom, to my parents' room. I screamed again and ran down the steps.

The television was still on in the living room, laughing voices filling the room with sound. I took hesitant steps toward the room, not wanting to see what was in there. I clung to the wall, pressing myself as flat against it as I could. When I reached the edge, I stopped. I breathed deeply once, twice, three times, before summoning the guts to look beyond the wall. I knew that if my father was dead, the television set would illuminate his face, giving me sight of his final expression. I didn't want to see that. I didn't think I could take it. But I had to know.

I peered into the room, gripping the wall tightly. The light from the television flickered and bounced. I saw my father's hand in his lap, his fingers covered in black.

With weak legs I staggered out of the house and into the night. The police picked me up behind my old high school the next afternoon. My aunt took me in, helped me get back on my feet. They never found out what happened at my house that night. But I know. Me and my shadow.

It watched me as I stepped through the door and into the house today. I could almost see it smiling.

The Woman in the Sepia Picture

The woman in the sepia picture was dressed in her Sunday best—light suit, white gloves, her hair in a bun. She sat with her legs folded, pressed together tightly as though two were one. She was regal, demure. A trail of blood ran from her mouth to her chin.

The Interview

"Why do I watch, you might ask. Why do I stay there, standing in the shadows, an unseen voyeur?" A smile crept across his lips as he pondered his response, the effect more hellish than attractive. Will sat without moving, all of his nerve endings, his entire being at attention, hanging on the silence between them.

Will looked at the subject of his interview and wondered how the session had come to be. He didn't remember contacting the man or setting a date. He didn't even know what topic they were discussing nor what question he asked that had elicited such an interesting response. It was as if he had woken up from a dream and found himself sitting there, embroiled in conversation. Will didn't have any notes in front of him, his trusty pad discarded, cast aside because he knew, somehow, that he wouldn't need it. The usual fanfare was absent as well; no cameras, at least none that were visible, no booms or hot lights, no gofers running around in the background on one trivial errand or another. It was just himself and the man, if you could call him that, sitting in two unadorned chairs set close together in a room with walls that appeared to be draped with a black sheet.

Funny how he had come to know the details of the studio's set up so quickly: the cameras and props were expected rather than fresh and new. He had only held the job for a week, but it felt like he had been doing it for years. It was what he was born to do, he thought. He was right where he deserved to be. Will had been pining for the anchor position for a while, working B grade beats and long, solitary hours for what seemed like years, waiting for a slot to open up. He had invested his entire career in the station, clawing his way up from the bottom rung; he had been an intern there when he was in college, starting as a gofer in his sophomore year. After graduating, Will worked at the station full time, coming onboard as a Production Assistant. His day was filled with research, copy writing, and fact checking; all things he had done while he was an intern. It felt like a step backwards, but he stuck with it, always keeping his goals in mind, even when the days were long and the pay was low.

If one were to plot his career, it would resemble the upside of a bell curve, every new position a step up on the ladder. He had worked almost all of the professional positions below middle management and had even tried his hand at that the previous year. He had received accolades from all of his bosses, had gotten a sizeable raise every year, and a nice bonus around Christmas time. He looked great on paper, and he knew it. When the job he had always wanted opened up, he went for it with everything he had. And his hard work had finally paid off. Getting the position was a long time coming, but he was finally there. He was damned proud to call the anchor's chair his own.

Will's eyes rested on his subject again, watching him deliberate. The man sat reclined in the chair with a look of amusement on his face. He seemed comfortable in his surroundings, and appeared to genuinely enjoy the discussion they were having. Will suddenly realized that he felt uneasy. His shoulders were hunched and his back was pressed into the chair so tightly, he was sure the imprint of it would show on his skin. He tried to relax, willing himself to settle down and enjoy the interview for what it was worth.

Still, his mind remained unsettled.

The man's right hand rubbed the base of his chin as he thought, forming the reply to his own question carefully. His olive skin appeared agitated and flushed, as if it were about to break into a rash. His hair was dark and brushed away from his face. The color was the deepest shade of black Will had ever seen. The man had a high forehead, and it gave Will the impression that his hairline was receding. Something about it bothered him. The look of it, the drastic slope of his forehead, made Will stare. The space between the man's eyebrows and hairline seemed vastly disproportionate, elongated, the way the mirrors in a carnival fun house make a person's reflection appear. The skin at the man's hairline was inflamed and had formed a welt, as though he had scratched himself. The welt itself seemed to be pulsating, throbbing as his blood rushed through it. Will became enthralled with its rhythm, watching it beat, thump, thump, thump, in time with his pulse. An itching on Will's own hairline pulled him out of the trance he had fallen into, clearing his eyes of the welt that had taken over his vision and blurred the rest of the room. Will coughed nervously; the sound was deafening, bouncing off the walls. Embarrassed, he waited for the moment to pass, certain that his interviewee thought him a fool. He was sure the man was annoyed by his behavior. He didn't know how long he had been staring at the man's head or how obvious he had been while doing it. Will glanced at him, trying to read the emotion on his face. The man appeared unfazed.

Will remained silent as his subject continued to ponder. His eyes were drawn again to the man's face, the distinctness of his appearance.

His features were sharp, disturbingly so, the perfect edges seeming unnatural and sculpted from rock. His chin was strong, dusted with five o'clock shadow, as were his cheeks and upper lip. His cleft struck Will as peculiar; its shape a perfect circle, its placement aligned dead center in his accommodating chin, looking as though it was drawn on rather than formed while in the womb. Will's eyes lingered there, staring at the depression as though it was a foreign object.

The man's smile compelled Will to blink. He turned his attention to another of the oddities the interviewee possessed. His lips remained closed, drawn up at the sides in a grin, yet they seemed to convey a message to Will, one that he couldn't quite decipher, but that sent a chill through him, nonetheless. Though his mouth held a smile, his eyes remained cold, trained on Will with pressure so intense, it was almost palpable. His coal black irises appeared abnormally large. Indeed, both of his eyes seemed larger than they should have been. Either he had fair eyelashes or none at all. The effect left his face looking eerily nude. Again, Will found himself staring at the man, as if trying to look into very his soul.

The man was dressed in black, from head to toe; black sweater, black pants, black boots. The hem of his pants caught Will's attention and he looked down at it with a paranoid veil over his heart. At the bottom, where the cuff of the pants met the smooth leather boot, something slithered just out of sight. Will blinked rapidly, his mind conjuring images of tentacles bunched within the leg of the pants, writhing together in slow motion, their movements like the lick of a lover's tongue. He realized he was leaning closer to the man, his sweat-soaked shirt sticking to his skin where the chair back had pressed into him. He was tense. His body was reacting to the strangeness of the situation by contracting his muscles and making his senses stand at attention.

He was in a room conducting an interview on a subject that was unknown to him with a being that was becoming less human in his imagination as the seconds passed. And no one else was there. No one else witnessed the odd manner of the man who sat before him. No one else was there to see the subtle nuances of his face; the features that seemed distorted or out of place, too perfect. That he was alone with the man made him uneasy. Will strained to listen, hoping to hear the sound of feet rustling in the hallway, or the chatter of his colleagues as they passed by, but of course, he didn't hear anything. He shouldn't have. The studios were situated far away from regularly traveled hallways and were soundproof. Knowing he couldn't hear anyone beyond the door, nor would someone hear him if he yelled out, made him all the more anxious. Fear he had never known coursed through his body like blood.

Will made himself blink, realizing he had been staring at the man in silence for quite some time. He diverted his eyes as he tried to pull himself together. Will chastised himself for his conduct. Strange or not, the man had accepted the interview and sat before him a willing subject. Surely staring was still considered rude, even when in the company of the odd, the unexplainable. Will decided that, regardless of the way the interview had come about, he had to finish it with the professionalism it demanded. He had to do his job.

A rich baritone reverberated in the room as the man laughed, bouncing from wall to wall, assailing Will from all sides. The laughter recycled itself each time, projecting new tones and inflections. The laughter troubled Will, but not that he couldn't pick out a singular voice — that was the least of his concerns. What bothered him most was that the voice in his mind, the one he relied upon to keep him grounded, was laughing as well.

Will looked up quickly, catching sight of the man as he laughed heartily. His mouth was open in a madman's grin, brandishing teeth of all shapes and sizes. Molars misplaced in the front of his mouth crowded incisors that appeared to be filed to a point. Both rows of teeth were a cluttered mess set in blood red gums. His tongue was home to abnormal taste buds, ones that were swollen to twice the normal size. Will couldn't control his urge to cringe as he imagined the taste buds were moving of their own volition, like maggots upon dead flesh.

The man's laughter ceased in a scaled decrescendo and his expression turned pensive as he prepared to speak. Will cleared his throat and looked away, casting his eyes downward, feeling he needed to do something to control his anxiety, to calm himself enough to be able to carry out the interview. He needed to focus on the task at hand and stop letting his imagination get away from him. *It's just nerves,* he told himself, though his inner voice didn't sound believable anymore. He had been riding high since getting the job, celebrating and partying like there was no tomorrow. The week between getting the offer and that day was a blur. He felt like he had been living in a fog. *No wonder I don't remember setting up this interview,* he mused. Will told himself that he just needed to settle in and do the job they were paying him to do. After that, he would treat himself to a drink and get a good night's sleep. That was all he needed, he assured himself. *All I have to do is get through this.*

Will looked up at the man with feigned calm, trying to prove to himself there was nothing wrong with his guest, that his overly tired mind was playing tricks on him. The man's face held no expression as he returned Will's gaze. His features were as they had been before, slightly off kilter, but without the fantastical extras Will's imagination had conjured up. Will exhaled, releasing the breath he had unconsciously been holding, and rubbed his hands together. He wasn't surprised to find them clammy.

Will began thinking of a lead in, some question he could ask to get the conversation back on track, but he was still distracted. Although the laughter in the room had stopped, the laughter in his mind continued ever so faintly.

"Let me offer a story to explain, if I may," the man continued, breaking the silence. He lifted one leg to fold it over the other. Will's mind tugged at his eyes, telling him to look down, to look at the hem of the man's pants and see, see what was there, see what his psyche couldn't bear. But he didn't. Instead, he shifted in his seat, stretched his legs, tried to appear comfortable. He straightened his tie and smoothed his pants. He did anything he could to occupy himself, to turn his attention away long enough to avoid seeing whatever might have been beneath the hem of the man's pants, bidding him look.

Will breathed deeply through his nose and exhaled soundlessly. His heart was still pounding rapidly under the weight of his fear. He felt light perspiration at his hairline and under his arms. Self-consciously, he touched the bottom of his jacket, thankful he had kept it on. *Get control of yourself*, the voice in his head admonished, its old spunk returning. The cackling laughter was gone, stopping as quickly as it had started, and the old kick-in-the-pants tone was back. Hearing the voice sounding the way it used to gave him a sense of calm, and he found that his next breath came easier. He was back on track. He was beginning to feel sane again.

With a nod that conveyed the assuredness of a seasoned interviewer, Will acknowledged the man's request. The man folded his hands in his lap. His face took on an animated expression as he began to set up his scenario, one that startled Will with its severity, threatening to crush his confidence and send him back into the throes of his fear.

"Imagine, if you will, a man in his mid-thirties. He is career oriented and ambitious with a lifestyle that reflects his extreme and, in most cases, expensive interests. He's married to a trophy wife in every sense: she's got a perfect face, perfect tits, and a perfect ass. They like the same things and enjoy each other's company. She does everything he wants her to do, when he wants her to do it, because he doesn't overstep his bounds. He doesn't ask her to cook, but she does. He doesn't ask her to clean, but she does. He asks her to suck his dick every now and then, but he doesn't say it that way, at least not to her. He couches his request, asking her to do something special for him on the nights he wants it, give him a treat. She knows what he wants and she does it every time. The way she sees it, she's getting off easy, if that's the only thing he asks her to do. Liking it the way she does is a bonus.

"So this guy, this ambitious man, seems to have it all, right? Nice wife, nice car, nice house, career, all the standard trappings. But for him, it's not enough. There's a longing in him that is not sated by the things he has acquired. He wants more. So he pushes himself, pressing ahead, working long hours, eating breakfast, lunch, and dinner at his desk. The great relationship he used to have with his wife begins to change. They used to have sex four times a week and go out on dates with each other on Friday nights, but now they only have sex once or twice a month and the dates are a thing of the past. She's upset. She misses her husband, but the last time she mentioned the distance growing between them, he bit her head off with comments like 'I don't have time for this' and 'Find something to do with yourself'. His favorite response to use when she complained was 'I'm doing this for us.' That one always seemed to work. So she keeps her mouth shut. She watches him come in and go out in a whirlwind, hoping that things would go back to normal sooner or later."

The man's lips curled at the edges, the beginnings of another of his heinous smiles. He continued,

"The guy doesn't see it, though. No, that isn't true, now is it? The guy doesn't care. He knows his wife is upset, but it doesn't matter to him. *I can take care of it later* is what he tells himself when he thinks about how everything is affecting her, if he ever thinks about it at all. His mind is so wrapped up in his wants and desires, his quest for validation, that everything else takes a back seat.

"He's up for a promotion that he wants more than anything. The new job would mean more money, relocation to the coast, corner office, the works. He sets his sights on it and never lets up. He doesn't even remember the day he said he would do anything and everything possible to get ahead, to get what he deserved. He was alone in his car when it happened, driving home in the dead of night. He drove at a leisurely pace—it was 11:30 at night and he knew his wife was already asleep, so there was no need to rush. He hadn't been home in time to go to bed with her in a while, but that didn't bother him. Not much of anything concerned him anymore except getting that job.

"He rehashed the day's events in his mind as he drove, thinking about what his early morning tasks would be, how he would stand out during the course of the next day and make an impression somehow. It was then that, with a voice filled with determination, he said the words that marked the end of life as he knew it, and the beginning of the life he leads to this day.

"He thought he was alone when he said them, thought no one could hear him within the confines of his car. But someone did hear him speak those words. And they took them to heart.

"The next day came and went with no change. In fact, the next couple of months were the same; the man struggled to get ahead, the wife pined away at home. Finally, after almost a year of neglect, she decided she couldn't take it anymore. She didn't believe him when he said he was at work all night, until one, two, three o'clock in the morning. She had mistaken his disinterest for distraction long enough. It was time to see things as they were instead of through rose-colored glasses. She didn't want to be made to feel as though she were just part of the furniture anymore, seen but not seen, passed by and ignored. He seemed to think that a kiss on the cheek before leaving for work would suffice for her the way a little cleaner would make a wooden table look refreshed and new. She was tired of him, tired of it all. She was done.

"She left her husband one day while he was at work and stayed with a friend who had an apartment nearby. The man came home that evening and found her gone. He called her mother, his mother, and their friends until finally finding her. She was staying no more than twenty minutes away from him. He asked her to come back. She said no. He asked again, she said no again. He decided he could deal with it. She could leave if she wanted to. He didn't need her anyway.

"A month later, the job he had been trying to get was given to someone else in the office, a man three years younger than him and with less experience. He was livid. He threw things about the office, broke his coffee mug against his manager's door, and cursed the secretaries who stared at him from behind their desks. His manager tried to calm him down, offering conciliatory responses like 'It's not the end of the world' and 'There will be other positions'. The manager even threw in 'It's not that we aren't satisfied with your performance' but was met with a vicious look that silenced him before he could finish. After more shouting and banging of tables, the man stormed out of the office, yelling threats to anyone who tried to restrain him or get in his way. He never returned to the office again.

"He went to see his wife later that week. She was still staying with her friend. He got ready to knock on the door but heard voices on the other side. He waited and listened to the inflections of the voices in the apartment, the giddy nature of the talking. The sound alone infuriated the man, but there was something else that bothered him that night as he stood outside the door. He thought he heard his name amidst the chirp and chatter. They were laughing about him.

"Inside, his wife and her friend sat on the sofa talking with a male guest. The friend and the guy were going out on their first date and were about to leave for a night on the town. The guy came in and took a minute to speak with his date's friend, being cordial, as would a teenage boy with his prom date's parents. He told them about his good fortune at work earlier that week. He had just received a promotion at work, one that he had been trying to get for a long time. He told them what happened next with a storyteller's animation, excitedly recounting the details of how the other guy in the running lost control of himself and stormed out of the office, leaving broken glass and strewn papers in his wake, and how he hadn't been back to the office since. He added an offhanded, 'poor sucker' chuckle for good measure. Something about the story bothered the women. The friend asked him where he worked. Before he could answer, the door flew open and banged against the wall behind it.

"The man raced in and punched the friend's date in the face with a quickness and fury that he had never known before. The date crumbled to the floor, hitting his temple on the side of the coffee table with a dull thud and died instantly. The friend screamed and tried to run out of the room. He caught her by her hair as she tried to speed by. With a quick twist of his hands, he made light work of her; her lifeless body fell to the floor next to her would-be lover. The man turned to face his wife. She was still sitting on the sofa, exactly where she was when he burst into the room. Her mind and body were paralyzed by shock. He regarded the tears on her cheeks with some enjoyment and it showed on his face.

"She gasped as he walked towards her; he was already too close for her to escape. The man took another step and leaned into her. Still, she kept her tongue, hoping that she would wake up from what had to be a nightmare. She could smell his breath and shrank away from it. It wasn't the sour smell of liquor that made her move away, but that of damp soil. The image of bloodworms and spiders sprang into her mind and she blinked through her tears several times to wash it away. She looked into the face of her husband, the man she vowed to love and cherish until death were to part them, and emitted a shrill, piercing scream at what she saw.

"I am the thing people see in the eyes of their killers, the crawling beneath their skin. I am the heat on their flesh and the chaos in their minds just before they breathe their last breath. It was me she saw that night in her friend's apartment. My face upon her husband's, there but transparently so. It is my face they all see at the moment of death."

The man fell silent then, staring at Will with eyes that could bore through stone, watching, waiting for a reaction. Will had only one, a question that had been forming on the edge of his subconscious since the beginning of the interview. Ignoring the cold that consumed his stomach, and the rapid pumping of his heart, increasing with every breath, Will opened his mouth to speak. With the controlled voice he was so used to projecting, he asked,

"Wouldn't the soul be enough?"

The man unfolded his legs and leaned forward, never breaking his gaze. A tear ran down Will's cheek before the man uttered a response, his mind drifting back to a time when grief and self-loathing were his only emotions, to when he felt jagged glass cut into the soft skin of his neck. He looked away, finding that he could no longer return the man's stare.

Grinning terribly, the man countered, "Was it enough for you?"

The Properties of Blood

His mother had been a sensual woman. She enjoyed men and had two children with different fathers to prove it, as well as countless other babies that never saw the light of day. She worked during the day, from six in the morning until six in the evening, as a chambermaid at one of the hotels in the city. She also cleaned the houses of the affluent in Georgetown three times a week for extra money. She worked hard and was often tired when she came home. Too tired to pay attention to him and his sister, Elizabeth. Bailey couldn't help but think of her then. Even when he could smell his own excrement, he thought of his little sister. He would do so when he drew his last breath, he was sure. She was a pretty little girl. He couldn't help but look at her, to admire her good looks, even when he didn't want to. Even when he shouldn't have.

His mother had loved Elizabeth. She'd spend hours brushing her hair, fussing over her clothes, making her feel special. Bailey remembered how his mother would smile when Elizabeth dressed up in her nicest dress and modeled it for them. She was beautiful. She captivated them both.

Bailey had never known his father, and Elizabeth's father had left before she was born. He had always been the man of the house. He was eight years old when Elizabeth was born. He was the one who ran down the hall to get a neighbor to help. It was him who brought the towels used to catch the baby, him who held his mother's hand and felt the pain of her grip, who wiped his mother's brow and kissed her sweaty lips when the ordeal was over. He could still feel her hot, panting breath against his face as she inhaled and exhaled rapidly, recuperating from the exerted energy. The memory still comforted him.

Bailey walked in front of her as he had walked in front of his mother while she was giving birth to Elizabeth. He knelt and looked into the dark of her vagina, remembering how ruined his mother's was after his sister had come out of it. His mind drifted to his well-kept memories of that day, preserved for posterity.

He had approached the doctor whose hands were deep inside his mother, guiding Elizabeth out to greet the world. The doctor smiled down at him and said, "You're gonna be a big brother soon." His voice was enthusiastic if not strained by the process. Bailey didn't react. Not a smile, not a flinch from the blood, nothing. Under normal circumstances the doctor might have found that odd. But he was too preoccupied with the matter at hand to notice that the boy seemed less interested in the coming of his sibling than in the blood that flowed freely from his mother.

Bailey stood close, as close as he could to the doctor before being shooed away. When his sister was born, he looked at her for only a second. Her body, covered with blood and fluid from the birthing canal, was of no interest to him; it was secondary. As the doctor whisked the baby away and the neighbors who had congregated in their apartment after calling the doctor rejoiced at the far end of the large bedroom room, Bailey moved between his mother's spread legs to look at her. Her vagina — a word he still couldn't say aloud, not when he could just as easily say pussy, cunt, or snatch — was wide and bloody. It looked to him like a gaping mouth, large and black inside, oozing with thick liquid streaked red with blood. He was hypnotized by it. He leaned closer, smelling the scent of his mother much like he would later with his other girls. He loved the smell of blood even then.

The doctor saw Bailey retracting a bloody finger from his mother's stretched labia. She didn't feel it, didn't even know her son was there. She was exhausted from the strain of birth, weary from the delivery. After what she'd just experienced, the light touch of a finger went ignored, if it registered at all. The doctor hurried over to usher Bailey away from his mother's prone body, a crease forming on his brow.

"You don't need to see things like that, Bailey. Go on, now. Play in the other room."

Bailey remained silent as the doctor guided him toward the door. He'd had the forethought to curl the bloody finger into his palm, hiding it until the time was right.

"What's the matter, doctor? Was Bailey bothering you?" his mother called out from the bed where she laid sweaty and fatigued.

The doctor hesitated before answering, measuring his words. He had never seen a person stand unmoved before blood and disfigurement, not child nor adult, unless they were in the medical profession. Christ, even the police were affected by the particularly gruesome. Yet this child stood still in front of his mother's bloody genitalia unaffected. He did not run away crying, shielding his eyes from what even grown men could not make themselves look at. Instead, he seemed to enjoy it, to relish it in the most primal of ways. It bothered the doctor. The child himself bothered him.

"No. Quite the contrary, actually. I think we have a burgeoning doctor in little Bailey here," the doctor said, trying to affect a sense of gaiety to mask the uneasiness brewing within him. He was sure, though, that his face portrayed his true emotion. As everyone in the room chuckled at his observation, the doctor felt off kilter. He looked at Bailey and saw that the boy was looking back at him in kind. His eyes, the blackness of them, were disquieting. The doctor had a niggling sense that something was wrong with the child. Very wrong.

"Albeit an honorable quality, young Bailey, I'm afraid we have to curb your tutelage for now. Let's allow your mother and sister to get acquainted with one another. Ok?"

The doctor almost expected the boy to say no, to stand there in defiance with his feet rooted to the floor staring back at him with his haunting eyes. A crazy thought occurred to him that if the boy's head should spin on his neck and his eyes shot fire beams like lasers out at everyone in the room, that would not be beyond what he had come to expect from him. It wasn't Bailey's infatuation with blood or the unnatural desire to see, touch, my god, smell his mother's vagina that bothered him. It was the child's eyes that tormented him to his core. It was those eyes that were visible in the doctor's mind even when he blinked. He had seen them before, watching him when his mother brought him in to be treated for chicken pox, staring at him through the bloody caul that covered his face in birth. The boy had always troubled him. He had bedeviled the doctor since the very moment he breathed his first breath.

The child Bailey looked up at the doctor then. As an adult standing in a festive, if not gaudily decorated living room before his victim, Bailey remembered hearing the tone of the doctor's voice that day. It was jovial sounding in most respects, but a cover just the same. The doctor was trying to hide his real emotion, trying to hide his fear. Bailey remembered wanting to smile at him, to laugh at the doctor for being afraid of a little boy like him. He remembered the way he felt and the daydream he'd had while looking up at the doctor. He'd fantasized that he laughed right there in front of the open door. Laughed at the doctor who had delivered his sister and him before that. His mother would have been appalled at his lack of manners, at his dismissal of authority. 'It's all right, Victoria,' he imagined the doctor saying. 'He's a growing boy. He's just sowing his oats.' He fancied that the doctor would smack him on the bottom. Not a disciplinary action. Just a tap on the bottom to urge him on. Bailey thought the doctor would have said something like, 'Ok now, enough of this. Go in the front room. We'll be done in here soon.' He remembered how much the thought, the mere idea that the doctor might strike him, had enraged him. He remembered the daydream vividly then, standing before his lovely as her body stiffened in rigor mortis. He saw his dream self, forever stuck in the body of a child of eight, turn toward the doctor with unnatural speed. He kicked the doctor in the shin in his daydream, and then, when the doctor bent to rub his leg, Bailey bit him on the ear. He ripped a chunk of the lobe away, the remaining skin left jagged from the bite of his teeth. Bailey's child countenance kept laughing with the doctor's blood running down his chin.

But he hadn't done any of that. Bailey remembered what really happened with disappointment. In reality, Bailey turned to look at the doctor, staring at him for only a moment, then obeyed his wishes and left the room. He heard the doctor exhale the breath he had been holding during the tense moment as the door closed behind him. Bailey then stood in the living room of the house he shared with his mother by himself. The room, looking as overdone to his young eyes as it did to him then (yes, he decided, it *is* gaudy), was silent and still. Bailey raised his hand, mimicking the movements he made years past, playing out the memory in present time. His mind replayed for him the moment when he uncurled the fist he had balled his hand into when he was interrupted by the doctor. He remembered himself plunging the soiled digit into his mouth, cleaning it of his mother's blood.

There, in the very room where he had first tasted of it, he again enjoyed the tinny substance and the pungent smell, as he savored the blood of his beloved, his sweet Elizabeth.

One

I sat back firmly in the hard chaise, crushing the pillow underneath my weight. The room looked as though it was moving around me, taunting me, echoing the words, those damning words, loudly in my head. The sound reverberated off the placid walls like bass from a speaker. I covered my ears and squeezed my eyes shut, wishing the nonsense away.

"No! It's not true," I said through the sleeve of my sweater.

The doctor sat across from me. His face showed confusion. Usually patients are elated to learn that they are not, in fact, insane. Hooting and hollering and jumping up and down is uncommon — those reactions are a bit of a stretch — but some sort of happiness is usually displayed when it is confirmed that you are a sane and rational human being, all contemporary quirks withstanding. He peered at me — I could see him searching to understand what was happening to me through my mesh sweater. He was looking at me like I was a caged animal playing possum just long enough to lure the over-zealous tourist to put their hand into my cage. I pulled my hands away from my ears and tried to regain my composure. The sooner I got out of that stuffy office the better.

"Ms. Wallace, did I say something to upset you?

Damn right, you did.

"No, doctor. I-I've just been so tormented with this. I guess I'm just relieved to know that it's finally over."

The doctor smiled thinly, the kind that never makes it out to the cheeks, but suffers painfully on the lips, finally acquiescing to the meaning. I straightened my sweater self-consciously, wanting to know more about what was wrong with me, what was in me, and not believing a word that came out of the quack's mouth.

The doctor glanced at me as though he was unsure of his previous diagnosis. Fondling the rim of his dramatic glasses pensively, he said,

"Fine then. Our session is over, Ms. Wallace."

Thank God!

"Thank you, doctor." I turned to the door. I remember feeling as though she was laughing at me. It seemed so loud, surely the doctor could hear it —

"Ms. Wallace?"

I jumped like I had been shocked. The laughing was gone. A thin layer of sweat sat on my brow, cooling in the breeze from the window. I snatched my coat off the coat hanger and left. I tried.

That was two weeks ago, before I killed her.

It's better this way anyway. Not like they'll miss anything. Dead. Gone. Pushing up daisies. No more shit from people who are gonna die too. The way I see it, they're one up on the rest! Like me. Like we're going to be.

I did it. I don't care. Know why? It was inevitable. Destiny, fate, whatever those theologists whackos call it, it was mine. Was it theirs? Could it have been someone else's? Doesn't really matter now, does it? It's better this way. No, it doesn't matter at all for those sorry suckers that I've put away. You know what? Every one of them was different. But in the end they were all the same. Isn't that funny? Y'all live your lives thinking that you are different from the next person. Better somehow. But in the end the same wide, blank eyes stare aimlessly up. The same fear consumed faces plead with the unknown not to take them. No one dies slowly. You start to die when you know you are trapped. Yeah, I say you got about five minutes from that point to defy death -- or think you can.

They all fight like they can win.

But they can't.

You can't win.

They can never win.

People used to be afraid of getting caught by the high and mighties by being captured in the dead person's eyes. That the writhing, gasping, dying person would have the image of their killer's face forever reflected in their eyes.

Lifeless, dark eyes.

Yeah, right. Not me. There's not much I didn't like about the whole thing – the killing. I'd venture to say that everyone has a secret desire to kill. Something even as small as a bug has life, but humans kill those without though by the thousands per day! It's a rush! The totality of it. The control of it.

Even a bug has life. Has blood.

Most of y'all are closet killers, suppressing the urge to do what comes naturally.

People like her always lose to people like me in the end.

The Keeper of Souls

It's foggy again. Just like it was the first time I saw him.

He came from the town at the bottom of our hill, the lights that glowed from their front porches looked like fireflies in the summer night sky. The heat brought him out, pulled him from his slumber to collect the souls of the townspeople while they slept in their beds, while they made love to their spouses. That's what happened to Calvin Thompson. He was enjoying his new wife's strip tease in the privacy of their bedroom when he came face to face with him, The Keeper of the Souls. Annie Thompson's dance was cut short when Calvin's face drooped and his eyes rolled in their sockets.

Maybe he wasn't sleeping at all. Maybe The Keeper of the Souls was in another town, touching his scaly hand to another family's door, taking from them a mother or a father. A child. He always came back to the town at the bottom of our hill, though. And I always saw him.

When Mom and Dad got the house on Carriage Hill, they were ecstatic. It was over a hundred years old and in great condition, a historical site, to be sure. The house had been in my father's family since it was built, the land even longer. When my grandfather died, Dad inherited it and moved us in. They loved it. The ornate molding that ringed the ceilings of the entertainment rooms, the white columns that graced the front of the house, the winding stairwell that led to the bedroom level — they loved everything. I liked it all right, but there was something about it that made me uneasy. I didn't know what it was until I saw him from my window.

He came in the dead of night when the crickets were chirping their loudest and the humidity felt its thickest. He came when most people were asleep, either from fatigue or heat exhaustion, their bodies glistening with sweat in the moonlight. Fans whirred, swirling around the hot air that came in through screened, open windows. He came on a night when I couldn't get to sleep, the new cast on my wrist proving to be more cumbersome than it looked — which was a feat in and of itself — the heat mixing stickily with my frustration.

I sat up in bed, the sheets sticking to my arms and legs as though coated with paste. I was hot despite the fan that was blowing directly on me. My window was open but the air that came in wasn't cool; it was hot and humid.

The skin under my freshly set cast was starting to itch, the skin underneath sweating in its plaster shell. I hadn't learned the trick to scratching with a cast on yet — the end of a wire hanger down the thumbhole — so I banged it as lightly as I could with my good hand. The break was still tender, so I felt every hit. The itch persisted. I was miserable.

I looked out of the window at the night sky, at the moonlight shining brightly on the lawn behind the house. The bricks Dad had laid out earlier that day were still out there and a patch of land was roped off and hoed. He was going to lay the concrete for the patio in the morning, one big enough to hold the grill, a table and chairs set, and a couple of chaise lounges. There would still be ample room to play even with the new addition. He was thinking about getting measurements taken for a pool. The idea of having a pool made Mom really happy. I had to admit, it got me pretty excited too.

I was thinking about what it would be like to have the pool when he came up the hill. My mind was filled with visions of me and my friends inviting some girls over for a dip. Bikini bathing suits and sunscreen blinded me to the sight of him on our lawn until he was right in front of my window. He was a good distance away, but I could still see his face. He wore a flowing black coat, black pants and shoes too, I guess. In the black night, I couldn't see the hem of his coat against his pants, or the tops of his shoes. It all ran together. His head was bald and sickeningly pale, seeming to glow white like the moon. Ridges cut into his face like slices from a knife, deep gashes crisscrossed, mirrored, usurped each other along his cheeks and head. His chin seemed elongated, drawing to a point in line with his nose. He didn't have eyebrows or facial hair. The corners of his mouth were smeared red.

His appearance, as unsettling as it was, wasn't what stuck with me most, what frightens me still as I look out of the window into the interminable night. It was what he had with him, what he had come for. Dangling from his hand were heads, opaque, tormented, gruesome, held by the hair.

I gasped, sucking the hot, thick night air in so loudly, the crickets silenced their night song. He turned toward me, looking up at my window with bottomless black eyes. A hideous smile spread across his lips, revealing jagged teeth that appeared filed to sharp points. It is that face that torments my dreams to this day, that face I fear will greet me when it's my time to go.

I see him every now and again, walking up the hill from town to some space behind our house where he keeps his collection, one that only he can see. I went in search of those souls once as a boy, but I didn't find anything in the woods behind our house.

I stayed in the house after my parents died, inheriting it as my father had, preserving our heritage. He visited with me once. The night my father died. I sat with my father that evening as he laid dying on the bed he shared with my mother. Mom had passed away years before Dad, leaving him with only me for company. I was on the cusp of sleep when my father died, the absence of the sound of his breathing, raspy and wet, being the thing that woke me fully. I raced to his side, waiting to hear him take another breath, but none came. The window above his head was open and I happened to glance out of it when I rose to leave the room. The man stood on our lawn looking up at the window. His face was straight as he held his prize out in front of him. My father's open mouth, frozen in a terrified scream, looked back at me, dangling by the hair held by the man's hand.

I'm old now. At 88, I've lived a full life. I've had women, money, fast cars, and liquor. I have a son who lives in Virginia and a daughter who just moved to New York to start her own business. My wife died ten years ago in her sleep. I didn't look out of the window then. I didn't think I could survive seeing him holding her soul captive for his collection.

The night is as dark and oppressive as it was the first time I saw him. I wonder, not for the first time, if I'll see him coming my way through the hazy summer fog.

Ole Hallows Eve

Do you know de real story of Halloween? No? Ain't no s'prise ta me, no suh. I's sho' lots a folks don't know de truf 'bout Halloween. Ain't like I wants to know dis horrid tale. But I do. I knows it like it be de bac' a' my hand, yes I do. You wanna know what really be happenin' on Halloween night, do you? You really wants to know? Gader 'round, chil'ren, while I tell you dis story. You be frozen in fear when you hears it, yeah. Just like I wuz when I saw it be true.

De night 'fore Halloween has a ancient history, dates back furda den I kin r'memba. De kids like to call it Gate Night nowadays. Dey ain't all that far from de truf, really. It used to be dat de town would gatha togetha on Ole Hallows Eve ta sit in front de cemetery all night. Dey wuz tryin' to keep de dead in. You heard me. Erry Halloween de dead be walkin' dis eart' wit us. Even now, dis day. You don't be seein' dem 'cuz yo' mama and pappa be makin' sho' yous safe. But deys scared cause dey can hear dem a'comin'. Dey feet be draggin' on de groun' cuz dey done been sleepin' dey death sleep and dey ain't got no kind a' coordination to speak of, you know. Sometimes, if dey fresh, dey guts be fallin' on de groun' and lettin' off de foulest stench you ever did smell. Don't boder dem none. Deys busy tryin' to get where dey be goin', and dey gotsta hurry, 'cuz dey ain't got but one night to do dey business in. We wuz tryin' to keep dat from happenin'.

Seem like a mist start to form 'round 10:00 p.m. erry Ole Hallows Eve. It travel 'cross town to de cemetery an' hover over de tombstones. Dem thar gates started a shakin' and de leaves wuz whippin' up a storm. Folks say dey hear moanin' and rustlin' in de cemetery. I don't know 'bout dat m'self. Alls I heard when I wuz down dere wuz screamin'.

I went wit my daddy one year to ward off de dead. We wuz all dressed up in our scariest masks to disguise our faces sos our dead relatives wouldn't be knowin' who we wuz in case dey got out. My daddy tole' me dat as long as dey cain't recognize us and we looked dead an' evil enough, dey would tink we wuz one a dem. So, we and 'bout fiteen uders sat in front de gate of de bigges' cemetery in our town. Dere wuz 'posed to be people sitting at de lil' cemeteries too, but I don't belie dat happen like it wuz 'posed to.

It got to be 'round 12:00 'clock befo' we started to hear de noises. It sounded like dey wuz tryin' to come out de groun'! De fog wuz so thick I couldn' see my own han' in front of ma' face! It happened so quick! I called out fo' my daddy, but he didn't respon'. I saw figures moving t'ward where we wuz sittin'. Dey didn't look like my daddy an' de men I went out dere wit. Dey wuz tall and dey shadows wuz long. Dey looked ragged in de shadows, and dey wuzn't walkin'. Look more like dey wuz glidin' t'ward me. I got up and ran off to my right, scared out of my wits. Seem like dem ole stories I had heard wuz true! I figured I could outrun dem cuz dey wuz movin' so slow. Just when I got past one of 'em it said ma' name, low and gurgly-like. It scared me so bad I wuz stopped in my tracks. Den it reached for me. A cold, lifeless hand tried to grip ma' arm, but I pulled away...and took off runnin'. I screamed bloody murder all de way home.

De next day when I woke up, mama asked me where daddy wuz. I tole' her I couldn't find him out dere and dat I think I lef' 'im. Her face clouded over in grief and she held back a sob. I tole' mama I would go back an' look for 'im but she said he wuz gone. Ain't notin' we could do now.

I went anyhow. I had to find my daddy. But mama wuz right. Wuzn't nobody dere. De cemetery gates looked like dey had been taken out de groun' an' de plots wuz all torn up. Some of de caskets has risen to de top, and de doors wuz broken off. De gate wuz splattered wit blood. All over it looked like all de blood a body could hol' wuz dryed on it. Infront de gate wuz one thing that I will never forget. My daddy's wedding ring shinned brightly in de mornin' sun, while his finger decayed underneath it.

I wore a diff'nt mask that Halloween night. And I've worn a diff'nt one ev'ry since. Me and mama.

Section F

I bought the newspaper from a kid without eyes. He gave it to me as aptly as a seeing boy would, no tentative lean, no hesitation. I turned to walk away, catching a glimpse of his smile from the corner of my eye. The jagged, yellow teeth crammed in his mouth sparkled in the afternoon sun.

It was a nice day. The sun was shining and there was a light breeze. I opened the newspaper, flipping through the sections leisurely as I strolled the city block. Voices spilled out onto the concrete from an open church door. I could hear the 'Ha, Glorys' and 'Lawd, helps' from where I stood. I stopped walking and looked in the door of the church. A one room building, the altar was done up in velvet red and gold. A body lay prone at the head; a woman dressed in a lilac purple Sunday dress with white gloves on her hands. I looked closer and saw that she was lying on a table covered with a white lace throw rather than placed in a coffin; her entire body was visible from the street. The pews were filled with people, all dressed in black. Elaborate hats adorned the women's heads, and all the men wore black double-breasted suits with white dress shirts with a thin black tie in line with the Adam's Apple separating their chest cavities, like a coroner's stitch. They turned to me all at once, every living head looking out into the brightness of the day to see the intruder. The music stopped. The singing was silenced. The pressure of their stares made me weak in the knees. A man stood and walked down the aisle, blocking my view of the woman in the lilac dress. His eyes were trained on me as he approached the door. As he drew closer, his features blurred. Where once I could see clearly eyes, a nose, and a mouth, I now saw a vast blankness. The man's entire face vanished gradually with every step. By the time he reached for the doorknob to close the ceremony off from the street, the shape of his head was indiscernible. The slam of the door rattled my soul.

I turned back to the newspaper and continued my walk along the barren city street. Somewhere in my mind I found the solitude strange; a nice spring day, well into the afternoon, and I had the street virtually to myself. Whatever thought I gave it was washed away when I saw the picture.

My thumbs held open the newspaper to a section I usually passed over. There was enough death on the front page, so I never had a need to look at the obituaries listed. But for some reason, my unconscious made me stop to take a look that day. The picture stilled my step and I found myself breathing heavy on the sidewalk for the second time. A couple stood posing for a picture in the Caribbean. The turquoise water, turned black by the cheap paper and ink, was behind them. They both held glasses garnished with umbrellas and filled with one tropical concoction or another, toasting the good life. Us.

My eyes watered as I stared at the picture. I remember the day we took the picture like it was yesterday. Our first vacation turned out to be our only vacation, but we didn't know that then. We were so happy. Everything was so new. It was the height of life for us and we took it all in. Could it be that we had become so distant that I wouldn't know this had happened? How could we have grown so far apart? As I cried in the open, daring a passerby to comment, I realized that I was mourning both her death and the loss of our relationship. My bitter tears stung my eyes.

I trudged to a bench against the side wall of an abandoned storefront to read the account of a life I once shared. The words rang true: a lover of life who jumped in with both feet. My mind flooded with the image of her on the street where we met, pumping gas into her car that winter day. I remembered how she looked when I asked her to marry me, how she looked when she said yes, how she looked when she told me she never wanted to see me again. I cried again as the memories taunted me, teasing me with the smell of her hair or the feel of her skin.

Oh God, Jen. I'm so sorry.

She didn't deserve this. How could this have happened to such a young woman? I always thought that, at some point, we might have had another chance at love.

I skimmed the obituary, searching for the details of her death, new anger welling within me. She was stolen away in her prime, her life cut terribly short. Our life together forever over. I wiped away the new tears streaming from my eyes, leaving smudges of ink on my cheeks.

The last sentence. Somehow that one was the hardest to read. It signaled the end. The end of the obituary, the end of my connection with Jen, the end of what we had. I hesitated, but forced myself to read it, making myself say goodbye. The bile rose from my throat and out of my mouth before I could suppress the urge.

Centered under the rest of the text were the words: I will always love you, Eddie. Rest in Peace.

Dear Monique

Dear Monique,

Hey girl! It's been a while since we've talked — well, a while for us is anything more than 3 days! I can't believe we've remained so close for over 30 years! I can remember the day we met at McAllen Day School. Nicole, the bully, was picking on you and I felt a jolt of assuredness — don't ask me how or why. I marched my little self right up to that mountain of a girl and told her to get away from you (oh by the way, I saw Nicole this week in California. She was at the convention I went to. She looks great. Even though I've got about 20 pounds on her now, I still felt a little twang of dread when we recognized each other!). I told her that you were my sister remember? We don't look anything like each other, then or now. You with your long blonde hair and piercing green eyes and me with my dark-brown locks and copper-toned skin. Who did I think I would be fooling? But I got Nicole off you that day and we've been friends ever since.

Wow! Can you believe it's been just over 30 years? Through junior high and realizing that boys existed for something other than to annoy us (I'm still not too sure about that), to high school and going on our first dates. You went out with that jerk Tommy Kern. What a bum! I thought he was a bum then, only I didn't want to tell you that. Even though we had been friends practically all of our lives, you were so into Tommy that I was afraid to let you know how I felt about him. I thought you would hate me for it so I kept it to myself. Things worked out for the best, though. Right after you broke up with Tommy the loser you met Greg, dear sweet Greg.

My choices in high school weren't much better than yours. I dated Calvin and Robert - two jerks who never should have gotten the time of day from me. I went to the prom with a friend of mine because Calvin and I had called it quits two weeks before. I still can't believe that! What timing! Remember Will? I had a crush on Will for years! We grew up with him from McAllen Elementary all the way to college. He was a year older than we were and fine as all hell so I thought it would be a cool stinger to bring a college man to the prom with me. A fine college man. And it worked! I got Calvin good! I'll never forget how his face looked when I walked in on Will's arm. Ooh girl, do you remember just how fine Will looked in that tux? He was a vision…until we went into the city to party after the prom. He drank the whole way down! When we got to the club I practically had to hold him up so he didn't fall on his face. I have never been more embarrassed. That was the worst possible prom night anyone could ever have.

College wasn't that much better than high school for me, was it? We followed each other to UCLA. Even though you two were across the country from each other you and Greg were still hooked up. I still can't believe you didn't date anyone else during college. I mean, we were only 20ish — prime time for dating around and experimenting. I can't believe you gave up all of that. But when I take a look at the man you gave it up for, I can't say that I wouldn't have done the same if I were in your shoes. Greg was a wonderful man, Monique. A truly wonderful man.

Let's see, I dated Rick, Troy, Nigel, and Michael my first year. Not too shabby. Second year I dated another Rick, William, Bradley, Travis, Ronald, and Steve, right? Or was Shaun in that year too? Third year is when the love bug bit me. It was when we went down to Huntington Beach that Friday night to hang out. We were staying with Carol in Irvine for the weekend and we wanted to get some good seafood. You and I went to Huntington thinking more like we were going to City Island in New York. I was craving shrimp like the ones that are served up on the end of City Island's restaurant strip. To this day I haven't found anything like it.

Anyway, so we went down there and ate at some joint that wasn't worth the trip and then we took a stroll on the beach. You spotted him first, remember? He was walking along the beach with some girl. They looked like they were having a really intense conversation about something. I remember that he looked annoyed. His brow was furrowed and his shoulders were hunched. But when he looked over at us his eyes softened. I should say when he looked at you, really. At least that's what I always thought. I always thought that he was checking you out that night on the beach. It probably sounds really silly coming from me after all of these years, but I did… and still do.

I don't know. Something about the air out here makes me go back in time. I can see it all like it just happened. We were on the beach, they walked by us, and we turned our heads. He is as attractive now as he was then. Tall, muscular, smooth, deep chocolate skin; he was breathtaking! I was nervous. I was never the kind to approach a guy and try to start a conversation. Eye contact still bothers me sometimes. It's so intense. But you, well you never really had that problem, did you? You looked at him like he should have been privileged to be walking on the same beach that we were. You turned your head with a quick little twist; your hair floating in the breeze lightly; almost like it was being carried in slow motion. And he kept looking at you. He just kept looking.

I swear had it not been for you pushing me off on him he would never have taken a second glance at me. I mean it! But thank goodness you did step aside and let him see me for me. It took a little time before I really let him break the shell, but when I did, I gave him my all. That's what I don't understand about this, Monique.

I remember the day we met Greg. He was playing basketball in the gym. I remember the gym being hot and muggy all the time. Muggy and smelly, like old shoes. We were walking to the track for cheerleading practice. It was our day to do laps (oh joy) and we were dreading it like usual. I went to the water fountain to get a drink and I thought you were right behind me. When I turned around you were still at the gym doors peering through the glass. You looked like a lost puppy. You should have seen yourself! Greg was practicing his foul line shot and he was totally engrossed in it. But that didn't matter to you. Every move he made, every dribble, every pause, every shot you followed with immense intensity. It was almost like you were holding your breath with each release of the ball. I'll never forget the way your face lit up and then turned beet red when he looked over to the gym doors and spotted you gawking at him. He smiled cockily and turned back to his practice. You were on cloud nine! It was all you would talk about for months! It got so bad that I was wishing he would just ask you out already so I could stop hearing about how great Greg was. And he did.

It seems like we're always there for each other's spectacular moments. Like when I had Jessica. You were the first person aside from Russell to see her. She adores you, just like we do. I always thought it was a shame that you and Greg weren't able to have any children. I know that you guys had been talking about adopting — what ever happened to that? I think it would be a wonderful idea, especially now that Greg is gone. You need someone to keep you company, to keep you busy. I worry about you, Monique. I really do.

I know it just sounds like I'm rambling on and on in this letter. I've just got so much on my mind right now that I need to talk to you about. I mean it's really only one thing but it seems so massive, so intangible, and I really need you to help me put this in perspective. I don't want to lose control the way other women do. I don't want to be like them. I just don't want it to seem like this has shattered my life. But it does, doesn't it? I mean, after all, things will change — must change — as a result of this. I guess I am like those women who completely fold up and crumble when this kind of thing happens. I share two things in common with them: I never thought this could happen to me, for one, and then it did; and no matter what I did to prevent it or how much I tried to block it out, it happened. I know it did, Monique, I know it happened. It happened, and God help us all.

Russell has never been happy with the amount of traveling that I do, you know. He has always said that it was going to cause problems if it got out of hand, and I have been traveling more than usual this year. I guess that's what you could call 'out of hand'. But Monique, the business has really been booming this year. I have to travel to take care of my clients. Their needs are growing and I have to be able to accommodate them all if I want to keep them. I have to go to any training opportunity available if I plan to remain competitive, right? Cutting edge is the name of the game and I have to be able to convince my clients that I am on that cutting edge, if not defining it, or they won't stay with me. Do you know what I mean? Of course not! You have the luxury of not having to work. Greg left you a very nice nest egg when he passed away so suddenly. Trust me Monique, you wouldn't want to be out here in this dog-eat-dog world. The competition is fierce and sometimes I want out too, but when I come home and see my little girl's face grinning up at me I know why I'm doing it all. At least that's my rationale for now.

That being said, I have to work like this. Russell's job is decent but the growth potential is not substantial. Mine is, so I do it. Well, for the past couple of months he has been acting really funny. Different, you know what I mean? For a long time I couldn't put my finger on exactly what it was. For a long time he was pretty good at hiding it. He would do little things, you know? Things out of the ordinary but not big enough to raise any flags on their own. Sometimes he wouldn't be home when I got in from work. Now you know I don't set foot in the door until at least 7:30 p.m. every night and he is usually back with Jessica by 6:00, so that struck me as odd. It only happened a couple of times, but it happened, and when you're dealing with a man who prides himself on being so routine you could set your clock by him, it looks a little funny. I mean he always had a good reason for not being there. Once he said he had taken Jessica shopping, but there weren't any bags (she didn't like anything, he said. She's 5 years old! She likes everything she sees!), or the time when they went to see the clown in the town center. Ok, maybe, but I don't know... something really bothered me about his behavior. But I never said anything - what could I say? Then, when I was away on business, he would come home really late at night. I mean I assume he was coming home late. All I know is that he would be wide awake at 11:45 p.m. when I would call in a last-ditch effort to speak to him. He would be awake and sound right chipper too. That's not like him. Russell usually gets in bed at 10:00 p.m. on the nose. It's been that way for years. It just didn't make sense to me. When I would ask him what he was doing up so late sometimes he would say that he had been doing some reading. Another one he frequently used was that he heard Jessica stir and he had just come back from checking on her. That never happens when I'm home. It just seemed odd.

I know you think I'm overreacting, but I'm not. I know what I know. There's more to this than what I've told you so far. When I came home he would be really nice, almost too nice. Know what I mean? He would shower me with flowers and kind words, so much so it became nauseating. He knows that I can't stand too much of that sappy stuff. If you say I love you too many times in a day it makes my skin crawl. I'm not like most women. I don't like all that togetherness, that all over you, got to touch you kind of love. I just don't and never have. Russell knows that about me. But yet and still, he is all over me like I'm the best thing going when I get home. Like he has been waiting all of his life to lay eyes on me. Monique, Russell didn't used to be so hot to see me when I came home. He never used to be so affectionate. I asked him once what got into him. I didn't want to hurt his feelings but all that touching was getting on my nerves. He said that he just loved me and he wanted to make things right. I told him that things were right; at least they were the last time I checked. He said that he wanted things to be the way they were before and then he hugged me fiercely. I was pinned in his embrace. I couldn't move. For a second I thought I was going to suffocate. I know you think what I'm saying is cruel and callous but that's the kind of stuff you go for, not me. I remember that Greg used to shower you with trinkets and tidbits and you just ate it up like it was candy. Me, show me your strength, your integrity, not your taste in jewelry. That's' what does it for me. I thought that was what Russell was all about.

So, as you can imagine, I was really suspicious of Russell by that point. I checked his drawers and didn't find anything out of the ordinary. I swear to you, Monique, I don't know exactly what I was looking for. Something, anything that would clue me in to some devious act. What that something was I didn't know. A number, perfume on his clothes, lipstick on his collar; I didn't know. I wasn't ready for it to be what it was, though. Nothing could have prepared me for that.

About a week ago I came home early from my appointment in Rockville. I went into the house and nothing looked out of the ordinary. Russell was home; he was upstairs in the shower. I came in, yelled hello, and went into the kitchen. My usual routine. See, at this point I was just thinking my husband was acting freaky, not anything else, especially when I hadn't found anything substantial to use against him. I hadn't formed any ideas in my head about what could be happening other than maybe he was going through some thirty-something crisis which was a mild version of what was waiting for him during the real middle-aged crisis. Just a preview of what was to come. I hadn't concocted any scenarios on this yet. I swear I hadn't.

I went into the kitchen and saw two plates, two glasses, and some silverware in the sink. Nothing strange about that. I had some toast with my banana that morning, so I walked right by the sink nonchalantly, assuming that Russell hadn't had the time to put the dishes in the dishwasher after I left. I pulled out a glass from the cabinet, got some cranberry juice from the refrigerator, and drank it down quickly. I put the glass in the sink and got ready to run some water so that I could rinse the dishes and put them in the dishwasher. That's when I saw it. I don't know how I saw this. The lighting wasn't right — remember it was really rainy a week ago — and I wasn't looking for anything, but lo and behold, there it was, as clear as day. I picked up the fork that was in the sink and looked at it closely. What had caught my eye was the pale frosted pink smear of lipstick left on that fork. Pale frosted pink lipstick that I do not wear. I am strictly earth reds and browns, Monique, reds and browns. Not pale pink. Never pale pink. And just like that Russell appeared in the kitchen. God, it took everything I had not to throw the fork at him or say something damning. But I didn't. I didn't! He came to me and hugged me tightly, and you know what, I took that hug. I hugged him back, girl. I hugged him and dropped that fork into the sink like it was hot metal. Russell jumped when he heard the fork clink against the plates in the sink and I think he realized then that I had seen it. He nudged me out of the way lightly but deliberately and immediately turned the water on, destroying the evidence of that pale pink frosted lipstick. I couldn't keep the smile off my face. It was a poisonous smile, one that could have bored holes right through him if given the chance, but I made it as sweet as possible. Do you understand that right then and there I realized that my husband, the man I had trusted my life to, the man I trusted my child's life to, was a cheating bastard? At that moment my world changed dramatically.

I let him clean the dishes and I went upstairs and took a shower of my own. I put on my soft robe and snuggled on the bed watching the tape of my soap opera. I couldn't even focus. I picked up a book and tried to read a little, but I couldn't do that either. My mind kept running over his behavior in my head. Over and over again I saw him being really fidgety when alone with me, being overly animated when I came back from a trip, and then today using every ounce of will power he had to keep himself in check when he knew I saw that fork. It all made sense. There was another woman, there had to be. That son of a bitch had gotten himself a whore to fuck him when I'm gone. Monique, I work like a dog to get us in a position where we don't have to work for the rest of our lives. I wanted us to be able to watch Jessica grow up rather than work and miss it all. He just works his same job day to day. He takes no initiative to get moving, move up in the ranks; he's content. Damn it if he didn't let me be the man! That bastard!

Well, I remembered that pale pink frosted whore's color. That afternoon after I picked Jessica up from kindergarten and we went to the mall. I went to two or three beauty counters and looked for something that matched it. I found a lot of things that came really close — Poppy, Raspberry, even Mostly Mauve. I didn't find the actual color until the next day on my lunch hour. I went to a different mall and I saw it. Matterhorn. I bought a tube of it and took it home. I tried it on my hand and forearm trying desperately to remember the color on the fork. I wanted to make sure that I had the right lipstick. If I didn't, my plan wouldn't work. I put the color on my lips anyway, thinking that if it didn't work and I had the wrong color it would go in the cabinet with all the other colors that I've bought over time that I don't like but can't bear to throw away. I put it on and lined my lips nicely. The color was nice enough on the right woman. A woman with considerably lighter skin and hair could probably carry it off much better than I could. It made my lips look like they were taking over my face. The urge to take it off and scrub my face clean was about to overcome me when Russell came home, late again. He usually ran up the stairs like a bat out of hell so that he could get to the restroom to unwind. But today he seemed to be dilly-dallying for a while. Just add that to the list of strange behavior he had been displaying for the past couple of months. I called down to him and *asked him to come up. He did, taking the stairs methodically, almost as if he was counting them one by one. He came to the bathroom door and looked at me in the mirror. His eyes squinted as they fixed themselves on my lips, as pink and bubbly as they were, set in a sappy sweet smile that would have charmed any man. He looked a little while longer before saying something like, 'Honey, is that a new lip color?'. Something pitiful like that came out of his mouth. I played along with his little game. I told him that I went to the store and it jumped out at me, but that I wasn't all that sure I still liked it. I told him that you had it and I wanted to try it, but that it doesn't look good on me. Come to think of it, that's not really a lie. You wear this color, don't you? Matterhorn. It sounds familiar. I thought that then. Maybe you'll want this tube of barely used lipstick when this is all over.*

That night went smoothly. To be honest with you, my mind wasn't really there. I had to leave and come out here to California the next day and I really couldn't wait. I felt like I would spill the beans if I stayed. I didn't want to just come out and tell him that I thought he was cheating on me without some kind of proof. I mean yeah, the lipstick is a little bit of proof, but that's a pretty thin piece of evidence, don't you think? It could have been anyone's lipstick! That doesn't account for his strange behavior, though, but that's all perception. I needed something real. So I left for California to come to this dry-assed conference. Not exactly the thing I needed while I plotted how to find out if my husband was being untrue, but I guess it will have to do.

After two days I couldn't take it anymore. I had to find out something somehow. I came home early. I came home on Thursday instead of Sunday. I stayed at a cheap motel on the outskirts of town so that no one would know. I wanted to catch him so badly, Monique, and I did.

I went up to the house one night and hid in the woods. I felt really stupid seeing as it was my own property that I was slinking around on, but I did it anyway. Part of me didn't think that he would be stupid enough to bring the bitch to our house with Jessica being there, but hell, he'd done it before, hadn't he? My car was parked three blocks over, so there' s no way he could have spotted me, and I was wearing all black. You know how thick our woods are. No one would ever see me out there. I stood there for two hours before anything happened, but then something did happen. My God, I never thought it would be –

Monique's hands shook as she read the letter. She tore her eyes away and looked up at the sky. She had been frozen in place, standing in her driveway reading the letter for God knows how long. She couldn't believe what she was reading! There was no way it could be true. She distantly heard herself reaffirming that over and over out loud; convincing herself that it simply wasn't possible.

"Oh, but it is possible, Monique."

The voice came from behind her, close behind her. She could feel the breath on her neck hot and sour. She could hear the belabored breathing and the crazed wheezing that rose lightly with each exhale. She was terrified. She shook as she turned towards the familiar voice. The voice of her friend. The voice of a woman who was beyond the edge of her sanity.

"Christine, what—"

"Don't talk, Monique. Just read. Read it out loud so I can hear you say the words. I want to hear you say them. But let's go inside first. No need to let the world in on our business, is there?"

Monique felt the muzzle of a gun pressed firmly against the small of her back and she jumped. Christine smiled, satisfied with the fear emanating from Christine's pores, wafting the tinny smell adrenaline to her nostrils. She continued,

"Good. Now let's go inside."

Monique turned slowly towards the door and walked cautiously. She wanted to run and hide but she knew Christine wouldn't allow her to get too far. Christine was in better shape than she was and Christine had always been stronger than she was, both mentally and physically. She knew she had no chance to get away.

She opened the side door and walked inside followed closely by Christine. She sat down at the kitchen table and waited. Christine shut the door and locked it. She walked around the kitchen holding the gun lackadaisically and said,

"No, we're not going to read the rest of the letter here. We're going to read it in the bedroom. I've always liked your bedroom."

Monique looked up at Christine who was standing over her, piercing her with eyes full of hatred. She said meekly, "Why are you doing this, Christine?"

Christine snickered and said, "Just get up, Monique. You'll understand everything in a little while."

Monique got up from the chair and started up the stairs to her bedroom. She was scared to death of what Christine might do to her and also of what she might do to herself. She had never seen her so out of control.

Monique opened her bedroom door and saw Russell tied up and gagged. He had been shot in the head twice and there was coagulated blood on his face and shirt. Monique screamed and dropped the letter on the floor. She turned to run but Christine shoved her onto the bed. She fell on top of Russell's mutilated body and came close to passing out.

"Read the rest of the letter," Christine ordered.

Monique jerked her body away from Russell's oddly warm corpse and onto the edge of the bed. She groped for the letter on the floor, afraid to take her eyes off Christine. She found the letter and brought it slowly up to eye level. Christine sat in the rocking chair next to the bedroom door with the gun pointed at Monique with a lazy arm.

"Read it now, Monique," she said coarsely, making herself comfortable in the chair that she had given Monique just before she and Greg lost their baby. "Read it to Russell."

Monique's face crumbled as she looked at Russell lying dead on her bed. She looked back at Christine with pleading eyes.

"That's right," Christine said coldly, "Face Russell and read the letter to him. I think it's only fair that he hears it too. Anyway, I can't stand looking at you anymore."

Monique turned around and looked at Russell reluctantly, her back turned to Monique. A sob rose in her throat and she choked it back. Her eyes took in the sight of her murdered lover. His skin was drained of color already, his normally rich brown skin taking on grayish blue overtones. It made her sick. She couldn't bear to look at his ruined face.

Christine grew impatient.

"Get on with it," she shouted. "Start where you left off."

Monique swallowed hard; her throat had become desperately dry. She cleared her throat loudly and dramatically. Christine rolled her eyes and waived the gun in the air. Monique's voice came out in a whisper at first.

— My God, I never thought it would be you. How could it be you? Can you tell me, Monique? How could it be you? How could you sneak around behind my back after all our years of friendship? After all the love I have shown you, how could you sleep with my husband? I should have killed you both right then and there. I almost did. When I saw him kiss you at the front door and pull you into the house I was sick. I looked through the window and saw the two of you groping at each other like two dogs in heat. It was disgusting! Downright nasty...but sensuous. I didn't know that watching you two could turn me on. It got me to thinking about how Greg's hands felt on my body, and how intense he looked when he was really aroused. I used to like it when he would just rip my clothes off me and smack me on the ass nice and hard—

Monique's head jerked up and her fiery eyes turned to Christine who was sitting in the chair with her hand on the rim of her unbuttoned jeans. Monique's lips snarled as Christine turned her head back in erotic, contemptuous laughter. Monique's anger filled her completely, blinding her to the situation at hand. Her body tensed as she prepared to lunge at Christine. Before she could move, Christine held up the gun and said,

"Not so fast. We're not done yet. Read the rest."

Christine smiled evilly, amused at the surge of anger adding color to Monique's cheeks. After snickering under her breath she said,

"Go on, read it, bitch."

Monique sat down slowly, enraged at what she had read, wanting to rip Christine apart with her bare hands. She picked up the letter and continued reading, through her clenched teeth.

— Yeah, when I think about Greg it makes me really hot. I couldn't help but think of how ironic this is. I mean, I trusted you all of my life and you slept with my husband. That was something that, up until then, I had been feeling pretty bad about doing to you. Well, that's not the only reason I had been feeling bad. I felt bad about the whole thing, really.

There were so many times that I wanted to tell you about it, but how do you tell someone that you had their husband murdered by mistake? There was no easy way to do it. But now I think you deserve to know. Greg wanted to call it off. He wanted to leave me and go back to you. He said his conscience was killing him and that he couldn't deceive you anymore. Well, I didn't want him to do it. You know what kind of man Greg was! He was wonderful! He was a great cook, considerate but not nauseating, and a great fuck. I wanted him to be mine for as long as we could keep it a secret. I didn't want him as my husband. I didn't want to confuse Jessica and, truthfully, I didn't want to hurt you. So I thought I could keep him on a string for as long as I wanted to. But he changed his mind.

When it came time to let him go, I couldn't. We met in the city and grabbed a bite to eat downtown. He told me he wanted to leave, I said no, on and on, and then he got up and walked out. Well, I just couldn't let him go. I got angry. I found some bums that wanted a fix so bad they would have killed their mother if they had to. I paid them to tail him to Metro Center and take him down for me. I told them that he was carrying a lot of money and jewelry, so it would be a good score. I tailed the bums to make sure they got the right guy.

They caught him a block or so away from the train station. They pulled him into an alley and rifled through his things. They had knocked him unconscious by the time I got there. I peeked my head in quickly and kept walking. I couldn't afford to be caught down there while they were mugging him. I don't know, I guess they got carried away. The next thing I knew, you were calling me saying that Greg was dead.

At first I didn't believe you. I knew what happened in the city but he looked alive when I saw him. I guess I was wrong. The coroner said that he suffered extensive wounds to the head as a result of being hit with a blunt object. That's really too bad, Monique. If he had cooperated with me this would never have happened to him. I cried as hard as you did at the funeral because I too had lost a wonderful man.

So now you know everything. My slate is clean and I have nothing else to share. I have something else to give you, though, dear friend. Turn around. It's ready for you.

With love,
Christine

Monique lowered the letter slowly and turned around to face Christine. Christine was standing with the gun pointed at Monique's head, a sardonic smile dancing on her lips. She chuckled and said,

"Good. I wanted you to be looking at me when I did this. Goodbye, old friend."

Monique threw her hands up to try and knock the gun away, but she was too late. The bullet ripped through her forehead with frightening accuracy. Monique fell limply onto the bed, her eyes staring blankly at Christine while the pages of the letter fluttered to the floor, splattered with blood.

With a sigh, Christine closed the door quietly behind her, got in her car, and drove toward Jessica's school to pick her up.

The Awakening

The fluorescent light above me is so bright, it's blinding. All around me, nothing but this bright light. I hear music—an old Motown tune, early era. The upbeat rhythm sounds tinny and far away. Muted footsteps approach me and suddenly I feel cold. A body leans in, mercifully blocking the light from my eyes. The person is framed by the light, their shape accentuated by the contrast. I see a strand of blonde hair peeking out beneath the green scrub hat on her head. Her eyes reflect a brilliant blue in the scalpel she holds over my chest.

Of Body and Blood

It mixes with the water that pools at my feet. It runs from me, out of my hair, off of my skin, racing toward the drain in search of release.

She wanted it this way. Wanted me to touch her, to feel her, no matter the cost. I warned her. Told her what would happen. What inevitably would. She said she understood and wanted it anyway.

Her skin beneath mine was hot from the fire that raged within her. It had been so long since we had been together, so long since we had sampled each other. The cover of night made my travel swift. She laid waiting for me just beyond the door. I stood outside for a while, fancying that I could see her from where I stood. My mind's eye pictured her lying upon the crimson chaise lounge that was in her bedroom, inches away from her bed. A wine glass filled with a sweet blush was in her hand. I could see her lips pursing to sip from it, could feel their softness upon my own. The vision of her made me anxious to enter and obey her call.

I was in her room before she knew I had arrived. She was as I thought she would be; her makeup perfect, her body clad in a revealing black negligee. Soft music sounded in the room and the smell of spring flowers tickled my nostrils. Such accoutrements I no longer needed, nor would she after this night. Passion would be borne of need, the desires of the flesh as one with the cravings of hunger. All this she had been told; she had been counseled of the consequence. Still, she had prepared for this evening. And now, alas, it was finally here.

Her head whipped in my direction, her senses detecting a presence in the room. I stepped from the shadows to reveal myself to her. The moonlight illuminated my body as I disrobed slowly, letting each garment fall away from my slender frame. A smile played at the corners of her mouth as I did.

She stood and walked toward me with a confidence that sured her step. Her lips parted, she leaned into me; an invitation to a kiss. I pressed my lips against hers in an adolescent peck before opening my mouth and introducing my tongue. The heat from her mouth was exciting as we danced inside and out. Her chest rose and fell against mine rhythmically, keeping time with the throbbing I felt within. She was flushed with passion, her body imbibing every touch as though it were sustenance itself. The power of her desire was entrancing. She was ready. I kissed her with increased urgency at this, searching for the slightest hesitance and finding none.

My lips traversed her cheek and earlobe, charting a path to her neck. She tilted her head backward, enjoying the touch of my lips upon her delicate skin. My conscious questioned if she had reconciled the reservations she expressed years before, praying that she had made her decision knowing both sides. I opened my eyes to search her face, silently begging her to show me, tell me that she was certain. An airy moan escaped her lips as if in response to my unspoken question. She was sure. I could feel it in her touch, in the thrust of her hips. Still, I waited a moment longer to be sure.

It was the pressure that made her cry out. The intrusion of teeth in skin, the initial sensation so exhilarating for me yet so startling for her. Then came the pain. Her blood flowed from her freely, rushing as if in escape, and I drank from her in great gulps. Her hands fluttered upon my shoulders, pulling me closer. I closed my eyes and drank more, blocking the thought of her eyes pleading in their death that I stop, begging to be let go, to be allowed to live. I knew that such a vision couldn't be real if she had chosen this, had wanted it as much as it seemed. The question lingered, but I pushed it away. I drank thinking only of the taste of her, the feeling of her blood as it mixed with mine.

I left her on the chaise lounge in her bedroom and retreated to the shower. Her blood washed off of me and rushed down the drain like so many regrets. So many lives. The hot water sometimes makes me think about the past, of the days when the pleasures of the flesh could be satiated by the touch of another's lips rather than the taste of fresh blood. She entered the shower just as my thoughts transitioned from the aching need for satisfaction to the pleasures of blood.

Moonlighting

"You think you can get them cheaper than that? They want a lot of money. I'd just as soon stand out there myself for a couple of hours a day. I only need the thing every once in a while. You know, for sales."

"Yeah, but you wouldn't look half as cute as the real thing." Mark laughed at his own joke and walked toward his car. "It'll only cost you $75.00 for one. Does that sound okay to you?"

Bill was blown away. "Okay? That sounds great! Those sons of bitches want $250 at least! And that's if I don't want a head on it." Bill smirked and said, "They're nothing but fiberglass dummies. I can't understand what the big deal is."

"Marketing is everything, Bill. How else are you gonna get those old biddies into your store to buy up all that secondhand crap you got in there?" Mark got into his car and turned on the ignition.

"You got a point there," Bill said as he strolled toward the car. He looked at his cousin and smiled. Mark always seemed to be able to come up with something, some plan, some way to fix everything. This one just added to his long list of saves.

"Thanks a lot, Mark. I really appreciate this. It will save a whole lot of money for the store. But how are you going to get it so cheap?"

Mark winked at Bill and put his car in gear. "You know I always I find a way. Just tell me when you need it and I'll get her for you. Give me the clothes and I'll dress her for you too."

Bill smiled and said, "Hang on a second then, 'cause I need one tomorrow. Is that too soon for you?"

Mark smiled and said, "No problem, cuz."

Bill ran into the store to pick out some clothes. He tossed them into the back of Mark's car and said, "I don't know how you do it man, but you always come through. See you tomorrow, then?"

"Bright and early."

"Don't forget my girl!"

They shook hands and Mark drove down the street.

Mark had been working the night shift at the funeral home for three months. It was part of his apprenticeship: take the late calls, pick up the bodies, prep and embalm, and wait for inspection in the morning. The manager came in at 7:00 a.m., checked his work, and relieved him of duty until the next night. He had done well so far, only one body had bloated up on him, and he fixed the problem before morning. He'd had all types come in: gunshot wounds, heart attacks, even one decapitation. He had to go back to the books for that one. It wasn't the stitching that threw him, it was the embalming; it was trickier than he thought it would be. He'd had enough post cases to last him a lifetime.

He only had six months left to his apprenticeship before he would be a full-fledged funeral director. He had already been offered a position at Crift Memorial across town, and he was excited about starting. They worked only two shifts a day instead of three; no one ever got stuck with the graveyard shift. Regular hours seemed like a luxury to him, especially when his watch read 3:00 a.m. There was something eerie about a funeral home in the middle of the night. It didn't matter where you were, the same cold hung in the air, the kind that chills you to the bone. It was unnaturally silent, even with the radio on. Maybe more so with it on. The tinny voices seemed to cut into the air harshly, like knives into supple flesh, ripping through it with their affected voices. That he was the only person alive in the building was disconcerting. Being home alone could not compare to being the only breathing person in a full house. He was surrounded by death, was a servant of it.

The nights were usually quiet. He came on at 11:30 p.m. and stayed until 8:00 the next morning. He got maybe two calls a night, and one of them was from a kid who had nothing better to do than to prank call a funeral home. It was always the same kid trying to disguise his voice to sound like something returning from the grave. He probably spooked himself trying to play his trick.

Sometimes the second shift would leave a body for Mark to finish up. There would be a note waiting for him on the table telling him to check the fridge for a treat. That usually meant a post case with sloppy stitches, or a jagged head incision on a bald man. Whatever it was, it meant more work and less sleep time.

Mark's shift that night started with a pick-up at the morgue. He wheeled the station wagon like a pro, getting to the hospital in ten minutes. He picked up the body and brought it back to the home all within a half an hour.

He unzipped the bag and saw a young woman. Her brown hair was limp and dull and her eyes stared up at him without seeing. He couldn't help but think of how attractive she must have been when she was alive.

Her body was slender, her breasts perky. Her lips were full and alluring. He sucked his teeth and said out loud, "Such a waste. Too bad I didn't meet you before today."

Mark heard the stories about lonely funeral directors taking an unnatural interest in their work, but he couldn't understand it. Dead is dead. He didn't delude himself that the woman might enjoy it if he touched her breasts, and he wasn't about to find out how satisfying the vaginal cavity might be in rigor. It wasn't his cup of tea. But he could respect beauty when he saw it.

He washed the woman, Miss Janet Stevens, closed her eyes, and set her jawbone in a look of contentment. That was his favorite part. He could give a face any expression he wanted, and in that, he found immense power. For this woman though, he had a specific purpose. Her face couldn't look completely at rest, nor could it look vibrant. Neutral, with a hint of attitude was needed. He manipulated her cheekbones and jaw until he achieved the perfect look.

The formaldehyde took less time to flow through the body than normal; the orange fluid replaced the woman's blood on the drain table in less than an hour. She died of a kidney infection in the hospital and there was no autopsy masking to slow up the process. Mark glanced at his wax kit and smiled. He wouldn't have to use it that night.

Mark rinsed the body again and patted it dry. He shaved the woman's hair and dressed her in the red and white sundress he had set out. He applied light makeup, just enough to make her look healthy and alive, and put her back in the station wagon. Hungry after a night's work, Mark drove to an all-night diner and had a sandwich.

Bill got to the shop at around 8:30 the next morning with coffee in hand. He was surprised to see Mark already inside, sitting comfortably in his office chair. Mark sometimes covered for him when he wanted to take off, so he had a key. Just another one of the ways his cousin always came through.

"Hey man! You're here early! I didn't expect you for another hour," Bill said.

"Slow night last night so I got out right at 8:00."

Mark smiled and motioned to the left of where Bill was standing.

"So? What do you think?"

Bill looked over at the mannequin standing in the corner. She was wearing the sundress he had given Mark the day before. He stepped closer to get a better look. It was the most realistic dummy he had ever seen.

"She's a beauty, isn't she?" Mark said, suddenly standing directly behind his cousin, whispering in his ear.

Love Nest

It's in my closet now. I can hear it rustling around in there, knocking over boxes of shoes, pulling at my dresses that hang on the rods. It grunts as it paces in the small space, waiting for me to drift to sleep so that it can come out.

I hear a clicking sound. It could be its nails colliding with one another in impatience, or it could be the sound of the heels of my good shoes knocking together. God, I hope it hasn't picked my red pair to destroy. I haven't worn those since the night Willie took me out on the town. We went to see a chitterling circuit play and had dinner at the diner around the corner from the mall, the fancy one that has a mirrored wall along the back and the waitresses wore pants instead of those short pink skirts. I've always hated those short pink skirts. Every time the girls bent over, whether to refill a cup of coffee or set down a plate of bacon and eggs, you could see clear up to their you know whats. I was glad the girls were covered there. I didn't want to have to compete for Willie's attention that night. The only person's you know what I wanted him looking at was mine.

I remember that night, how cool it was outside, how happy I was to be out with Willie after wanting him for so long, how he couldn't keep his eyes off my breasts. That was all right. I was going to give him some anyway. There's nothing wrong with taking a look at the merchandise before you buy it, I always say.

I know it's in there tearing up my shoes. The red ones. The ones I wanted to keep forever because they were the ones I had on when I went out with Willie. They were the last women's shoes he ever saw. I wanted to keep them for him.

Its grunting sounds almost like talking, like it's forming words under its breath. Words I understand. They sound like the ones Willie used that day, cutting and harsh. The voice it's using tonight is more real than it has been the past couple of months. More solid, angrier. The sound of it brings me back to that day, puts me right there in the thick of it all. He was standing there in broad daylight talking to another woman. The girl was one of those slender numbers with big, round breasts and a shapely behind. Willie was sizing her up with his eyes the way he had done me the night before, damn near salivating over her body. I watched him from the window of Lumley's, the corner store where me and all the other people on the block had been buying our candy bars and sunflower seeds since we were kids. It made me sick to see him looking at her, his eyes as hungry as a wolf's. He liked the way her lips formed the words she spoke, the way her tongue caressed the syllables. He was undressing her with his eyes, imagining what her body might look like in slinky black lingerie. I could tell what he was thinking. I could see his dirty thoughts like they were my own. That's how in tune we are. He couldn't hide anything from me, no matter how hard he tried. He must have felt my eyes boring into him after a while, because he looked over in my direction. He didn't crack a smile, didn't act like he saw me at all, not even when his eyes met mine. He acted like I wasn't even there!

The girl went one way and he went the other. I watched from Lumley's as he got in his car and drove off. I hurried out and got in my own to follow him, burning up mad. How dare he look right at me and not acknowledge me? I knew he was ashamed of what he did, but what kind of man runs away from things? Stand up and take it like a man. Give me what I deserved. I wanted an apology and I wanted one right away.

He made a stop for gas and then went home. I sat in front of his house, trying to decide what to do. How could he have done that to me? Cheating on me after what we shared the night before? No, we hadn't made a commitment yet, but we were going to. It was just a matter of time. And he screwed it all up by gawking at some chick on the street. Lord knows he would have taken it if she had thrown it at him. And that pissed me off. Willie wasn't going to step out on me, the way the others did. He didn't know who he was messing with.

It doesn't stop, that moaning. God help me if that thing speaks again. I might lose my mind right here.

I sat outside for a while, long enough for the afternoon sun to set, thinking about what I was going to say to Willie. I was so angry at him for being like all the others. He was nothing but a dirty dog going after anything that would give him the time of day. I didn't want to believe it, but I saw it with my own eyes. Momma always said to believe what your own two eyes showed you. And I saw Willie sidling up to that girl. Like it or not, he was going to have to pay for it. As sure as my name is Carrie Jones, he was going to pay for making me out to be a fool.

I knocked on the door and waited. He must have been sleeping because it took him a while to answer the door. He opened the door slowly, like he was afraid of who could be on the other side. I couldn't help but take some joy in that. He should be afraid of me after what he'd done. When he got the door all the way open, he seemed confused. He looked at me strange, even had the nerve to ask me who I was. I lost it. I pushed him into the house, stepped inside, and shut the door. He cussed.

I cussed back.

"Willie, don't you dare use that language with me," I yelled. My blood was boiling. If a fight was what he wanted, I was game.

He looked stunned. He took a step toward me and said,

"Look, I don't know who the hell you are, but you need to leave my house right now." He grabbed me by the arm and tried to usher me to the door. I'm a full-figured woman, honey. Nobody moves me unless I want to be moved, especially not some feather of a man with hardly enough meat on him to feed a cat.

How I loved that little man, though, even then.

I snatched my arm away from him and said, "You can't get rid of me that easy, Willie."

His face showed his brimming anger, but I ignored it. "I saw you with that hussy today."

"What?" He genuinely seemed confused, like he really didn't remember. Somehow that made it worse.

"I saw you in front of the supermarket with that girl. You know what I'm talking about, Willie. Don't try to act stupid."

Willie's face contorted in confusion, but I knew it was a lie. He knew what I was talking about just as sure as I was standing there in his house. Men lie. They try to throw women off with their sweet words and tender kisses. They buy candy and flowers, jewelry and clothes to make women believe whatever they say. That kind of thing works on most women. But not me. Carrie Jones was no push over. He couldn't worm his way out of this one.

I took a step toward him, my shoulders squared, my hands clenching and unclenching unconsciously.

"How could you do that to me after all that good lovin' I gave you last night?"

I was right in his face, my bosom bearing down on him.

Still, he protested,

"I don't know what you're talking about! You weren't with me last night, that's for sure. You've got the wrong man. Lady, I don't even know you."

I smacked his lying face with everything I had. Willie ain't but a string bean of a man, so the slap sent him flying. He hit the opposite wall and staggered, trying to stay on his feet. Humiliation and rage flushed his face red. I couldn't help but feel a twinge, like butterflies in my stomach. I always did like a high-yellow man. That color flooding his fair skin made him look all coppery, sexy. I took a deep breath. I had to force myself out of grabbing him and kissing him all over. He didn't deserve my lovin'. Not yet, anyways.

"Look, lady," he said in a voice that was trying to mask his pain, "I'm not above hitting a woman if she's already hit me. You need to leave here before something you're not going to like happens."

I couldn't help but laugh at him, this little man, trying to bully me. He couldn't hurt me if he threw his whole body on me at once.

He was serious. His lips curled in a snarl, trying to scare me away. I got angry again, all laughing and lusting pushed aside. He ruined it all, threw away everything we had. "We were supposed to be together," I said, backing him up to the wall. "But you messed it up for us."

Willie must have realized that I wasn't leaving and that I meant business. He picked up the phone book and knocked me over the head with it. He was fast, I'll give him that much. The blow pushed me to the side, and he was able to get out of the corner and around me before I recovered. He was on his way to the front door when I caught him. I threw him to the floor like a rag doll and plopped down on his chest. I covered his nose and mouth with a pillow from his sofa and pressed down. He pushed and pulled at me, his touch growing less and less urgent by the second. Finally, he stopped moving all together.

I took him out of the house after dark and brought him here, where it's quiet at night and nobody knows us. It's a nice place. Just out of town, up a grassy hill. They put the place up after they tore down the old crazy house that used to be here. Back when I was a young girl, we could hear the people in there crying at night, screaming and hollering like they were being tortured. Some people claimed they never heard it, but I did. It used to keep me up at night. I was glad when they knocked the walls to that evil place down.

Willie and I have been here ever since, sharing a bed the way we did the night before he betrayed me, the way we would forever. I brought the things I knew he would like: some skimpy outfits, the recipe for my famous chocolate cake, and of course, my red shoes. He has everything he could ever want: a woman who adores him, would kiss the ground he walks on, and a clean, secluded place where he can do anything he wants to with her. I mean anything. I even made sure the walls and bed frame were covered with cushion, and it's a good thing I did. Sometimes we get a little rough, if you know what I mean. No, Willie wouldn't ever think of leaving me again.

The thing in my closet keeps grunting, spinning madly behind the closed door. It calls itself Willie, says it's here to take back what's his. But I don't believe it. Willie is here with me and he's all mine.

I'll pull the cover up over Willie's head and mine so that it can't find us when it gets out.

Carrion

He knew the house was a fixer upper, but he wasn't ready for this.

Rick had spent the better part of the summer working on the house. He had it reshingled and treated, had put in new windows, replaced the front door, and had mended cracks in the foundation. He had built a new stairwell, sanded and polished the hardwood floors that ran throughout the main level of his two-story tract house, and repainted the walls. The first floor of the house looked excellent with its warm colors and up-to-date furniture. It was the basement that still needed work. A lot of work.

The basement was done with dark wood paneling and chocolate brown floor tiles. The tattered drapes that hung from the rotting bar were a mix of burnt orange, burnt sienna, cinnamon, and brown. The room was partially underground; what little light came in was through mini, just barely above ground windows. It was the kind of room that was cold all the time. To walk the floor in the basement with bare feet was to sign up for a cold the following day. The times that Rick had ventured into the cluttered room that ran the length and width of the house, he felt the chill on his skin so intensely, it seemed to permeate the flesh and muscle underneath to burrow into his very bones. And it was dark. Abnormally so. Shadows seemed to stick to the corners, hovering on the outskirts of the sun rays, surrounding them. Rick had avoided the basement in the past couple of weeks, even when it was roasting outside and the coolness of the room would have been refreshing. He couldn't put his finger on what it was that bothered him about the basement, but something made him uneasy.

On the evening before a trip to the mountains with his girlfriend of two months, Rick ventured into the basement to gauge the work he would have to get started on when he got back. The bare light at the bottom of the steps turned on when he flipped the switch, casting a yellowish ray over the dank smelling room. Furniture was stored there, left by the last family to live in the house some twenty years prior. They had left the area and moved to Arizona, deciding to keep the house as an investment. They were never able to rent the house and eventually paid it off, thinking they would give it to their only son when he graduated college. Their son never did graduate, dying instead in a car accident at the end of his junior year.

They buried their hopes and dreams, their sanity, and any recollection of the house they left behind in Spring Valley, New York with him. It was sold as part of the estate sale after the wife, who had survived her husband in a world of suffering for eight years, died in her sleep.

The house was dirt cheap and Rick snatched it up in a heartbeat. He loved to work with his hands and, because he was a schoolteacher in the county, he got a lot of time to do it. He dedicated the summer to it and had thrown himself into the work, getting better at it every day. But the basement was going to be hard. How do you turn a depressingly cold storage area into a game room with a pool table and a big screen TV? He didn't know, but he was about to find out.

Rick surveyed the room, trying to figure out where to start first. He would have to haul all of the furniture out and get rid of it, no question. Then he'd have to pull the paneling and the tile, gut the room, and start from scratch. Right. With a sigh, Rick, put his hands on his hips. It might take longer than the three weeks he had left before school started again. He made a quick mental goal, as he did with everything in his life: Get the room in order in time for the Super Bowl.

Rick's eyes cascaded over the covered furniture as he wondered if there might be anything under there that he might want to use. His mind shifted quickly with a thought that wasn't completely formed. A distorted image flashed in front of his mind's eye, a grizzly countenance with long, jagged canine teeth and a mouth ringed with blood. Classic horror movie stock. He chuckled at the thought, remotely registering that the sound of his laugh in the otherwise silent house was less confident than he would have liked.

Rick lifted the sheet in front of him and dust burst into the air like a cloud of gnats. He waved it away, sneezing violently as he did. Through watery eyes, he saw the first of the furniture, a maroon and walnut sofa. The piece was adorned with spiral walnut veneer. Rick started thinking about his girlfriend Tracey and how much she would love something like it. The sofa was right up her alley. The guilty feeling that had been sitting at the edge of his thoughts for lifting the cover and skimming the contents like he was at a yard sale disappeared with the thought of Tracey's smile. He yanked off the next sheet with zest, eager to see what was waiting underneath.

Lamps, loveseats, armoires. An ornate mirror. Nice stuff, but nothing as stunning as the sofa. There was one sheet left. The piece was behind the sofa, its back slightly lower than the one he would give to Tracey. Rick thought it might have been another loveseat, possibly a match to the one he had just uncovered. Rick put his knee on the Tracey's gift and reached over its back to remove the sheet from the smaller piece. The dust that kicked up from the sheet made him sneeze and his eyes watered as they had before. Rubbing his nose and sniffling, he peered at the piece. It was the match to the loveseat that he had already uncovered, its paisley design identical to the first. On it laid the decaying body of a young man.

Rick recoiled and fell from the antique sofa, landing on his back. He inched backwards reflexively, using his elbows and buttock to push away from the furniture. As he watched, the man sat up, turned toward him, and stood. Blackened flesh hung loosely from his face. His mouth was open in a skeletal grin. Tattered clothing swung about him, some swatches of cloth falling away, some clinging to the strands of muscle that had yet to completely decay. The sound of his bones cracking as he took a step toward Rick was petrifying.

Rick's scream died in his throat as he watched the dead man approach him, his body immobile from fear. His mind flooded with voices his conscious had long forgotten, telling him the stories about the owners and their abandonment of the house. He could hear his neighbor, a little old man of eighty, telling him that the house wasn't fit for a young man to live in.

"You don't want that place. You don't need a place like that," he had said on their first meeting. Rick told him that he had already signed the paperwork so it was too late to do anything about it. He joked with the man, tried to make light of whatever situation the man had brewing in his mind. He hoped the joke might have taken the edge off, but it didn't. The old man went on to say that he should be careful being there alone. Told him to watch with a dog's eye. Rick had nodded and excused himself politely, writing the advice off as the ramblings of an old man.

On another occasion, the gossiping socialite of the street had come by the share what she knew about the house and its previous owner.

"I've lived on this street all my life. Knew them when they lived here. Nice enough people, I guess. Kept to themselves mostly. Then they moved away and we never heard a thing from them. I heard they were trying to rent the place, but nothing ever came of that. The house just sat here empty." She shook her head slowly, recounting the story.

"We took care of the yard," she continued. "My husband Moe cut the lawn and kept the bushes trim and what not, trying to keep it neat looking. Didn't want an eyesore on our street, you know what I mean? Things went like that for a while. Years. Then they came back. They brought the boy here."

"So it hasn't sat empty the whole time," Rick said, just to feel like he was contributing to the conversation. The woman had been talking nonstop since she had gotten there.

"It has. They didn't stay long, didn't even set foot inside."

Rick couldn't help but wonder if she had been watching their visit through binoculars from her window. He didn't put it past her.

"They parked in the driveway and went around back with him," she continued, chewing her gum rapidly as she took a breath. "Cheryl and Barry had a doozy of a time carrying the casket, but they still moved pretty quick."

"What?" Rick cut in. "What are you talking about?"

"The casket. They brought their son here and buried him in your backyard so that he could be in his home forever."

Mucus ran freely out of Rick's nose and onto his upper lip as the dead man approached him. His mind was spinning, a battle between fright and logic ensuing. Some part of him screamed for him to get up, to run out of the house. It told him to move, to do something other than lie there and wait to die. But he couldn't. The magnitude of his fear and disbelief was too heavy for him to carry.

The boy, undoubtedly Aaron Carter, son of the Carters' from whose estate Rick had bought the house, stood over Rick. Decayed matter fell from Aaron's body and onto Rick's shirt as he knelt down, looking closer at the man who would inhabit the house with him forever.

Baie Rouge

The hot sand engulfed her feet with every step she took toward the shore. The smell of salt water caressed her nostrils and the warm breeze tousled her hair. The turquoise water lapped along the shore, depositing shells with intricate designs on the sand. The day was perfect for a dip in the water, warm with a breeze, the sun still high in the sky, but she didn't notice. The tropical backdrop that Mayaguana provided was wasted on her. The salty air did nothing to mask the smell underneath. The smell of blood, pungent and strong.

Sandra had gone for a swim at Baie Rouge, taking advantage of the beautiful Wednesday afternoon. She knew when she awoke that morning that she was going to do it, was going to call out sick from work to bask in the sunrays at the beach. The morning had been so warm without the humidity typical of the island in the summer months; the sun felt so good on her face. She couldn't help it.

Sandra packed a salad—prawns cooked with spices, guava, passion fruit, melon, grapes, tomatoes, and avocado on a bed of lettuce— and something to drink—a bottle of White Zinfandel—and headed to the most secluded beach on the island. She wanted to be alone with her salad and her wine, alone with her thoughts and the sound of the surf.

She set up her beach chair at the water's edge, allowing the tide to come in and caress her legs and buttocks before traveling back out to sea. Her towel and basket were further up on the sand, warming in the sunlight. She squinted at the horizon through her shades and beneath the brim of her straw hat, her wine glass filled halfway in hand. So far away, intangible, like Vickie was. The thought of her made tears well in Sandra's eyes. She took a sip of her wine and sighed as the water rose to cover her legs once more.

Vickie. So beautiful, alive. It didn't make sense that she could have been taken away so suddenly. She had been walking to the store from the hillside villa they shared to get odds and ends for dinner. Sandra had already been to the supermarket and had forgotten to buy fresh garlic for the Alfredo sauce she was making that evening.

"Mi Dios!" Vickie exclaimed, "The garlic is the best part! How could you forget that, kerido?" Vickie spoke with such a carefree lilt, it was hard to take her agitation seriously. Her petite frame didn't inspire fear either. Sandra looked at her face, and through her frustration, could see a smile playing at the corner of her lips. She couldn't help but notice how beautiful Vickie was, the setting sun casting golden rays on her face. Her hair was shoulder length, her features dainty, a testament to the European side of her heritage. The sun had kissed her skin to a copper brown over the years that she and her family had lived on the island. Vickie couldn't remember living anywhere else in her twenty-three years.

"I know," Sandra said, snapping out of the trance Vickie's eyes usually put her into. Sandra turned away to stir the sauce. The back of her neck was hot. She knew Vickie was looking at her. When she turned back, Vickie was smiling. She could never stay angry for long. "Can you go and get some?" Sandra asked.

"Sí, sí. At your service, madam." She bowed and Sandra playfully popped her in the head with her hand. Vickie stood up and put her arms around Sandra. Their lips met while Vickie's hands caressed Sandra's back. To Sandra, Vickie's kiss was like fresh water splashing over her face; her touch was invigorating.

Sandra felt herself responding to her, wanting to abandon the Alfredo sauce and take Vickie into the bedroom. Everything about Vickie excited Sandra. Her touch was like satin on her body. Men had never caused that reaction before. At first Sandra had been frightened, nervous about what it all might mean. But Vickie was patient with her. "I'm Caribbean. It's my way," she was fond of saying, but it was much more than that. Vickie was a caring girl who allowed Sandra to take her time. She knew that Sandra didn't understand what was happening. Vickie had always known how she felt about women, but for someone who had just come out of a heterosexual relationship, it was a big blow. When everything you thought you knew about yourself is false, there's a lot of readjusting to do. Vickie knew that. So she waited.

They had been together for three years. Sandra moved to Mayaguana from New York and made a new home. Vickie left her apartment and moved to the other side of the island with Sandra. They were good together.

Sandra pressed her body into Vickie's and let her hands trace her shoulder blades as they kissed. Vickie cupped Sandra's buttocks gently, squeezing each glute and letting her hands linger. Their kisses were becoming deeper, their tongues probing each other's mouths unabashedly. The sauce began to bubble. Sandra pulled away and said breathlessly, "E garlic, beibi." (*The garlic, baby.*)

Panting, Vickie pulled away and put distance between them. Her eyes lingered at Sandra's lips then at her erect nipples. She bent down and took

Sandra's shirt-covered breast into her mouth, closing her lips around the nipple and sucked lightly. Sandra's eyes closed and her back arched, but she held firm.

"Kuandu abo buska bèk," she said in stilted, unaccented Papiamento. (*When you get back*). Vickie had been teaching her bits and pieces since they had been together, but she was just starting to use it without being prompted.

Vickie cocked her head and clapped. "Masha bon! Masha bon, Sandra!" (*Very good*). She took a deep breath and one last look at Sandra's breasts before saying, "Now we have to work on the accent. You're butchering a perfectly good language with your New York accent." Angie laughed as she turned to stir the sauce.

"I'm getting there."

"That you are. Soon you'll be able to carry on a conversation in Papiamento at the market."

Sandra nodded. Vickie gave Sandra a kiss on the cheek before leaving. "Just garlic, right?" she asked at the door. "Did you forget anything else?"

"No, that's it, smart-ass," I said.

"Just checking." Vickie left.

That was the last time Sandra saw her alive.

Some thugs saw Vickie walking the street alone. They grabbed her and tried to take her money. When they got a good look at her, they decided to take more than that. She fought them off the best she could, ruining one of the guys' eyes forever. But they forced it. They choked her to keep her in place. The guy violating her didn't even notice she was dead until after he had finished.

That was two years before.

Sandra got up from the chair and waded into the water. Its soothing touch reminded her of Vickie's lips on her body. The tears fell freely as she thought of her lover, cold in the grave, gone to her forever. Sandra dipped below the surface and swam underwater for a while, letting the images of her and Vickie fill her head. How many times had they swam at Baie Rouge? Skinny dipped in the setting sun, picnicked in seclusion? They were able to enjoy life as a couple better in Mayaguana than they would have been able to anywhere else, but the freedom was not without its limits. People still turned their heads and snickered when they walked by hand in hand. Baie Rouge's seclusion offered respite from that. They felt like it was their own little corner of the world.

Sandra resurfaced and breathed deeply, letting the air fill her lungs. It smelled differently then, tinny and metallic. She wiped water away from her eyes and looked back to where her towel and basket were. She was getting hungry and could almost taste the salad she had prepared. It was one of hers and Vickie's favorites.

There was someone standing in front of her picnic basket.

Sandra looked up and down the beach from where she stood in the water and could see no one else. Mid-day beach going was not the norm for the natives of Mayaguana, and the tourists found that beach to be too remote for their tastes. No Jet Ski rentals, no restaurants. Just unspoiled beach and white sand surrounded by lush mangroves and palm trees. The other side of the island had several more popular beaches, leaving Baie Rouge deserted most of the time.

Sandra walked toward her camp, grabbing her lounge chair out of the water. As she dragged it behind her, she noticed that the woman standing in front of her towel and basket seemed familiar. Though her back faced her, Sandra thought she recognized the woman's shapely form. She was wearing a bathing suit, black and tiger print that hugged her body. A black sarong was tied loosely at her waist, the sheer material revealing her toned legs. Her hair was pulled up in a bun revealing a slender, delicate neck. Sandra looked away, embarrassed. She hadn't looked at another woman since Vickie's death, hadn't been able to. She felt bad that she had done it then. It was still too soon.

Sandra placed the chair and sat down in it as soon as she reached the picnic basket.

"Bon tardi, madam," Sandra said before she took a sip of the wine that had grown warm in the afternoon sun.

The woman turned around and looked at Sandra with the warmest of eyes.

Sandra jumped, spilling some of the wine onto her leg. The woman's eyes, her mouth, the arch of her brow, every feature on the woman looked like it belonged to Vickie. The resemblance was uncanny. It was disconcerting.

"Sorry. Abo parse algun ami gewon konosé." (*You look like someone I used to know*). Sometimes Sandra shocked herself at the ease with which she spoke Papiamento. *I guess Vickie was right*, Sandra thought bitterly.

The woman cocked her head and said with genuine emotion, "Masha bon, Sandra!"

Sandra's fingers felt like ice.

"Oh my God, this can't be!" Sandra whispered. She tried to inch backwards but found that she couldn't move. Her lips quivered and fresh tears fell from her eyes.

"But it is, kerido. It is."

Sandra sat in confused silence, staring up at a woman who looked, sounded, smiled like Vickie. Her body was shaking, but she wasn't aware of that. The glass of Zinfandel fell from her hand to the sand.

"My love, I wanted to come before, but I didn't think you were ready."

"What?" Seeing Vickie again was intoxicating and frightening all at the same time.

"You weren't ready to see me, to understand. But I thought now, in this place, maybe you would hear me."

Vickie's voice was like velvet. She sat on the towel beside Sandra's chair and folded her legs beneath her. She reached for Sandra's hand and clasped it between hers before Sandra could blink. It was pleasantly warm.

"This can't be happening," Sandra said under her breath.

"Why can't it? Why can't I be here, sitting next to you on our favorite beach, our favorite place in the world? Why is that so far-fetched?"

"Because you're dead!" Sandra said louder than she meant to. Her voice hitched. "It can't be true because you are buried in the ground." Sandra turned her head to the sky and said, as if asking God, "Why do you put me through such torment?"

"Yes, it's true. I am dead." Sandra brought her head down to face Vickie as she spoke. "But I am alive at the same time."

The confusion registered on Sandra's face as her tears dried.

"Those boys left me for dead on the street between home and the supermarket. No one would help me. The bums receded into their shacks, people closed their shutters to the noise of my screams. It was when I lay there dying that she came to me."

"Who?" Sandra's eyes were wide with wonder. To hear Vickie's voice again was pure ecstasy.

"Vanessa."

The name rolled around Sandra's mind, finding no placement. "Who is that?" she asked finally.

"She lived on the other side of the island near my family. People always shied away from her because she wasn't a native. But I always talked to her, said hello when passing by, in the market, or on the street. I've known her all of my life but never did I see her age. When I was five she was our age, as she is now, after twenty years have passed."

Sandra wanted to ask her what she was talking about but couldn't form the words. "I know it's a lot to take in, but try, Sandra," Vickie continued, her eyes gazing into Sandra's the way they used to. Sandra felt herself melting.

"She gave me her gift, kerido. She saved me from a life of aging, of withering away to nothing, of dying. She made me whole again."

"But your body," Sandra sobbed. "I saw them put you —."

"I had not yet awoken," Vickie cut in. "I did that night. My hunger was so great, I had to stay away. I was afraid of what I might do. I was so young then."

"Hunger? What-what does this all mean?"

Vickie leaned into Sandra slowly. Sandra's mind protested, but her heart couldn't make her turn away. The touch of Vickie's lips upon hers felt incredible, like life anew. Sandra kissed her deeper, kissed her for all the years lost, kissed her for spent tears.

Sandra joined Vickie on the towel, reclining so that Vickie could lay on top of her as they kissed. Their hands explored each other, touching places that hadn't been touched since Vickie's death. Sandra felt exhilarated.

"It means," Vickie said as they parted lips, "that I am here with you and will be forever. I will not age. I will not die."

Vickie put her hand on Sandra's chest, feeling the rapid beats of her heart against her hand. "I want to share the gift given me with you."

Sandra's eyes blurred with tears. What she had wanted, what she had prayed for for two years was finally happening. She looked at Vickie, the beauty of the tropical setting her backdrop, and knew.

Wordlessly, Sandra agreed to receive Vickie's gift. Vickie kissed her once more, nibbling her lips and cheek as she made her way to the supple flesh of Sandra's neck. Vickie looked at her lover — her love — once more before taking her. She was so beautiful. How Vickie had missed her. Cradling her head as she did it, Vickie pressed her teeth to Sandra's neck, puncturing her jugular vein. Tasting her sent chills down Vickie's spine. She could feel herself stir in anticipation of an eternity with Sandra. A tear of blood fell from her eye as she watched her lover die. She strolled the beach as the sun warmed her skin, waiting for nightfall when her lover would be reborn.

The Last Port

The warm water soothed Bill as he stood in the shower of their cabin. Michelle had turned the lights off in the room, leaving it pitch black. They loved inside cabins for that reason alone. There was nothing like going out on a dive, coming back to your room, and sitting in blackness at 4 o'clock in the afternoon. They would take a nap and be fresh for dinner. He almost couldn't wait to join her in bed.

The dive had been good. Lots of tropical fish, but nothing out of the ordinary. Sergeant Majors, Parrot Fish, a couple of Moray Eels hidden in the rock, a Guitarfish blending in with the sand. It was only their second dive with the camera, and it was his turn to fiddle with it. It was like the fish knew he was a novice. They would swim in front of his viewfinder, teasing him with beautiful shots of them. A second before he took the picture, though, they would dart away, leaving him with a shot of nothing but the water in front of him.

As usual, Bill and Michelle swam side by side, gliding in the water, becoming one with it. He saw an eel poking out of its cave and motioned for Michelle to look at it. When he swam closer to try and get a picture, Michelle's eye caught on something else. She swam toward it, gliding in the opposite direction from Bill, to get a closer look. Bill gave up on the eel after about a minute or so and turned around to find Michelle, but he didn't see her anywhere. With visibility at 80%, it was virtually impossible to lose sight of someone unless they had swum far ahead. He turned to look for her but saw only coral and rock formations in the distance. It was times like those when he wished they had invested in facemasks with the microphone, speaker, and regulator included. Then he could have called out to her instead of having to swivel around in search of her fluorescent pink fins. Bill had ogled over the facemasks in the catalog, much like he had over the underwater digital camera and the plastic video camera casing. Michelle nipped his spending spree in the bud after the digital camera. It was a good thing too. If he had bought all the gear he wanted, they would never have been able to afford the trips to use them.

A minute is a long time underwater, especially when you're alone. What was once relaxing turned frightening; the vastness seeming claustrophobic and stifling. Bill began to chastise himself for doing the dive without a guide. True, they had been diving for years and understood navigation well enough to go out on their own, but there is comfort in numbers. The beach was so inviting, though, and with so many spots to just walk off the beach, swim out a ways, and descend to 60 feet, they couldn't help themselves. It was easy to rationalize. They intended to dive anyway. They brought their gear on the cruise, expecting to dive at the last port. The rates were high, so they thought they would find a local shop on the island and go with them instead. They were on their way to a shop when they saw a guy renting tanks at a dock. It seemed like a great idea, so they did it. And now he couldn't find Michelle.

Bill could feel his breathing increasing after about ten seconds of swirling in the water and not seeing anything. He looked at his watch, but it was a useless gesture. He couldn't remember at what time they had separated, didn't think he had looked at the watch at all after their descent. He tapped his tank knocker hoping that she would hear it and come out from wherever she was, show him that she was okay. Nothing. He looked up. Nothing. She wasn't anywhere.

Bill was sucking up a lot of air, using much more than he would normally have. He finned over to the other side of the rock where he had attempted to get a shot of the eel. His mind conjured up terrible images. He saw Michelle being attacked by curious barracudas, or a Tiger shark. He saw her regulator snagging on the jagged coral and dislodging from her mouth. He saw her unable to reach her back up regulator and drowning to death. His mind was running wild and he knew it. But he couldn't stop the images from coming.

Bill looked behind the rock but saw nothing. When he looked up, he saw a flash of pink ahead. He kicked strongly, propelling himself through the water to reach the pink flash ahead. Michelle's suit had a fluorescent pink line down both sides, and her fins had pink on the underside. It had to be her, he told himself as he approached.

The sand had been kicked up and it hung in the water like a tan veil. Bill slowed down as he approached the oddly heavy space, extending his arms as he swam into it. Thousands of tiny needles pricked his skin as he swam through, fire coral protesting his intrusion. There was something in front of him. Something his size.

Bill's mind warned against continuing. He couldn't see what was in front of him, lying in wait. He couldn't scream if something was there, couldn't call for help. He was 45 feet under water, diving off a dock. No one knew where they were. Bill breathed in deeply, depleting his air even more, and forged ahead.

His hand hit the thing in front of him first. It was coated with a slippery skin. Bill tried to close his hand around the thing, to grab on to something so that he could figure out what it was, but he couldn't. He reached his free hand out to grab the other side of the thing, to bring it closer to his mask so he could see it. Something moved under his touch, wriggling away from his grasp and out into the freedom of the sea. He turned his head to see what had escaped but couldn't see through the wall of sand in front of him. Bill grabbed onto the sizeable thing with both hands and pulled it toward him. He could see that it was dark and long. Bill's fear threatened to make him release it and swim away, but he held firm. His wife's face jutted out at him, staring at him with wide eyes.

Startled, Bill recoiled, his breathing increasing. Michelle blinked and signaled: pointing at him (you), index finger rounded to thumb (okay?). Bill looked at her eyes through her mask. Water had seeped into the seal, pooling at the bottom, just under her nose. He watched as she cleared it with ease and looked back at him. She furrowed her brow and gave him a thumbs up: a request to ascend. Bill stared at her, trying to figure out what was wrong. There was something different, something not quite the same about what little he could see of her face. Her eyes were clear and focused, sure, but they seemed somehow vacant. They were dull. Bill stared at her eyes, ignoring her signal. Michelle shoved his shoulder and signaled again, but he didn't respond. She hooked her hand into his BCD and began to ascend, dragging him with her.

When they resurfaced, Michelle automatically turned Bill on his back and leaned his head and shoulders against her chest. She removed her regulator and said,

"Just relax honey. I'll get us back."

Bill removed himself from her hold and turned toward her. "I'm okay. It's you I'm worried about. You seemed… strange."

Michelle cocked her head to the side and said, "What are you talking about? I'm fine."

"Where were you? I couldn't find you for a long time."

"A long time? I couldn't have been gone for more than a minute."

Bill looked down at the water, feeling his cheeks starting to burn. Suddenly the time they had been separated didn't seem that long at all. Not more than a minute or so, like she said. Maybe he had overreacted. A smile spread across his lips.

"You sure you're okay," Bill asked again.

"Yeah, I'm fine."

Something about Michelle's face seemed disingenuous. Her right eye twitched as she spoke, moving in time to her words. Bill's mind called up the feel of slime that coated her and the thing that disappeared into the water.

"C'mon, let's get back. I'm starving now. Aren't you hungry?" Michelle asked.

Bill let the subject change. He couldn't put his finger on what he thought was wrong, and asking the same question over and over would, after a while, irritate anyone. They swam back, made their way to the ship, and ate on the lido deck without talking about their underwater encounter again.

Bill blinked the memory of the day away and turned off the water. He dried off and joined Michelle on the bed. She stretched out her arm and he rested his head on it, snuggling close to her.

"What's on?" Bill asked, knowing that he would only see ten minutes of the movie before falling asleep. The darkness of the room, the mellowing hot shower, and the physical exertion earlier combined would knock him out.

"I don't know. Some love story. It had already started when I found it."

Bill had started to drift already. He grunted a response and let himself fall to sleep in his wife's arms. She felt normal to him, if not just a tad bit cold. He let his concerns about her float away.

Myrtle and Roy sat in the dining room along with many of the other cruise passengers. They were back in the States, back home to continue on with their everyday life. The paradise they had visited would soon be just a memory.

They had been waiting to disembark for an hour. They had already passed through Customs on the ship and were ready to get their bags and start on the four-hour drive from Baltimore, Maryland to Nanuet, New York. The drive was going to be a pain in the ass. She tried to get Roy to fly, but he said, "Why should we fly if the port is only right up the road? I could see if we were leaving out of Florida, but fly to Baltimore?" If he drove the speed limit it would be fine. If he let her drive, that would have been even better. But no, he hogged the wheel and poked his way along the highway. She sipped her cooling coffee and tried to mentally prepare for the trip home.

"What's taking so long anyway? What's the hold up?" Roy asked. He folded his legs and twitched his foot back and forth rapidly.

"Some people still haven't cleared customs yet. That's what the cruise director said." *Over the loudspeaker*, you idiot, she wanted to add. *If you had been listening, you would have known.* But she didn't. She saved the sarcasm for later, when she wouldn't be able to stop herself.

The cruise director's voice cut through the noisy chatter in the dining room for the fifth time that morning. With his Italian accent that had been seducing women all week, he said,

"Ladies and Gentlemen, as I've said before, it is necessary for everyone to pass through Customs before anyone can get off the ship. Right now we are waiting for the following people: Bill and Michelle Gunner. If you are Bill or Michelle Gunner, please come down to the Stardust Lounge and complete the Customs process. If you know Bill or Michelle Gunner, please alert them. Thank you." He tried to mask his anger, but he didn't succeed.

Mumbling erupted in the dining room. People were asking to be let off, telling the staff to go to the room and get the couple that was making everyone wait, cursing them for their laziness.

"What could they be doing? Everyone knew the process two days ago!" Myrtle said, unable to hold her tongue.

"What do you think they're doing, Myrtle?" Roy said, agitated. *Use your brain, woman,* he would have said if he felt like dealing with the hour of arguing his comment would bring. He was going to be stuck in the car with her for hours. He didn't want them to be filled with her bitching. So he changed his tone, and said instead,

"They're probably having some last-minute sex before they have to get off the ship." He giggled and got up to get some fruit from the food bar. *Good for 'em,* Roy said in his mind as he walked away.

The cruise director met the cabin cleaning staff in front of Bill and Michelle Gunner's stateroom.

"Have they not replied at all?" he asked.

"No. Not all morning," said the cabin steward from Yugoslavia. She shifted from foot to foot nervously. She wanted to get off the ship as much as anyone else. This was her first time in Baltimore and she wanted to see the sights. She sent a picture of herself at a port along with some money to her mother every week. She only had four hours in between cleaning the rooms after the guests disembarked and going over them a second time for new guests. She was anxious to leave.

The cruise director cleared his throat, knocked on the door, and said, "Mr. and Mrs. Gunner. I am Nick, the cruise director. Please open the door. You must settle with Customs before anyone can leave the ship."

No response.

He waited a minute before knocking again. "Mr. and Mrs. Gunner, I will have to open this door if you do not comply. Please."

Nothing.

After two minutes of waiting, Nick motioned for the cabin steward to open the door. She inserted the master passkey and the light flashed green.

Nick announced, "I'm coming in Mr. and Mrs. Gunner."

He pushed the door open and was met with darkness. He turned on the light and, almost immediately, backed away in horror. Bill Gunner laid in the bed, his body turned on its side, facing his wife. He was coated with a thick slime over his entire body. His stomach was flayed, the muscle and fat beneath his skin open to the air. His eyes were missing.

Michelle Gunner laid opposite her husband, her arm beneath his head, supporting it. Her mouth was open, slack. Her skin was lacerated in several spots, torn open, exposing the soft, bloody flesh beneath the skin. Her stomach was ripped open, a hollow cavity remaining where internal organs should have been.

While the cruise director and cabin steward watched, a tentacle reached out from Michelle's mouth. Another poked through a laceration in her cheek. A terrible throbbing started in her chest cavity, slowly at first, then increasing until the skin could no longer contain it. Her sternum gave way with a sickening crack. Two more tentacles pushed through the skin above her breasts. They seemed to survey the air, to smell it. The creature that inhabited Michelle's body lunged toward Nick, the Italian cruise director, with immeasurable quickness. It had probed his brain through his nose before he could flinch.

Room 3708

Jerry is really sick this time, I thought to myself. The doctor told us to watch his diabetes, told us what could happen if we let it get out of hand, and we tried to change. We started eating salads instead of fried chicken, and I started putting apples in his lunch bag instead of potato chips. Less mayonnaise on his sandwiches. Less sugar in his iced tea. He started dropping weight. And so did I. That gut of his that had started to resemble the stomach of a pregnant woman had slimmed down to nothing more than a little pouch in six months and I was fitting dresses that I hadn't been able to get into in years. His legs, which had gone rubbery and unhealthy, started to show some of the muscle they once had. We started walking more. We started by driving to the lake that sat at the edge of our community and walking halfway around. Then we'd walk the whole thing. After a month or two, we started walking from our house to the lake: a full mile! It became our Saturday date. Sometimes Jerry would get up early and surprise me with fresh picked flowers before we started our walk. He would hold my hand as we strolled the lake, beautiful in the noonday sun. It was our special time.

On Sundays, he would take our grandson out to play at the park. Michelle and Ryan would stop by to drop Jeffrey off before they spent the day at the mall. I would get ten minutes with Jeffrey before Jerry whisked him away to play on the monkey bars or in the sand dunes. I was so proud of Jerry, so happy to see him tackling the disease head on. He was more fit than he had been in years and he looked great.

It was the dessert that got us.

Jerry loved cherry pie and I love to bake. I used to bake a pie every week, until he got sick. Then I cut it down to two pies a month, maybe less. At first, Jerry went after the pie with the same gusto that he used to, taking big slices of it and topping it with two scoops of rich vanilla ice cream. I got on him about the size of his plate, and after a while, he listened. The portions got smaller, at least in front of me. I worried about him sneaking pie here and there. He was the one who took out the garbage, so if he cleaned the plate before dumping it, I would never know. I was concerned, but I didn't stop making the pies.

Our first scare was two months ago. Jerry woke up on Friday and went to the bathroom like he always did. He took a shower, shaved, and got ready for work. I went into the kitchen and made his lunch for the day with the usual stuff: tuna fish sandwich, a slice of pickle, and an apple for later. He came downstairs and kissed me good morning. Everything seemed fine. He started talking about something, a guy at work who wasn't pulling his weight, or some other story, I can't really remember the details anymore. He was distracted by it and wasn't watching what he was doing. He reached out his hand to grab the handle of the coffee pot without looking and touched the glass flush. I know the pot was piping hot, hot enough to make you yell out in pain if it only brushed against you. The coffee had just been brewed and the burner was on high. But he didn't even flinch. Some of the coffee splashed out of the pot and onto his hand. I could see the steam rising from it as it rolled down toward his wrist, but still he didn't utter a sound.

I called his name cautiously. I didn't want to scare him and have him knock the pot off the burner and onto himself. He looked at me and followed my eyes back to his hand. He saw the brown liquid wetting the cuff of his shirt and jerked his hand away from the pot.

"But I didn't feel anything," he said, his voice full of disbelief.

We went to the hospital right away.

The doctor told us we had to reduce his diet even more to keep him healthy. I racked my brain, trying to think of what we were eating that could have done this to him. On the way home from the hospital, I decided that my pie making days were over. It was the only thing I could think of that was bad in our diet. I knew he wouldn't be happy about it—the man had been eating my pie for the better part of thirty years—but I had to do it. The doctor told me that, if we didn't make changes to the way he ate, he would die sooner than he would if he followed the right plan. If I had to choose between pie and Jerry, Jerry wins every time.

The next two months went fine. He was angry about the pie, but I put my foot down. He got used to it after a while, and life without pie became normal. He started falling asleep earlier than usual about three weeks ago. He'd come home and complain about being tired. I mentioned going back to the doctor but he refused. He said that he didn't have to go to the doctor for every little thing. He assured me he was fine. I believed him.

He fell into a diabetic coma at work. They thought he had just nodded off at lunch, finding him bent over the table with his head resting in his arms in the break room. But when he didn't report back to his register after lunch, someone went back into the break room and found him still sitting in the same position he had been in an hour before. When they tried to rouse him, he wouldn't stir. His manager called the hospital and then called me.

That was yesterday. He still hadn't woken up, hadn't moved a muscle since being checked in. The nurses had him propped up for the better part of the day, but at night, they laid him flat on his back. There was an IV in his arm and oxygen in his nose. The nurse put lip balm on his lips to keep them moist. Something about that frightened me more than looking at him with all of the tubes coming out of him, more than all of the beeping and buzzing of the machinery around him. It seemed like they were planning for him to stay a while, like they didn't expect him to wake up.

They let me stay with him. I sat in a chair next to his bed. I stared at him for a long time, at his unmoving eyelids and his closed mouth. His hands lay motionless on the sides of his body. He was completely still. I cried for a while, then I paced, then I sat next to him and stared again. Nothing. I picked up his hand to caress it. The familiar warmth was disarming and it left me cold. How could he feel so alive but be gone from me? I started to tell him to wake up, to open his eyes. I whispered it at first, but my voice quickly rose to a shriek. I lost myself for a moment. His body was so still, so quiet, it was as though I was standing before a corpse. But his hands were warm.

I finally heard myself yelling, the sound seeming to push itself out from a bubble, and I settled down. Tears wet my face again, and I brushed them away absently. Jerry's face remained the same. If he had heard me, he didn't show it.

Defeated, I sat back in the chair. It was more comfortable than it looked, and my weary body began to relax. Before I knew it, I had drifted off to sleep. At least that's what I think I did because the sensation of waking up was so real. I looked over at the clock. Six hours had passed and it was 3:00 a.m. I stood up and stretched my legs. I looked over at Jerry and saw that he looked the same. He hadn't moved, hadn't shifted at all. The sight of him that way filled my heart with dread.

I looked away from him because I had to. I felt that I would fall away from myself if I didn't, that I would join him in the silent world that kept him disconnected from life. I walked toward the bathroom to splash some water on my face.

The bathroom was just inside the door of the hospital room. I looked into the hallway with its bright fluorescent lights and sterile walls. I could hear the nurses at the station three doors down chatting, could hear the beeping of other patient's machines. The whole atmosphere seemed surreal to me. I just couldn't believe I was there and that this was happening.

I reached out to open the bathroom door, but something across the hall drew my attention. The door opposite Jerry's room was open. The patient in there was probably sleeping, as the lights and television were both turned off. A person stood over the patient, at the foot of the bed. I took a step forward to get a closer look, forgetting about the bathroom door. Something about the visitor was strange. The person had a man's build with wide shoulders and straight hips. He didn't wear a doctor's coat or a nurse's uniform, but that didn't strike me as odd. The hospital let me stay the night with Jerry, so it made sense that a family member might be in the room. But something about the person seemed different, odd. I looked closer, straining my eyes to see, but not wanting to give myself away. The person stood about six feet tall, medium structure. He wore dark clothing, making it hard to decipher where he stopped and the darkness of the room began. I could see the man's hands; one of them was at his side and the other was on the patient's feet. The skin on his hands seemed bright, cutting into the darkness with some kind of inner light. It was almost as though he held a flashlight that shined on his hands, but not quite. The skin itself seemed to be moving. The thought of migrating ants came to mind as I looked at the man's hands. My hands became clammy as I stood in the doorway in plain sight, all too obviously eavesdropping on the patient in room 3708. I knew I shouldn't have, but I couldn't turn away. I couldn't stop looking at the strange man.

The man's face was shadowy and dark. I could barely make out the outline of his head. What I could see had to be wrong. His head was oblong and with more curves than a normal face has. Where the eyes, nose, and chin would be, there were coiled protrusions that seemed to reach out from his profile. Those too seemed to move, to sway in an imaginary wind, bobbing up and down independently. Like snakes. I stood frozen in the doorway watching as the man stood over the patient, staring intently the way I had at my husband. A scream rose in my throat, but I was able to swallow it back.

I could hear the padding of feet coming down the hall. I desperately wanted to move, to turn away and act like I was doing something else. I didn't want to be caught looking into other people's rooms. I didn't want anything to jeopardize my nights with Jerry, however many there might be. Moreover, I didn't want the man in the other room to look my way when he heard the footsteps. More than not wanting to be caught snooping, I didn't want to see the man's face.

I backed away from the door. I had moved to the mouth of it without realizing I had, and I needed to take two steps backward to fade into the shadows of Jerry's room. The nurse stopped in front of our room with her head turned toward room 3708. I couldn't help but wonder if she saw what I saw, felt the strangeness of the man visiting in that room. She walked toward the door slowly, as if trying not to disturb them. She reached in, grabbed the doorknob, and shut the door, giving them privacy. I furrowed my brow, realizing that she hadn't seen what I saw, if there was anything to see at all. I sighed imperceptibly, chalking the vision up to my nerves being on end. This thing with Jerry was taking its toll on my mind.

I was about to take a step out of the darkness and go to the bathroom like I had originally planned, but the nurse turned towards me. Her brown hair hung in a straight cut, framing her face. It was parted in the center perfectly, providing an unobstructed view of her attractive face. Her expression was unreadable, blank in most respects; her red painted lips were neither smiling nor frowning. I couldn't conceal the gasp that escaped my mouth as I backed away from her. Her face, beautiful in every way, was missing the eyeballs that would give her sight. The empty sockets were as black as the night that blanketed the city. A tear of blood ran down her cheek as she turned away from me and continued down the hall.

I kept backing up, clutching my chest as I did it. My heart was beating rapidly, faster than it ever had, faster than it should have been. The back of my legs hit the side of Jerry's bed and I lost my balance. I felt onto the bed, right on top of Jerry's unmoving legs. I turned to him to see if he stirred. He was sitting up in front of me. His eyes were open, but they were as hollow as the nurse's had been. He spoke in a voice that was as familiar to me as the back of my hand. Black spittle shot out of his mouth as he spoke, dusting his chin and hospital gown with a gritty dirt-like substance. He said in the voice I had loved for most of my life,

"Make me a cherry pie, Evie. Make me one more before I die."

He touched my face with fingers that were as cold as ice. My body trembled as I screamed.

"A nurse's gentle but insistent tapping woke me up this morning. As soon as my eyes fluttered open, she told me to leave the room, that they had to tend to Jerry. I left, still groggy, and stood in the hallway. The room was full of people, doctors and nurses, all shouting commands and responses. They were too busy to shut the door so I was able to look in at them while they worked on your father. I knew he was gone before they came out to tell me. A pretty young nurse came out to tell me the news. While she was talking to me in the hallway, telling me how sorry they were and that they had done all they could, I had this odd sensation, like I was in another room overhearing them speaking to someone else. I felt like I was moving in slow motion, nodding at all the right times and wringing my hands. Then, in a moment of clarity that seemed to come from nowhere, I looked to my left at room 3708. All the sounds that had filled the hallway were silenced as I looked into the room unabashed, no longer concerned about being nosey. It was as though I had to see, had to know who or what was in there." Evelyn paused for a moment, shaking her head slowly. "But both beds were empty."

Evelyn tried to stifle her sobs as she told her daughter of her father's last moments. Michelle and Ryan had come straight to the hospital that morning but had not been able to see their father alive.

"Mom, I wish you had called us sooner," Michelle said through her tears. The family huddled together in Jerry's hospital room until it was time for him to be transported to the morgue.

***

Evelyn unlocked her door and went into the house. Michelle and Ryan sat in the front room, breaking the news of the death to their son. Evelyn left them, giving them time to be alone, and walked into the kitchen. She went to the refrigerator to take out the orange juice. Her mouth had been dry since she had woken up to find her husband dying. She put the juice on the counter and reached up to open the glass cabinet. Her hands barely touched a glass when her eyes wandered to the countertop. A foil covered dish sat on the far end of the counter. Evelyn dropped the glass onto the counter loudly, her arm losing all strength as she stared at the dish. She approached it slowly, dragging her hand along the counter. She stood in front it for a minute before reaching toward it. Pulling at the edge of the foil slowly, she found a cherry pie underneath. The sweet, fresh smell of it filled the room, making her nauseous. A slice, wide and jagged, was missing.

Island Girls

The air was heavy. I could feel my clothes clinging to me as I stepped off the plane. I breathed deeply, taking it in, welcoming it as I did the layer of sweat above my brow. This is where I wanted to be. This is where it will all begin.

I carried my bag on my shoulder and left the terminal. A young woman moved slowly ahead of me, struggling under the weight of her suitcase and carry on. I passed her, smelling her perfume as I did. Could she be the one?

Ahead a woman wearing black capri pants, a turquoise halter-top, and black sandals crossed the street. She swung her summer purse as she jogged to beat the light. Her brown hair swayed like palm tree leaves in the breeze. A smile crossed my lips as I quickened my pace to catch her.

She'll do. She'll do just fine.

To Die A Fool

I tried my best to be good.

To be godlike, holy, a servant of the most high. I worshiped and fellowshipped. I tithed and studied. I did all of the things that He asks us to do to be looked upon favorably. I ministered to others, gathering souls for the Lord. I gave out pamphlets and ushered Sunday service, taught Sunday School and brought food to the homes of the bereaved. But now, as I lay on my deathbed in a room made stagnant by my uncontrolled releases, I wonder.

I recount my life in moments of lucidity: I had a wife, two kids, and a dog. A nice single-family home in a quiet neighborhood with a big backyard and a two-car garage. I worked a modest job and brought in a nice salary. I provided for my family, giving them everything I could. I offered my time at the church where my parents were married. I sat with the old and infirm in their time of need. I did all those things through my love for the Lord and my search for salvation at the end of my journey.

Still, I have sinned.

All of us have. We were born to do it. He Himself says that not one among us is more holy than the next. That passage of scripture always made me feel good, safe in a way that nothing else could. No matter how deep my sins, there were others out there with the same indiscretions and we would all be forgiven them. I was not alone.

My sin was that of unkind thoughts. I couldn't control the demon in my mind that would shout negative, hateful things at some of the people in my lives. No, I never expressed them aloud, but the Lord knows all of us inside and out. Satan put the thoughts in my head, an evil spirit to roam through my mind and body, tempting me to go against the word of God that I know to be true. He wanted me to speak the words, to give them voice and let them lay upon the shoulders of the receiver. I wanted to also, wanted to tell that jackass of a boss I had where he could shove it, wanted to tell the guy who cut me off in the rain to kiss my ass. And I almost did. But God gave me the strength to resist the urge, to shut my eyes to the temptation that laid before me, and keep my mouth shut. Still, the thoughts remained in my head, festering there, growing more intense.

There were those that I'd met in the church who challenged God, challenged His word for merit. They brought up the theory of evolution and Big Bang. They talked about Adam and Eve and passages like it as though they were merely parables, stories to guide us in our faith, and nothing more than that. I fought vehemently against them at every turn, quoting one scripture passage after the next to no avail. Finally, after they rebutted me time and time again, challenging me and the word as though we were one and the same, I told them that they had to have faith to believe in the Lord as I did. Faith and faith alone would help them. With a smile, they would walk away from me, their faces plainly showing their amusement with me, the satisfaction of their win. My wicked tongue would lash out at them then, calling them bitches and whores, sinners of the highest degree. My head filled with such profanity as to make my temples ache.

My life is slipping away. My eyes have grown cloudy, my eyelids heavy. Now that I am at death's door, I find my mind drifting toward the concepts that had been brought to my attention before. One in particular troubled me most. The thought took over my mind in those last minutes I would have on earth, pushing out all attempts at prayer and repentance. I met my death with doubt in my mind and fear in my heart.

The darkness gave way to the light of my childhood street. I took a step forward, disbelieving my eyes, the feel of the sidewalk beneath my feet. I looked at the back of my hand and found nothing but clean, unblemished skin instead of an IV and tape. The clothes on my back were heavy; I was clad in a navy blue blazer and tan dress slacks. My knees gave way and I steadied myself on a bench. From the looks of it, it was the same bench I had spent many an afternoon on with my buddies after baseball practice. I took a closer look. My initials were engraved in the wood in the same spot I had carved them more than twenty years before.

I rubbed the wood, enjoying the feeling of its grain against my finger. I could feel it! The roughness of it, the splinter that leapt from it into my hand. The sensations were real. I chuckled despite my fear and confusion, my mind pushing the two emotions aside in favor of happiness. Even though the memory of my suffering and death was not gone from me, I lived. The last breath I took was linked to my first in this place, all part of the whole. My mind cleared, all thoughts erased like rolling fog. This was Heaven. I had made it at last.

I looked up from the bleeding cut on my hand and started to take a step when I saw a man sitting on the opposite end of the bench. He was dressed in rags and oversized garments, everything seeming to hang from him. His face was dirty from the grime of the streets, his lips red and chafed. His hair had grown long and matted, his mustache and beard were unkempt.

I took my step in a wide berth, putting space between the homeless man and myself. The smell of urine wafted from him to harass my nostrils. I couldn't contain the wince that spread over my face.

I was almost past him when I heard a voice call out a name.

"Clayton?" the voice gargled. I knew no man with such a name so I took another step.

"Clayton!" he said insistently, his eyes boring holes through the back of my head. I turned to him and tried to ask if he was talking to me but my mouth wouldn't function. I started to shout, to scream in my head, 'I am not Clayton! I know no one with that name!' but my protests went unheard. I couldn't feel my lips moving either, or my tongue within my mouth. I raised my hand to the place where my lips should have been and found nothing. It was as though fused skin laid beneath my nose, blended together to form a smooth plain.

The man's eyes smiled before he did. He seemed a benevolent sort, his demeanor radiating calm. I let my hand drop to my side and temporarily forgot my lack of lips, tongue, mouth. The man's eyes had entranced me.

"I know what you're thinking. You're wondering why I am calling you Clayton, right?"

I felt powerless as I nodded in agreement, as though I was being led to do so. My mind was reeling. None of the images that I had ever seen or formulated in my head could have ever mirrored what sat in front of me. Could this be God?

"You will be soon," the man continued in a phlegmy voice. He laughed heartily and I felt my face flush. There was something about his laughter that left me cold. It didn't have any of the jovial qualities one would expect from a kind being. Instead, it had a sinister feel with a swarthy bottom. I was suddenly terrified of the man on the park bench.

"Why are you here, you're wondering. Didn't I die? I hear the questions echoing in your head as if they were in my own," the man said, suddenly interested in the frayed belt on the dingy coat he was wearing. "Here is there. There is here. There is no difference."

My eyebrows wrinkled in confusion.

"I know they never told you that, but it's true. They led you to believe a lot of things were true, but they aren't. The truth is more difficult to face, as is damnation. To know that you are already in Hell is hell itself."

His words frightened me. All of the answers to the questions I had when I was alive were starting to come clear. The man wasn't giving me the answers, I could feel them, could deduce them from the tone of his voice, from the cold pit of my stomach. The reality that was revealing itself to be true was more than I could bear. I sank to my knees in despair.

"There's no need for that, dear boy. You tried that before and look at what it got you."

The vice on my mouth loosened its grip and I could feel my lips and tongue moving again. I forced myself to speak, to ask the questions that were choking my mind.

"Are you the devil?" I croaked.

He laughed again, but his eyes never left mine. Within them I could see his fall from grace, his plummet to the abyss, his condemnation. I could feel his anger and rage against God, could feel mine brewing inside me.

"Am I in Hell?"

The man got up from the bench and gathered his garments around him, piling more of the raggedy cloth on. He took a step away from me, leaving me in silence just as he had come. I dared not reach for him, grab his arm and turn him around to face me. I feared the face that would meet mine, the heat that would surely consume my soul in that instant.

He walked away from me, trudging along as an old man would. In the distance I saw a woman spinning slowly, her heel raised off the pavement, her head upturned. Her face showed sheer delight and amazement as mine must have to a passerby. Only there weren't any passersby. Just souls on their way to reincarnation in another body, sent to live in the façade that was life; a movie screen for the enlightened.

The man turned back and looked at me just as I felt myself growing light. The smirk on his face told me everything I needed to know.

The Visitor

I can't believe she still has that look on her face. That tranquil, utterly at peace stare. Her lips actually turn up at the corners, even after all this time. She held the same face when I looked in on her through the window. She was gazing out, seeing but not seeing, caught in the fabric of a daydream. She was so still, so calm, I thought my work might already be done.

I opened the front door, complying with the nagging need within me to replicate the motions I had performed on many other occasions—Christmas parties and game night, not to mention the one time we stole up to her bedroom and had the sex we had wanted to have for twenty years but never had before. We never talked about what happened. Not afterward, not ever. I just got up, left her crying softly in bed, hugging the pillow her dearly departed husband had left behind, and went home. I hadn't touched the doorknob that opened into her house since.

Until then.

She didn't stir when I came in. I saw the hair that rested on her forehead shift as the faint breeze drifted in. I shut the door quietly and walked toward her. My feet were soundless against the hardwood floor. I could barely feel the wood beneath them, and even the slight sensation I was able to feel was manufactured. The pleasures I felt before, the mere touch of another's hand in mine, were things of the past. I grew used to the lack of sensation, the white numbness of my existence long ago. I made my peace with the fact that it was gone. Forever. Still, sometimes I feel the need to feel things I once felt, smell things I once smelled. It's during those times of longing that I conjure up the memory of their sensations, the feel of things taken for granted. Often I miss my mark. I think of the wind blowing and what returns is the smell of burning hair. I try to remember my mother's voice as she sang me to sleep when I was young yet what returns is the sound of thunder clapping violently in a darkened sky. I deal with the misfires and keep trying, grateful for the sensation that came, regardless of what it was. It broke up the monotony, the silence, the blankness. When I entered the house I tried, with every fiber of my being, to feel the wood beneath the balls of my feet. Instead, I was met with the smell of fresh blood, its subtle sweetness making it all the more horrible. My senses wrapped around the smell, embracing it, wanting to make it last, to fill the empty spaces, to awaken the things in me that have lain dormant for what seems like an eternity.

She didn't move, not even when I stood behind her, staring down at her graying hair. How she'd changed over the years. She had been allowed to live life through her forties and fifties, to greet her last sunrise in her late sixties. The hair I ran my fingers through was once black and full, but now the rich black was peppered with gray. The wrinkles that framed her mouth and eyes were unsightly to me as I remembered the smooth skin of the young woman she had been when I last laid my eyes on her. Though tears filled them when I left, her eyes were mesmerizing to me. The emotion they carried within them was paralyzing. Once, I loved to stare at them, watching them move as she talked, coloring with animation. I had the urge to turn away when I saw them so close to their end, the light in them all but extinguished. I decided before I entered the house that I would not look at her again, would not look into her eyes, nor let mine linger upon her face. It was too painful to see what time had done to her. I couldn't bear to see her that way.

Her hair hung loose, draping over the back of the cushioned chair in which she sat. The desire to touch her hair was met with the vision of congealed blood, vinaceous and still.

Always the blood.

I've come to expect it now. It seems to follow me from the moment I hear his call until I have completed his work. It's as though the one who will perish puts it in my path, trying to dissuade me from continuing, as if their spilt blood might make me feel for them and preserve their existence. Unknown to them is my torment, the knowledge that their blood is as symbiotic to life to me as it is to them, my need for it as great as theirs. Maybe greater. There is nothing they can do. Once he has made the call, I must abide.

He calls frequently now, more so than he had in the beginning, his need increasing as time passes. He never tells me who, just that I must find someone to give to him. Anyone. He said it was my role in this existence, that I belonged to him as ordained by the Lord of the Dark. This I didn't question. I expected punishment in some form in one dimension or another.

I started with killers and rapists, but their blood made me ill. I tried the homeless, but got no joy from it. Finally, I called upon a friend. Nicholas was sick with cancer when I heard the call. I went to him in an effort of kindness, to free him from his misery. In return, he supplied me with a memory that drives me in my servitude. He gave me peace.

Since then I have visited my brother and sister, my wife, my grandchild, and my neighbor of ten years. And now I am visiting the only woman I ever truly loved. My beautiful Rebecca.

Her back faced me in the moments before her death. I wished she might turn to me and speak, see me as no one had since I closed my eyes. But she didn't. She continued to stare out of the window, recounting memories of the past when she was young and free.

I touched her shoulder with an unseen hand and watched her body twitch beneath it. The blood that coursed through her veins funneled into me, grounding me, making me feel the tingle I have grown so enamored with. Soon I was covered in her blood, the viscidity of which was alarming. It strangled me in its intensity, gave me the sensation of needing to gasp for air. In that moment, that feeling of desperation to free myself, I found what I was looking for. The colors of the room, where muted before, became alive and vivid. The walls were done in bright coral instead of lackluster bone, the pallor of her cheeks was that of a girl, rosy and blushing, showing nothing of the dull tincture of old age. I felt more alive in that moment, while her heartbeat slowed to a stop, than I had when air expanded my lungs. It was for those moments that I continued to serve with vigor.

In their deaths, I live.

I waited long after she had taken her last breath, as the day drew to a close and the world woke up the following morning. I wanted to be with her until the very end. The next morning the front door was blown open by a wind that affected no other house or lawn. The mailman who always gave Rebecca her mail in hand saw that the door was ajar and began to call out to her. I could feel the vibrations his voice made on the air, could sense his concern heightening, yet I could not hear these things. The mailman, dressed in his summer uniform, revealing sun-starved legs with white socks pulled up just under the knee, found Rebecca sitting in her chair, her blank eyes fixed upon the window, her mouth fashioned in the same curious expression.

I waited until the police came and the coroner's van parked in front of the house. He walked in, the usual solemnity etched on his face. He kneeled in front of her, my beloved Rebecca, and saw me standing behind her chair. As the EMT unit rolled the stretcher in behind me, he nodded his appreciation.

Last Request

The clink of the bars at the end of the hall was a welcome sound. My brother, Jerry, was coming to see me and join me while I ate the last meal I would ever consume. I didn't care for the company, I would just as soon have eaten my meal alone where I could lick my fingers and grunt my appreciation in privacy. But Jerry had shared many a meal with me. Surely he wouldn't be one to judge, and what did it matter anyway? In a couple of hours I would be gone and no one would care whether I ate like an ill-mannered child, or if I took each bite with the poise of royalty, my pinky finger extended away from my hand.

This will be my last meal and I'll eat it whatever way I please.

Momma really came through this time. She sent Jerry over with the meal I asked for, fried chops sandwiched between two pieces of white bread with black bean soup on the side. At first, I didn't think she'd be able to get it in here. When I told the guards what I wanted for my last meal, they told me I couldn't have it. It had to be something they prepared, nothing from the outside. But my Momma, she talked to them. Showed them her tears and pain. And it worked. Somehow it worked.

I could smell the food from where I sat long before Jerry was let into my cell. They had checked it up at the front desk, mutilating the meat with their jagged cuts, probing to see what might be hidden inside, re-pouring the soup into another container, tearing the bag it was transported in. They had checked Jerry out too, almost to the point of subjecting him to a strip search before he was let in. He could have been carrying anything on him in a last-ditch effort to free me, the way they figured it. If they knew him the way I did, they wouldn't have looked at him twice. Jerry couldn't hurt a fly. He just didn't have it in him.

Jerry looked disheveled when he finally got to my cell, holding the tattered bag of food in his trembling hands. He was a sorry sight, but I smiled at him anyway. My mouth was watering over the aroma coming from the bag.

We had the whole thing planned out for months. Momma and I talked about it during one of her visits. We had to be careful not to tip anyone off, what with them listening to every word of our conversation. But Momma was a pro. She never got flustered, never once lost her cool. I learned everything I knew from her. Except how not to get caught.

When the guards told me Paulette had died, I faked tears like a champ. I should have gotten an award for that performance, if I do say so myself. I lobbied the warden for permission to go to my fiancée's funeral, telling him how important it was for me to be there for our little girl, to be there with the family. My request was denied, of course. I knew it would be. The warden hardly ever let people out to be with their families if a loved one died. I knew an inmate whose mother was killed, run down by a bus, but he wasn't allowed to go. Even when the guy argued that he was the only living relative and that there wasn't anyone to make the necessary preparations for her burial. The guy's mother was taken to Potter's Field over that, buried in with the homeless, the crack heads, and stillborn babies all on account of the warden's hard ass. Paulette and me wasn't even married yet, so I knew he wasn't gonna let me out. Plus, I'm on death row, a hardened criminal, a rapist and killer of women, and a bunch of other things the law didn't know anything about. That guy was a thief, a bank robber, small potatoes. If he couldn't get let out, there wasn't a way in hell I would have.

But I didn't need to get out. I just needed it to seem like I did. I couldn't have cared less about Paulette. She got what she deserved as far as I was concerned. She was a whore, pure and simple. After I got locked up, she started going around with one of my buddies. It didn't take her long to start up with him. It kind of made me think they might have had something going before I got locked up. She came to see me pretty regular at first, but then all that tapered off to nothing once they got started. I guess she had better things to do with her time. Everybody that I knew on the outside seemed to have something more important to do than to come and see a dead man, to visit a living grave. Can't say I blame them, but that doesn't make it right.

Momma is the one who told me about Paulette and my friend. She saw them one day carrying on in the supermarket parking lot, grab-assing and feeling each other up. She took offense to it and said something to Paulette about it. "I don't know how that boy got his hand around her wide ass no way," Momma said, her words shooting venom from every syllable. Momma was mad.

The next day Paulette came up here and told me we were finished. She said she wouldn't carry a candle for me anymore, she wasn't going to wait no more 'cause there was nothing to wait for. I was going to die as sure as my name was Willie Dean Campbell, and it was silly for us to stay together anymore. I didn't say nothing. I just sat there and listened to her. Momma and I had already talked, so I knew she was on her way. I didn't have any feelings about it, except a sense of amusement. See, I know my momma and I know how she thinks. That's why I wasn't surprised when they told me Paulette was dead.

Momma came in the next week, her face all lit up and excited. She told me that she had just got some meat and that she was going to try out her mother's recipe for rump roast on it. That's when I made sure to tell her what I wanted for my last meal. I made her day.

Jerry came in the cell and started with the pleasantries to throw the hacks off.

"They out there picketing you, Willie," he said as he sat down. His skin was wet and clammy, streaks of motor oil shining beneath the sweat.

"Oh yeah? What're they saying?"

"Some of 'em want you to fry. A bunch others say it's inhumane. They want you to get life imprisonment instead."

"Shit, it's all the same to me. If I'm in here I'm dead anyway, ain't I?" I couldn't keep my eyes off the bag.

"I reckon so."

The hacks were out of sight, milling around a desk at the end of the hall. There was a prize fight on that night. Somebody stood to make ten million bucks on the night they turn my lights out. At least this day would be good for some poor sucker.

I wasn't afraid of death. It's probably the best thing for me. When I was on the outside I raped women, even my cousins. I beat them until their faces were destroyed, and then I killed them, just because I wanted to see more blood. I loved what I did. I loved to smell their fear, like musk after a day's work. I loved to see their faces contort into grimaces of pain and anguish. I loved the taste of blood. When they caught me I pleaded guilty because I was. I knew if they let me out again, I would kill another girl that same day. Because I wanted to. So the punishment is just. All those picketers out there wasting time on me should go home. They're lucky I'll be dead in a couple of hours. If not, I might have knocked on their door that night.

My brother was taking it hard. Jerry had always been a soft touch. He was so different than the rest of us in that way, always wanting things to be just so. He couldn't understand why I had done what I did. He was the only one who didn't know what I had done before I got caught. I didn't share it with him because I didn't think he could take it. His world didn't include the darker side of life. Death was an unfortunate thing rather than a necessity. I didn't want to break his already fragile heart with the news that his brother was a killer.

Momma knew. She always did. She made me that way, is what she said one night when she sat me down to talk. She saw me going into the field with a little girl from down the street. She followed us in and, after an hour, she found me on top of her. The girl was long dead by then, her lifeless eyes staring up at the darkening sky. Momma helped me hide her body, digging the hole alongside me. That night we talked about things Jerry will never know about. Momma told me about what she had done as a teenager, the men she'd slaughtered, where the bodies were hidden. She told me I had nothing to be ashamed of, that my grandfather and great-grandfather had all been murderers, rapists, and worse. Information like that would have made Jerry wretch his guts up. But they gave me encouragement. I was proud to belong to a family like ours.

Momma taught me how to prolong pain, how to remove vocal cords and render my victim mute, where to cut if I wanted to see blood spurting out like a fountain in time with the beating of their heart. She showed me how to get rid of bodies, how to cover my tracks. Then she showed me her storeroom.

Momma had always told us to stay out of the storeroom. She made her face look so menacing, we didn't dare step foot inside. She took me in there that day though, while Jerry was out on a date with a girl from our high school. The room itself was basic, a typical storeroom with boxes packed together lining the walls, an old file cabinet, antiques from the generations before. But in the corner, separated from the other junk, was an icebox, long enough to fit me with space for more. Momma walked over to it with a mischievous grin on her face. "I'm only showing you this because I think you can handle it," she said, her hand resting on the lid of the icebox, "Between you and Jerry, you have always been the one who understands the practicality of death." Her voice was hushed, almost whispering. She leaned into me conspiratorially and I moved closer to her, wanting to hear every word she was about to say. "This is between me and you, right Wille Dean?" I nodded in earnest, anxious to see what was inside. "Between me and you," she repeated just before she lifted the lid.

There were cuts of meat wrapped in plastic and stored in bags. Filets, chops, round, bacon. I felt let down. Momma stored meat. So what? Based on our conversation, I had expected to see more than that. What exactly, I didn't know, but something more than frozen venison and the occasional rabbit. I turned back to Momma and said, "What's the big deal? Ain't nothing' in here but meat."

"Ah, but what kind of meat?" Her smile frightened even me. I turned back to the icebox and looked closer. I lifted some of the wrapped meat to check the pieces below. And that's when I saw it. A trunk of meat lay beneath the individually wrapped cuts waiting to be divided into portions. The trunk was not skinned, its pale white pallor almost glowing from within the icebox. I leaned closer, disbelieving my eyes. A smile spread across my face when I saw the nipples, frozen areolas diminished to pale pink atop rigid flesh. Momma stood close behind me, her warmth a pleasant contrast to the cold of the icebox that beat my face. "I always like the meat from a buxom female most, but you and Jerry fancied a slender male, seeing as you like your meat tough and dry, cooked through." She put her arms around me as I laughed.

Momma and I shared our secrets with each other over the years. Sometimes we would hunt together, other times I'd bring something back to her as a present. She'd cook the meat up nice, just the way I liked it every time. Jerry didn't know what he was eating, had been eating all of his life. But I did. And it was out of this world.

One night, during our talks, I asked her what happened to Daddy. He had up and disappeared one day ten years back, without a trace. He and Momma had been arguing something awful, and it was better when he left. I didn't miss him none, I just wanted to know if she knew what happened to him. She stood up and walked away after I asked her, staying silent for at least five minutes. I got nervous. I didn't want her mad at me. I didn't know what she might do. Tell the cops about what I'd been doing? Kill me and serve me up to Jerry? I didn't know. My imagination went wild with scenarios.

Finally, she said, "Some things are better off left alone, Wille Dean. You get my meaning?"

"Yes ma'am," I said, eager to let the subject lie. I knew what happened to Daddy. The gurgling of my stomach was answer enough. I didn't need her to say it aloud.

That night Momma cooked up the meat of a roomy girl. It was tender and juicy, better than any pulled pork sandwich I'd had before. Remembering that meal makes me salivate as I did that day. I just couldn't get enough.

"Well, here's your meal," Jerry said, and handed over the bag. His eyes were watery and red around the rims from crying. I patted him on the back in thanks and he nodded solemnly. He turned away from me while I opened what was left of the brown bag Momma had sent for me. It was all too much for him, seeing his brother eat the last meal he would ever have. I could hear him sobbing in the corner when I took my first bite of the tender, juicy sandwich.

Phantasma

It calls to me

The dark

From the shadows of cast by rotted eaves

Or with the voice of the wind.

It calls to me

Beckons me forth

To greet it with open arms

Cracked and chaffed from nightly encounters of

Its hateful whims.

It calls to me

Softly at times

Like a mother might a child

Like a lover would another,

Of which it is mine.

Then loudly

Mockingly

Painfully divine.

It calls every night

Its only desire that I not see the evil beauty of my love,

The beast controlling me.

—*What Voice Does Speak* by elle wood

Everything She Wants

She sucked her teeth and hissed, "It figures."

Darren was asleep. Again. He always fell asleep after sex. Always. There was no drinking of water, no flicking through television stations, no talking, not even a breathy moan about how good it was. Nothing. When he was done, he was done. She barely got a peck on the cheek after he rolled off her and onto his back, settling into his position for the rest of night. Just before drifting off to sleep he might mumble 'Goodnight' but that was the rare occasion.

He sucked.

Real bad.

Laurie liked affection. She wanted to snuggle up next to him after sex, wanted to ply him with kisses and tell him how much she loved him. The times she tried to cuddle up after sex he complained that he was too hot and needed to catch his breath. That one never ceased to piss her off. Yeah, right, he needed to catch his breath. Maybe if he did more work during their lovemaking she would agree, but as it stood, that excuse didn't fly.

His snoring drowned out any of the night sounds she might have been able to hear: crickets chirping outside, the hum of the furnace, the whistling of the wind. She frowned as she looked over at him, his mouth agape as he lay on his back atop rumpled covers. He never pulled the sheet over himself before drifting off to sleep, leaving his sex exposed. Though she had enjoyed it moments before (at least somewhat), she was now repulsed by it. Back in its normal limp state with a dollop of dried semen on its head, his exposed penis reminded her of what an anticlimactic experience the whole thing had been. It was times like that when she hated Darren and everything he was.

It wasn't just the snoring or the lack of affection, or the sex, really. She knew that. But that was when she felt it most. During the day he didn't appear to be the unfeeling ogre that he was, even to her. He seemed like an average guy. He had a good job, held the door open for her to walk through; he had all the qualities one would expect of a doting husband. Only she knew the truth. It was all a façade, one that hid secrets even she had yet to uncover.

His snoring, which sounded more like a growling ape than air being sucked in and pushed out through his nose, deafened her. It persisted and persisted, pushing itself into her mind, permeating her usually placid shell. She decided she'd had enough.

She was going to shut him up.

She'd tried pushing him while he slept before, nudging him over to his side when his snoring became unbearable. At least that would turn his head away from her, if not quell the snoring. But that didn't work. She'd asked him to turn over, speaking almost directly in his ear to get his attention. He muttered a groggy 'ok' but never really moved. He may have thought he did, but he didn't. So she knew at least a little about what kind of window she would have to work within.

Laurie pushed Darren with her index finger. Nothing. She jabbed him with her fingernail. Not even a flinch. She slapped his skin, just hard enough to make a dull *clap*. Nothing. He slept like he was dead.

Good.

Laurie started with his hands and feet, that way when he woke up he wouldn't be able to move. Industrial strength ropes and bailing wire did the trick. He could struggle all he wanted to as long as he didn't mind ripping into the soft flesh of his wrists while doing it. She mounted him, his penis becoming erect even as he slept. Men are so easy. A few touches and they're ready. She almost couldn't conceal her laughter at their simplicity.

Darren's eyes fluttered but didn't open as she moved on him, still not quite making it to consciousness. He was disgusting to her then. He couldn't even recognize a good fucking when he was getting one. She'd show him. He'd never forget that night. Of that she was sure.

She pinched his nipples with her fingers. His face contorted uncomfortably, like he had just passed gas. She was infuriated. She hardly realized she had bitten the nipple off until she tasted the saltiness of his blood in her mouth. Chewing the severed areola and swallowing it down, she smiled as he finally opened his eyes. And screamed. A laugh that Darren had never heard before emitted from her lungs as she ripped at his skin with nails that had been filed into sharp points. She clawed him as a cat might, drawing four lines of blood with each swipe. Darren tugged his bindings and shrieked in surprise as the bailing wire cut into his skin, biting into his vulnerable veins. Laurie saw the blood running down his forearms and laughed even harder, her body racked with it, shaking uncontrollably. Her laughter became cries of pleasure as she slammed her hips down harder on Darren, pushing him deep inside her, further than he had ever gone on his own.

She leaned in to kiss him, letting her hairbrush against the blood that flowed from his wounds. He tried to bite her, the effort driving the bailing wire deeper into his flesh. She sat up abruptly, crushing his testicles under her weight. Her face, which he once thought was angelic, was now a mass of crazed emotions. Her eyebrows were furrowed, her lips pursed. Her skin was flushed and sweat dotted her forehead. But her eyes were the most disturbing things. They were wild with enjoyment, satisfaction. They were giddy in the most hideous of ways.

"That's not nice," Laurie spat at Darren whose teeth, once bared in attack, were now bared in a grimace of fear and pain. "I guess I'll have to teach you a lesson."

Laurie reached over the side of the bed and grabbed the hammer she had put there before tying Darren up. She held it in her hand long enough for him to see it—long enough to feel his legs tremble—before plunging it into his chin. Teeth flew from his mouth in splintered pieces as his jaw collapsed. One or two of them fell from his bloody gums onto the back of his tongue. Instinctively, he tried to either swallow or push the teeth forward to clear his throat, but the tooth got lodged in the soft skin.

Laurie didn't know if Darren was turning blue because of the obstruction in his throat or the loss of blood from his veins. And she didn't care. All she wanted to do was come. And she did, even as Darren lay dead beneath her, she had the best orgasm she had ever experienced in her life. Spent, she rolled off of him and laid down on the bed. Cutting down Darren's arms, she wrapped herself up in him, nuzzling her head in his chest and feeling his arms around her the way she always wanted.

Nigh

Her grandmother warned her about them. She said when the time came and shadows started to show themselves along the wall, hovering up high, where the ceiling and wall meet, she was on her last dance. The party was over and the last song was almost finished. She told her this when she was nine years old, right after she started seeing shadows of her own. "It's how they call you home chile," she said while thumbing a pocketknife. Pieces of chewed apple flew from her mouth to land on her apron, but she didn't seem to notice. Barbara did. She always did.

"I see your grandfather in 'em all the time," Addie Mae went on. "He gets closer and closer every time he comes."

"Grandpa wouldn't hurt you." Barbara's voice was low, nervous. The idea of the shadows was frightening enough without putting faces on them.

"I know it. That's how I know the shadows are good." She peeled off a sliver of apple and thumbed it into her mouth.

"What does he say when he comes?"

"Nothing. He just stands there and smiles." Her grandmother couldn't help but smile at the thought of his visits. That bothered Barbara more than she knew. "I see him dressed in his finest zoot-suit and hat, as clean as could be. He looks like he did when we used to strut up and down the avenue after church on Sunday. A fine man, he was. A fine man." She started to rock in her chair. Addie Mae shut her eyes and smiled again, seeming to smile at him.

"It could just be a memory," Barbara cut in nervously. The darkness that filled the sky outside seemed to creep in around her.

Her grandmother's eyes opened fast. They looked at her with a mixture of sorrow and anger. "I know the difference between a memory and a vision, missy. I ain't outta my head yet."

Blushing, Barbara hurried, "I'm sorry. I didn't mean it to sound—but Grandma, you're talking about seeing ghosts!"

"I know it. I see them," Addie Mae lifted her head proudly. Her eyes skimmed the ceiling, but there was nothing there.

"And so will you," she continued. "Just wait and see. Your granddaddy ain't the only one who comes to me. My momma and daddy have come before, my sister Sue comes from time to time. I expect more of 'em will come when my time gets closer. Like I'll come to you when it's your time."

"Doesn't it frighten you?" It sure frightened Barbara to hear about it.

"Nah," she said, peeling off another slice of apple and shoving it into her mouth. Some of the juice dripped over her lip and down to her chin as she spoke, but she made no effort to wipe it away. "It's how they wake you up from the nightmare."

"What nightmare?" Barbara would always ask. Her grandmother's musings were always interesting to her, even though she could never back anything up with any solid evidence. Faith was always her answer. Faith in yourself.

"This one," her grandmother would inevitably answer. "This is the nightmare."

"This?" Barbara asked, not wanting to know what she meant, but knowing somehow she would need to one day. Usually Barbara's grandmother didn't answer the question, but on that day, seventy-nine years ago, she did.

"Life, chile," she said, her eyes set firmly on Barbara, looking into the child as though she could see the intricacies of her very soul. "Life is the nightmare."

Barbara asked her grandmother why she thought that way, asked her to stop talking like that too. No child wants to hear their grandma talking about death — their death. Barbara already wondered what she would do if her grandma ever left her. She was her playmate, her historian, her model for proper etiquette, her confidant. She was the moon, the stars, the sun, and the clouds. Death wouldn't dare lay a hand on her grandma's silver-gray hair. Not as long as she could help it. Barbara tried to reassure the 91-year-old woman she would live forever, that she would be there to see her great-grandchildren. Addie Mae responded with a sincerity that chilled Barbara's spine with the implications, even then, "I'll see your children, all right. I'll pick out nice ones and send them to you with a kiss." That thought always made her feel warm inside, even after her grandma's death a year and a half later. Until that day.

Barbara was watching television the first time she saw them. Her stories had just gone to commercial and she was getting up to pour some more coffee. Muttering about why Loraine would ever give Peter another chance, Barbara stood up to trudge to the kitchen when they caught her eye. She lived alone, her daughter and grandson more than an hour away, so no one heard her when she gasped, nor saw her hand flutter to her chest. Her body stood rigid, straight as a board. The shadows were wide and oddly shaped, like inkblots spreading across white paper.

They were there, just like her grandmother told her they would be.

Dressed in their Sunday best, Gillian and Jonathan made their way up the steps to the church. The place was full of people who had known Barbara throughout her life. Most of them were in their nineties like Barbara had been. Wheelchairs and walkers cluttered the pews and aisle ways. Sniffles and muted cries filled the room.

The director from the center came and spoke a few words over the body. She talked about how pleasant Barbara had been and how she was a joy to have around. Everyone nodded and sobbed, a couple of people said 'Amen', others shouted 'Hallelujah' from behind their handkerchiefs. Gillian dabbed at her eyes as she looked on, nodding at the appropriate times, bowing when asked. But Jonathan didn't. He stared at Barbara, at her face unnaturally frozen and molded into a look of contentment he had never seen her strike, at her chest stilled and solid looking, like rock beneath the cover of clothing, at her hands drawn flat and forced to intertwine with one another. She didn't look real. She didn't look right. Jonathan looked at his grandmother, watching, waiting for her to move, to turn her head and speak to him. *Would she sound right?* he wondered. Or would she sound otherworldly, evil and beatific at the same time? Jonathan wondered if the darkened spot on the silk lining of the casket beside her head was the shadow of his grandmother, coming to bid them goodbye.

The shadow that hovered over Barbara's face as she lay still in the casket her daughter Gillian had picked out for her was there for only a second, seeming to dance on the end of her nose. It seemed, for a moment, she would reach her hand up and swat it away, like one would a troublesome fly. At least it did to Jonathan. But she didn't. And then it disappeared. But Jonathan had seen it perched there, just above her face.

He saw it and smiled.

Witchdoctor

I am dead. My limbs have no feeling. My skin is rock hard. I am dead. At least I want to be. But he won't let me rest. He comes with his roots and his magic to awaken me on the nights that he chooses, sprinkling dust over my body and making it tingle again. I revel in the feeling, my senses heightened to feel the coolness of the night breeze, to smell the musky scent of his unwashed skin. I am alert, the void that was nothingness filled with rich, vibrant life. He takes me then, where I lay, the smell of damp earth surrounding us as he presses. When he is done, sated by my loins and fatigued from exertion, he looks at me with eyes that turn me to stone.

I am dead. At least I want to be. Dead hurts less than the burning tingle of life on my dry skin.

Blue Sally

Blue Sally picked up the osteotome with shaky hands. She knew where she wanted to cut; she just couldn't muster the nerve. Clifton was out cold. She had knocked him over the head pretty good with the shovel, and he was out like a light. But still. She didn't think it prudent to hesitate for too much longer. He was knocked out, not dead.

She thought about starting on his mouth, that gaping cesspool that did nothing but spew hatred at her. 'You're too fat, Sally. Huge, like a blue whale.' She imagined cutting away the skin and crushing in his jawbone. Or maybe cutting through it and watching the shavings pile on the rosy flesh of his muscles like snowflakes on frozen earth. Yeah. He'd never be able to utter mean words again after she was through.

Or maybe she'd go straight for the heart.

She could cut away his ribs with the tool she lifted from the hospital. She'd been looking for one of those head splitting jammies, the ones that coroners used to crack open the chest cavity, but she could only get her hands on the handheld. With the mallet from Clifton's toolbox, the tool might prove to be quite versatile. It would have to do. And if it didn't, there was always the saw.

Clifton would surely wake up once she started to split him. Sally imagined his arms flailing and him gasping for precious breaths. He'd be helpless to fend her off though, with his organs exposed to the elements and her grinning over them, salivating at the sight like she might over a home cooked meal. He wouldn't be able to swing at her the way he always threatened to or scream more obscenities (if he didn't have a potty mouth, she didn't know who did). He would only be able to gasp, like a fish out of water.

She searched his body, finding the right place to make the first cut. As she sipped her wine and listened to his contented, full-of-himself laughter, Blue Sally could almost feel the weight of the shovel in her hand, could still feel the velocity of her swing.

"Laugh now," she said between her own calculated chuckle, masked so well no one heard her say it, not even Nosy Nellie, Clifton's best friend Wallace's wife, and company for the night. Over the lip of her half-filled wine glass, Sally whispered, "Die later."

The red wine, a smoky blend with a particularly bitter bite, went down like sweet nectar, waking her tongue in preparation for the night's sampling.

Verity

The produce looked good. Jeremy picked up a green bell pepper, dripping with water routinely sprayed on the vegetables to make them look appetizing. He supposed that wasn't the only reason they did it, but that was what the drops glistening in the light from the fluorescent bulbs did for him—made him want to eat every vegetable in the display case. He must have caught them in their cycle; the water was cool to the touch. If he remembered right, there would be another dousing in about two minutes. He'd been caught with his hand in the cookie jar before and learned to time the bursts lest he come away with a damp cuff.

He reached in and grabbed a cucumber, putting it in one of the plastic vegetable bags off the spindle. Grabbing another bag, he reached in for some scallions, then for a head of green leaf lettuce. The mirror behind the produce reflected the crisp greens of the lettuce and vibrant reds and yellows of the peppers. The light was bright enough to make the face of his nails appear buffed to a natural sheen. Yeah, they knew what they were doing at that supermarket. They had suggestive selling down pat.

Jeremy sifted through the lettuce, looking for the perfect head. His fingers were growing progressively colder as he sorted out the good from the bad. He hated getting a head with a lot of dirt on the leaves. Sure, he cleaned it before eating it, but there was something about seeing the dirt fall from it, muddying the water as it swirled down the drain. That an occasional dead fly fell from the core didn't help either. He could imagine them, settling their disease-ridden legs onto a fresh head of lettuce, crouching and sleeping, defecating on the leaves. The thought made him sick. Sometimes he wondered why he even bothered.

He turned the lettuce on its side, checking for punctures or discoloration. The fluorescent light seemed brighter now, and hotter; he could feel its heat on his skin. Water fell from the lettuce onto his hand as he inspected the head. He could feel the drops of water slide down his hand and onto vegetables beneath it. They were warm. Growing progressively hot. Jeremy was about to yank his hand away to rub it with the other one—his skin felt as though it was cooking—when he caught a glimpse of his reflection in the mirror. His hand was bloated and discolored, black and blue like it had been battered.

The skin was flaking away as though peeling from a summer tan. He tried to move his turgid limb from the display but couldn't. The bone itself seemed nailed to the grid beneath the vegetables, rigid and stiff. Caked brown dirt covered the rich green head of lettuce and something microscopic, almost intangible writhed within it. Jeremy peered at it, wanting to look away but needing to see. Bile rose in his throat as maggots forced their way to the surface and crawled along the dirt. A spider followed close behind them, massive in its size with long, black legs and beady eyes. It walked the length of the lettuce and rested on Jeremy's hand, which had formed puss-filled blisters under the relentless heat of the fluorescent lights. Sweating, Jeremy watched as the spider rose on its legs in attack, its body pulsating in time with his heart. Jeremy's scream was drowned out by the sound of water spraying from the sprinkler above the vegetables.

Waking up was like falling. His body jerked, making him feel like he had fallen onto the bed from the ceiling. His eyes snapped open and darted around the room. He was home, in his own bed, albeit empty. He jerked his hand in front of his face. It was fine. No blistering skin, no swelling, no spider bite. No wet cuff.

The room was dark when he sat up in bed, pushing off a sweaty sheet. His heartbeat was erratic. The sweat on his face felt cool and clammy. Christ, he hadn't had a nightmare in years, certainly nothing that had made him get out of bed. He hadn't missed the feeling.

Trudging to the bathroom to splash water on his face, Jeremy's mind spun a collage of images from his dream before his eyes. Scallions and cucumbers dripping with water. Vibrant green lettuce. A black spider. White light. God, he could almost smell the onions in the display, could almost feel his shirt sticking to the sweat that coated the small of his back. He tried to shake off the chill the dream covered his body in and went to the bathroom, turning on the light before stepping into the darkened room. For a fleeting second he was afraid of what might have been hiding behind the shower curtain. Even with the light on, he thought he could make out a shape behind the curtain, a hunched over, round-backed creature with a head as big as an elephant's. He thought he could hear it breathing, a wheezing mix of phlegm and air being pushed through cracked lips. His chest was warm where he thought the thing's eyes might rest, keeping him in its sights. Jeremy's leg shook ever so slightly as he raised his foot to take a step into the bathroom. His heart threatened to stop before he could reach the sink, but Jeremy forced another step, then another. With a deep breath, Jeremy looked over at the shower again. He pulled the curtain back with a tentative finger. He moved slowly, hoping, praying that nothing was looking back at him, waiting to say hello. And there wasn't. Jeremy released his breath with a nervous chuckle, turned on the faucet, and cupped his hands beneath it. As he brought the water to his face, he thought twice about closing his eyes, opting instead to splash the cold water on his face from his nose down. He knew he was too old for schoolboy fears of the dark, knew damned well that there was nothing in the bathroom with him, in the house period. He knew it was all in his head. But still, he wasn't ready to close his eyes. Not just yet.

He pulled his cheeks down, rubbing the skin beneath his pronounced cheekbones, and stared into his eyes reflected in the mirror above the sink. They looked strange to him in the fluorescent light. Darker than they should be, larger somehow. It wasn't obvious, just a little hint of a darker hue ringing the color that should normally be there, the blackness of it seeming to run into his natural reddish-brown like oil. Jeremy leaned closer, staring at pupils that seemed to be moving, writhing, imploding. And there was something about his mouth that didn't sit right with him either. Something about the shape. It resembled that of a cherub with painfully pink lips.

Behind him, in his peripheral vision, he thought he saw something move. In the second before he pulled away from the mirror, sucked in a gasp, and whirled his head around the room, his mind conjured up a heinous visage of a spidery beast with glowing red eyes and a massive body that was translucent like that of a jellyfish. His mind's eye could see pink and purple veins in the clear, hazy body, pulsating, bulging. He only caught a brief of glimpse of it, but what he saw was enough to bring him nightmares for the rest of his life.

Jeremy spun around, drop of water dripping from his chin onto his chest, flinging to the floor. His eyes scanned the small room, always ending up on the shower curtain. Nothing. He released his breath, only realizing then that he had been holding it. The air he breathed in smelled of mint.

"What the fuck?" he muttered under his breath as he walked out of the bathroom and back into his bedroom. He tried to be as silent as he could, hoping that the floor didn't creak as he stepped or that the light from the street didn't illuminate his position when a car passed. He wanted to sneak up on whatever the hell had decided to come into his house and fuck with him. Whatever it might be.

Jeremy inched along the walls of the room, cloaking himself in shadows. He imagined that he could hear the thing breathing in the family room down the hall from where he stood; it was a husky sound, full of mucus and blood. Though his stomach turned over at the thought of it, he kept on, needing to see if there was someone there.

The door to his bedroom creaked open so loudly he thought the sound might wake the dead. A distant thought nagged at him: *Did the door creak when the thing left the room?* He didn't know but he didn't have time to think about that. The thought that the thing might actually be in the room Jeremy was leaving, might be so close to where he stood that he would have no time to protect himself, was terrifying and he decided not to let his mind dwell on the possibility. The thing—whatever it was—was out front. It had to be.

Jeremy took a step into the hallway, realizing for the first time that he was weaponless, completely defenseless against whatever might be waiting for him save for his bare hands. A chill ran through him, doubt coursing through his blood like rust. His last fight had been in the 4th grade. Bobby Carmichael. The class bully. Bobby kicked his butt too, if he remembered correctly. No matter how hard he tried, Jeremy couldn't get a good shot in, hitting Bobby's arms with a barrage of pitty-pat smacks and kicking his feet in the air instead. The memory of that day at the park between school and home didn't bring fond memories, or the embarrassed flush in his cheeks that thoughts of his childhood garnered. It brought fear.

Jeremy clenched and unclenched his fists as he took his second step, this one more tentative than the first. Sweat coated his face and chest and chilled in the breeze. *Shit,* he thought to himself. *I must have left the window open in the family room.* Jeremy shook his head in disgust, pulling his eyes away from the darkened room at the end of the hallway to look at the floor. He reasoned that must have been the way the intruder got in. It was probably a burglar looking for something light to lift so he could make it back out the way he came. Garden apartments were terrible for that reason alone. It was all too easy to slip through a patio door or climb in through one of the windows. There was no climbing, no scaling of the wall. You only had to step out and you'd be at ground level. And if you had a mark that was stupid enough to leave their window open…

Jeremy raised his head quickly. Something about the breeze had changed. It was colder now, like ice. He felt like he was standing in front of the freezer; the cold blast of air surrounded him like a funnel. He took a hurried step forward and pressed his back against the wall. He looked into the dark family room, suppressing the urge to clank his teeth. He didn't know if it was because of the cold or because he was terrified, and he didn't want to know. All he knew was that he wanted to get out of the house before whoever was inside saw him.

When did the mission change from 'get that fucking thing out of my house' to 'I better get the fuck out of the house'? he asked himself but didn't dare allow an answer to formulate. All he knew was that he wanted to get out and get out right then. He had to figure out a way to get to the front door. It was on the other side of the apartment, through the family room and opposite the kitchen. A 70s design if he had ever seen one. So much like his aunt's apartment, he sometimes pictured her things in the places that his stuff occupied. She put her sofa where his bookshelf was; she had a fish tank along the wall where his entertainment center stood. Jeremy couldn't imagine a more inconvenient design. Especially then.

Jeremy's eyes scanned the room and stuck on a figure standing by the patio doors. The moonlight that should have illuminated half of the face lit only the floor. Smoke hung in the air where the body should have been. There was nothing there; no shadow was cast on the opposite wall, no silhouette against the darker backdrop. Nothing. But still he knew someone was there. And that they were looking right at him.

"Look, whoever you are, just take your shit and go," Jeremy called out, his voice sounding uncertain. "I don't want any trouble."

"What did you say, honey?" a female voice asked from within the shadows. Jeremy took a step forward, his gait steadier even though he was more confused than ever.

"Natalie?"

"Who else would it be?"

Jeremy still couldn't see her but he imagined that she was sitting cross-legged on the sofa with one arm propped up on a pillow. He pictured her wearing a teal spaghetti-strapped nightshirt with striped bottoms, teal and blue on white satin. Her hair would still be short with blond highlights, the way it was when they were dating. Her face would be soft in the moonlight; he enjoyed looking at her when the night's shadows danced on her angular face. She wouldn't have on any makeup, not like she did the last time he saw her on the sidewalk in front of the coffee shop they used to go to when they were together. She was all done up that day, black mascara and eyeliner, blood red lipstick, some kind of powder that made her face look sickly pale. He couldn't help but stare that day and wonder why she was wearing all of it, wonder what she had done to herself. Her stockings had holes in them and her hair was unkempt. Her clothes were different; it seemed her style had strayed from her usual professional attire to something younger, streetish.

The change happened overnight, it seemed. They had only been apart for seven months. Jeremy and Natalie said hello to each other, him with a look of surprise on his face, her with a look of what could have been called shame. She was hardly the woman he had known. But there, in his living room, he could imagine her the way she used to be. He could almost smell the coffee she would have brewed had she really been there.

But she wasn't there.

The moonlight didn't reveal the beautiful line of her cheek. He didn't smell coffee, didn't smell anything at all, in fact—not the remnant of pizza hanging in the air, not the air freshener he used to cover it up. Neither did he hear anything, only the oddly detached voice and his own heart beating loudly in his chest.

"Natalie?" he asked again, planting his feet. He wasn't sure he wanted to get any closer. He didn't know what was going on, but he knew that Natalie had given back her keys when she left. Could she have made a copy before returning them? Why?

"Yes, Jeremy. It's me. Who else could it be?"

The darkness was impenetrable. He couldn't make anything out. That, somehow, frightened him more than anything else.

"What are you doing here?" He suppressed the urge to back away, to turn and run back to the safety of his bedroom.

"I came by to see you, that's all."

"What? I don't understand. I thought you said we were finished. When I saw you a couple of weeks ago it certainly looked like you had moved on." He was careful not to say too much.

"I know, and that's why I'm here. I wanted to see you again without all of the baggage I was carrying. I'm done with all of that now."

"All of what? What happened to you, Natalie?" Jeremy took a step forward in the dark, bumping his shin on the speaker stand in his haste.

"More than you need to know, Jeremy. But I'm ok now." The pause between them was weighty. It covered Jeremy like a familiar coat. Still, goose bumps sprang up on his arms.

"What are you talking about, Nat?"

"Nothing." Jeremy could almost see the expression on her face. It was just beyond his vision, teasing him. "I just wanted to tell you that it's ok. I wanted to tell you not to worry about it anymore."

"What?"

Jeremy took the three steps he needed to reach the place where he thought Natalie was sitting. He reached under the lampshade to turn on the light before she could say anything more. Before he turned the knob, a screeching sound like metal grinding against metal attacked his ears and he put his hands up to shield them. Through his squinted eyes he saw Natalie's face. Her hair was stuck to her forehead and cheeks, the blood and sweat that painted them had formed a clot-like glue. One of her eyes was gone, the empty orb looking back at him was filled with blood, torn flesh, and tendrils. The other eye was open, looking out into some unseen distance. Her nose was compressed, pressed flush against her face as though part of her cheek. Her lips were horribly split and distended, more like cuts of fresh meat than the mouth of a beautiful woman. Her front teeth were gone and part of her tongue had been severed.

The image stayed with him for only a moment before a deafening roar engulfed the room, shaking it. Jeremy staggered then fell to the floor. A piercing *beep* filled his head, making him shut his eyes against the room. He gasped for air and moaned; the beeping seemed to rip his head apart. The house shook like an earthquake hit it and his head pulsed from the shock. And, as abruptly as it started, it stopped.

Jeremy opened his eyes slowly, terrified of what he might see. He was curled in a ball on the floor; sweat coated his body like a second skin. He opened one eye and took a cursory look. In the dark, everything looked normal. All the shadows were in the right places — the pictures were still hanging, the speakers and television were still on their stands. He expected to see glass and broken furniture strewn everywhere, but everything was in place. He opened his other eye in disbelief. He got up from the floor and turned around, surveying the living room and dining room. Surely there had been some sort of earthquake. He felt as though the world was going to end not a minute before! But the house didn't show any signs of disruption. Everything was as it was before he went to sleep. Before he reached for the light.

Jeremy turned his head toward the sofa, afraid to look but knowing he had to. What he had seen was the most horrific thing he had ever laid eyes on and he wasn't in any hurry to look at it again. But it was Natalie. Dear God, something had happened to his beautiful Natalie. He had to look.

Jeremy reached under the lampshade with a shaky hand. He grabbed the knob and turned it, closing his eyes when the light illuminated the room. Finally, with the heat of the light bulb warming his chin, he opened his eyes to face what might be waiting for him on the sofa.

No one was there.

Before he could blink, before the incredulity of the situation could take hold, Jeremy was accosted by probing fingers. They poked at him, seeming to lift his shirt and press upon his chest with cold palms. Some of the hands were slimy and wet, others dry but cold, so cold as to chill his very bones. Claw-like fingers peeled back his eyelids, exposing his eyes to a blinding white light. The light filled his vision, removing the contents of the living room from view. His head was tilted back by some powerful force, his arms cast out to his sides. His mind half-heartedly joked at how awkward he must look, but the sentiment was all but ignored. Jeremy struggled against what held him, commanding his body to thrash about, thinking the whole time that the effort was futile.

Finally the creature loosed his eyelids and stopped probing his body with its many digits. Jeremy relished the darkness and only remotely wondered if he might be able to see again once he opened his eyes. He drifted off there, opting to keep his eyes shut instead of opening them to whatever might lay waiting in the darkness. He only vaguely remembered that he was in the living room of his apartment; indeed he didn't remember how he had gotten onto the floor, or if that was where he truly was. All he knew was that he was laying on a cloud, as soft as feathers from a dove. And that he was so tired.

Jeremy was behind the wheel of his dream car. A 1965 Cobra Roadster, blue with white racing trim. It was a beauty. Jeremy had loved that car for over thirty years. He used to frequent car shows in the hopes that they'd have a model on hand. He almost bought an original when he was young and foolish, but the price tag was more than he could scrounge up. He even toyed with the idea of making a kit car replica so he could have one of his own but never got around to it, and the parts weren't exactly cheap either. It was his dream. His baby. Even though it changed his life forever.

Jeremy's mom and her lover died in a '65 Cobra up the coast in New York. She had left him and his dad behind to gallivant with her young lover, a marginal actor who happened to have a gig on Broadway at the time, John Nathan George. She met him after one of his shows, took up with him in a great number of New York hotels, and decided to go off with him, without a care in the world, least of all her family. Three days later, as the happy couple sped along a winding road in Piermont, the great John Nathan George lost control of the car and flipped, crashing both of their unprotected heads into the cracked concrete. Jeremy never forgot the details of his mother's death. Not even the make and model of the car.

The air felt good on Jeremy's face as he rounded the corners of the road at speeds he would never have attempted in an ordinary car. He couldn't believe he was touching it, driving, it, moving such a beauty up and down the roadway. He laughed at nothing in particular, the sound disappearing into the wind as soon as he released it.

The body of water on his right glistened in the afternoon sun, the light shimmering on the easy waves.

"It's beautiful, isn't it?" a woman's voice asked airily, blissful. Jeremy turned to look upon his mother's face, full of youth and radiant. It was the face he had seen in so many pictures. A beautiful woman with medium length brown hair and smooth skin. Her eyes were a delicate oval shape, accented with thick, luscious eyelashes. She was beautiful. She couldn't have been more than 33 years old.

"Don't you just love the Hudson on a sunny afternoon?"

Jeremy couldn't believe what he was seeing, hearing. His mother, of whom he had no memory save for the details of her death, sitting next to him on a day that mirrored the day she died? How could he imagine such a thing? Why would he want to? The Cobra's steering wheel suddenly felt too hot to touch.

"Why are you afraid, darling?" his mother asked, turning away from the water to look at him. "Didn't you know I'd come for you?"

"What are you talking about?" Jeremy couldn't conceal the fear in his voice.

His mother placed a gnarled hand on his thigh. The skin was greenish-black and putrefied and fell from the bone in puss-filled clumps. Jeremy gasped and looked back at her face. It was gone. Nothing but the skeleton remained, discolored and chipped, staring at him through sightless eye sockets. The front row of her teeth was missing.

"I wouldn't let you go alone," she hissed, the words gargling from her rotted vocal cords.

"We're losing him," the nurse said in a voice that had no emotion. Just a colleague informing another of a fact. Jeremy's body jerked spastically, not for the first time since admission. But that was nothing more than his nerves settling down. He was a goner and everyone knew it.

"I can't believe he's lasted this long. This guy should have been dead when he got here." The doctor shook his head as he lifted Jeremy's right eyelid and shined light into his exposed eye again. They couldn't save the other eye and it had since been removed. Pulse of light then darkness. Again. It was dilated.

"The woman who called it in is in the lobby," another nurse started while she straightened up the ER. "She overheard Larry and Chris talking about that jumper today and freaked out."

"What jumper?"

"You didn't hear about the girl who threw herself in front of the train in Rosslyn? Big mess. Well anyway, as it turns out, the girl who killed herself is an ex-girlfriend of this guy's."

"Christ," the doctor said, as he watched Jeremy's vitals slow.

"Do you think he knew? Maybe that's why he shot himself," the emotionless nurse said, perking up. The status of the guy on the table was suddenly more important to her now that she knew some of the juicy details behind it.

"There's no way he could have. They just brought the girl in about ten minutes ago. Right after this guy came in."

The crystal blue of the Caribbean Sea always enchanted Jeremy. Ever since his first visit as a child, he loved the islands and everything they had to offer. The tropical backdrop was breathtaking. Rock formations jutting out of the water to his right, palm trees, Heliconias, and Birds of Paradise growing behind a long patch of white sand. His palapa was close enough to the shore that he could sit his chaise longue at the water's edge and still be shaded from the noonday sun.

It was warm. He could feel his shirt sticking to the sweat that coated the small of his back. The air was humid but not uncomfortably so. The white sand felt like silk beneath his feet. The turquoise water called to him, lapping against the shore gently, enticing him to take a dip.

Peeling off the sweaty shirt was like lifting a load from his shoulders. Jeremy wadded in the water slowly at first, the way he always had, allowing his body to get used to the cool temperature of the water. But he didn't need to. The water was as warm as bathwater, swirling around him, welcoming him. Jeremy smiled before dunking his head.

The heart monitor's flat beep startled everyone as it cut into the conversation, even the doctor.

One Night Stand

His eyes were shut when it happened, when the monstrosity overtook him, blanketing his legs and arms with its mass and leaving his flesh raw. Sucking mouths engulfed his face, pulsating as they devoured him to some unseen beat. And then, sated, at least for a while, it left him there, a mass of exposed muscle and blood. Before closing the door behind me, I tossed in dessert: his bitchy little wife.

The Shower

She stood under the warm flow of the water with her eyes closed. She loved feeling, the beat of the spray as it hit her back and cascaded down her spine to crest over her buttocks. She always had, ever since she was a little girl. She used to stand in the shower for as long as a half hour, way past the point where her fingers and toes started to prune, way past the duration of the hot water. She loved to feel water on her skin, fresh water with every drop. She couldn't stand baths. Her mother made her sit in stagnant bath water once a week to clean herself, claiming that taking a shower was like rinsing off, but sitting in a bath would truly cleanse the body. She never understood that logic. Sitting in a bath filled with water that carried the dirt that came off your skin was better than letting that same dirt run down the faucet? Right. So she showered anyway.

She used to play in the shower, finding new things to do every time. She filled her mouth with the water from the faucet, sometimes spitting it out like a fountain, other times swallowing it. She folded her arms and made a dam, catching the water above her navel and watching as it rose, and rose, and rose until spilling over. Sometimes she poked her middle finger out of the bottom of the dam and pressed her arms closer to her body to play Drowning Man. She enjoyed watching as the water crept up her finger until it overtook it completely. Sometimes she made pleading sounds, being sure to keep her voice low so her mother didn't hear her. He was drowning, after all. Wouldn't a drowning man cry for help?

She did different things in the shower. She urinated more than once. She pleasured herself, sometimes with a man, sometimes not. She meditated. She thought over a hard day at work. She dreamed about going to an exotic island, dreamed about having children. The shower was her sanctuary. The shower gave her peace.

The water was growing cold, yet she stood in the same place, right under the nozzle where the water could wet her hair and face. She was doing something new in the shower that day, something she had never done before. It was great fun, much like watching soapsuds chase each other down the drain, disappearing without a trace. Only, blood clots stain the tub as they swish around the drain, chasing each other and streaking the water pink in their wake. Smiling, she added that to her list of games.

Issue

1

"What the hell?"

"That's a big boy right there."

"At least the fucker got off."

"That's always important."

The cops snickered as the coroner's assistant took pictures of 50-year-old Mitchell Pinegrove. Pinegrove had been about 5'11", 230 pounds. He was a teacher at the local high school and lived with his ailing mother. He was found dangling in his bathroom from a noose made from one of his best neckties. He was naked, his body graying center mass, darkening to black in his extremities where the blood had gathered. He was holding his penis in his hand.

"He's a bagger," one of the cops said, flexing his investigational muscles.

"Really? How'd you figure that out?" Charlie Carver asked as he walked toward Pinegrove's body. "Couldn't have been the bag on his head, could it?" Carver and his partner had been the first car dispatched to the Pinegrove home. He had known Mitchell well enough; he taught his daughter's 10th grade Science class a couple of years back. Carver had never pegged Cassie's teacher to be the kind to get off on breath play, but then again, he'd never understood why anyone did. Sure, Carver had a dick like every other guy, and he could understand beating off every now and again. He did it himself. But to choke yourself while doing it? Carver was all for getting as much pleasure as he could, but autoerotic asphyxia seemed extreme to him. "To each his own," he muttered under his breath, shaking his head.

Carver was trying to make detective, so he was scrutinizing the case a little more than the other guys were. All they saw was some freak hanging from the showerhead in the bathroom with his dick in his hand. They pitied him, laughed at him for his stupidity, his loneliness. They silently thanked God they could get a date or had a wife to go home to when they felt like getting it on. But Carver saw more than that. Much more.

"The mother says this guy was 50 years old on his last birthday," Jackson, Carver's partner, said. "Isn't that a bit old for this kind of thing? Usually it's high school kids that do this."

"Not if you're lonely."

Carver stood in front of Pinegrove's blue, distended face and sighed. The plastic bag covering his head, the tie around his neck, the position he was found in: it all leaned toward him killing himself by accident, but Carver didn't buy it. It would be a day or two before the coroner's report would reveal ligature marks around both of Pinegrove's wrists and even longer for the tests to raise doubt whether the plastic bag was on his head before he died or put there as an afterthought, but Carver already knew something wasn't right with the case. He didn't think Pinegrove killed himself, but the lack of sperm on his hand wasn't the only reason. He could feel it inside, gnawing at him like termites on wood.

2

Morris wondered if he'd given too much away already. What he could see clearly was that his first foray into the story was filled with errors. He sighed as he thought about all the fact-checking and theory-proofing that lay ahead. He was nervous starting this, his third book. His first two books, *A Man Alone* and *Fallen Angel*, had been huge successes. Everybody seemed to want another Mo White mystery. After writing the first book, he sat down to write the second one within three days. But the time between novels two and three was vast—seven months. He hadn't so much as thought about a third novel for five of those months. He was enjoying his newfound celebrity. And why shouldn't he, he thought. It's what he had been working for. He got invited to premiers and low to mid-level Hollywood bashes. After the first Mo White mystery was optioned for a screenplay, he was suddenly part of the 'in' crowd, and he loved every minute of it. One day he was begging the girl next door for a date, the next day he was waking up beside models and aspiring actresses who knew how to play the part. Morris was living the life.

As he stared at the computer screen glowing in the all-encompassing darkness that shrouds 5:00 a.m., Morris started to wonder if he had been partying a little too much.

Carver, his old pal, his trusty wannabe detective, was feeling more like a stranger to him than he had when Morris had first brought him to life. Morris was having trouble sorting out his feelings, his motivations for this next book, and that was bad. If there was anything Morris needed to know going into a new story, it was the why. Without it, the story could never move forward. He couldn't just sit in front of a keyboard and go for it. He had to know where he would end up and why the 'big thing' that was supposed to happen later on in the story would come to pass. Usually the why came pretty easily. Right after coming up with an ending — putting the cart before the horse as his mother called it — Morris usually figured out the why. It hung out there like a beam of light from a lighthouse, just waiting for acknowledgement. It didn't take much effort. But that day, as the blank screen glowed in the dark, he couldn't see the why. Hell, he couldn't see the who, what, where, when, or how either.

"Shit." Morris cursed under his breath. Usually, when what he refused to call writer's block hit, Morris fancied that Carver cursed too, his New York accent hardening the edge all the more. But either Carver was asleep, or he just didn't give a damn that morning because he didn't say a word.

Morris pushed himself away from the desk, the wheels on the chair sounding incredibly loud as they moved along the plastic carpet guard. He trudged into the bathroom like a man asleep. Writer's block did that to him. Not being able to write was akin to being in a tranquilizer-induced fog, and Morris' body reacted in kind, barely moving the muscles necessary to get him to and fro. He ran the cold water and splashed some of it onto his face. He stared into his eyes as he let the water drip from his sleepy countenance back into the sink, only somewhat aware that the basin was overflowing. He looked like shit, he surmised after studying the bags under his eyes and the pallid tone of his skin. Maybe 5:00 a.m. was too early to get started after all.

The water in the basin rose to meet his hands where they rested on the sides, but he didn't move. There was something in his eyes that had snagged him, that called his attention, all of it. The world around him was beginning to white out, as though a bright light had been turned on, obscuring the shower curtain behind him, his neck, his face. He could only see his eyes, the whites streaked with red from months of fast fun, the brown irises seeming abnormally large and smooth. He only had a second to wonder where the ridges that make up the iris were before he saw Pinegrove hanging from his neck in the reflection. He flinched but only slightly, as the room behind him changed from opaque nothingness to a crowded bedroom where the body of a middle-aged man hung by the neck. And there was Carver, looking at Morris with an intensity in his eyes that commanded heeding. Finish me, Carver said, his lips barely moving. No one else in the room seemed to have heard him. They continued to mill around the body aimlessly, touching everything and nothing at once. Even the coroner seemed to be idling, walking around the body with his camera retaking shots he had just completed. And then, all of a sudden, the image was gone.

The smile spread across his face before he knew it. It was the one he hated, the one that always frightened him away from the mirror. It was a smile that he was almost positive was not his own, but the resurgence of some 'thing' inside him that only came out during episodes like that, when Morris wasn't in control. Morris turned off the faucet and dropped a towel onto the floor, averting his eyes from the mirror. He was afraid to see that face — his face — again. Sitting down to the keyboard, he got started right away, new ideas flooding in with every keystroke. Carver was back. The fact that the voice Carver used wasn't one that Morris had ever heard before never registered; his rapid-fire ideas were all that were important. Morris and Carver had a case to solve.

3

Carver knew the detective on the case — Jenny had been a friend of his since high school. More than a friend, really, but that was ancient history. At least, for her it was. She still looked good to him. Even though he was married with two kids at home, she still made him stir. He loved to see her when she was intense; the cute way her brow furrowed over her gorgeous brown eyes always made him wonder 'what if'. The tapered business slacks that hugged her curves didn't help either. But that day, Carver had other things on his mind. He couldn't stop thinking about Pinegrove hanging from his neck in his bathroom.

"What did the coroner's report say, Jen?" Carver asked as he sidled up to Jenny's desk and took a seat.

"Why do you care so much, Charlie? Haven't you moved on to bigger and better things?" Jenny was buried behind stacks of paper. Carver tried to figure out which stack was Pinegrove's.

"I knew this guy. He was Cassie's teacher, for chrissakes."

"All the more reason to stay out of this." Jenny could be hard when she needed to be. But Carver knew how to soften her up.

"Something about this thing is sticking with me, is all. I feel for the poor guy." He could see the ice melting before Jenny said anything. The charm worked every time.

With a sigh, Jenny acquiesced. "All right Charlie. Take a look for yourself."

Charlie flashed his best appreciative smile, even though it took everything he had not to snatch the folder from her hands. Jenny turned to her computer and started banging away on the keyboard, muttering something about finishing a report under her breath. Carver snatched a glance at her again, checking out her profile as he did often when she wasn't looking. *Damn, she's still a looker*, he thought. *Shit.*

Carver was right. His hunches never lied.

"This is why they put you on it?" Carver asked as he finished the report.

"Bingo. The ligature marks could go all the way back to the guy we're after in New Paltz. The marks on the victim's hands in NP were similar to this DOA. Might have been made with the same kind of material. We're checking fibers now."

Carver nodded absently, his mind focusing on another detail of the report. He wondered if Jenny noticed it.

"Where's the jizz?"

"What?"

"The semen. The report says he ejaculated before death. So where is it? There wasn't any on his hand and I didn't see any on the floor —."

"You looked?" Jenny tried to hide her amusement as she turned to look at him.

"Yeah, I looked." Carver smiled the way only Jenny could make him, broad and uninhibited. "I'm a cop. I'm supposed to."

"I really think you need to sit for the detective exam, Charlie," Jenny said as she turned back to the monitor. "You'd pass it in a heartbeat."

Carver blushed. He couldn't help it.

"So, what about the sperm? What if he shot and it landed on the wall or on the bathroom rug? What if his mother saw it and cleaned it up, trying to protect her son?"

"Come on Jen. The man was 50 years old. He'd be lucky if the shit didn't trickle out like water." Jenny wanted so badly to keep a straight face but was failing. "I doubt he shot that far," Carver continued. "But if he did, and it landed on the floor, that would be the last thing his mother would worry about. The bag on his head, his nakedness in general would have been tended to first. The sperm would have been an afterthought, you know? I mean, if you were in her situation, which would you pick?"

Jen nodded in agreement. "So, what are you thinking?"

"Someone took the sperm. For what, I don't know."

"Mrs. Pinegrove didn't say anyone else was in the house."

"Maybe she didn't know."

Jenny turned back to Carver, looking him right in the eye. It made him a little nervous. And a little excited. "It's a rambler, like your mom's place.

What, 1500 square feet at the most? She'd hear someone if they were in the house. Hell, even the neighbors would know!"

Every once in a while, Jenny brought up the past, something about Carver that she remembered. It always made him drift into the past, thinking about when they were a couple. Back then she was the only girl that 'got' him. She knew he was more than just a jock. She knew that he was deeper than that, more introspective than the average guy in school. And she liked it. All the other girls he dated wanted him because he was on the football team. But Jenny really cared, really saw him for who he was.

Damn, he missed her.

"Yeah, but she's old, Jen," he said, trying to push the memories away. "And it was 12:30 when we got there. If she turned in early, she might not have known."

Nibbling on a pencil, Jenny pondered that. She added, "Maybe Pinegrove had a date over and was trying to be quiet?"

"Are you saying that maybe he was kinky?" He wondered if Jenny was kinky now.

"If you don't have to get off by yourself but you let yourself be tied up like that, you might be," she replied.

She said might. Yeah, Carver decided, Jenny *was* kinky. He shifted in his seat.

"So, Pinegrove gets a date, brings her to the house, engages in, let's call it foreplay, and what? She — ."

"Or he," Jenny admonished.

"Or he," Carver said reluctantly. He couldn't imagine Pinegrove as gay, but then again, he wouldn't have thought he would find him hanging dead in the bathroom with his dick in his hands either. "Whoever. They get evil all of a sudden and let him die? Or is that person too caught up in pleasuring themselves to realize that old Mitchell was kicking the bucket?"

"Or was it planned? Staged?"

"By who? The lover? Pinegrove? The mother?"

A wry smile spread over Jenny's lips. "The murderer."

Jenny turned back to the monitor and started punching at the keys again. "Do us both a favor and take the test," she called over her shoulder as Carver got up.

"Yeah, yeah," Carver said as he walked away, a new bee in his bonnet.

4

Morris was moving slower than he wanted to on the new novel. That rush of ideas was short-lived. He couldn't seem to get into a groove. Normally he could bang out five to ten pages every two hours, but now he was stuck at one, maybe two, if any. There were days when relaxing by the pool or going to dinner with the new love of his life seemed more exciting than sitting down and writing. He had just met her; the magic hadn't worn off yet. He loved everything about her; the way her hair smelled, the way her lips curved when she laughed—everything. He didn't want to do anything but be with her, lay near her, feed her, sleep with her, snuggle with her—whatever it was, it had to be done with her. Rose Marie. God, she was perfect!

He could rationalize his procrastination too. Who knew when the gravy train would end? Maybe this was the high point. Maybe this was his time. He shouldn't waste it. He should live it up while he still had a chance, while his name still resonated pleasantly on the critics' lips.

Something about the way the new Mo White mystery was going didn't sit well with him either. Things were happening. Lines were being written that he was sure weren't his own. Sure, he told many a fan that he gets into his characters, starts to think the way they would, becomes them to the point that he requires down time after each book just to find himself again. It worked with the chicks who only read a line or two of text from anyone's book, let alone his. The intellectuals? Well, he didn't imagine they would read his stuff anyway. But this story was becoming too real, too strange. Like what was the deal with the sperm? He had made his bad guys collect things before—a finger (the middle one, to be precise) for the serial killer, a tongue for the gangster, a heart for the Bocor—the standard stuff. But sperm? What the hell would the murderer want with sperm? For some reason, even thinking about the storyline freaked Morris out.

Carver and his newest case would be there for Morris when he was ready to jump back in. Right now, Morris decided, he would live a little.

5

Carver and Jackson had just finished lunch when a call came in over the radio.

"We're close. Let's go," Jackson said as he started driving toward the address. They got out of the car and were met by a hysterical man in front of the house.

"She's in there. My-my wife, she's in there. Oh my God, how could this have happened?" The man's face was wet with tears and his gait was shaky. He started to walk toward the house to show Carver and Jackson where the body was, but Jackson stopped him, urging him to remain outside. It didn't take much. The man sat down on his steps with an audible thump and held his head in his hands.

When they entered the home, they found a woman pinned to the floor. She had bled out long before they had gotten there, before her husband came home and found her. A piano leg had been thrust through her stomach and out her back to penetrate the floorboards beneath her.

"What the fuck? What kind of person could have done this?" Jackson said, his voice tense, edgy.

"A stronger one than you or me," Carver answered in awe.

Carver inspected the piano leg and found that the top was splintered, rough. "Looks like he wrenched this leg free with his bare hands."

"What would make someone do this? I mean, kill her like this?"

"Takes all kinds, my friend."

Carver and Jackson hung around while the team collected evidence and dusted for prints. Carver did a little snooping – just enough to satisfy his curiosities, but not enough to get in anyone's way. The woman had only been married to the guy on the front steps for a year. They were thinking about starting a family, based on all the baby magazines in the bedroom on her side of the bed. Did the piano leg in the stomach have anything to do with that?

Maybe the husband didn't want kids as much as she thought he did. Maybe the husband took it out on her after she told him she was pregnant. *If* she was pregnant, that is. Or maybe she didn't want kids and the side of the bed Carver had been looking at was the husband's. Carver dismissed the thought. He couldn't imagine the guy out front being the type to buy a bunch of baby magazines and coo over them before drifting off to sleep. He'd been wrong before, but he didn't think he was wrong about that. Anyhow, if he followed that train of thought, the wife would have taken herself out. Carver could think of plenty of ways to off yourself if you really wanted to—he had seen more of them than he liked to remember. Plunging a piano leg into your stomach didn't make the list. No, somebody killed her, more than likely, because she was pregnant. But why?

The husband told Carver that his wife had something to tell him, but that she was waiting until their anniversary that weekend. "I think she's pregnant," the husband said, profound loss coating his words. "My Jenny, I think she was pregnant."

An unwanted thought flitted through Carver's mind, and once it showed itself, he couldn't shake the implications it left in its wake.

Two bizarre crime scenes.
Then the name.
Jenny.
Carver shivered involuntarily.

6

Morris shelved the novel for weeks, deciding instead to travel the world. He saw London, Switzerland, and Brussels. He went to the Caribbean and South America to soak up the sun. He never gave Carver, Jenny, or any of his other characters a second thought. Life was good, and he wanted to experience all it had to offer.

When Morris came home from his trip, he languished around the house, avoiding the novel at all costs. He always found something else to do, something else that required his attention immediately. The book sat for months without a single word being added. But, inevitably, his insides were getting restless. Morris wasn't surprised, not really.

After all, the book was a part of him.

7

Jenny being in trouble – such a stretch of the imagination. Carver knew it, but it was the only thing he would allow himself to think. He didn't want to admit that his desire for her, to feel her soft skin beneath his calloused hands, was bringing on unhealthy thoughts. Admitting that would show weakness and that was something he would never do. Even when he found himself outside Jenny's house that night, watching her bedroom window as avidly as a peeping tom might, he wouldn't admit it. He called himself protecting her, though she was capable of protecting herself. He was only watching out for a friend.

The office was buzzing the next day. Another dead body was found in a compromising position — a man was found dead on a makeshift sex table equipped with metal ties and harnesses in the basement of the library. Though he was yet unidentified — the skin on his face had been cut away with a razor — the common thought was that it was Lyle Coleman, early fifties, head librarian.

Two men in positions that could be considered reputable with personalities that could be deemed kindly, if not meek, were found in compromising positions at their death. Sexual positions. That their fantasies could drive them beyond the breaking point, reputation be damned, was not a stretch in Carver's mind. Not really. He had a fantasy or two of his own that might raise the eyebrows of those around him. But to the point of death? He wasn't so sure about that.

Who, then? Who would murder these men, men in midlife with no spouses and no prospects? Men with jobs that required patience and compassion, and in so demonstrating, made them quiet and tame. Men whose deaths would shock the community because of the compromising positions they were found in and, of course, their proximity to the children. And speaking of children, why was it that both men's sperm was removed from the scene as soon as they had spilled it? Lyle Coleman's testicles had even been sliced and bled. Could a man do that to himself under the guise of pleasure seeking? Carver doubted it.

A jilted lover perhaps, or an admirer whose advances had been thwarted, maybe? But neither man had been dating. Lyle had never dated, at least his coworkers claimed. And Mitchell had lost interest in the fairer sex since his divorce six years ago. Internet dating? Maybe so, given the times. But for some reason the jilted lover theory didn't resonate for Carver. Call it instinct, but he thought it was something else.

A student, perhaps? Maybe a kid was getting a bad grade in Pinegrove's class, snuck in the house and found Pinegrove in a compromising position. It would be easy to slip the bag over Pinegrove's head while he hung. But then what about the ligature marks? Pinegrove had been tied up before dying and let free to bring himself to orgasm. Carver rationalized that if you buy the theory that the mother heard nothing at all, and Pinegrove had someone with him when he hung himself, then maybe that person snuck out before the mother came downstairs, fleeing so as not to be caught. Why would they run away? Married woman? Married man? Frightened kid?

And what about Coleman? Surely the same student couldn't be having an affair with the librarian. Or could they? Both men were older, but not too old. Both dressed in a distinguished fashion—sport coat and slacks, polished shoes. Both men had a similar look—short cut hair, graying slightly, same height and weight give or take a few pounds. It might be feasible. But why kill Coleman? He couldn't affect a grade, so maybe the student idea is out the window. Maybe he threatened to tell the husband or the wife of his lover about their affair and was killed before he could? Could both Pinegrove and Coleman pose a threat to the same person within weeks of each other?

Unlikely.

There was something else.

Carver sat in front of Jenny's house trying to figure out the connection between Pinegrove and Coleman. Aside from the sexual position of their bodies, there was none. Or was there?

8

The doctor visit was no fun. Morris' carefree lifestyle had bought him a nice case of Chlamydia. He wished he knew which bitch had given it to him. He kept trying to think back to when it started hurting to urinate. The doctor said that there are, often times, no symptoms of it, that it could have been in his body for years. Yeah, well, he *had* been fucking around for years and it had finally caught up with him. He couldn't have kids. He didn't know how much he wanted them until they told him he could never have them. He felt as if his life was over.

What was the point of anything anymore? Sure, he wasn't at the point of settling down, not yet. But he always knew he wanted a house, a wife, 2.5 children, and a black Lab for the kids to play with. He wanted a family. And now all of that was gone.

He was depressed. He spent days sitting at home alone. He didn't answer his phone, didn't answer the knock at the door. He told Rose Marie to go and find someone else. He told her about the disease and made sure she got herself checked out. Thank God, she wasn't affected. But after that, he made her leave, made her promise to forget about him. Why should he bring her down? She wanted kids too and he knew he could never give them to her. So, he let her go to find someone who could.

He didn't accept his agent's phone calls either. Why should he? What was the point in busting his hump to finish a book made up of meaningless words? Even if he made money on it, what was he going to do with it? He had already seen everything he wanted to see, gone everywhere he wanted to go. Without a family to leave the money to, what good was it? Morris turned over in bed when the phone rang, not caring who might be on the other end.

9

Jenny saw Carver pull up in front of her house and came outside. He wondered if she knew he watched her every night, wondered if she liked it. The thought made him excited.

"What are you doing here, Charlie?" Jenny's voice was crisp, aggravated.

"What?"

"In front of my house. What are you doing out here? I saw you here the other night too. Why?"

Carver bristled at her reaction, more than a little annoyed that she was speaking to him that way. Didn't she know he was there to protect her?

"I just stopped by to say hello and you came out. That's all." He cursed himself for sounding like such a wuss.

"Bullshit, Charlie, you've been sitting out here for the past couple of days. And I want to know why."

Jenny was starting to raise her voice. Carver couldn't have that.

"Jenny, settle down."

"Charlie, you better tell me why you're out here or I'll have to call the Captain."

Carver gave Jenny his best smile and, like usual, it disarmed her. "I've been out here because I was concerned for you."

Jenny sighed, but she believed him. "What are you talking about?"

"I didn't want to tell you about this, but I guess I have to now. You caught me."

"That's why I'm a detective. What's all this about?"

He had her. "Just this case the other day. Really, all of them recently. There's something tying these people together, but I just don't know what."

"Yeah, but what does that have to do with me and why you've been out here in front of my house doing a crappy job of hiding? I gotta tell ya, your stakeout practices have got to be better than this if you want to make detective."

Her laughter sealed it. "It's just – her name was Jenny."

"Who?"

"The case midweek. You know, the woman who was found dead with the piano leg stuck in her. That was her name – Jenny. It just – it seems a little strange."

Jenny's chuckle was genuine. "Charlie Carver, you think too much."

Charlie smiled and looked down into his lap. It might have been an endearing look to her, but he was just making sure he had settled down enough to get out of the car.

"Come inside and let's get something to drink since you're here."

They drank beer and ordered pizza. They talked about old times and people, high school and what happened after. There wasn't sadness in Jenny's voice, just a longing that Carver hadn't noticed before, hadn't allowed himself to hear. That he was a married man was not a topic for discussion, not a topic to ponder. At least not then. Who knew what would happen later? Who cared?

Jenny didn't talk much about men. She didn't seem to have any use for them, no time for the games that men play. Work was her life and she was happy with that. Or tried to be, at least.

Charlie couldn't have hoped for better. Jenny got herself blitzed enough to accept a pass. Charlie wondered if she hadn't made the pass first, subtly, but there true enough. She kissed him like she hadn't kissed in a long time. Carver suspected she hadn't. He took her up to the bedroom and made love to her the way he had wanted to for years — hard, fast, unyielding, the way she liked it. It was like heaven. Like rebirth.

10

Morris was working at a fevered pitch. He poured every waking moment into the book. It was like a light switch went on, casting away the shadows of his lost legacy, obliterating the burning in his loins. Morris didn't think about asking Rose Marie to come over to celebrate his lifted malaise, didn't consider going to a bar and toasting his writing streak with a buddy. All he wanted — all he could think about — was the book. He threw himself into it, adding his blood, sweat, and tears to every word. It satisfied him the way Rose Marie never had. Morris coddled the pages he printed off, laying them next to his bed, touching them like a mother might a child as it drifted to sleep. He was possessed of it and he knew it.

The scary thing was that he liked it.

11

Jenny turning up pregnant was the least of Carver's worries. Keeping his wife from finding out was the problem. He wanted her to keep the baby, to have his child. But she didn't. To her, being pregnant was like a death sentence. No amount of talking could seem to change her mind, either. Jenny wanted to get rid of the baby — his baby — no matter what.

"How could you want this?" Jenny asked him incredulously. "This baby could ruin your life."

"No Jenny, don't you see? This is perfect for us. It's the way it should have always been."

"Charlie, you're a married man, for God's sakes! Are you crazy?"

"I love you, Jenny."

Jenny shook her head in disbelief. "You fucking idiot. This is not going to happen."

Carver had heard it all before.

"I'm not having this baby, Charlie."

"Of course you will. It will be beautiful." Charlie grabbed Jenny's arm, putting more pressure on it than he should have.

"Charlie, you're crazy."

"You *will* have our baby, Jenny."

The look in Charlie's eyes frightened Jenny, filled her with base horror. "Get the hell off me."

"It will be wonderful, you'll see."

"Charlie," Jenny almost growled. "Leave me alone. I will do what I want with this baby and you will have nothing more to say about it, or your wife will find out."

The threat stunned Carver and he loosened his grip. Jenny snatched her arm away from him and walked off. Watching her go burned Carver up inside.

How dare she threaten him?

She wouldn't do anything to their baby. She couldn't. He'd see to that.

12

Morris' dreams that night were hazy, clouded. It started with he and Rose Marie. He was pounding her with an intensity he had rarely exhibited. It was exhilarating to hear her scream for more, to press him further into her as she gyrated against him. Sex had never been as good as that between them. His orgasm was more disappointing than fulfilling; he wanted more of her.

But then she was gone and he was in a different place, a different time. He could still feel the tingle of climaxing in his thighs and the balls of his feet. He could still smell her, the tangy sweetness of her sex, caressing his nostrils. A blackness surrounded him that was as heavy as an overcoat, though the air was crisp. He was doing a book signing in a field. His table was surrounded by tall, overgrown grass and weeds. A line of fans snaked through the field as far as the eye could see. He'd be happy to draw a crowd a quarter of that size at a real live event.

Morris was signing copies of the last Mo White mystery. He was cranking them out too, doing his best 'S&S', as he liked to call it (signing and smiling), as quickly as possible. He hadn't looked up to see the people in front of him until a fly rose from someone's hand to buzz in his face. Swatting the fly away, Morris finally laid eyes on the people in line, the ones who would wait in such a secluded place to get him to sign their books. The woman in front of him smiled shyly, her hand fluttering up to her mouth to hide her girlish, toothless grin as it spread across her decaying face. A fingernail dropped from a fingertip filled with puss and discharge. The nail landed on the title page of the new book. It was painted the color of blood. The nail alone was disturbing enough, but the fact that he recognized the woman sent Morris into a panic.

The pleasant face of a wife and soon to be mother stared back at him. The woman he had killed with a piano leg in his book.

Morris couldn't make himself look at her stomach, at the gaping hole the piano leg left in its wake.

"Just sign it 'To Jenny'," the woman gargled, her voice straining on ruined vocal cords. "I can't wait to read it!"

"We love Mo White!" someone from the middle of the line yelled. The voice was so degenerated, Morris couldn't tell if it was a man or a woman. Morris looked beyond Jenny to see that all of them, the entire audience—all of his fans—were dead. Not only dead. They shouldn't have existed at all. One by one, the characters of his books filed behind the other, waiting for Morris. There was Joe from the first book, who perished under the hands of a serial killer with a finger fetish; there was Mitchell Pinegrove, as naked as he had been when he died, his face bloated and discolored from lack of oxygen; there was Lyle Coleman, a bloody mess below the waist. And there were more, scores more, lined up in the darkness. Waiting for him.

Morris recoiled in disgust laced with fear so prominent, he could smell it on his own skin. The woman before him smiled wider, reaching a rotting hand toward Morris as he pushed himself away from the table. He stood to leave, to run away, but caught a glimpse of something more heinous than his "fans" in the corner of his eye. What could only be described as a thing staggered toward Morris, its legs of differing lengths and thickness. One leg was nothing more than bone from pelvis to foot. The other was covered with unblemished skin, as smooth as that of a newborn. His back was hunched over, curled like a fetus in the womb. The bones of his spine were visible in places and covered with paper-thin skin in others. His arms were almost complete. The skin on them, like one of his legs, looked healthy. His hands, however, were mashed, broken, crushed. His face was a mass of broken bones, split skin, and blood. His features were almost indistinguishable, with gaps in the skin that revealed muscle and bone. His eyes, though, were piercing. Their iridescent brown bored into Morris, chilling his very soul.

The thing said something that sounded more like a grunt than a word. Morris didn't want to hear it, didn't want to be there at all, but knew he had to. Stepping close enough that Morris could smell its breath, a scent both sweet and putrid at the same time, the thing spoke again, clearer somehow.

"Finish me!"

Morris awoke with the sound of his own screams in his ear.

"Are you all right?" The voice of a woman he didn't recognize spoke to him softly. Someone else shrieked from far away.

"A-are you all right, sir?"

Morris opened his eyes and saw the kind face of a matronly woman, hair dusted with gray and roller set like his grandmother's had been, standing in front of him. She was clutching his book to her chest. His own penetrative stare looked back at him from the back cover. She clutched the book so tightly that her knuckles were white.

Another woman rushed over with a cup of water, which Morris greedily downed. He was starting to get his bearings. He was in a bookstore, one that he'd been in before, to sign and to buy books. He was seated at a table, a stack of his books next to him, pen in hand. Okay. Made sense. He had a couple more venues on his tour for *Fallen Angel*. He just didn't remember how he got there.

"I'm fine," Morris said unconvincingly. "I didn't get much sleep last night. That's all." The women were still worried. "The life of a horror writer, what can I say?" He smiled but it felt wrong. Some of the people in line, mostly women per usual, chuckled but still looked at him with concern in their eyes.

Morris didn't know what was wrong with him, why he couldn't remember getting to the bookstore, coming in and sitting down, why he daydreamed such a horrible scene in broad daylight. He didn't know anything except that he wanted to sign as many books as he could and get out the hell of there.

The next woman in line smiled and handed him her book. "You can just sign that to Jenny, Mr. White. I can't wait to read it!"

Morris caught a glimpse of the title on the cover before he passed out with the smell of wet grass in his nose and a baby crying in his ears.

Jennifer's Rose, A Mo White Mystery.

Things That Lovers Do

The last time he looked she wasn't there.

But she is now.

She moves beneath the black satin like a snake coiling down a dune, so fluid, so rhythmic, just watching her might make him explode.

Usually.

But not that night.

She moved.

Slowly at first.

Then faster.

She knew he was there, watching her. Seeing her body move under the cover of the black satin sheet. He could taste her skin on his tongue, taste her sweat, her saliva, her sex, like he could every night, every time she moved for him. And she liked it.

Barry stood watching her from the foot of the bed, feeling himself rise, but trying not to satisfy himself just yet. He wanted to make it last this time, draw it out.

He wanted to see what she would do.

Her breasts pushed at the material, forming it around them. Barry could see the outline of her areolas imprinted there. How he wanted to press his mouth to them, flesh upon flesh, sucking them, tasting her again. But he stayed away, watching instead, willing himself to wait.

Her hand, delicate and tiny, caressed the skin beneath her breasts, traced the line of her ribcage and stomach, and dove past her pelvis. Her hips gyrated and bucked ever so slightly beneath the sheet. Saliva, tinny and cold, sprang into his mouth, wetting his tongue. He could almost smell it, could almost feel the warmth of her juices on his finger. He brought it to his lips and plunged it into his mouth, imagining that he could taste her as he had so long ago, as he had before he put her in the ground next to his mother and father to rot. It was sweet, the taste of her, unlike any of the ones he'd tasted before or after. He could never find the right one, the one who would be his Mindy, his sugar. All the others that writhed beneath the sheet stopped after a while, the dance boring them. Some never danced for him at all, bleeding out instead, right when he was about to release. But

Mindy, she never bled out, never cried for help, never made a sound at all, except for the sensual moaning that shook her body and aroused his.

He fancied he could taste her when she visited him, could smell her in the air.

And for one lucid moment, he could.

Congratulations on your Wedding

It's not that I still carry a torch for her. At least I don't think I do. Not really, anyway. We broke up five years ago, for God's sake. That should be a long enough time to get over a person and move on, wouldn't you think? We remained friends and even got together every once in a while for lunch since our offices were so close. That's all they were though, lunches between two friends who just happened to be ex-lovers. Lovers who had explored each other's bodies and souls more closely than they had ever explored anyone else's. Lovers who, if they had made it work, would have grown old together, sitting on the front stoop of their old house laughing and joking about their younger days. Being friends had been hard at first but we worked it out, hadn't we? At first, I would cross the street when I saw her coming, getting myself out of view before she even knew I was there. The breakup was still raw for me, even after three months. It's not easy when the love of your life says she needs to move on, says she doesn't think you're the right one for her. It took me a while—longer than I wanted to admit—but I got over it. I got over her.

And now we're just friends. Right?

Seeing her walk down the steps and into the parlor toward the man she had chosen to spend the rest of her life with made me question myself. It wasn't me she was walking toward. It was Cliff. Cliff was a nice enough guy, I guess. Good job. No discernable vices except Jasmine. She seemed to be the only thing he needed, the only thing he couldn't do without. God help him, I knew the feeling.

The wedding was in one of those bed and breakfasts that Jasmine always wanted to stay in. The ones I said were nothing more than old houses with a fresh coat of paint thrown on the walls. Standing there in Ridgefield House I still thought I was right, but a little shortsighted. The house was a 100-year-old brick Colonial with an elaborate fanlight and a decorative pediment with 'Ridgefield House' engraved in Olde English lettering to greet you as you walked up the stairs to the door. The molding for the windows was painted white and shingles of the same color were mounted on either side of the windows on the second floor. The hallways were narrow, the walls bordered by decorative molding. The wood floor blended nicely with the high chair rail in the parlor. A modest chandelier hung from the ceiling in the parlor and candelabras sat on the mantel. Oil paintings of cherubs adorned the walls and crystal figurines cluttered an antique curio. Period furniture done in cherry wood and maroon fabric ringed the room, adding to the aura of the place. The bed and breakfast was old but it was elegant.

I guess Jasmine got her way after all.

The wedding was small. Her mother and father, Cliff's parents, and maybe thirty of their friends. I didn't expect to be among their number, but here I am. I felt out of place, like I had 'jilted beau' tattooed on my forehead in big red letters.

Jasmine was radiant; her smile lit up the room. I was captivated as I was sure everyone else in the room was. The sight of her was breathtaking.

Why wasn't it me she was walking toward with such light in her eyes as to blind anyone who dared to look at her? What did Cliff have that I didn't? The answers to those questions came far too easily and I pushed them away before they could form fully. It wasn't me that Jasmine was marrying. It was Cliff. And that was the bottom line. To hell with the reasons why.

The service was your usual variety. *Anyone here object?* (Yeah, me!) *Recite these vows; you may now kiss the bride*, etcetera. Afterward, I went to the bar and got a glass of red wine, hoping it would help me relax. I barely noticed when the bartender handed me the cork to examine from the new bottle of Cote-Rotie La Turque. Jasmine's dad was rolling in it. I wasn't surprised that he'd shell out $375.00 per bottle for the wedding. Only the best for his little girl.

I mellowed with my second glass. It's easier to take all the laughing and smiling and happy feelings people emitted for the bride and groom when you've got a bit of a buzz going.

Finally, the moment of truth. It was my turn up at bat. I had to go and congratulate the lucky couple.

I leaned over to kiss Jasmine on the cheek, taking in her scent as I did. I hope no one noticed.

"You look beautiful," I said, trying my best to keep my face jovial. What I really wanted to do was kiss her deeply, tell her I love her, and whisk her away. But I smiled instead and repeated, "Really beautiful."

"Thanks Steve," she said, still beaming, "I'm so glad you could make it."

"So am I," Cliff chimed in, not to be ignored. "It means a lot that you're here."

I shook Cliff's hand and said, "I'm honored to be. You're getting a wonderful woman, Cliff."

"Don't I know it."

His smile was nauseating.

I started to walk away when Jasmine reached out and touched my arm.

"Steve, hang on a sec. I want to talk with you." She cast a glance over her shoulder at her new husband and he nodded and left us alone. Within seconds he was mingling with the other guests. It was just me and her.

Man, she's such a looker.

"I just wanted to tell you how much it means to have you here," she said. "I'm so happy you came."

"I wouldn't have missed it for the world." The words sounded foreign coming from my mouth.

"I am happy, Steve. Cliff is a wonderful man."

I nodded. What could I say to that? He was wonderful and I knew it.

"Steve," Jasmine said, stepping closer to me and talking in a hushed, conspiratorial tone. I couldn't focus on her words at first. I was too caught up in the view to think of anything else. Her breasts were beautiful. I remember holding them in my hands, caressing the nipple ever so lightly, coaxing them to stand pert. They were so delicate, so soft. I wished I could see them one more time. If only she'd take a step closer and I could see a little more…

"…ok? I would really appreciate it."

"What?" I stumbled. "I didn't quite catch that."

"Can you go in there and check on the caterers? I wouldn't ask, but since you did that catering gig way back when…" She chuckled, looking nervous somehow. "Cliff's mother chose them and, well, I don't think they're doing things right. The dip tasted bitter to me. My God, if they can't get the easy stuff right, just imagine how they might screw up the rest of the meal."

I looked at her eyes while she spoke. So beautiful, even now.

"Anyway, so I was wondering if you would go in there and see what they're doing. If something looks off let me know. Ok?"

How could I say no to her? This was the most important day of her life. The fairytale that was coming true to the letter up until this point. I couldn't let her down. I couldn't be the one she walked down the aisle with, but I could at least do this for her. As a friend.

"Sure. No problem."

The smile she gave me made my heart jump. I missed her so badly it hurt.

Jasmine walked me toward the kitchen and then casually slipped away, mingling with the crowd. I looked at her once more before I went inside, but she didn't look back. She was too busy laughing with a girlfriend of hers from college. Amy. Amy never liked me. The feeling was mutual.

The catering staff was working furiously, cutting, shaving, trimming, stacking, dousing. One woman cut the ends off the bread, another placed kale on a large round plate for garnish. The room smelled of tomato sauce and grilled shrimp.

I noticed immediately that everyone looked incredibly gaunt. Dark circles under their eyes, cheekbones poking sharply against sallow skin. Thin. Emaciated almost. Like skeletons covered with the thinnest layer of skin. That the finger food, which would normally be prepped and brought over ready, was just being worked on hardly registered.

"Hey guys," I said, feeling a little off kilter. "What's for dinner?" I tried to ham it up, patting one of the ladies closest to me on the back and leaning over to get a better look at things.

"Jambalaya," the guy standing over a pot on the stove said. His voice was gravelly and without inflection. It seemed to drone in my ears - like an insistent bass drum.

I walked over to the cook stirring the pot of jambalaya. I scanned the immediate area on and around the stove but didn't see the rice that should be added to the dish.

I saw a woman dicing something that resembled a cow's tongue.

Celery was lined up on the cutting board, waiting to be knifed.

Someone that I didn't see banged a metal rod into an oyster shell, shucking it.

"Did you throw anything good into that jambalaya? Some mystery meat?" I joked awkwardly as I peered into the pot. I laughed trying to draw a smile from the stoic, anorexic cook whose brown skin looked as though it had been roasted over the fire and made tough.

"Lotta things in this pot make this dish good," he said in a rich baritone that made my teeth rattle.

"Like what? I can smell the shrimp. What else? Chicken? Ham? That's all standard stuff. What's your special ingredient?" I was talking too fast, I knew that. I couldn't help it.

"Brains."

I had been ready to laugh at whatever he said in an attempt to egg him on, keep him talking so I could see what was in the pot. It wasn't until I felt the cool wind on my neck, the one that had been whipped up by the arm that swung the rip hammer into my head – yeah, the blow that crushed my skull and made blood drip from my eyes - that I realized what he said. And by then it was too late.

The cook's assistant hit me once more, opening a sizeable hole in my skull and exposing my brain to the open air. He used the forked end of the hammer pry my skull away, breaking bone off in chips, to get easier access to the soft meat of my brain. My body convulsed as my head was held over the pot, my hand falling onto one of the burners and filling the air with the smell of burning flesh. But that didn't matter, not anymore.

All I wanted to do was shut my eyes.

Before I did, I caught one last glimpse of the cook's face, alight with excitement now, sporting a rotten tooth smile that spread from ear to ear as he held my bleeding head over the pot of jambalaya for Jasmine to see.

Malady

The air was thick, stifling, oppressive. Heavy with water. Her body felt so weak, she could hardly stand. Darkness covered the place so completely, nothing could be seen for miles ahead or right in front of her. It was comprehensive, like blindness, unyielding and whole. A shriek welled in Sabrina's throat, though she dared not utter it.

She took a step forward, needing to feel the familiar press and pull of her flesh as she moved, needing to feel anything at all aside from the air, so palpable it felt like a hand caressing her cheek. But there was nothing. If the step had moved her forward or backward, she couldn't tell. The nothingness in the new space was the same as the nothingness where she stood before.

Sabrina stayed silent for what seemed like hours, her eyes darting to and fro, trying to make out buildings or cars or people walking along a sidewalk. That's what she should have been able to see: a bustling New York City street lined with skyscrapers and crowded with people in a rush to get to a restaurant, a meeting, or to a cab. Whatever the reason, it should have been happening. But it wasn't. She didn't hear the familiar beeping of a cabby's horn as he darted in and out of traffic. She didn't hear the *clicking* and *smacking* of shoes on the sidewalk as the mob walked from one end of the city block to the other. Instead, she heard nothing. Saw nothing. Sabrina started to wonder if she herself was nothing, as everything around her had become.

Was this death? It certainly could have been, given the silence of it all. But when? How? Sabrina remembered being on the street, heading toward the corner. She needed to get to a building a few blocks over for an appointment, and she was late. She was running… did she trip and fall? Did she dart out into traffic and get hit? She wondered if she might have remembered something if that had happened. A flash of light or the screeching of tires, maybe. But she couldn't remember anything other than being on the sidewalk.

Did people just drop dead?

Sabrina's breathing hitched, startling her. She didn't have the impression she was breathing at all, especially with the concept of death floating around in her head. She tried to take a deep breath but couldn't.

She tried again but got even less air in her lungs than before. She gasped, beginning to feel starved of air, like she was choking. She *was* choking; something in her mind affirmed it. She was lying on the city street choking while people walked by, too busy to stop and help her. An old lady was sitting on the ground with her, holding her head up and shouting for someone to get help. A homeless man ambled over to look at her with morbid curiosity shining in his eyes. He gazed lasciviously at her legs, more of which was showing as her skirt was hiked up from the fall. He wanted to touch her and he would as soon as no one was looking. Saliva dripped from his discolored lips and onto her heaving chest. Her purse garnered that reaction; the bum had hit the jackpot.

Sabrina gasped again, trying to suck in elusive air that stubbornly blew away from her. It moved the hair on her forehead and chilled the sweat that glistened on her face, but wouldn't travel to her lungs, wouldn't give her sustenance. A scream pushed through her closing throat, forcing its way out into the air to cut at it for its betrayal. As it crescendoed from her diaphragm with all the force she could muster, Sabrina's eyes flung open. The sound of her scream echoed loudly off the walls of her darkened bedroom, surprising her with the intensity of it; the sound of her fear was raw and shrill. And then there was silence.

The radio Sabrina had left on had been turned off and though she found that odd, it wasn't the only thing that caught her attention. Kramer, her golden retriever, sat on the floor at the foot of her bed. He rose up on his haunches to look at her as she sat up, jarred from his sleep and desperately wanting to return to it. Sabrina looked at him, love filling her up as his sleepy eyes blinked slowly and he rested his head on the mattress.

"Kramer," Sabrina whispered, her voice thick from sleep and emotion, "What are you doing here, sweetie?"

Kramer blinked again, even slower. A tear cascaded down Sabrina's cheek.

She heard the top step creak under the weight of a foot and smiled. She knew what he was going to say before he said it and was tempted to recite the line for him.

"Honey, what are you doing up?" Jeff started, as he always did on Saturday nights. "I thought you'd be asleep by now. I fell asleep downstairs." Jeff leaned down to kiss Sabrina on the forehead. She raised herself up to meet his lips as tears streamed down her face. She wanted so badly to turn the light on, to see Jeff and Kramer without the obstruction of shadows, but she knew she couldn't.

She never could.

Maybe this time will be different, she told herself. *This time I choked first.*

Jezebel

Her hands rest upon my back to strum my spine like the strings on a carved maple upright bass. I wonder what sounds she will conjure when her nails pierce my skin.

The Bathroom Door

It was closed.

It wasn't when I walked by it this morning, but it is now.

Both of the cats are in here with me, have been since I rolled out of bed and schlepped into the baby room turned office once the divorce was settled. Normally I would have yelled downstairs to Marty to ask him if he'd closed the door for some reason. He would have come upstairs to see what I needed, claiming he couldn't hear me from downstairs (and, of course, he'd take a minute to berate me for yelling into the vent). I never bought that line. If he couldn't hear me, then why did he come up? That was what damned him the times he chose to ignore my calls, what damned him after all was said and done.

Normally, I would call out and ask Marty if he'd done it, but I couldn't anymore. There was no Marty to call. Marty was gone.

"Sonofabitch," I muttered under my breath. This was yet another thing that Marty had stuck me with. The house, all three floors of it, and every stick of furniture. The cars. Most of the money. He left me everything, told me I could have it all if I'd just let him go. He didn't even have a chick on the side, didn't have any place in particular to run to. He just wanted to get away from me. "Fuck him," I said, a little louder this time. Jean, one of my cats, raised her head and looked at me with sleepy eyes. I regarded her, taking in her black and gray coat, her green eyes. She stared back in silence, in scorn. "And fuck you too." She laid her head down and closed her eyes in response.

The computer was on, but I wasn't looking at it. It was always the same old thing – chatting in groups, playing internet games. Who gives a fuck? Marty could have taken it with him; he was the one who got more use out of it anyway. But I guess he wouldn't have, would he? It reminded him too much of me.

Bastard.

I trudged into the hallway and started down the stairs, but the bathroom door – pulled to, but not quite closed – bothered me again. I squinted my eyes and stared at it, trying to remember if I got up in the middle of the night and closed it after using the bathroom, or if one of the cats might have rubbed themselves against it and pushed it closed. Maybe, but unlikely. I never shut the inside doors, hell, I don't even pull the shower curtain across after I've gotten out. I always feel like something's behind it, lurking there, waiting to catch me unaware. And wouldn't the cats have shut themselves in if they had rubbed against it? A quick glance into the office proved they were both in there, their green and yellow eyes staring out at me accusatorily, pityingly, perhaps. I looked back at the door and sighed.

Marty used to make fun of my fears, used to concoct little ghost stories just to freak me out. I'd jump and shake and tell him to stop and he'd laugh, a great hearty sound, beautiful and condemning at the same time. But then he'd wrap his arms around me and pull me close. He'd swear he wouldn't let anything hurt me. Ever.

Right.

My hands were sweaty as I approached the door, its gold knob glistening against the bone backdrop. Images of ghosts flooded my mind, the dead swathed in rotted clothing, their faces melted as though acid had gotten to them, their eye sockets nothing more than black holes, their mouths gaping maws ready to bite at my living flesh. I didn't hear Jean jump off the chair and walk into the hallway. All I could hear was the incessant moaning of the dead, calling out my name to join them in Hell.

Jean purred as she rubbed against me, startling me so badly, I leapt from the floor. Her delicate *meow* enraged me more than soothed so I kicked at her, pushing her away. Her hissing was background noise as I put my hand on the doorknob.

It was cold to the touch, the kind of cold you feel when your leg presses onto the plastic mattress of a waterbed in the winter, the kind of cold you could feel in your bones. I yanked my hand away as though burned and lurched backward. I looked down at Jean who seemed to stare at me with eyes that could bore through stone. And then the door called me back to it, beckoned me to look at it. It seemed to pulse, to writhe ever so slightly, like an enthralled lover might from the touch of her intended. It rolled from top to bottom in an effortless wave. I stepped toward it, my hand outstretched, wanting, needing to touch it, to have it ripple beneath my hand as Marty once had when I touched him on his special spot. I could see him, could feel him bucking against me when I found it, when I teased, when I drove him to the point of release. I used to make him moan like a boy toy, but now all I make him do is run.

I opened my eyes, not remembering when I had closed them, and saw the door beginning to open, slowly widening the blackened mouth behind it. I gasped as I pulled my hand away again. A breeze from the bedroom window chilled the sweat on my forehead and back, cooling it much as the doorknob had my hand moments before, making me feel numb, rubbery, dull. The hand before my face hardly looked like my own, but I knew it was, its color paled to gray, the veins seeming rigid and firm.

Jean looked away from me, but I didn't notice. She smelled the air from the bathroom with her lips parted and her ears pert. Carmine, my other sleepy head cat, joined her in the hallway, casting a quick glance at me before sniffing around the bathroom door. But I didn't notice that either. Carmine and Jean nosed their way into the bathroom as I turned away in what felt like slow motion. I ran down the steps with the sound of lapping ringing in my ears.

Office Visit

"Does it really have to come out?"

"Sally, I suggest all four come out, not just the one. You're just going to have the same problem in three months. Look," the dentist said as he motioned to the x-rays posted on the light board. "The top two teeth have erupted. The bottom two are covered by your gum. Don't you feel the top tooth pressing into the bottom when you chew? I can see the indentions myself."

Sure I felt it. I just didn't want to admit it. I'd been having pain when I ate on and off for four years. I knew full well that something was wrong with my wisdom teeth. I just hadn't done anything about it and wouldn't have if my gums hadn't become so enflamed and sore I could hardly open my mouth the day before. As a public speaker with engagements on Thursdays and Saturdays for the next five weeks, I can't afford to have that happen again.

"I'm amazed you've been able to last this long, frankly," Dr. Crammerton continued in the same chastising voice he used on me when I was a kid. I could almost quote his next sentence for him. "You can't possibly be flossing back there," he said, as I knew he would. "I can't see how you'd be able to slide the floss between the tooth and back wall of your mouth. The tooth is pressing almost flush."

Always with the flossing.

"So we're going to take out all four today and wrap this thing up. No sense in you coming out here twice for the procedure to be done on the other side."

I must have looked confused because he continued, "That's what would happen, you know, if you only pull the one. In three months you'd be back with the same problem. It's better we to get it done all at once, especially since you'll be going to sleep for it."

There it was. So he was going to put me out. I was terrified of the whole thing—the pain I was experiencing, the needle, the yanking of my poor teeth out of my head where they meant to stay forever—all of it scared me. But being knocked out was the worst of it. Everyone always told me that it was like going to sleep, that you rarely dreamed. Even Dr. Crammerton had launched his spiel about it, and soon Colette, his dental assistant, would reiterate the speech. It's all designed to calm me down, I know, but they don't understand. It's more than just getting the needle — which, trust me, for a chicken like me, is scary enough. It's being put to sleep. Forced to close my eyes, forced to be oblivious. Even in my sleep I can hear the sounds of my house settling or my cat shifting positions at the foot of the bed. But here, they were about to knock me out so that I didn't know anything. Sure, I didn't particularly want to feel or, God help me, *hear* Dr. Crammerton wrench my teeth out of my gums, but to be completely unaware of it at all didn't sit well with me.

There was something horribly wrong with the concept.

I had a concussion once. I fell down the stairs at school. Well, really, I was pushed. I was talking to my girlfriends and not paying attention. This girl — Janice Pembrose, the bitch — was pissed that her boyfriend had a crush on me. I knew he liked me but didn't do anything about it. Ricky wasn't my type, to put it nicely. Anyway, Janice saw her chance and shoved me when I wasn't paying attention. My head hit the floor at the bottom of the steps. Hard. They said I was unconscious for three minutes. It was the worst three minutes of my life. There was darkness, thick like wool: impenetrable. I was suspended in it, walking on it as thought it was a solid floor, surrounded by it. Voices called to me almost instantaneously, shouting my name in different tones and inflections. They weren't the voices of my girlfriends who were gathered around me, their tears dropping onto my face like rain. They were voices that I knew somehow were otherworldly. They were haunted, ethereal, urgent. Some sang my name, other shouted it. All of them beckoned me to them, to walk in the impalpable darkness and find them. I almost went. Underneath the eerie tones, I heard the voice of my grandfather who had died only two months before. He called to me, his voice, the beautiful husky sound I remembered, tinged with the slightest of Creole accents. And I almost went to him. My imagination, my desire to see him again, softened the tones of the less frightening voices, made the ones with an odd lift on the second syllable of my name less alarming, made me less aware of the chill down my spine. I imagined that the people calling me were relatives that I had never met, people from as far back as the beginning of time. A family reunion, that's what it was. The gang all came to see me.

That's when I began to wonder if I was dead. Had the fall killed me? Had I broken my neck at the bottom of the stairs, my open eyes staring at the crowd of students that surrounded me, gawked at me? How did Janice feel? Was she happy? Scared? Sorry? I never saw the creatures as they came for me, hunchbacked and deliberate, grabbing on to my outstretched arms that held up my groping hands. I was too caught up in the notion that I had died. By the time I saw their faces, like leather masks made from the skins of animals with jagged cuts oozing puss, blood, and discharge, I was already in their grasp. They ushered me forward. I tried to escape but it didn't matter. Their strength was indomitable. Their hands, hot like fire and as tight as a vice, clamped onto my skin and held me firm.

The darkness lightened to a brown-influenced shade of black and I was able to see a chair, a grand throne upon which sat the most heinous being I have ever laid my eyes on. His eyes were upside down in his blotchy face. His skin was jaundiced and wrinkled, seeming to tear away from the muscle at the hairline and the base of the nose. He didn't have any hair and his bald head was coated with blood like a gel cap. His smile was accentuated by long jagged teeth. One of his legs was that of a horse, strong and muscular, though misplaced on his human frame. His other leg was as hairy as a bear's. The scepter he held in his hand glistened, supporting a murky crystal knob upon which he rested his hand. I could have sworn I saw something move within it, swimming in circles as though lost.

He grinned as I screamed, his eyes dripping bloody tears of glee every time he pushed out the sound that seemed to ring inside my very mind.

And then I woke up. I was in the nurse's office by that time, waiting to be picked up by an ambulance and taken to the hospital. I was shivering and I remember that my friends called the nurse over, afraid that I was having a convulsion. But that wasn't it. The cold hand of the devil in my mind had reached out to caress my cheek as I lay awake in the real world.

The chill of the dream never went away. It still haunts me from time to time. Especially when I sleep hard and late into the day. He is always there, leaning closer, always with his hand outstretched.

He wants me.

Only me.

I wish the smile the plays at the corner of my lips at the thought wasn't there.

"…ok? Just a few minutes now. Relax."

I hadn't realized Dr. Crammerton had given me the needle already. He held my hand as the medicine did its job, the sweet elixir that would keep the pain at bay taking control.

This time he didn't wait for me to fall into the oblivion that was his domain.

Dr. Crammerton's smile, jagged, bloody, and vicious, bid me goodnight.

Shadows

Day turned to night as I sat in the room staring at the walls, never moving, not even to use the bathroom. My bladder was screaming and my back hurt from the pressure on my tailbone, but I remained still. I hadn't had anything to eat except for the bunless hotdog he left me. I ate it after it had already gone cold, after the oil that had bubbled from within it to sit upon the skin like little drops of sweat had solidified into dollops of fat. I ate it, but I vomited it back up minutes later, never raising a hand to wipe the chunks of meat from my chin.

Shadows do weird things on the walls as the light changes. I didn't know that before, but I do now. They move with the wind, along the windows of passing cars. They make branches look like the crooked fingers of a skeleton, make a fern that beautifully adorns a corner look like a menacing intruder. I wonder what I look like in the shadows. Do they soften my looks or give them an unnatural edge? Do they show the truth or do they lie for me in a way that harsh light never would?

When he comes back tonight I won't speak to him as I usually do. I will, instead, let him peer at me through the shadows and be amused by his reaction to what he sees.

The Coming

The women moved quickly through the dark and winding corridor towards the reservoir entrance. Their long black robes dragged along the floor, tracing their paths in the dust, smearing the blood that fell from their legs. The woman in front, an old woman with salt and pepper hair, and sallow, wrinkled cheeks peeking out from under the black hood, stopped in front of the metal door and closed her eyes. Swaying slightly, with her arms outstretched, she mouthed a prayer. Her hands traced the letters of the sign rhythmically, spelling 'Echo Dam and Reservoir, Employees Only'. The younger woman, not much older than twenty, nervously crossed herself when the old woman finished. Without a sound, the women entered the pump station. As they made their way to the supply, the door shut behind them, as though pushed closed by the air.

Slowly, deliberately, the two women moved, turning the tight valve in unison and opening the duct. The old woman dipped her hand in the clean water, letting the droplets fall between her fingers. She brought her wet hand to her lips as she looked at the running water ruefully. After minutes of concentration, she looked at the young woman and nodded slowly. The young woman took an ampoule out of her robe and opened it over the duct. With shaky hands, she poured the solution into the water. The old woman lifted her head to the ceiling, her eyes filled with tears of resignation.

"It is done," the old woman rasped.

Brad Foster and Charlie Dixon would never be able to explain what happened that day. The reservoir was usually quiet and uneventful; perfect for their games of 5-card stud and porno magazines. Sometimes they would work on a 5th of Jack to pass the shift away. Nobody cared because nobody knew. Brad had been working at the reservoir for 20 years, Charlie, 14, and there had been only a handful of visitors on their shifts since the beginning. Nobody cared and nothing ever happened at the reservoir.

Brad trudged slowly down the darkened hallway to the pump room. He fumbled in his pocket, looking for the key. His vision was blurred - they were halfway through the Jack with a Budweiser chaser. Brad pulled the contents of his pocket out. Some change fell to the floor as he sifted through it. Brad groaned as he bent at the waist to pick up the change. He leaned against the wall on his way up, feeling queasy.

"Shit"" he mumbled under his breath, steadying himself.

He put the change back in his pocket and put the key in the keyhole, releasing the lock. As the door started to open, he brought his hand to his face. Bright red blood glistened in the light.

"What the hell?"

Brad frowned over the blood, rubbing it between his fingers. Shrugging, he wiped his hand on his shirt.

Brad opened the door wide enough to walk in, his eyes trained on his shoes, riveted by the bend of the leather with each step. The women were standing in front of him, side by side. They looked at him blankly as he entered the room. As he shut the door, he noticed them. Terror rose in his throat as the women stared at him, through him, with pupils as dark as ebony and as big as almonds. They seemed to be, almost, floating.

Brad shouted loudly as he ran out of the room. The slam of the metal door echoed through the basement. He shook as he locked the door and ran toward the stairwell.

"Charlie! Charlie!"

"What?"

Charlie staggered over to Brad. He burped loudly and laughed at his friend.

"You look like you done seen a ghost."

"I might have."

"What are you talkin' about?"

"There's two women in there," he wheezed, trying to catch his breath. "They don't have no eyes."

"What?" Charlie exclaimed in awe. "That ain't nothin' but the liquor talkin'. Got you thinkin' you seein' chicks with no eyes."

"They're in there, man. I ain't that drunk."

Charlie looked at Brad's sweaty face. He was obviously shaken, but by what?

"How could broads be in there? We got the only keys."

"See for yourself. I locked them in there."

"Alright. C'mon."

Charlie started down the hallway. Brad didn't move. Charlie turned and saw Brad

standing in the stairwell.

"Ain't you comin'?"

"I ain't goin' back there. You go."

Charlie shook his head as he walked down the hall. "Chicken shit," he said under his breath.

Charlie tried the doorknob, but the door was locked. He took out his key and unlocked it. He hesitated for a second and looked back at Brad, seeing his shadow sitting on the steps.

Charlie took a deep breath and pushed open the door. A strong gust of wind whipped past him, knocking him into the metal door so hard, he imprinted it. Seconds later Charlie screamed. The sound of whirling wind filled the basement and then it was silent.

"Charlie?"

Brad reluctantly walked slowly down the hallway to the pump room and found Charlie on the floor clutching his back.

"What was that?" Charlie gasped. Brad shook his head as he stood in the doorway. The blood was gone.

It snowed the next day. In the middle of August, a cold front as strong as winter in Antarctica moved over the East Coast, dropping snow that was measured in feet instead of inches. Even Florida was covered in the cold wetness. The kids in Florida ran outside dressed in shorts and sneakers, throwing themselves in it, loving every minute of the unexpected downfall. Their parents stood staring at it, then at the sky wondering how — why — it came to be. The ones who played lived to see day turn to night. The ones who didn't die after their morning coffee, after showering, after eating breakfast.

The ones who were left, knowing no better, ate, drank, drowned their sorrows. Not waking up to the next morning didn't seem so horrible a prospect anyway, given all they had lost. When taking his last breath, Brad felt that way. As his legs grew numb and his hands stilled, he wondered if Charlie felt the same way.

Noon

Orange. That was his favorite color. He wore it the day they caught him. An orange shirt, more melon than the color of Florida's finest, beneath a brown blazer and Khaki pants. Mom gave him that shirt a couple of Christmases ago. It worked for him, that color. It always seemed to match anything he combined with it: tan, brown, green, black. It was covered with blood the last time I saw it, brownish red where the drops had landed.

Orange. An odd color for a man to fancy. At least that's what I think. But he liked it from the very beginning, almost as soon as he knew how to walk. I remember that he picked that color out of all the flashcards Mom showed him, learning how to say that word first, or at least some variation of it. 'O ran' was what he called it until he was four. I still think of it as 'o ran' when I see it. I can't get it out of my head.

They say he'll come for me but I don't believe it. How could he? I'm his brother, the only one he's got left. It was he and I against the world before all hell broke loose. Before the rain that drew smoke from the ground like mist. Before they came. It was just he and I, out here alone. Both our parents were dead and there wasn't any other family to speak of. I didn't have a girlfriend and him, well, the supposed love of his life left him a month or so ago. We only had each other. How could he do to me what had been done to him?

Corey was at work when it happened, sitting in his office, minding his business much like I was on the floor above him. We both sat in cubes, were both on the phone with customers when they came, were both thinking about what we were going to eat after the call. I know that's what he was thinking because we always thought alike. It was foolproof. If I was thinking about a ball game, so was he. If he was thinking about fishing on the Chesapeake on a Saturday morning, you'd better believe I was mulling over the same possibility. They said twins were like that, but we had five years between us. We always joked that Mom had the longest labor known to man: the second twin came out five years later.

Maybe Corey was thinking about lunch and maybe he wasn't. There's no way to know for sure, but I think he was. I'd bet everything I had that he was. It makes me feel better thinking that he was, that we might have been in tune one last time. So I'll go with it. There's no one left to disprove my theory anyway.

Corey's office didn't have windows so he couldn't see them coming, couldn't see what was happening. Mine did. I remember looking out at the noonday sun and thinking that it looked a little strange, like a widow's veil was draped over it. It was bright outside, sure, but not the same kind of bright you get at noon in the middle of August. It was muted somehow. Strange, but not enough to pull me away from my conversation. I looked out a minute or so later, silently wishing the West Coast would wrap it up—I hated getting on calls with them. Their 9:00 a.m. was my 12:00, and while they sounded fresh and ready to begin their day, I was already over it. I remember that I pitched my pen across my desk when one of the project managers asked yet another erroneous question.

When I looked out at the street below the second time, I didn't see people walking to lunch or talking at the outdoor café on the corner. Instead, I saw things chasing people down and attacking them. Cars blocked the intersection in a maze of accidents. People backed up or plowed forward, trying to push through the stopped cars. They were panicked and suddenly so was I.

They're hideous, those things, with discolored skin that seemed to fall from their bones in putrefied globs. Their faces were human, but almost indiscernibly so. Some of them had skin that had all but rotted away, leaving their all too white skulls exposed to the sun. Others had smooth skin that was intact for the most part, save for the rips at the corners of their mouths and the base of their chins caused by reanimated jaws. All of them walked with stiff legs, bumbling lurching movements that seemed easy enough to dodge from the safety of my cube. It was an altogether different thing to be down there with them, though. Fear alone would paralyze you, as it did the people I saw being mangled.

The beasts clenched people in their rigid hands and drew them close. Their gaped mouths must have smelled like death itself, fouled by the earth within in which they had lain. They bit people in the neck, in the temple, in the eyes, taking the supple flesh into their mouths and devouring it, chewing and chewing with teeth that were so loose they soon fell from their mouths. I watched people die from my office and I was powerless to do anything, unable to move at all.

I don't know how long I watched in open-mouthed fear; I don't know how long my phone line was silent except for the grunting and gnashing of teeth. All I know is that when I got my wits about me I called Corey. He needed to barricade himself somewhere before whatever the hell was outside made its way in.

Corey's phone rang but no one answered. My heart dropped as I dialed two, three, four more times. The thought never occurred to me that he could have already left for lunch. Even if it had, that wouldn't have stopped me. Being out to lunch could have been as dangerous as being inside unaware.

In that instant—when the incessant tone of the phone ringing was about to drive me mad—I decided to go to Corey's office. Going out of my cube, my office, and into the hall was almost unfathomable, was sheer suicide, but I had to do it. I couldn't let them have Corey. He was my little brother. He was all I had in the world.

I didn't know what to do if I encountered one of those things. None of what the people outside had tried seemed to work, and that included running them over with cars. I hadn't stopped to think of a plan. I hadn't thought much of anything except getting to Corey. As an afterthought I grabbed a letter opener. It felt insufficient in my hands as I inched along the wall of in my office space, exposed and vulnerable.

My boss's office door was closed and locked. I vaguely remember him calling out for people to come in, to hide. I wondered how many of my colleagues were holed up in there, cowering, whimpering, crying in fear. I would be in there too were it not for my brother. I had to help him even if I died trying.

Corey was only one flight down so I took the stairs. Of the two methods for getting there, I thought the stairs might be the safer bet. God help me if I was trapped in the elevator with one of those things. At least on the steps I would have room to fight (or run) if I had to.

The sound of the door on Corey's floor opening was obscenely loud. I imagined a bunch of those things lifting their heads at the sound, smelling the air like dogs. The letter opener felt slick in my clammy hand.

Silence. Only the sound of someone's radio, its tinny broadcast distorting in the distance, could be heard. I didn't have time to think about what the silence meant, couldn't think about the fact that everyone—all 65 techies and support staff—was probably dead, that the pretty receptionist with the brown hair and piercing black eyes that I had finally gotten the nerve to ask out on Friday had probably turned into one of those hideous things, one of those horrible creatures that seemed to have taken over D.C. and who knows where else. I couldn't think about that. All I could do was think about getting to Corey.

His office was down the hallway and to the left. I made it there without an encounter (I half expected to be met by a slew of them, all reaching at me with mangled hands). I called for him over the tops of the cubes, whispering at first, then yelling as loud as I could. I went to his cube and looked. It was empty. I looked into every cube in the row. I opened the conference room doors and banged on the ones that were locked. Nothing.

"Corey!" I yelled one last time, fear and anguish overtaking my voice, choking it into a sob as I walked back to his cube. I leaned against his desk for support and let the tears flow. He was gone. Dead. My little brother. My best friend. I couldn't stop the tears even if I wanted to.

In a tear-induced blur I saw orange streak in front of my face, pass the cube I was in, then come back to block the doorway. I blinked my tears away and immediately wished I hadn't. Corey stood in front of me, the light gone from his eyes, a dull pallor on his face. He was dead. He had been bitten in the soft flesh of the temple. The wound was fresh, blood dripped from it and onto the shoulder of his shirt.

Having found Corey, I know that I was supposed to. I had no choice in the matter. The movies say he'll come for me, that he only knows the desire to feed. But I don't think so. Not my brother.

Corey stood there staring at me as I cried for him and for myself. I wonder what he was thinking when I plunged the letter opener into my right temple.

Patty

Patty cowered in the corner, unsure of what to do. She could hear him coming but felt stupid running away. She didn't know what kind of mood he was in, she never did. Maybe he felt like hitting her, maybe he felt like insulting her, maybe he felt like shouting obscenities, or maybe he would only stare at her in disgust. She didn't know which scenario was worse. Every time she thought she was seeing him at his angriest, he would come back with two times the intensity. She never knew what to expect, and it frightened her. He'd stomp around the house and throw things at the wall. He'd make a whole lot of noise, but that wasn't the scary part. Nor was the endless yelling and shouting and harping and belaboring. He was the master of beating a dead horse. But none of that was what frightened her. It was the look in his eyes that really got to her. A silent, slow-burning hatred that had been there for years, growing more intense every day.

She wondered if she saw it there—that look—when they were dating. It may have been there from the beginning, but in her love-struck ignorance, she might have missed it. There was always some major fault he saw in her, even then. If it wasn't the way she chewed her food, it was the way she dressed. If it wasn't the way she dressed, then it was the way she walked. If it wasn't this, it was that. There would always be something that he didn't like, couldn't stand, didn't know if he could live with. He never said that kind of stuff outright back then. He would allude to not liking a particular outfit, or hairstyle. Of course, being in love and wanting desperately to please her mate, she would change her hairstyle, or give away the dress that he didn't like to make him happy. She was determined not to let anything come between them, especially something that she could easily rectify. As time went on though, there were things that he didn't like that she couldn't change, like her voice, or her height. Little things. Things that sound almost comical when you hear them. He didn't like the way her voice took on a rich alto glide, kind of like the sexy voice of Anita Baker. He thought she sounded too much like a man. Patty would joke that he should have asked another woman to marry him, maybe Olive Oil would do the trick. She never forgot the icy cold look he gave her at that remark.

Another thing she would never forget was what happened the weekend before they got married. Two days before the wedding, they drove to Hampton to meet up with his parents. She was so excited. She and her soon-to-be mother-in-law went off in their own little corner of the house to whisper about the upcoming events. They settled in the next room and cracked the door open so that they would be able to hear if one of 'the boys' was trying to sneak a peek and listen to what they were saying. A couple of minutes later, voices that were both boisterous and joyous emitted from the other room. At first, she wasn't paying attention to them. She was engrossed in the fantasy of her upcoming wedding. But the sudden drop in tone made her listen. She didn't know at the time what was making her eavesdrop, but she knew that she had to do it. Something was making her do it. She heard her fiancé say to his father the phrase that lingers in her mind to this day, almost two years later.

She heard her soon-to-be husband say, "Dad, I'm not sure I'm doing the right thing here. I mean, I'm just so tired of her bullshit that I don't know if I should do this. Look at her! She's the most plain-Jane girl I've ever seen in my life!"

She remembered standing there, her feet glued in place, in shock. She had been thinking that, in the next few days, she was going to have the best day of her life. That's what every woman thinks of their wedding day. She was going to marry the man she loved more than anything in the world. She hadn't listened to that little voice in her head, the one that told her she was ugly and stupid, mediocre and simple. She had ignored that little voice, the one that whispered things to her at all the wrong moments. The one that told her what to do and how to behave. The one that she usually trusted. That little voice in her head told her that she wouldn't be allowed to have a fairy-tale wedding, or a fairy-tale life, for that matter. It told her that no one would ever love her the way she thought they should. No one. But she didn't believe it. She thought things would be different. Like her mother used to say, when she was sober, that was, 'That's what you get for thinking.'

As she sat dumbfounded next to her soon-to-be mother-in-law, who was pretending she didn't hear anything, Patty scolded herself. 'It shouldn't have been a shock', that mysterious, cynical, mean-spirited voice chimed in her head, the sentiment seeming to reverberate from ear to ear, 'You were forewarned.' Still, she couldn't believe it.

She was crushed. His words put her in tears. She explained them as pre-marital jitters when his mother asked her what was wrong. *Could she really have not heard?* His mother seemed genuine in her concern. Patty began to doubt herself then, like she always did. *Did I hear what I think I heard?*

Patty decided to lay down upstairs. She told herself that she heard him incorrectly. That it really was just a case of pre-marital jitters, and it was making her misconstrue his words. She talked herself into believing that everything was fine. It was an easy notion to accept when you factored in his behavior later. He hugged and kissed her in front of all his high school buddies that night, acting like the happy groom-to-be. He seemed proud to take her as his wife. So she talked herself into believing that her ears had played a trick on her earlier. He cuddled up as close to her as he could that night, and when they made love, when he made love to her, it was proof that he truly loved her, deep in his heart. And more than that, it proved that he was *attracted* to her. That's what she told herself. That's what she made herself believe. But over the months, through all the apologies, after all the roses had died, and after all the chocolate had melted, her mind's eye started allowing the rest of her to see what he was about. It revealed all the memories she had thrown in a mental lock box, like the way he had dominated her since the very beginning, and how he never considered her well-being in any situation. It was always all about him. The resurrection of these memories jarred her flowery sense of contentment. It jerked her into reality. It prompted her to do something about it. It prompted her to make a move.

He had a sharp temper. Sometimes he would come home and wage a verbal war with her for no apparent reason. He was quick, cold, and cutting. He knew all of her weak spots, and how to push all of her buttons. It was like sport for him. He would come home and insult her about anything: how she kept the house, or how she kept herself—let the games began. A game that only he could win. One way or another.

Patty tried to retaliate, to talk back, to stand up for herself. But none of that worked. He just ate it up. He said he liked a woman who would show a little spunk now and then. He told her that she never struck him as that kind of woman, but he welcomed her little outbursts. He would say that just before he smacked her into a wall or kicked her up the stairs towards the bedroom where he would continue to punish her for being a bad girl. He would force her into a corner and stand over her, spouting threats (she never knew if they were empty or if he fully intended to do the things he promised), and flailing his arms as though he were about to hit her again. She never knew what to do during those moments. Her mind told her to kick him in the balls as hard as humanly possible and run for dear life. Go to the kitchen, pick up a knife, get some money and her car keys, and leave the house. But that thought was always dissolved by the realization that if she ran, he could catch her. And when he did, that would be all she wrote. He would probably beat her to death and leave her body lying around on the lawn so that the neighbors could see how she died in disgrace. She knew that wasn't a rational thought, but she believed something similar to that would happen for sure. She knew that as well as she knew her own name.

So, more often than not, she cowered in the corner, the very same one she was crouching in then, and waited.

He was abusive. Both physically and mentally. She never knew which one she was going to get. If he had been out drinking, which he did often, she would get physically abused. He would come home frustrated about some game on television that he made a sucker's bet on with some drunk at the bar and take it out on her. He would smack her around a little, to make sure she knew her place, and then he would demand that she take off her clothes so that he could fuck her. It only lasted about two minutes from start to finish. He would push his way inside her, painfully splaying her legs and laying all of his weight on her stomach. He was oblivious to the shriek that escaped her as the friction of his erect penis rubbing against the flesh of her dry vagina chaffed her, or the tears rolling down her cheeks from the degradation. He'd hump her maybe ten times, and then pass out on top of her, blowing his sour-sweet smelling breath in her face: a combination of beer, vodka, and cigarettes.

She would lie still for a couple of minutes to make sure that he was completely knocked out, and then push his body off of her in disgust and dissatisfaction. Sometimes she would satisfy herself after his accost. Sometimes the idea of having him inside her aroused her senses. Sometimes. Most times it just made her feel like her stomach was welling with a greasy film and she wanted to throw up.

After he was finished doing his business and he lay next to her knocked out by the booze and the exerted energy, she would lie there in the dark, staring up at the ceiling and cry. Patty felt used, embarrassed, ashamed. She wanted to crawl into her own little shell and never come out. She hated him for it. For everything. But when he woke up the next morning, everything was peachy and rosy, and he acted like nothing had happened. No, it was more like he acted as if maybe he did something he shouldn't have, and that if he was extra nice and extra kind to her she would forget about the whole thing. He either ignored the situation, and made sure to stay out of her way, or he smothered her with flowers and dresses and shoes on some impromptu shopping spree. She saw right through it but didn't say anything. She kept thinking that maybe he really was sorry and that she was being unfairly judgmental of his actions. She would berate herself for not believing in him, and not being a loyal wife who never contested anything her husband told her. She would guilt herself into thinking that somehow, she *deserved* that kind of treatment, and that when he was nice to her, he was showing her unbelievable mercy. Mercy that she didn't deserve from him.

Her father had been that way with her mother. She remembered hearing him shout and break things. Most of all, she remembered her mother's helplessness. Her father would come into the house in a rage most nights, stemming from something that happened at work, or at the track, or anything that rubbed him the wrong way. She could tell from the moment he closed the car door whether or not he was in a bad mood. He would storm into the house calling for her mother. She would come out looking innocent, looking afraid. He wouldn't always hit her, no. What he would do instead was probably more damaging. He would slap her with insults about the tidiness (or lack of) of the house, about the laundry, about her appearance, about dinner, about the sun, about the moon, about the air. He would say anything he could think of to belittle her mother. He would reduce her to tears, but she would not, could not leave the room. She would not cover her face. She would not respond. She was like a caged prisoner that was bound and gagged and forced to hear the lecture from a warden or a prison guard. It was difficult to see her mother looking frightened to death, but not moving from the line of fire. To see her father with his huge, broad shoulders hulking over her like she was a small child terrified her to the core of her being and affected her throughout her life. She felt defenseless. There were so many times that she wanted to go to her mother. She wanted so desperately to help her get away from her father's fury, but she couldn't do anything. She was caught up in his trance as well.

Her mother died when Patty was fourteen years old. Her body (her shell) still walks around and talks to the people she comes in contact with. It still dances at parties, and drinks with the girls on Ladies Night Out. It still does all those things, but without a soul; without the essence of *her*. Her mother's soul died a long time ago at the hands of her father. The day her mother died pops into Patty's mind from time to time. It comes to her when she is frightened; when she thinks she is in trouble.

Patty's father came home one day after work. He was annoyed, she could tell that by the way he slammed the front door shut. Her mother walked slowly out of the kitchen and timidly said hello. She went to take his coat and hang it up for him, but he cringed away from her. She asked what was wrong and he slapped her so violently that her body was thrown into the china cabinet…and it came tumbling down. The crash was deafening. It reverberated through the house. But what was worse was the shriek her mother made when she was thrown. It was a high-pitched yelp, almost like a wounded animal's cry. Patty wanted to go to her. God, how she wanted to run to her mother and pick her up and take her to safety. The next-door neighbor's house, or even the corner store would do. Anything to get away from her father. But she was too afraid to move.

He seldom hit. He liked to cut with his words too much to diminish the intensity and sting with physical force. He used to always tell her that a person who settles matters with his hands is not a man but is an animal. He said that a person who could handle his or herself with their mind was far superior and would be the one who would evolve. He rarely abandoned that thought process. But when he did, he had good reason, at least in his mind. And there was hell to pay when he lost his temper. You'd better believe that. If he struck you with his hand, something must be seriously wrong. And there was no running from it, and no stopping it. It was going to happen one way or the other.

She hated to see her mother holding herself in a fetal position amidst the broken glass and china that was given to them for their wedding. She knew that the mess would prompt another beating later, before the bruises she was about to get could heal. Her mother would offer a meek apology for something or another, usually whatever she thought he wanted to hear, but it never worked. Nothing ever stopped him when he was like this. Nothing.

Her mother sat up to face him as he demanded. She was frozen. Her face was full of fear and distress. Her eyes called out for him to stop, to look at her and feel the love he felt when he asked her to be his wife. As he hulked over her and his ominous shadow crossed her face, something changed. Her eyes, which had always begged forgiveness, now pleaded with him to get on with it. To end it all for her in one fell swoop. To shit or get off the pot. And, in a way, he did.

Her father stood over her shaking mother who looked as if she were melting under his hot glare. She was so afraid to move. She waited, as she always did, for the next blow. It came. He hit her squarely on the side of her head, just under her temple. She fell sideways into the broken glass, cutting her right arm and leg. She yelled out in pain and begged him to stop.

Go ahead! Finish it, you bastard!

And he did. He stopped hitting her. He picked her up and carried her out of the glass. He dropped her heavily on the stairs and began screaming at her. He told her how much of a slut she was and how unfaithful she would be if he closed his eyes for just one minute. She asked him what he was talking about and he threatened her with his open hand.

"Shut up, or I swear I'll hit you so hard you'll wish you were never born," he yelled. She lowered her eyes and began to weep.

"You'd better stop all that crying. What kind of woman lets her man see her cry? A weak one, right? Well, I guess that's just what you are, isn't it? A weak, needy woman. I don't know why I married you. You aren't worth the ring you wear on your hand. The ring you and your stupid friends coo over. You ain't worth shit."

He paced in front of the stairs Patty's mother laid upon, broken and bloodied. Anger welled up from his diaphragm as he continued,

"You are nothing but a whore. I thought you might be the trophy wife I had been searching for. The one who would look pretty, yet say nothing. You certainly haven't turned out the way I had hoped you would. You are neither pretty nor obedient. Instead, you're wrinkled. Old, worn, and sassy. Just my luck.

"I have never wanted you, not even when you were young. You repulse me sexually. I wanted a woman who would do her duty and take care of my kids. But you wanted a job and I let you do it. Why not? It's not like you could ever make more money than I do or ever accomplish more. I figured you had to be good for something in your worthless existence. But I was wrong. No, the only thing you are good at is flaunting what little you do have to my colleagues and bringing shame to my good name. How dare you?"

Confused and afraid, she said, "What are you talking about? I have no idea what you mean. I have never flirted with anyone, you must know that."

"I don't know much when it comes to you, my dear. Sometimes I wonder if I should have my head examined for even continuing this farce of a relationship with you. The only reason I am still here is because it looks better in my profession to be a married man. Even if I can't stand the sight of my wife."

Her eyes gave way to her tears. She couldn't take the abuse anymore, and it was breaking her down. She tried to hold in her tears, to hold in her emotions. She had been trying to learn to do that ever since he started coming home in these rages. But it never worked. She always ended up sobbing and shaking. She was sure she'd be able to take another smack for it, but she couldn't stop.

"Go on. Cry. That's all you seem to do well, anyway. You and your family are just a bunch of paupers. All of you walk around with your hands out looking to get some spare change from a person who works hard for every dime. No, you may not be exactly like them, but the apple sure doesn't fall far from the tree, does it? All you ever want to do is whine about your job and the inequalities of men and women. What makes you think you should be equal? What makes you think that you have enough smarts, enough where-with-all, enough gumption, enough common sense to stand toe to toe with a man? Huh? Who ever told you that?"

He changed the subject often when he got angry enough. It was almost as if his mind was so full of hatred he couldn't decide what he wanted to lash out about next. He liked to badger her on a variety of subjects so he could make sure he beat her self-esteem down to nothing. Sitting on the stairs, her face drenched with sweat, she didn't have much self-esteem to attack.

Her mother wanted to shout back, to retaliate, to clear herself, but she fell mute. And maybe that was a good thing. When he was like this—so headstrong and stubborn, so irate—you never knew exactly what he was capable of doing. She sat in silence looking up at the man that she had married for better or for worse.

"Whoever told you that was lying, I will say that much. Get in the kitchen and cook my dinner, you worthless whore. And while you're at it, clean up this pigsty we try to call a house. You and that little bitch don't do anything in this house but eat the food I buy and sit around. Worthless. You were worthless when I got you, and you're teaching her how to be worthless also."

From her hiding place in the hall, Patty saw her mother's light diminishing. She didn't know what half the stuff her father said meant, but she could tell by the look on her mother's face that he said something damaging. Her mother looked like a wilted flower on its last legs of life as she walked into the kitchen to find something to use to clean the mess up. The light that had always shone in her eyes, even when he was being abusive to her flickered out that day, never to resurface. Not even after his death. Patty hated her father for breaking her mother spiritually and mentally. The woman that lived on was nothing like her mother. Nothing like the woman who had a positive outlook on life, who loved her unconditionally. What was left was a woman who barely knew where she was. A woman who didn't voice her feelings or her thoughts. A woman who cringed at the sound of a loud voice. She always blamed her father for the disintegration of her mother. He took her life in the blink of an instant, in the slice of a word.

Now, on the floor, in the corner of the bedroom she shared with her husband, with her knees pulled tightly under her chin, she knew that her light was gone too. She knew that she would never love the smell of freshly cut grass or feel the warmth of spring sunshine on her skin the way she once had. She knew that all the happy moments she would have from then on would be clouded with despair and fear, as her mother's life was. She felt trapped. It was the same feeling she had when she hid in the closet while her parents fought. She was afraid to get out of the closet and venture down the hall to her bedroom. She was too afraid her father would see her and turn his anger in her direction. She didn't have the courage to stand up in front of her father and shout at him to stop it. She could always feel the words welling in her gut while she cowered in the darkness. She could always feel them gurgling in her throat, threatening to come out. But she stifled them because she was too afraid. Too afraid of him.

Her mother always told her to be quiet when daddy yells, and to make sure she stayed in her room when mommy and daddy were talking loudly. She said that daddy had a bad temper and he might get mad that she was around. She said something like eavesdropping, and something about a child's place and some other catchy phrase that would pacify her for the time being. They never really worked. She just did what her mother told her to do because there was no other recourse. Disobeying mommy when it pertained to daddy could result in a whole lot of trouble that she didn't want. She was scared to death at the idea that her father could be angry at her. That meant he would shout at her the way he shouted at mommy…or worse. She felt like she would melt right into the floor if he looked at her with his black, menacing eyes. She was afraid. Then and now. She shivered as she heard footsteps coming up the stairs.

He'll kill me if he finds out.

The days grow colder and colder now. When she looks out of their bedroom window she sees nothing but gray in the bright sunlight. There's nothing but gray inside also. She hears angry voices shouting incoherently, as though they are trapped in the depths of her mind. Except one. There is one voice looming just under the surface, with horrifying clarity. Whispering cunningly, coaxing her to do unspeakable things.

She wrung her hands as she listened to the footsteps ascend. The car had pulled up just as she spilled the juice. It ran across the countertop and dripped onto the floor. She heard the garage door opening, creaking, signaling his arrival. The gentle hum of the motor cut off and the car door slammed shut. Frantically, she reached for a paper towel to sop up the mess that started pooling on the floor. Bright red trickles fell relentlessly on the paper towel, saturating it. The garage door slammed shut and she heard the paced footsteps, rhythmically approaching the basement door, as if in slow motion. Instinctively, she ran upstairs, trying to hide herself.

He'll kill me if he finds out.

Then she saw his eyes. Big and horribly bloodshot, as if someone had poured red dye into them. He saw the mess. He was not happy. Not happy at all.

Then there was nothing. The house was silent, except for the scratching sound of the tree branches grazing the window. There were no footsteps climbing the stairs and no irascible eyes threatening her. She was alone, cowering in the corner of the bedroom she shared with her husband. Her gentle, hard-working husband who was on a business trip in Florida.

Is he?

(you ungrateful bitch)

He had been gone for three days.

Is the trip really business, or pleasure?

(fucking bitch)

and she was supposed to be packed and ready to go when he got back. They were going to the beach for a week and he wanted to get on the road as soon as possible.

I'm leaving him.

(Do it)

She got up hesitantly, wondering if her mind was playing tricks on her. She couldn't tell if it was just trying to make her think the coast was clear when he was really waiting around the corner to pounce on her. She looked over at the packed bags on the floor. She had packed them herself, not five hours earlier. Still, she wasn't sure why she had done it, nor where she was going.

She peered around the door and saw nothing. Just an open hallway. She was alone. Alone except for that terrible whispering that echoed in her head.

She walked into the hallway feeling confused, but grateful that she had been mistaken. She turned to look at the grandfather clock in the foyer downstairs. It was almost 4:30 p.m. He would be gone for another day or so on a business trip. True to form, he would probably come home cranky. He was loud and belligerent when he was cranky.

Wouldn't he?

She decided that she wasn't going to stick around for it this time. She was going to leave. She was going to get up her nerve and leave him, like she had been telling herself to do for months (*had she?*)…but just for a little while. She couldn't leave him all together like the voice in her head kept telling her to do. She wasn't ready to start a life without him. She wasn't ready to be alone.

She went back into the bedroom they shared and packed some of her things, forgetting that she had already packed clothes for the beach vacation. She walked right past the vacation bag, pulled out an overnight carry all, threw a nightgown, shorts, underwear, and sandals in. She only wanted to scare him. She wanted to make him *think* that he was losing her forever. That way he would do everything he could so straighten up and try to get her back. At least, she hoped that would be his reaction.

As she packed she thought about the good times they had, like when he picked her up from work one day with roses in one hand and concert tickets in the other. He was so handsome, so stunning. She couldn't help but be swept off her feet. His beautiful brown eyes always seemed to see right through her. He would smile at her innocently, shy almost, like he was unsure if he should be so forward, even now. They had been married for a while, but he still had a timidity about him that was intriguing and captivating. It was part of his charm. He rendered her defenseless when he complimented her on her dress and then lowered his head, as if he was too bashful to look her in the eyes. She missed the times when he would kiss her so gently she questioned if their lips were even touching. He used to caress her feet after a long day at work. He would whisper in her ear about how much he loved her. He supported her decision to stop working so that she could stay at home and start a family. And when Michelle came along, Troy treated her and the baby like they were his most prized possessions.

Michelle. Their bundle of joy. She was a gift that rejuvenated their relation for a short time. That was until Patty realized that Troy cared more about the baby than he did about her. Michelle could do no wrong. She was precious: a gem. With him she was good, she smiled at him the first time, walked to him, said 'Dada' first. Daddy's little girl. For mommy, all she had was defiance, messes, vomit, and mischievousness. Didn't he hear that incessant crying in the middle of the night when she was an infant? Couldn't he see how she was warming up to him in an attempt to alienate her? Couldn't he see how manipulative she was? At two years old, that little girl knew exactly what she wanted and how to get it.

Something you used to know.

(ungrateful bitch)

Patty thought about Michelle sleeping in her crib/bed combo, surrounded by plush teddy bears – presents from daddy. She shuddered despite herself.

Troy used to love her the way he loved Michelle…once. As tears welled in her eyes, she realized that those days had been gone for a long time. She wanted them back desperately. She just didn't know if those times could be again.

(Or if they had ever ended)

She went into the garage and loaded up the car. It was unseasonably cold for October — with the wind whipping around, it felt like it could have been 10 degrees below zero. She could see the leaves blowing around her driveway from the little window in the one car garage door. It gave her a chill. She started the car to warm it up for the drive ahead. She wasn't exactly sure where she was going yet. She was having a mental tug of war with leaving him for good, or only leaving for the night.

And there was something else too. Something she was missing.

Or forgetting.

Life with Troy had been bittersweet. The ups were magnificent, yet few and far between. The downs had been more prevalent and damaging. They didn't fight like normal couples. They could never figure out how to have an argument, agree to disagree, and then end it. It just didn't work with them. Instead, they would yell and scream and rant and rave until he had enough. When he reached his saturation point he would hit her and she would be silent. From that point on the ball was in his court. Whatever he said went and nothing else could carry any weight. Depending upon how angry he got, he would hit her several times beckoning for her to tell him if she understood the rules of the house. His rules. She would say yes time and time again, but he would still beat her until he got tired. Then he would storm out of the house and do God knows what for a couple of hours. They fought like that a lot.

She closed the trunk and leaned against the car. The low, steady hum of the engine was soothing, and it lulled her into a daydream. She thought back to when they were in Jamaica walking along the beach, him in shorts, her in a short sundress. Looking out at the turquoise water and enjoying their love. They were so happy then. It was their first trip together, and they had been planning it for months. They were staying in a rinky-dink hotel, but it didn't matter to them. They just wanted some time to get away, to relax, and to learn more about each other. They made love for the first time on a secluded beach at midnight. They held each other under the stars and dreamt of their lives together. It was like a fairy-tale. One that didn't come true. She wiped the tears from her eyes and opened the car door.

She sat in her car unable to move for a while. She felt weak with despair and simple with love. The sun was going down, and a branch from a willow tree cast a shadow on the dashboard on the passenger side of the car. It was in the shape of an index finger. It pointed directly at her, either shaming her for staying so long, or shaming her for leaving.

(Or shaming you for Michelle)

"Shut up," she screamed aloud, covering her ears with her hands and rapidly shaking her head back and forth. She didn't know which one was true. All she knew was that she felt helpless and lost. She didn't know where to turn.

How long had she been sitting in the car? A minute? An hour? She guessed it had been even longer than that. It had been bright and sunny when she ventured into the garage, and now night was threatening its entrance. In the gray light of her car, she opened her diary and scribbled in it. There wasn't much to say, really. She expressed her indecisiveness daily to the pastel pages within that book. It was her only outlet. She couldn't yell back at her husband for fear of being beaten, so she used the diary as a sounding board. She couldn't express her feelings (love? hate?) to Michelle aloud anymore. She choked on the words. So she wrote them all down. The entries were usually very short and jagged. Her thoughts were rarely in eloquently phrased sentences. This time, the last time, was no different.

As the smell of exhaust filled the air thickly, she cried into her hands. She couldn't make herself move. She felt like she had nowhere to go and that she was worthless. The big family that she had when she was young was gone. They had died off or distanced themselves. Seeing each other only rekindled the memories and the rumors, so no one made an effort anymore. The last time she saw her family was when they gathered together for her Aunt Clairese's funeral. She was in her Aunt Clairese's house, trying to remain contained when she saw the thing that unraveled her. She and her aunt had never been close. They had never played together, or talked silly talk, or even taken walks in the park. All they had ever done was see each other at family functions or funerals. They would hug, talk for five minutes, and that would be all. There wasn't a tight connection between the two of them. But when she stood in Aunt Clairese's living room and saw an old picture of herself sitting on the very top of the mantel, dusted and clean, she buckled. The sofa caught her fall. She had never, not in a million years, thought that her aunt cared enough about her to think of her outside of when they saw each other at family gatherings. She thought that her aunt regarded her as just 'one of those relatives' that you could take or leave. She never thought that her aunt might actually care about her, that she might actually love her. Years of guilt engulfed her at the moment.

In the years after Aunt Clairese's death, the family broke apart. It wasn't a surprise, there was always a storm brewing underneath the facade of happy faces and family love. She hadn't seen her cousins in years, probably since the funeral. There was nothing to say, really. Whatever happened before they were born was too great to overcome. So everyone dropped the ball. They dropped the ball and kicked it in the corner.

All the friends she had a couple of years ago were gone. They moved on with their lives and rarely kept in contact. She missed the nights when she would go out drinking with the girls and checking out guys. They used to sit around and talk about nothing, but that was OK because it passed the time. She used to go shopping with Troy's sister Cheryl and they would stay out all day not buying a thing. That all ended when Troy told her that he didn't like Cheryl and Patty spending so much time together. He said that he never really liked Cheryl and didn't want her to be a negative influence on Patty. His own sister! She did what he wanted because she thought this was the man she would live with for the rest of her life. She did it for love.

That's what the voice told her to do.

Cheryl faded out of the picture without much of a fight. It wouldn't have mattered if she protested anyway, there was no changing the plan. If having Cheryl out of the picture would make Troy happy, then, by God, that's what she was going to do. She lost a lot of friends because of Troy. They either didn't want to be around her because all she ever did was talk about Troy, or Troy didn't want them around. She compromised her dignity to feed his ego. She geared her life toward making him happy and in the process, forsaking her own happiness. She wasn't doing things for herself anymore. Everything was for Troy. She lost her road. She also lost herself.

The voice in her head told her so.

The Blackout

Click. You almost feel like you hear it when the lights go out. At least you think you should. You imagine that the sound will be like the flicking of a light switch when you turn out the lights for the night. So that's what you hear when the lights go out unexpectedly on a weeknight at 8:21 p.m. when you're just getting into the movie you're watching, especially when it's not raining and the only electronic devices that are on are in the room with you, not the hairdryer upstairs or the computer in the office. Just the TV, the portable heater, and the halogen lamp.

Click.

"Oh!" Rich yelled, reacting to the sudden darkness. "That was the best part of the movie!"

"Yeah," Jessica said, trying to conceal how freaked out she was. The lights went out during a countdown to New Year's Eve in the slasher film they were watching, some low budget flick about a teen couple who get hacked up by a satanic cult at the stroke of midnight. The movie wasn't any great shakes, but it was more than a little eerie that the power shut off right before the count reached one.

They waited for thirty seconds for the lights to come back on, both of them holding their breath unconsciously. Nothing.

"Damn, they might be out for good," Rich said as he moved the drapes that covered the sliding glass patio doors aside to see if any of the other houses on the street had power. At least twice before the blackout had been theirs and theirs alone, a product of running everything electric in the house at the same time. But not that day.

"Yup, it's all of us," he said, confirming.

Jessica took a deep breath and let it out slowly through her parted lips. It wasn't that she was afraid, but there was something about being in a dark house, unable to see anything, that made her uneasy. Things that normally provided comfort like the love seat she curled up in on winter nights, seemed like ominous creatures lurking in the shadows, waiting for her to get closer, within its reach. And hallways were worse. She always imagined something waiting for her on the stairs, some infernal creature with bloody eyes and long fangs whose pointed tips touched the base of the thing's chin. It stood in the dark with its arms open, waiting for her to walk into its deathly embrace. She got chills just thinking about it. Because they were in the basement.

Rich bumped into the coffee table upon which sat an open bottle of soda and a box of pizza. "Shit!" he exclaimed, rubbing his stinging shin. "There goes dinner." His cusses fell on deaf ears. Jessica was still thinking about the dreaded walk from flight to flight and how she would get by the creature on the stairs.

"Here we go," she heard Rich say just before he turned on the flashlight, filling the room with a tannish glow. "And then there was light."

Jessica looked at Rich standing in the laundry room with the flashlight in hand and screamed loud enough for the neighbors next door to hear. With every contortion of Rich's face—his furrowed brow and squinted eyes when he asked if she was ok, his opened mouth, so much like a gaping maw, as his concern heightened— Jessica screamed louder. Circling Rich's head were creatures that looked like smoke at first, swirling as they took shape. Demonic heads, scarred with boils and slashes atop snake-like bodies writhed on either side of him, licking their serpentine tongues in his ears, on his cheeks and forehead. The more Rich talked the more he came to resemble a beast with horns that grew out of his brown mop of hair, bonish brown in color, and as sharp as a tack. Clumps of hair and blood adorned the points of the burgeoning horns, residue from the skin they had broken through. His eyes grew darker, the pupils widening until the eye was nothing more than a pit of blackness. His nose was split in two, the pink flesh of his nasal passage flayed. His mouth was a mass of jagged, pointed teeth.

Jessica screamed until she passed out, catching the reflection of her elongated countenance in his inhuman eyes. Slumping into an unconsciousness she prayed was permanent, she heard the multiple voices of a crowd yelling joyously,

"One!"

'Tis the Season

Police car lights and Christmas lights flash one in the same to me. Red. White. Blue. Red. White. Green. Blue. Against the wall, they're like two lovers at a dance having a spat: maybe she's irritated because he's flirting with the girl across the room, or maybe he's sick of dancing and wants to go somewhere to be alone, but she doesn't. The lights flicker, bouncing off one another in the strange ritual, pawing and pulling away at the same time.

Or maybe that's just the way I see it.

Muzak and Christmas carols sound the same. Both have droning voices to carry a fabricated happiness—the whine of a French Horn and the shrill screech of a Soprano Two share the same ear-piercing tone—the same patronizing cadence. Like hellions screaming from the depths of Hell, they shout their holiday wishes at you, their soothing façade in place to mask their Lovecraftian countenances.

I shudder as the two accost me—wretched Muzak and Christmas lights bound to puncture my flesh, spiraling toward me in a seductive and deceiving whirlwind. (Or is it Christmas carols and ambulance lights?) Someone's attempt at levity to celebrate the coming season, hanging garland and lights, ornaments with little pink angels and obese Santas all over the cube walls and in the lobby of the office. Folderol, to be sure. I'll have to find them—I bet Molly did it, that busybody— and share the image their effort conjures in my mind. I'll show them how close to laughing screaming can be.

Hell

The corner was dark but he rounded it swiftly, shutting his eyes to the demons that lay in waiting.

"Take me," his final cry.

Idol

"God, she's so beautiful. I mean, her caramel-colored skin and her shapely body are the most beautiful things I've ever seen. She's got these gorgeous pouty lips and a smile that has movie star written all over it. Her hair is always perfect, short cut and close, straight, soft, jet black. Damn.

"I look for her on magazine covers every day, collecting everything I can find that has her pretty face on it. She's everywhere right now; her career is finally heating up. Good for her! She deserves it. But better still, I'll get to see more of her. More movies, more interviews, more gossip online, more pictures. More her.

"She's my model. The image I am molding myself into. She's perfect in every way, and if I can achieve just a sliver of her beauty in myself, I've got it made. The guys around here will know what they've been missing the day I walk outside looking like a million bucks. They'll be sorry they ignored me.

"I've been tanning a lot lately, trying to achieve her pretty skin color. It's not going as well as I hoped — I've gone from beet red to a sickly looking brown, one that resembles over-cooked meat. But I'm going to keep trying. I'll get it right one day.

"I thought about selling everything I had to get collagen injections to make my lips fill out like hers do. Even doing that, I can't afford them, let alone the Botox, breast and butt augmentation, and nose job I would need. Hell, I can't even afford the fancy haircut. So I'm doing it myself. My lips won't be exactly like hers, but they'll be damned close.

"I bought the hair product she pushed a couple of years ago. The no-lye perm took my blonde locks out. But that's ok. I bought a wig that is cut in the same style she wears, shiny hair and tapered back too. Losing my hair was a blessing in disguise.

"The dentist told me it would cost over $400 to get my teeth capped like her, at a minimum, if I have insurance, which I don't. But my grandmother has Medicare and can get her dentures through them, so as soon as the teeth come, I'll yank mine out. I love how straight hers are. I can't wait to see mine like that.

"I've been trying to arch my eyebrows like she does, like a sideways pyramid is the only way I can think of describing them. But it never works. Mine are too thin and light, like the hair on my head. I tried dyeing them but they still don't come out right. So I shaved them off and I draw them on every day. Now they look just like hers.

"I stole some dresses, like the ones she wears, from the Five and Dime. I almost got caught too. At first I tried to press my body into them, trying to make myself fit. But she's a size six and I'm a size fourteen. I didn't want to ruin the clothes, so I started on this diet she said she uses. The bottle says you can lose 10 pounds in three days and sure enough, I did. I kept drinking it, day in and day out, trying to lose more, but the weight was coming off too slow for my taste. So I cut it off. Yeah, I 'cut the fat' so to speak. A little off the sides and the inside of my thighs. There was more blood than I expected though, and I passed out before I could finish. And then I woke up here."

Iris chewed the pill they had given her a moment before and sipped water from the small cup. Satisfied, the nurse walked away, on to the next patient awaiting their noon cocktail.

"You see," Iris continued, talking to no one in particular, "I need to finish up. I can get into that dress if I just shave a little more off my butt. It'll work. And then I'll look just like her."

Day By Day

It was him. It smelled like him, felt like him. I can hear him as he approaches, his footfalls as weightless as air, yet still apparent to my ears. I've always been a light sleeper. Why should that change in eternal rest?

He comes without speaking most times; his thoughts are words enough. His gentle touch is barely felt anymore; so far away is the soft skin of his hands as they search for something tangible, something real. He is delicate, sweet. He brings fragrant flowers and places them for me, knowing that only he will inhale their intoxicating smell. He brings chocolates on our anniversary, eating them before me in despair. He writes poetry, brings a radio and plays our favorite song; he does all of these things and laments later, unable to continue yet unable to stop. I listen to his cries, his silent sobbing. I feel his hot tears as they penetrate the earth to lie upon my exposed skin. He is confused, enraged, saddened; alone.

I coo words of encouragement that he can never hear.

He suffers so.

In front of my picture, he disrobes nightly, stroking himself to climax while my smiling countenance looks on. His last image every night is of my nightgown spread over my side of bed. He has kept it there as a reminder of me. He snuggles next to it some nights, curling it into his arms and nuzzling it as he would me on bitter winter nights. His does this as a matter of habit, not because he wants to. He'd like not to, in fact. He would rather rid himself of me the way he once did, to be done with me completely. But alas, he cannot.

The next day, after his dreams were filled with images of me, he starts the cycle again. He is most often weary; his sleep is rarely calm. His dreams are interrupted by flashes of silver edged with bright red in the noonday sun. Most nights he can feel the warmth of blood on his hands, on his face. Can taste the metallic tanginess of it on his tongue. In the middle of the night he would awaken to find his hand in his mouth, his fingers vainly scrubbing at his tongue, his nails scratching the flesh raw as he tried to rid himself of the blood. He would run to the bathroom, cup water from the faucet and drink from it in hearty gulps. He would roll the water around in his mouth and spit it out, repeating the process many times, trying to obliterate the taste. But it would never work. He would look, then, into his eyes as reflected by the bathroom mirror, made grimy by inattention. He would search them, plead with them to make it stop, to make it end. But it would be my eyes that would look back at him night after night. My eyes that would answer his unspoken pleas.

He's here again, twice today as usual after a particularly frightening night of terror. He is weeping again, wishing he could will himself to abandon this place, to leave and never come back. He wants to beg for his life to return to the solitude he once enjoyed, but knows he dare not utter such a request. It would be as fruitless as fighting fate. I will always be here. And he will always come to me. My blood sealed our pact for eternity.

As he pours a glass of Chardonnay, the crystal glinting a rainbow of colors off the golden rays of the sun, his apprehension, his fear, begins to drain. With his first sip, he wonders why tears dried on his cheeks, why the muscles in his shoulders were tense. Settling in for a visit with his one true love, he forgets the terrors that befell him the night before and is oblivious to the ones that will meet him later that night.

Another

It came again, pressing against the fatty lining beneath her flesh, dying to be let out, set free. But the flesh didn't give. Instead, it pushed, turned it, maneuvered it through the urinary track and out of the host into the cold world where it smoldered, cooled, then died. And yet, as its sister lay dead on the forest floor, waste tangled in the roots of dead trees, another pressed ever so slightly.

Maybe

Every time I blink I see it there, glaring back at me with eyes that glow white and features that are hazy, but make up a face, nonetheless. He's always been there, that guy behind my eyelids; the bastard who frowns, snarls, bites at me each time I blink. I'm tired of seeing him there, tired of his devilish grin as he laughs at me from the safety of my mind. Maybe they'll understand if I explain it to them that way, if I tell them it's not me who's insane, it's him. Maybe they'll believe me if I show them his heinous face.

Old Friends

I never liked them, those tracks. From the day we looked at the house, I had a problem with them. A beautiful house with almost an acre and a half of land surrounding it bordered by bulky train tracks. The tracks weren't dormant back then. In fact, a train ran on them every day until the early eighties. We had kids, for God's sake! They could have run out onto the tracks and been killed. Didn't anyone think about that when they planned the route, zigzagging it through residential areas up and down Rockland County? Apparently not. Either that or they didn't care.

Every once in a while there was a passenger train, but that was the rare occasion. More often than not the big, hulking machines that traversed those tracks hauled everything from produce to coal, moving ever so slowly, their wheels squeaking and screeching along the rusted tracks. Ridiculous. Some delivery somewhere needed to be made and the train had to take the route that brought it through our backyard while we slept, sometimes before 8:00 a.m. An afternoon train ran every Saturday, a little quieter than the morning line, but just as slow. And there was always a night train. That one seemed to creep up on the house, gray smoke billowing from its stack against the darkened sky, the scratching of the wheels sounding more like nails on a chalkboard cutting through the silence of night. Oh, that sound used to make me sick. The kids too. None of us ever really got used to it. For months after the rail was shut down we still heard the night train approaching, our minds triggering the sound we had heard for the better part of fifteen years instinctively.

The kids used to make the best of it. They would run to the top of the hill to meet the afternoon train when they heard the grunting and groaning of the heavy machine less than a mile away. They waved at the conductor as he passed by carrying his load. The conductor always waved back and offered a pleasant, toothless smile at the kids. He tipped his faded red cap at me and I couldn't help but wave back to him from the deck. His wide grin and straggly bearded face always drew a smile from me, even on the days when the sputtering and spitting of the train seemed at its loudest.

The same guy did the morning and afternoon runs. I remember feeling sorry for him; he was an older guy, had to be in his sixties back then. I didn't know how far the train went every day, but I did know that wherever it was going, he was taking it. What about his family? Did he even have one? He worked all the time, every day of the week. I wondered if he drove the night train too, eating meals in the cab, seeing life pass by through the grimy windshield of the car. What a life.

The kids took a liking to the conductor, Mr. Bill as we came to call him. I don't know if that was really his name or not, but that's what the kids called him so it stuck. Sometimes they would race to the deck dressed in overalls and donning a battered cap. Mr. Bill's smile would grow wider than before when he saw them dressed that way, carbon copies of himself minus the light film of dirt that always seemed to coat his face. He'd laugh and grin until he rolled out of sight.

It's just me now.

There was a time when this house was full of laughing voices and pattering feet. Marty had his friends over every Sunday to watch the football game and Christine had friends over on Saturdays. When Michael came home from school he was always trailed by buddies he had known since he was a kid. They would spend the afternoon tossing the ball around in the backyard at the bottom of the hill. Below those wretched tracks.

But then Michael went away to college, married a girl out there, bought a house and started a family. Christine flew to California, deciding to pursue the acting career she always wanted. She hadn't landed a big role yet, but the minor ones plus a job waiting tables at a popular chain restaurant gave her enough to eek out a living. And Marty. Poor Marty. He died right after Christine moved. A heart attack snuck up on him while he was watching a movie in the basement. I was reading and didn't find him for hours.

Things changed in the twelve years since Marty's death. The neighbors on both sides of us moved, both opting for the warmer climate of Florida. New people moved in, but it was different. I had lived with the Tillmans and the Parkers for years. We raised our kids together, took pictures when the limousine picked them up for the prom, exchanged Christmas cards. We knew each other. I never really connected with the new neighbors. I did the expected 'welcome neighbor' visit and that was the last time I saw them except when we happened to be going to the mailbox at the same time. And even then it was just a short wave and a forced smile before we were on our way. Times were different.

I woke up early today, earlier than usual. The night before had been a doozy; my arthritis curled me into a ball. The pain had gotten worse over the past couple of months, crippling me to the point of staying home most of the time. And now there was a burning sensation in my chest that never seemed to go away. I stayed in bed for most of the day, only getting up to go to the bathroom.

There was a low rumble in the woods just beyond my backyard last night that kept me awake for a while. I looked out of the window but didn't see anything more than the moonlight on my overgrown grass. It was beautiful, reflecting off the trees, glinting off the worn railroad tracks left in place. I must have stared out at the night for over five minutes. I was mesmerized.

I didn't sleep well. I kept hearing things banging in the dark. My house is old, I know that. It settles in its foundation every night, the sound seeming to grow louder and louder as time passes. But it didn't sound like that. There was a low hum that seemed to permeate my mind, my soul. I couldn't sleep, I couldn't think. All I could do was listen to the incessant tone.

The morning sun was brighter than I remembered it being in a long time. I took my coffee on the deck as I had for years, sitting in the shade this time instead of in the warm rays. I raised the cup to my lips to sip the coffee, expecting to taste the rich brew. It would have been comforting to me, my reward for enduring such a harrowing night. But it wasn't to be. When I raised the cup to my lips and blew at the billowing steam above the rim, I knew something was different. I couldn't feel the heat of the coffee on my hands, even when I held the mug flush in my palm. I couldn't feel the steam as it coursed through my nostrils. None of the familiarity of my morning ritual was there either. I didn't remember brewing the coffee or stepping out onto the deck. I didn't hear the familiar creak of the floorboard just outside the screen door. The one I hadn't gotten around to asking Michael to fix the last time he visited. I looked down at it, puzzled. I stepped on it again. Nothing.

I took a sip of the coffee knowing I wouldn't taste anything, but it seemed like the right thing to do. As I suspected, there was no taste, not even the feeling of having anything in my mouth. I swallowed as I supposed I should when a sound broke through, intensifying the dull hum that had stuck with me the whole night. Over the top of the trees hung a cloud of grayish smoke. I stared at it, unsure of what to make of it, but knowing what it was. A puff of smoke shot upward as the train came into view, past the weeds and tree limbs, on vine-covered tracks that hadn't been in use in years.

I felt the smile inching across my face and wanted to take it back. It wasn't possible that there could be a train on the tracks. There hadn't been one in years — decades. But there it was, crawling along the tracks like a fat rat on its way back to its hole.

Mr. Bill sat at the helm as usual, his cap even more worn and tattered than it had been so many years before. His overalls were moth bitten and the film of dirt that usually covered his face was thicker, more prominent, like motor oil. My lips trembled as Mr. Bill lifted his hat from his head, taking clumps of hair and blood with it, tipping it to me as gentleman would a love interest.

I screamed as my hand rose, seemingly of its own volition, to wave back to an old friend.

The Gift

268

The box he gave me was red, as red as the one that would hold his head, red like blood against snow. Chocolates sat in sections, as would his eyes, nose, lips, and teeth, separated nicely, easy for the picking. I chose one that looked particularly tasty — a long mold of milk chocolate gathered at the top with a surprise filling. I bit into it, letting the filling flood my mouth like a sugary fountain. Cherry. Sweet and tangy. Much like the taste of his eyes.

Word of Mouth

I wouldn'ta had a problem believing it had someone told me about it at the grocery store or at Hog's diner. I'd've bought it lock, stock, and barrel had Willie or Charlie from the kitchen said it, that is, if they could pronounce it at all. And why not? Stranger things have happened, some of 'em 'round these parts. Nobody blinked an eye when Jimmie killed Wanda out by his barn, cutting her head clean off. When he said he didn't mean to do it, we all believed him. Hell, many of us wanted to kill Wanda ourselves and were happy the deed was done, to tell the truth. Sure, he served time, but not too much. Nobody asks him what he does out there by the barn now, 'cause we got our ideas of what that might be. There's a reason the Sheriff never found Wanda's head. 'Cause it ain't lost.

When Bobby said lightning struck his tree and knocked it into his house, right on the spot where his momma lay sleeping, crushing her underneath it, we believed him. Even if it wasn't raining that night, hadn't rained in weeks, we stood by him. When Susie said she saw something in the road, and that's why she veered off and lost control of her car and slammed it into a ditch, we ran to her side. That her husband, who she found out was cheating on her not a day or two before the accident, was thrown from the car and killed didn't bother us none. Even if he always wore his seatbelt and Susie's side didn't even have one attached. We believed the girl, by God, 'cause she was one of us. And we stick together in our little town, yes we do. For better or worse.

Nanny Tyler didn't understand us folks; she didn't fit in with our lot. Ever since she moved to Woodside, she acted like she was better'n us, somehow above the locals. We all got a kick out of the way she walked by us on the streets, barely speaking a lick to one of us unless she needed something. She turned her nose up to us like we were the scum on the bottom of her shoe. A number of us told Hog not to sell to her, but he did it. I guess you don't mess with a man's money. After all, green is still green. Some of the town folk boycotted old Hog for a while, upset that he would cater to that trash, but I suspect everything will go back to normal now that she's gone. Hog may miss her green, but he'll be happy to get the rest of us back in his seats, that's for sure. Green is green anyhow.

Nanny lived out in the sticks on the other side of town from where most folks settled. She rolled her trailer in from Alabama musta been ten years ago. She lived by herself and that seemed to suit her fine. Evil is what I always thought she was, but that's just my take.

Nanny and I lived on the same block of land, 'bout three acres apart. I didn't see her unless I meant to, that is, until she decided it was time for her to dig up some garbage on me. That's when things went south.

Nanny tried to get me turned in on account of my trucks. She said I was poluttin' the air around her and that I shouldn't have all them vehicles on my property. Sheriff didn't want to, but he had to pay attention to her, this being a call to his office and all. He made me tow off a couple of 'em and said I had to work on 'em somewhere else unless I got a license. I might've been mad at the Sheriff, but I wasn't. It was Nanny's doin' and she was the one who would have to pay.

Smokin' like I do, I keeps a pack on me at all times. And drinkin' like Nanny did, she was out of her head every night. She never heard me coming into the window in the kitchen, not even when I fell over in the sink and knocked her cheap dishes around. Even if she had gotten up I could have taken her. She was a big'un—'bout 235 pounds—but I've wrestled bigger. I meant to do what I meant to do and nothin' was go'n stop me.

Nanny sat in her patchwork chair snoring up a breeze. Her bottle of rum had already slipped out of her hand and hit the floor, wetting up the carpet. I looked at her for a minute and saw her for the first time ever. She wasn't half bad looking. If things hadda been different, she and I might have been able to saddle up. But not anymore. The deed needed to be done.

They say everything but her feet and a bit of her spine was gone. No skull, no bones of any kind left 'cept that bit of backbone. Her feet still had full skin; they hadn't burned at all. Neither had anything in her house 'sides the chair she sat in. That sounded peculiar to me but I wasn't gonna be the one to raise the question. Spontaneous Human Combustion is what they called it. Said she burned so bad 'cause she had so much fat 'round her middle. Said it lit up like the wick in a candle. Believe it if you want to is what I say. Can't nobody tell it any different. Only me and Nanny know what happened.

I wouldn'ta had a problem believing it, and I knew the sheriff wouldn't neither, being the superstitious sort that he was. He'd've believed Jesus had come again and knocked on my door last night if me or anyone else in Woodside told it to him. And he didn't like Nanny any more than we did. So when Sara Ellen told me 'bout it at the gas station, I didn't worry a'tall. Hell, it was as much a fact as aliens landing at Roswell if Sara Ellen said it. People tended to take what she said as gospel, they did. Yes sir, just like it was written in stone.

Cerulean Blue

The water that covers his face shines cerulean blue as he looks up at me. I smile back as I bound toward him.

Nouveau

Blood spills from the wound to warm his waiting hand. He brings it to his lips, tasting the familiar piquancy, the familiar loss. He smelled the odor that permeated his dreams, had since he was a boy, the coppery scent of fresh blood. And it did nothing for him.

The kills were no longer satisfying. Neither the look of flesh, either recently dead and still warm or in late stages of rigor, or the thrill of taking a life had done much for him in the past couple of months. He tried everything to keep what had once been his hobby but grew into his passion, alive. But it was slipping away. Snatching a girl from the parking lot of a bar and killing her before making it home had fallen off his list of good times years before. He had graduated to taking them from more crowded areas, like raves or concerts. He even took one at Times Square last New Years'. He made them feel good, whispering in their ear and grazing their earlobes with his lips. He touched their waists, his fingers a respectable distance from their buttocks, but almost over the line. They liked it, those naïve girls, those girls who knew they were hot and didn't mind showing it off, those girls who were so high he could have been their next-door neighbor and they wouldn't have known the difference. Everyone liked to be seduced.

Even him.

But the idea of taking a girl in the bathroom of a rave when the music outside pumped harder and harder, seeming to come through the walls in time with the beating of his pulse, had lost its thrill. He started tasting the blood then, trying to ingest it, to make it live within him. That worked for a while, but not long enough. Now the taste of blood was akin to the taste of water: a nothingness that was as indescribable as the features of his last conquest. His last, nameless girl.

Killing men was even less appetizing. When the women ceased to get a rise out of him, sexually or otherwise, he started to wonder if he was gay. Gay bars are the same as straight bars. Just a mass of people looking for someone to take home and fuck, be it that night or the next. Finding a suitable specimen for his experiment was easy.

That the boy, barely eighteen and proud of it, fought back was brilliant. Exhilarating. The women always did, but their attempts were futile. The boy, on the other hand, might have bested him were he not so determined to feel something, anything. When it was over, when the boy's neck was broken and his head split open to reveal pink, fleshy meat, he couldn't have been more disappointed. The thrill of the fight, the danger it presented, was profound to him a way nothing else was. He loved the rush it provided him. So he went back for more.

How many men and women had he gone through to find another spark like that first one years before? Countless. None of them matched up to his sweet Darlene. She was his first, his only perfect kill. Her blood flowed from her neck in a crimson deluge, beautiful to the eyes and silky to the touch. The warmth startled him at first as he rubbed it between his fingers. She was naked, but that didn't matter to him. He thought it might, but in the end, it was no big deal. He had sex with her first, this friend of his mother's who couldn't keep her eyes off him whenever they were in the room together. She made herself available to him like he was a grown man, even though he was only fourteen at the time. A 5'10" boy with broad shoulders and a mature frame, he wasn't about to turn her down. But she would have to give him something in return for her pleasure. And he took it swiftly, before she could protest.

His dexterity with a knife had been honed by years of slaughter and experimentation with the wildlife around the Blue Ridge Mountains. Opening her was easy. He stepped away from her body to watch the blood spread from her neck to her shoulders, and cascade over her bared breasts. He waited for arousal but it never came. Nothing else did either. Not repulsion, disgust, grief, or regret. Just a fascination for the brilliant red that leapt from her body to greet his stare.

And now, even that was fading.

It was time for something new.

Taking a girl from a bar in a town he had never slept a night in, he brought her back to his hotel room. She was eager to go; she was looking for a party and she thought she had found it. Moments after closing the grimy motel door, she began to disrobe, but he stopped her, wanting to be the only one exposed. Smiling, she watched as he removed his shirt, pants, and underwear, making note of how neat his pubic hair was, trimmed and shaped to a fine "V". As her mind began turning over that detail, comparing his to all the other men's genitalia she had viewed, he produced a razor blade.

"Watch. Please," he said, his voice exuding the desperation his heart felt.

She gasped and scooted backward, away from him and over the bed to the other side. A tear cascaded down her cheek as he sliced the flesh of his forearm lightly at first, then deeper and deeper until his arm was covered with blood. It was so beautiful, the sight of it. So exhilarating, the smell. The color, the essence, the feel of it on his skin: his infatuation with the blood brought forth a myriad of sensations that mingled within him. They were as succulent as sweet nectar from forbidden fruit. He salivated at the prospect of a taste.

Tears fell from his eyes and blood from his lips as he lamented.

Bored

The day draws to a close and still I sit in my cotton pajamas and my bootie slippers. Bored. All day I've watched the cycle of television, from court shows to crime investigations, from news to political debates — it's monotonous really, the drone of the television as it plays one show after another, feeding me until I'm stuffed, full up until I feel I might vomit. *Is that all there is?* I find myself wondering while yet another court show comes on, this time with a judge who seems slowed by anti-depressants with plaintiffs and defendants who have neither prepared for their case, nor dressed appropriately to stand before a judge, let alone the millions of people at home sitting before the boob tube as I am on this cloudy, nameless day. What day is it, I wonder before picking up the remote and checking the online cable directory. Ah. Thursday. Whatever.

I think of things to do — getting dressed and going outside are not among them — yet none of the things that make my list are particularly appetizing. Braiding my hair? Can't - too short. Listening to music? Not the God-awful garbage being manufactured today, mind you, but maybe some Jazz, traditional, like Coltrane or Davis. Or maybe some contemporary – some Joe Sample might be nice. But no. I don't have the interest in getting up, hunting for the CD, and actually putting it in the machine. So I sit and listen to the two young adults bicker about a scratch on a car door, suing for the actual and punitive damages. Give me a break.

I could pick up the phone and call a friend, but I don't want to put in the effort. I could play a video game or paint a picture with the acrylics in the closet, the ones that I long since abandoned and have probably dried up. But what's the use? I'll never finish the piece. I could read a book, write a letter, pull my fingernails out with the tweezer I use to pluck my eyebrows. That would be something to inspect: an intact nail. But why? What scares me is that I don't contemplate the origin of that idea. I only push it away because it would take too much effort.

Moonlight Kisses

3:00 a.m.

The crack of dawn.

Mid shift for some. Time to turn over in bed for others. For Jeremy, it was time to wake up from his tentative sleep. Time to prepare himself for her visit, once again.

She came every night, sometimes just to smile at him from the window, or hover over top of him, teasing him with her gentle touch. He loved to look at her eyes, such a rich brown, gleaming in the moonlight only for him.

He had a surprise for her this night. He planned to wake and greet her as she came, to see her as she materialized for the first time. Maybe, if he showed her how much he wanted her, she would take him with her to the place she goes when the clock strikes 3:02.

3rd floor window

They walk aimlessly, to and fro, their faces blank and emotionless, their steps gauged, as though controlled by a grand puppet master. I see them come and go every morning and night, watch them trod along worn sidewalks in the biting cold and the blazing sun. I watch their monotony from my 3rd floor window and laugh at the simplicity of their lives. I hardly notice as hot tears trickle out of my eyes to wet my gaunt, jaundiced face. I turn to lift a tissue from the almost empty box, casting a glance over my bare-walled studio apartment. My love sits in the corner in his favorite chair, the beer in his special mug gone flat and warm. His countenance is obscured by more than the late afternoon shadows that form grotesque designs on the far wall—fingers from Hell reaching up to grab, masked men speeding closer and closer, only to disappear in a haze of gray. He stares at me with his sightless gaze, seeing me for who I am. Finally.

My laughter, high-pitched, if not shrill even to my ears, cuts through the heavy silence like a knife.

Voices

A woman sobs. A man stands over her in condolence, in tongue-tied sorrow. Others sit near, behind my file cabinet, beside my whiteboard, but I can't hear them, not like I can her. Her voice permeates my skin, echoes within my very frame.

Her cries are deafening, all-encompassing, smothering. She calls out, ready to speak a name and give voice to the thing that ails her, but she stops, sobbing again, as she always does. As I bring my headphones to my ears, I wonder if the name that would pass over her lips will mean anything to me.

Abstract

"What's the big deal about this one?" Cameren asked as she stared up at the monstrosity that was Mitchell Peterson's work. "It just looks like... like — ."

"Say it. That's part of it, you know."

"Part of what?" she said, frustrated. "See what I mean? I don't understand all the hype around this crap."

"But you do," Matthew said, his voice oddly calm. "Don't you see?"

Cameren had already walked away, moving alongside Peterson's latest, a humongous billboard-sized blotch.

Shaking her head as Matthew approached, she said, "It isn't even that good."

"That's your opinion. I've known people who have come in here and been moved to tears by it." Cameren looked at him incredulously. "I do!" He shoved his hands into the pockets of his leather jacket. "I've heard of people leaving here and walking aimlessly into the streets, looking as though their lives had been sucked out through their eyes."

Staring at the painting, Matthew fell silent, introspective. "I also know someone who killed themselves after leaving it."

Cameren stared at his face, trying to read it. Matthew always had a flair for the dramatic, but she couldn't tell if he was using it then. His face was blank. No smile, no frown, no creasing forehead — no expression whatsoever. Bullshit. It had to be.

"Oh please Matthew. Gimmie a break. What moron would kill themselves over this crap? Save that one for the movies — that would actually be a great script idea. You should write it down."

Cameren laughed and shoved Matthew playfully, but his face remained the same. The serenity, the utter calmness of his features, was unsettling.

"Matthew?"

He stared at the piece, enthralled by it.

"Hey, Matthew, c'mon." Cameren nudged him and he looked at her with eyes that didn't seem like his own, the familiar glint of green in his rich brown had dulled to a mossy hue. His eyes looked dead.

"Matthew, cut it out. I don't buy it, so stop."

Matthew's voice sounded weighty, as though he had been sleeping. "I'm not kidding. Do you remember Lauren from school? The tall girl from Delaware?"

"Sure. I had a couple of classes with her."

"Well, she's dead. She killed herself after seeing one of Peterson's paintings. This one, in fact. It happened last week, on the last day it showed in Boston. She went to the museum like she had every day it was there. She closed the place down, and after a guard asked her to leave, she went home and slit her wrists."

Cameren's mouth was slack as she looked at Matthew. She didn't know how to feel about what she was hearing.

"If you don't believe me, talk to Dillon. He heard about it from some of the guys that still live by campus. I can probably get the obituary for you if you want it."

Lauren was a nice girl, but Cameren hadn't known her very well. It wasn't sorrow Cameren was feeling, though she was sorry for her, the same way she was sorry for the unnamed masses that die every day. It was something else. The hair on the back of her neck stood on end, and she was keenly aware of the back of her head, her nerve endings on high alert. After all, the back of her head faced the painting that Matthew claimed caused a woman to kill herself—a woman she knew. Even though she didn't believe Matthew's story—not really, anyway—she couldn't help but imagine an arm reaching from Peterson's painting to strum the back of her neck with a hand filled with sharpened barbs.

"Matthew you can't be serious," Cameren finally got around to saying. She had been so wrapped up in the elaborate fantasy spinning in her mind that she wasn't sure how long she had been silent. She noticed, though, that when she spoke, Matthew jumped. He had been looking at the painting again.

"Why can't I be? You saw it yourself. The painting elicits strong reactions in people. Is it so far-fetched to believe that maybe, in some people, it elicits violence? Or depression so great, the only relief is to kill yourself?"

"You don't know that this painting made Lauren kill herself. It could have been anything. You don't know what was going on in her life."

Matthew shook his head and smiled. Always the patronizing one when Cameren disagreed with him. She seethed inside but pushed the feeling away.

Instead, she said, "Frankly, I'm surprised at you for believing she did it because of a painting. This painting, no less." Cameren turned back to it and regarded its jumble of red, orange, and purple. The acrylic glistened under the fluorescent lights. "To fancy yourself an academic, yet you'd put stock in a story so… adolescent." If he wanted to patronize, she could most certainly cut.

Matthew walked behind Cameren and gripped her shoulders with more force than he needed to. He held her in place and hissed in her ear.

"Look at it, Cameren. Really see it. Tell me what you see."

Cameren sighed and shrugged her shoulders, hoping he'd get the hint to lighten up. He didn't. She stared at the piece, the eyesore, as she'd taken to calling it in her mind, and tried to critique it honestly. What had initially seemed like a spill from a can of Fire Engine Red paint had texture in the center, chips and flakes that jutted out from the canvas and created rolling hills of red. Lines extended from the blotch to the corners of the canvas, blending with orange and purple. Stucco framed one corner, absorbing the red paint and turning it pink, like pus blended with blood. Pennies were glued to the canvas and surrounded by a brownish red mixture, whipped with a palette knife. Glossier than the other sections was the top left corner, it's bright red hue pure, like blood from a gaping wound.

"What do you see?" Matthew spoke urgently in her ear.

With a swallow and an emotion she dared not realize, Cameren replied, "Death."

Matthew's death came as a surprise to everyone. People were in shock as they passed before his closed coffin and touched the strangely cold mahogany wood. The common theme for conversation at the house after the ceremony was how surprised they were to hear about Matthew's passing. And the way it happened, especially. He always seemed like such a levelheaded man, one person said to a nodding audience of two. How could he have killed himself?

Cameren wasn't surprised, not after seeing the way Matthew looked at the museum. He went there three more times after without her, sitting for hours in front of the thing, letting it fill his mind with horrible images. He'd come home and stare at the wall as if imagining the piece again, seeing it in all its wretched color. Cameren disturbed him once to talk about something that happened at work and he turned to look at her with the emptiest eyes she had ever seen. So when she found him in the bathroom with one eye already in the sink, plucked from the socket and severed from the optic nerve, and the other being dug out with his bloody fingers and a metal nail file, the day the painting left DC headed for New York, she wasn't surprised. She stood and watched Matthew as he worked, digging and pressing, until it came out with a comical pop. The shrillness of her laughter was the only thing that surprised her, though it didn't bother Matthew one bit.

Anathema

It's there

looming overhead

discretely

but blatantly

It does not move

rather mills atop

prepared

with its hind-legs

as smooth and long

humming a sweet,

treacherous song

- *Temptation and Consequence* by elle wood

Green in Brown

He looked back at me with green eyes that sported specks of red and brown in the deep crevices of their irises. Cat eyes, though I'm sure the man across the street who couldn't stop staring at me, even after I stared back at him with the most disrespectful of looks, or the woman who brushed past us in a huff, didn't see them as anything more than beautiful. Some might consider him lucky, especially those who shared the same skin color as he, who shared the same features. They might have envied him or disliked him because of them, his pretty eyes. Men and women alike would call him pretty, one group with less criticism in their voices than the other. But it would always be there, that jealousy, that desire to have what he has. Those beautiful green eyes. Cat's eyes to me, but to others nothing more than a gift from birth. Especially to those who shared the same skin color, who shared his features . But they didn't share them, don't you see? He was unlike anyone they had ever seen. He was from a place they would never know, with their narrow minds and their arrogant idealisms. His world was filled with beautiful combinations: green in brown, yellow in red, white in black. Where he was from, he was common, lackluster, plain-Jane. His green eyes were a dime a dozen. The magenta ones, now those were specimens to look at, with their specks of yellow and cobalt. Those eyes were mesmerizing, worthy of envy. I should know. I wanted them the moment I saw them.

His green eyes twinkled at me, speaking a language that the guy across the street and the woman who brushed past would never understand. They glistened in the sunlight, unflinching from its bright rays, even as they stared directly into them. Cat eyes. And no one knew it but me.

Skin

"It wasn't the way they said it was, the ones who think they can psychoanalyze me, prod and probe me like some deranged animal. He didn't control me. He never did. The whole thing was quite the opposite of what they chose to believe.

Sure I fed him, gave him what he wanted. And yes, I knew that he was crazy. I knew that there had been no mistake, that he wasn't remanded to the hospital by accident. I knew all about what he'd done to those women, how he'd treasured them, honored them in the only way he knew how. He loved them, savored the feel of their flesh. He wanted to be inside them, a part of them. He would cover himself with their blood, encase himself inside their skin, do anything he could to become them. But it never worked. That's what drove him to take another, and another, and another, one after the other, in search of the girl who would finally make him feel whole. He chose big girls because they could compensate him more. He loved the warmth of their flesh, the glove-like protection he felt when he entered them. Their skin covered him more fully, draped him like an overcoat. But still, they never truly accepted him. They grimaced when he took them, were repulsed when he entered them, grew cold after he killed them, and began to smell once he gutted them. He could be them only for an instant, wriggling into their graying flesh and wearing it like a suit, before the smell of rotting, putrid flesh enveloped him, made him want to gag. That's what depressed him, what made him hate them. The turning.

I knew that. All of it. I used it to suit my own needs.

Jeremy was the easiest patient to get along with on the ward. All of the other patients were lunatics, true crazies. Paulette thought the sun was the devil, and that it rose every day to watch her, waiting for the right time to claim her. Clifton, if that was really his name, thought the white walls were really ghosts standing flush and close together. He thought the room closing in on him was really the ghosts getting closer and closer, waiting to capture him. The other patients had similar delusions: One thought his doctor was his dead uncle, coming back to molest him from the grave. Another one thought the black specks in the tile were ants, killer ants that wanted to get at his toes, inject their venom, and turn him into an ant. He had terrible nightmares of the ants crawling over him, cannibalizing him as he lay beneath tall blades of grass. Yet another one of them thought he was the ghost of Christmas past, and he prophesized everyone's future as they walked by his room. Nut jobs, all of them. But Jeremy was different.

Jeremy sat in the middle of the hall, which made it difficult at times. During the day it was normal for me to visit him two or three times. I was the day nurse on the ward of willies, as I liked to call it: The fourth floor of Minisink Psychiatric Hospital. But at night, after my shift was over, it wasn't so easy. Jeremy was as far away from the elevator as he was from the back stairwell. Someone—loonies or staff—was going to see. I had to calculate that risk.

You might ask why I did it. Why I brought him girls to mutilate, devour, slaughter. I ask you to think of the silhouette of a woman in the moonlight, the curve of her breast, the form of her hips. I ask you to consider the scent of her love as she reaches climax, the taste of her sweat on your anxious tongue. I ask you to think of those things, let your mind course over them, and then tell me you would have done differently than I.

Jeremy faced the wall the first day I met him. He had just changed into his hospital pajamas—a uniform much like the one he wore in jail, but with toned down colors, designed to "relax" him—and his court suit lay in a mound at his feet. He was staring in the direction of the window, but not seeing out of it—it was a small glass pane mounted high up on the wall, higher than he or any patient could ever reach, and barred on the outside and inside, just in case they did. As the light bathed his face in gold, I could see why the women found him attractive. Too bad, I remember thinking. If only he'd been attracted to the ones who fancied him, he might not have had to take what he wanted.

Jeremy didn't have any use for the tall and slender women who dotted the campus upon which he worked as a drama teacher. He had no interest in the perky little breasts that sat up on their chests, nor the hourglass shapes of their waists and stomachs. He preferred a fleshier model, a woman who could give him more of what he liked: breasts, buttocks, and thighs. That's how I knew I'd be safe. That's how I knew we would work fine together.

I always envied my sister, Michelle, who had been a big girl since we were kids. She had naturally wide hips and added to them by eating whatever she wanted when she wanted. My hips? Well, they aren't exactly slender, but I fit a size ten just fine. Michelle had never been a size ten, twelve, fourteen, or sixteen. At least not that I can remember. I looked like a waif standing next to her. Like an undeveloped child. It drove me crazy to see her breasts, fuller than mine would ever be, bobbing up and down as she walked. I envied her more than I let on. She never understood why.

But it wasn't just envy. I always knew that. I would time her showers and make sure that I was in the bathroom when she stepped out of the tub. When she got out I'd be fiddling with my hair or flossing, doing something that made it seem like I had a reason for being there other than seeing her wet body. I would always move her towel from the toilet seat to the edge of the sink so she'd have to lean over more to get it. The way her breasts dangled, floating back and forth to rest on her ribcage when she righted herself, would send chills through my body. I had to fight the urge to touch myself right then and there. Every time.

Michelle caught me looking at her once, when we were at the beach. She had gone in first; I watched as her voluptuous bottom strode into the turquoise water. I walked in behind her, quietly admiring her form as the water cascaded over her skin. I was right behind her and she didn't even know I was there. She was too busy soaking in the rays of the sun, feeling the water on her face turn from cool to lukewarm as the sun warmed it. I couldn't stop myself. I pulled the strings to her bikini top, untying it, and making it fall from her. Michelle shrieked and then laughed in embarrassment as she whipped around to look at me, her full lips forming a beautiful 'O'. Her breasts, their wet, brown areolas glistening in the sun, were beautiful. I couldn't take my eyes off them. I didn't notice that her expression had changed, or that her laughter had stopped. I only saw her beautiful breasts floating on the water.

"Karen, what the fuck are you looking at?" she yelled. The sound of her voice jarred me out of my daydream and I pulled my eyes away from her breasts.

"What are you talking about?" I replied weakly.

"You're staring at my boobs! What the hell?"

"I – I didn't mean anything."

"Yes you did, you pervert!" She started to swim away, trying to slap her bikini top back on as she went. "I'm telling mom. You're a freak."

She couldn't possibly know what she was saying, couldn't understand the implications. Yes, I am a freak, a pervert, though I didn't know that much until later. I knew what I was doing was strange, looking at my sister, wanting her. And I understood why Michelle was angry. But telling mom would bring the wrong kind of attention to me. I had to do something. And fast.

"Fine, go tell mom, you fucking cow. I was only looking 'cause I can't believe how huge they are!"

Michelle turned back to look at me with pain on her face. I felt bad—I hadn't meant to hurt her feelings. But I had to do something. I couldn't let her tell mom I was staring at her tits. At least not that way. I remember wishing I'd had a chance to touch them before she got out of the water.

Michelle trudged up the sandy slope back to where our parents sat on towels and blabbed, "Karen's being mean to me! She took down my bikini top and then laughed at my boobs!" Perfect. Sure, I got in trouble for being insensitive to my sister, but that was far better than what could have happened had Michelle told them how I ogled her. I never stopped looking at Michelle and her ample bosom and wide behind. That's why I made her our first.

I didn't mention my plan to Jeremy until a month after he'd been at the hospital. I wanted to let him get comfortable, get used to his new digs. After all, he was supposed to spend the rest of his life here. I wanted him to settle in.

He didn't say anything at first. He looked at me with distrustful eyes that were red in the corners as I talked. He thought I was setting him up. I told him I wasn't. He worried about the cameras. I reminded him that the hospital had yet to install them, that it was specked out in next year's budget. He thought I'd report him if he even looked like he was interested. I told him I wouldn't. He said all this without speaking a word. I could read him like a book.

I pitched my plan twice and he still hadn't spoken. I was starting to get angry with him, I'll be honest. I couldn't understand how he could turn this opportunity away. Finally, on my last round before leaving, I gave him his meds and brought the plan up again. I told him to look at me and he did. I opened my jacket and pulled up my shirt and bra to reveal small, pert breasts—just the kind he hated. He looked at them, pawed one even, before he started to cry. Satisfied, I put myself back together and showed him a picture of Michelle. She was wearing a formfitting black dress that accented her voluptuousness. The rise under his smock was all I needed to see. I told him I'd bring her by in the next few weeks. I kept my promise.

Michelle was nervous, of course, but once I showed her his picture and told her that he was being railroaded, that he hadn't touched those girls and that it was a case of mistaken identity, she calmed down a bit. Telling her that I had shown him a picture of her and that he was interested helped a lot too. I brought her in after hours, using the back entrance near the nurse's lounge. I knew the orderlies—ex-jocks, the lot of them—would be in the cafeteria watching the game. The night shift was typically slow. The doctor's prescribed meds to knock the patient's out at their eight o'clock "feeding", so the orderlies congregated in the cafeteria to play cards or watch television. The nurse's lounge was on the other side of the floor, so even though I could hear the television playing, I couldn't see the room. I was able to slip in and out without being noticed.

It took a while for Michelle to mount the stairs—a fact that I incorporated into my plans for the next run. She trudged down the hall, trying to rein in her breathing before getting to Jeremy's door. I couldn't help but smile. Things were coming together nicely.

Michelle liked what she saw. Jeremy had cleaned himself up a bit, combed his hair and smoothed his beard. He liked what he saw. It took effort for him not to salivate. They got together easy enough, neither one of them realizing that I had slipped into the shadows of the corner to watch. She let him take off her clothing faster than I thought she would have and stood before him naked as he disrobed. I opened my pants and slid my hand into my satin panties, a pair I had bought specifically for that night. The feel of the material against my skin as I moved my hand back and forth, up and down, was like being in water: soothing and warm.

He laid her on the tiny hospital bed and penetrated her without much foreplay. Michelle grunted but didn't force him off of her, didn't make any attempt to make him stop. He pressed into her, wanting to be all the way inside her, as I knew he would. I slowed my rhythmic circle and waited to see what would happen next. I didn't want to miss a thing.

When he could take no more, Jeremy wrapped his hand around Michelle's neck. He reached for the knife I had taped beneath his bed with his free hand, deftly ripping it from the bed and wielding it at her neck. Michelle's eyes opened wide when she saw the blade. She fixed her mouth to protest, brought her heels down hard on the bed and set her legs to push Jeremy off, but she wasn't given the chance. Jeremy sliced Michelle's throat without blinking. He brought the knife between her breasts in the next motion and sliced her open. The blood didn't make me cringe like I thought it would. That it was my sister didn't affect me either, at least not negatively. It was the most sensual display I had ever seen. It was better than all of the ones that came afterward, better than any fantasy I had imagined. I climaxed on the floor sooner than I wanted to and watched Jeremy as he worked, hoping I'd be able to have another.

Jeremy modeled her skin for me that night on his trim frame. He played with her breasts and presented me with her clitoris while he stood covered in her, mimicking sounds of pleasure as I explored her. When it was time to go, when I had to clean him up and get what was left of Michelle out of the room, I knew we would do it again. Soon.

No one caught on for months, and even then, you only stumbled upon us by mistake. I brought him many girls, more than ten, and every time he would put on their skin and let me have my way with them. Every once in a while I'd suck his dick for him if he'd push it through the girl's skin for me to get at. That's what you think you saw, me satisfying him. But really, he was satisfying me.

A fluke, me being in here. If the idiot down the hall hadn't been launching herself at the walls and screaming like a banshee, she would have never caught us.

Nurse Bunn approached me the next day, when I came in for work. She fired me because of what she heard I did in the middle of the shift the night before. She thought she was doing me a favor by telling me in private and documenting it as a mutual parting. She said she didn't want to tarnish my reputation with allegations of sleeping with patients. Nurse Bunn is an older woman with considerable girth. Her bosom heaved while she spoke. I could imagine her nipples—brown or pink, it didn't matter—in my mouth, my heightened body heat combating her dwindling temperature. I wondered if Nurse Bunn would be Jeremy's type.

I didn't realize that I had reached out to touch them. That's how you got me. I let you win."

"Ok Karen, that's enough for today, don't you think?"

The orderly stood with his hand outstretched with her meds in a cup, as he'd done for the past 5 minutes. Doctor Kimble continued, "Maybe one day you'll tell us what really happened to you that day in the office, why you killed those people." He adjusted his glasses once more before continuing, "But for now, let's just take our medicine. Ok?"

Karen stared the orderly lasciviously with wild, unfocused eyes. It made him more than a little nervous, given her past outbursts—once she tried to bite his nipple off—but he didn't let it show. *Fucking wacko,* he said to himself as she grabbed the pill cup from his hand and scratched absently at her thigh.

Spinning

The class kicked my ass. After years of inactivity, I decided to jump into working out with both feet. A spinning class. An hour on a stationary bike with up-tempo music blaring in mine and ten other masochists' ears. All of this at six o'clock in the morning.

I must have been out of my mind.

That's what I was thinking in the shower after I left the class early. I had to leave; I was so tired, I almost fell off my bike. No one in the class seemed to notice as I dragged myself out of the room, my thighs trembling of their own volition, my crotch throbbing from the awkward, thinly padded seat. They just kept facing forward, sweat falling from their faces in torrents, their eyes trained on the instructor, a singer shouting unintelligible words at them through distorted speakers. They looked like robots. Like fine-tuned, chiseled humanoids.

The hell with that.

I trudged into the locker room, taking the walk of shame in front of the free weights and aerobics room in stride. So what if I quit early? So what if I was as out of breath as I would have been had I run up 30 flights of stairs? It was six o'clock in the freaking morning, for crying out loud. On any other day, I wouldn't have even been awake yet.

Telling myself that made me feel better, especially in the shower. The warm water cascaded over my body, washing away the sweat, relaxing my muscles. I put my face in the spray and let it wet the edges of my hairline. I stood that way for a while, not wanting to move a muscle. *I'll try it again tomorrow*, I told myself. *I'll do better next time.*

I closed my eyes in the spray, sinking into it, trying to push errant thoughts out of my head: The agenda for my meeting at 9:00 a.m., the project due C.O.B. today. The day's tasks invaded my mind, trying to force me out of the shower and into the routine, into the real world. I tried to focus on the water, on the way it moved over my body. I tried to imagine being in a pool or at the beach, where the water could engulf me, swirl around me, relax me. But the tasks of the day kept pressing, pushing their way in.

"Fuck," I muttered under my breath as I started to lather myself in short, choppy motions.

A shadow darkened the shower stall as I soaped my tired body. I tried to look through the opaque glass, but I couldn't make anything out. It was then that I noticed how quiet the locker room was, how utterly silent. The only sound was the water from the showerhead slapping against my body and the tiled floor. A light near the bathroom stalls shorted and blinked out, setting my heart racing. I tried to tell myself that it was irrational to be afraid. Lights go out all the time. People walk in front of the shower stalls to get to their lockers—the gym was designed that way. Just because I couldn't see the person go by doesn't mean it was something else. The glass was opaque, after all. But none of that mattered. My heart beat wildly in my chest and the water, so warm and comforting before, felt cold against my flushed skin.

I pressed myself to the back wall of the shower, afraid to move too much. I didn't want whomever—whatever—had walked into the locker room to hear me sloshing around. I flattened my palms against the formed walls of the stall, bracing myself, trying to control my heartbeat. It was so loud, I was sure it could be heard beyond the door. A shuffling sound arose from the locker room, as though someone was rustling the contents of a gym bag. Maybe the spinning class had let out and women were in the locker room preparing to shower. I had almost sold myself on the idea when the rustling stopped abruptly and gave way to silence. Painful silence, like the one just after death.

The lack of sound, any sound at all, was maddening. I felt like I would go crazy if I endured another second of it, yet I dared not open the shower door. My mind had concocted a vision of the thing in the other room, its beastly proportions immeasurable, its hunger insatiable. I imagined it was toying with me, waiting for me to come out, luring me with the insanity brewing in my mind. Its teeth were long, fangs really, and they were primed to bite me as soon as I stepped out of the shower stall.

I couldn't move. I could barely breathe.

Then I heard it moving.

Toward the showers.

Toward me.

Suddenly, I felt trapped. If the thing came for me, there was no way to escape. I was pinned in.

I had to move. I had to. Either I moved, or I would die.

In a burst of action, I kicked open the shower door and leapt from the stall. Nothing. I turned left and right, my hands up, prepared to fight, if I had to. Still nothing. With adrenaline coursing through my body, I checked the locker room, looking for the thing that had terrified me into immobility moments before. I came upon two women, mid-twenties and trim, clearly in upkeep mode rather than weight loss mode, like I was. I don't know if it was my naked body dripping water everywhere, or the crazed look on my face, but for some reason they stared at me, watching in silence until I walked away. They whispered to each other as I moved on, one asking the other what my problem was and joking that I needed to cover my fat ass, but I didn't care. There was something in the locker room and it was going to kill us all. But not if I found it first.

After three trips around the locker room, I still hadn't found it. Confused, I made my way back to my locker. I was cold and embarrassed. All I wanted to do was get my clothes on and leave. The lock on my locker was missing. I put my hand where it used to be, fingering the clip in disbelief. A thick, mucus-like film came off on my hand. As I rubbed it between my fingers, I heard the voice of one of the women I saw earlier. It was airy this time, detached, but had the same inflection, the same timbre. She was laughing.

Images of a hideous creature with four arms and legs and green skin covered with moss flooded my head. I couldn't turn around to face her — it. I didn't think I could handle laying eyes on such a horrific sight.

Then I felt its hand on my shoulder.

Inheritance

To his credit, the attempt had been a good one. He'd called Hattie into service faster than she'd been able to find a suitable slave. The argument had really burned him up so he went home that night and set to the business of concocting his potion. But Hattie had been easy to dissuade, at least thus far. Sharon didn't have to do much more than lock the door against her to keep her at bay. A quick sidestep and the old girl was lost. Wilson hadn't bothered to teach Hattie anything more than how to get up and walk again. He told her to go after Sharon and to kill her, but he hadn't told her how.

Sharon got used to the beating against her front door. Hattie could stay out there all night if she wanted to. It didn't bother Sharon any and there wasn't a neighbor to complain for miles. She figured Wilson would wait until morning to see if Hattie had done the job. After the funeral, just so it would look right. People would wonder why he wasn't in the family car, it being his brother-in-law's funeral and all. They would wonder if he was anywhere except right by his wife's side.

Sharon had time.

Hattie hadn't figured out that she would do better to bust in the windows yet. Sharon doubted that she would. The woman hadn't been a brain surgeon in life. How could Sharon expect her to be any different in death? Sharon sucked her teeth as she walked into the spare bathroom, the room where she brewed her potions and cast her spells. She thought back on how she and Wilson had gotten to the place they were—wanting to kill each other.

Their mother had left the shop to the both of them. She had been a respected woman in their village, a woman who was known to take care of people's problems. Half the time she didn't do anything except sell roots and dried fruit for one potion or the next; she told Sharon and Wilson herself that the whole thing was bogus. But it worked and she never had to put in a hard day's labor in the hot sun in her life.

Wilson played around with it, 'Momma's mumbo-jumbo' he called it. He was the oldest and the one who was supposed to inherit the business. He never caught on though, and was easily overshadowed by his younger sister, who seemed to have the real gift. When their mother died, she left everything to the both of them. And that's where the trouble started.

"You're making us look like fools," Sharon said, from the back room of the shop that day. "No one will believe us if you keep gallivanting around the street like a commoner."

"They don't believe us as it is, Sharon," he said, tired of the argument. It was always the same thing over and over. "People are smarter now. They know this is a bunch of bullshit."

Sharon burst through the beads that hung from the ceiling to separate the rooms and growled, "Watch your tongue in momma's house."

Wilson chuckled. "Sharon, momma's been dead for ten years already. When are you gonna cut it out?" He turned his back to his sister and fondled one of the dry herbs that hung from the ceiling.

"Her *ánimo* is still here, Wilson. She's angry that you speak of her that way."

"Right, sure," he said condescendingly. "Anyhow, I just came here to tell you that I'll be talking with a man about selling this dump. I'm gonna try and get whatever money we can out of this place and do something with it. Maybe I'll move to the mainland. Who knows?"

Sharon looked stricken. "You can't sell the place! This is momma's legacy!"

Wilson flicked the herb and sent it swinging on the string that held it. "It's not much of a legacy, now is it? You can barely live on what we make from it. I have to work a second job just to keep food on the table." He shook his head and stood to leave. "I'm selling it, Sharon. And there's nothing you can do about it."

Wilson walked toward the door, opened it, and turned to speak before leaving. "But you should have already known that, *bruha*."

Sharon cursed him then, vowing to stop him by any means necessary. She didn't utter a sound as she stood facing the closed door of her mother's shop, but Wilson heard every word.

The church was sticky and the mosquitoes were relentless. They couldn't resist the bounty they were getting: thirty people crammed in a small building with nothing but their hands to protect them. They feasted.

Wilson escorted his wife in and sat in front of the body of her brother. Clay had been a strong man, muscular and fit for most of his life. He worked out on the boats and was stung by a Portuguese Man of War during an afternoon pull. They didn't make it back to the dock in time to save him after he went into cardiac arrest.

As his wife sobbed, all Wilson could think about was Sharon. She wasn't at the funeral, so she must be dead. She wouldn't have missed Clay's service. She fancied him and was genuinely saddened by his death. Wilson tried to conceal his smile as he thought of Hattie taking Sharon by surprise. She must have been shocked to see her, considering she had attended Hattie's funeral a couple of days earlier. He would talk to the man after they put Clay in the ground, Wilson surmised. He would have his money in less than a month.

His wife's shaking grew intense and a cry was stuck in her throat, choking her. Wilson turned to her and said, "Honey? Honey, are you ok?" He didn't see Clay fidgeting in his tight casket, didn't recognize the sounds of grunting from his chest and the ripping of the stitches in his lips to be what they were. His wife's eyes were wide open, unblinking, in shock. "Honey?" He shook her slightly, trying to rouse her. She wouldn't look at him.

Wilson turned his head in the direction of his wife's stare in time to see Clay sit up in the casket. An audible moan escaped his chest as the air escaped his lungs. Clay forced his mouth and eyes open, ripping the stitches apart. He lifted his right arm and then his left, inspecting them in disbelief. The whole thing was so much déjà vu to Wilson that he didn't move.

Then Clay climbed out of the casket.

Wilson didn't hear the shrieks and screams that emanated from the congregation as Clay planted his feet on the floor. He only saw Sharon standing at the back of the church smiling prettily, devilishly.

Clay moved quickly for one of the undead. He closed the space between him and Wilson in three strides and pressed down on his shoulders, buckling his legs, making him submit. Wilson became aware of a pungent odor, the smell of meat that had been left out in the sun. Sharon had converted Hattie in the light of day and brought her along as backup.

With everything he could remember from Momma, with everything he had, he called Hattie inside. She came sluggishly, bewildered. She looked at Sharon who was too busy watching the show in front of her to notice. Then she looked at Wilson.

He intimated his command to her, deftly breaking Sharon's spell and reinforcing his own. Hattie was upon Sharon before she could turn around.

The smell of fresh blood permeated the air as Hattie ripped away Sharon's scalp. Sharon's scream was nothing more than an afterthought as was her limp hand against Hattie's decaying cheek. She was dead as soon as her skull was exposed to the summer air. Hattie banged Sharon's head against the wall like a squirrel might a nut and pawed at the brain inside.

Clay smelled the blood just before Wilson did. He turned his head, lessening his grip just enough so that Wilson could slip away. Clay lunged at Sharon, grabbing her leg and digging his nails into her skin, cutting through the flesh and muscle with determined swipes. He licked at the blood that spewed from the wounds before baring his teeth and biting into the supple flesh. Wilson slinked against the wall, trying to make a quiet exit while Hattie and Clay dined on Sharon. He noticed for the first time that the church was empty, including his wife. He'd have to remember that she hadn't tried to help him at all, that she had just left him in there to deal with two zombies. Yes, that was useful information indeed.

Wilson stood in the doorway to watch as Clay sank his teeth into Sharon for another bite, sinews and fatty tissue draped over his working lips. He looked at Sharon's face one last time, at her ruined eyes and what was left of her exposed brain and smiled. So much for her being the only one who "got it". As he closed the door to the church, he changed his face from satisfaction to fear to please the waiting crowd. His wife ran up to him, tears streaming wetting her cheeks. He hoped she couldn't see the hatred in his eyes.

He'd meet the man later that day. He'd have his money in less than a month.

Worthington Court

No one remembered what had gone on before Worthington Court became Worthington Court. Even the oldest resident of Smithfarm Junction had only a fading recollection, and she was almost ninety-seven. Alma could tell you that Worthington Court went by another name back when she was a child. Tolliver? Lynwood? She could never get the name right. She told the town historian that her grandfather used to play with a boy who lived on that street. When the historian, a mild-mannered man of 46 with a receding hairline and a nervous twitch in his eyebrow, tried to correct her and say it must have been her father that played with a boy there, she became adamant.

"It was my grandfather, I tell you. I know who it was," she croaked using weathered vocal cords.

The historian flipped through a mass of maps, going as far back as 1880. He scoured over the faded ink, peering through his reading glasses at the yellowed paper, while Alma took a sip of tea. She chewed absently, nothing but her tongue in her mouth.

"Ms. Roberson, there —."

"Alma," she said, tired of having to. Ms. Roberson was her mother-in-law, rest her soul, and Alma had taken to saying as much ten years before. Age is what you make of it. "Call me Alma, Henry, or don't call me at all."

"All right… Alma," Henry said as color flashed in his cheeks. He looked over the maps one more time before continuing. "I'm looking at the maps and…, well Alma, the street you're talking about just wasn't there."

Alma wrapped her arms around herself, shivering from the chill that was picking up on the porch. The sun was going down and the night's chill was easing its way in. *About time to go inside*, she thought. She braced her hand on the armrest of the wicker chair and prepared to stand.

Henry rose with her, before her, though he tried to keep her pace. "It's not there, Alma," he continued cautiously. "The road you talked about. Worthington Court doesn't come into existence until 1915. By any name."

He spoke louder that time and Alma didn't hide her frustration. She wasn't deaf, dumb, or senile and she grew weary of buffoons like Henry who liked to treat her as though she was. She declined his arm when he extended it to escort her back to the front door.

"I don't care what's on your map, Henry Goode. I'm telling you what my granddaddy told me. I remember it like it was yesterday. Granddaddy said he and the boy played over there every summer back when the family came out this way for vacation. He told me the boy didn't live on the street right then. He had lived there years before. My granddaddy asked his father if he knew his playmate's family one night since our family had been coming to Smithfarm Junction for years during the warm months. Great granddaddy didn't know anyone that lived where the boy claimed to live either, said no one had ever lived there back when he was young. He said it was nothing but trees. Granddaddy went back and told the boy what great granddaddy said the next day, but the boy insisted on it just like I'm insisting on it right now. The street was there, Henry. He said the road was there, that his family used to have a house on it, but that they had left." Alma reached for the front door, opened it, and stepped inside. "And that was that."

Henry looked at Alma with confusion in his eyes.

"All right?" Alma continued dismissively. "That's all I know. You take that and do what you want with it."

Henry stood in silence, looking at Alma, at the age etched in her face. Her stare, unblinking and direct, was mesmerizing.

"Ok, Henry Goode?" Alma was insistent.

"Y-yes ma'am."

Alma looked at Henry in disapproval.

"Yes Alma," Henry corrected himself. Alma smiled genuinely.

"I guess I'll be seeing you then," Alma called over her shoulder as she let the door close on its own.

Alma walked to the back of her house and pulled out her photo album. The picture of her great-grandfather was covered with plastic and sat alone on a black scrapbook page. "Handsome devil," she mumbled, as she did every time she looked at the picture. She sighed, wondering if she should have told Henry more about the street, or nothing at all. She knew he wouldn't be able to let it rest. They never could.

Henry scoured the microfilm the town had on hand about Worthington Court and the surrounding area. For a residential area, the street had seen its share of tragedy. Five car accidents with one fatality (a man backed out of his driveway without looking and killed his wife while she stood at the mailbox), three fires, construction accidents, you name it. A woman slipped on ice while walking on the sidewalk. She hit her head and died instantly. More dogs than Henry cared to count had run in the street and been hit by oncoming cars. Two missing children had been reported from that street in the past three years. There had been flooding and severe potholes that the state serviced every year.

Most of the occurrences seemed to take place in front of a specific plot of land.

Henry dug in the land records as far back as he could go to learn more about plot 197 on Worthington Court, tracing its owner as far back as 1910, when the road took on its current name. It didn't take much to find out who Harvey Kringle's only living kin was. Alma.

Henry drove to Alma's place the next morning with determination dotting his brow. Why didn't she tell him about it? She had no reason to be ashamed—Harvey's sins were his own. The blood he spilled wasn't on her hands. He was trying to think of what he'd say to her when he passed her street. Seeing unfamiliar houses pass on either side of his car, Henry realized his mistake. He banged the steering wheel with his palms and turned onto the next street, intending to turn the car around. He looked up at the sign and noticed he was on Worthington Court.

Henry couldn't remember ever having been on the street before, though he was sure he must have been. He lived in Smithfarm Junction all his life; there wasn't much about the small town he didn't know. But the ancient oaks that lined the streets and the small, abandoned looking houses weren't familiar.

He pulled his car to the curb, turned off the engine, and stepped out. A squirrel lay dead on its side with its paw stuck in a crack in the ground. Henry squatted to get a closer look, not so much at the animal, as at the crack in the asphalt. It was split in the middle of the road – the jagged break didn't extend to or originate from either curb. It was wide, the darkness inside it seeming to be endless, bottomless. It was as if the ground had opened up to ingest the squirrel.

Henry noticed the softness of the ground at the same time that he noticed there wasn't any blood coming from the squirrel. Henry squinted and looked closer; the asphalt seemed to be forming itself around the squirrel, swallowing it.

Henry turned to run away, but the ground had already engulfed his legs, the sensation like fire roasting his skin. He screamed out in pain, clawing at the ground looking for something to hold on to, but found nothing.

Alma snipped the article about the town historian's sudden death on Worthington Court and pasted it neatly into her scrapbook behind the others. *Quite a history,* she mused. Over the years she and her family had amassed scrapbooks upon scrapbooks of newspaper clipping and articles about their street, though the early ones were largely about Harvey and his insatiable need for blood. They talked about his exploits, how he took women who pleasured men for money and bled them to drink of and bathe in their essence. They talked about how he forced the family to drink too, believing that the blood would give them youth, special powers, eternal life. They called him crazy, applauded his capture, cheered his death. After the prison turned his body over to the family, there had been no more intrusion on their privacy. They buried him behind their house and tried to forget. Everything had been fine until a boy cut his leg while playing in the dirt on what is now the paved road of Worthington Court.

"Will you ever be satisfied?" Alma asked the sepia photograph of her great-grandfather. Her thoughts were disturbed by a parcel driver looking for an address.

Vices

Barry sat with $150.00 in his wallet. He tossed fifty on the table like it was nothing, like there was a lot more where that came from. He bet with reckless abandon on the first couple of hands, doubling on thirteen, splitting tens, and hitting on five when the dealer showed a three. He was a little more cautious with the next fifty, but still he missed twenty-one and pushed with the dealer. He thought things might turn around after he bet his last $15.00 on a hand, got twenty, and the dealer busted. But, like the fool he was (at least that's what his wife called him) he bet the entire $30.00 on the next hand and lost.

Barry trudged out of the casino, past the pawn shops across the street where he'd spent so much time, the lights glittering and flashing behind him as he walked away from the waterfront and into the city. He sighed. As he watched his feet take step after step on the dirty sidewalk, he lamented over his life. His wife had wanted to move out of Atlantic City, wanted to get a place in Maryland, right near DC. She said it would be easy for her to get a job there, especially with her associates degree. She could be a banker, a restaurant manager, practically anything. She had visited her sister out there and come home full of ideas. Plans for their future. But Barry said no. He said they would be fine where they were. He guilted her about leaving her mother by herself in a dangerous town, then spouted off about opportunities in the casinos. He told her she could be a banker in AC too, if that's what she wanted to do. She protested, but he didn't listen. He didn't want to leave the casinos. He couldn't imagine having to drive hours at a time to get to them. They were like a lover to him. They comforted him, made him feel like a man. He couldn't leave them. He wouldn't.

But Barry hadn't felt like a man in a long while. The casinos had turned cold, taking his money every time he stepped inside, which was at least three times a week. They only lived a block or so from the strip, and Barry walked over after work, before going home to kiss his wife and newborn son. He knew he shouldn't. He knew that even if he won that night, he'd only go back and lose it. But he couldn't leave it alone. The casinos called to him like nothing else did.

Barry stood in front of his house and looked at it. An attached home that had seen better days. He looked at the chipped paint, the dirty steps. It looked horrible. Like shit. It wasn't the kind of place he wanted for his wife and his baby. But what else could he do? He worked at the cemetery as a gravedigger. He didn't have the skills to do much else. It was hard to buy a fancy $250,000 house in the suburbs on $8.50 an hour.

Barry cast a glance over his shoulder at the strip—he could see the edge of one of the signs and its chasing lights. That old familiar warmth crept into him again. His nipples hardened and his stomach dropped.

Barry got into his car instead of going home.

AC Memorial's gate needed repairing. Barry was sure management would tell him to take care of it when they saw it, but they didn't come around that much anymore, so he let it sit. It was easier to get in with the door loose on its hinges and the lock dangling off. He pushed his way through the gate as he had many times before.

He didn't need a flashlight; he knew the place like the back of his hand. He walked over to the mausoleums and into the one set up for Gerard Mitchell without slowing. There was no need to look around, no need to check behind him to see if anyone was looking. Security never patrolled the place with any regularity and there weren't any houses for a couple of miles. There was no one there but the dead. And they wouldn't tell.

The door opened easier than it should have; Barry had hardly turned the key before the door slid open. Sucking his teeth, he made a mental note to fix it in the morning. Sometimes the new mausoleums came with loose or broken locks and he never found out until he opened it up for a family member. He snickered as he entered the dark space.

Barry tripped over something hard yet disturbingly pliable. *It must be the bench they put out for visitors,* he thought. He remembered that Gerard's mausoleum had some fancy doodads in it – stained glass on the back wall, a brass flower stand, a picture of Gerard's younger self encased in glass. It was a real piece of work. Must have cost the family a pretty penny. Barry's mouth nearly watered at the thought of what Gerard might have taken with him to the grave.

The wind whipped around outside, sounding almost like it was inside the mausoleum. *Sshht. Sshht.* Barry looked around in the impenetrable darkness in spite of himself.

Barry pried the casket open, breaking the seal with a crowbar, and hefting the lid open, his eyes clamped shut. He never got used to seeing them, lying there in their best clothes, their faces rock hard, just starting to go bad. The smell that greeted him was bad enough, but their faces, so statuesque and unreal, always gave him the shakes. So Barry prepared himself for it, keeping his eyes closed until he was ready, then opening them slowly as he exhaled. But there was nothing that could have prepared him for what he was about to see. Even the smell was faint, an afterthought.

Gerard wasn't in there.

Barry's hand felt pinned to the top of the lid. He couldn't move himself away from it, couldn't sort out in his mind what he was seeing. His eyes coursed over the satin lining of Gerard's ornate casket in search of something—anything that would explain what was going on. He hoped that he'd see a clean, unused casket. He hoped that the funeral home made a mistake and sent a new casket instead of the one Gerard was already in (it's hard to tell the difference once they're already closed, right?). But as much as Barry tried to force himself to believe it, to ignore the difference in weight the pallbearers would have surely felt if they carried an empty casket, to ignore the faint smell of decay, the disheveled satin liner where a body might have lain, the hair that dotted the satin pillowcase, he couldn't make himself ignore the *sshht sshht* sound that came from behind him.

"Gerard?" Barry said in a shaky, almost inaudible voice.

Sshht. Sshht.

Barry trembled as he felt the space behind him closing in. He could smell him now, the rot as pungent as it should have been after ten days of death. Tears mingled with the sweat that coated Barry's face as Gerard took his place behind him. Barry turned around to face Gerard out of instinct. He wished he hadn't. Gerard had been a tall man, reaching 6'3" during his life. He bent over Barry's 5'7" frame and stared into his eyes, a terrifying mix of fascination and hunger on his ruined face. Gerard's face was melting – the skin all but dropping from his skull. His clothes seemed to hang from his broad shoulders like they would on a hanger, limp and formless. His lips had curled away from his teeth, his gums were black and swollen. And, God help him, he was smiling.

Gerard trudged closer, laying his cold body against Barry and pinning him between himself and the casket. Barry could see a glint of gold around Gerard's neck and wrist. He laughed bitterly in Gerard's decaying face. Gerard joined in, adding his raspy rendition just before thrusting his fingers in Barry's eyes and plucking them out to sample as an appetizer.

The Color of the Day

The color of the day was like grains of sand, tan and brown, light and dark all at once. From beneath her nails I could see the sun and sky as she did when she took pieces of them for herself.

In the Morning Light

Enraptured as I was, I didn't notice. I awoke that morning to find her resting with the light shining on her upturned face and her hair splayed beautifully on the pillow, framing her head. I looked at her as I always did, admiring the way the sun highlighted her hair, the way the lift of her lips seemed to kiss the rays. Her nipple, her pink flesh touched by the golden glow, called to me. I felt a pulling so desperate from my loins, I shuddered in response. It wanted to feel my mouth around it, wanted to feel the warm softness of my tongue as it circled and licked. And I wanted to do it.

Her cleavage, darkened in shadow, called out to me also. It wanted my hand to separate her breasts, to caress the skin over her breastbone, to kiss it as I always did. And I wanted to. With everything in my being, I wanted to.

The sheet was draped over her hips, just beneath her navel. I imagined my tongue probing her there, circling her bellybutton, darting in and out to touch the sensitive skin inside. I fantasized about running my tongue along the line where the sheet met her skin, teasing her. I could almost feel the heat that would surely emanate from her arousal.

I succumbed. I leaned over her nipple, so perfect in the morning sun, and opened my mouth to suckle it. She hadn't stirred; my darling hadn't roused from her night's sleep. My heart beat faster in anticipation of when she would wake and find herself in the throes of passion. I touched her nipple with the tip of my tongue, wetting it, enticing it to react. I didn't wait; my desire wouldn't allow it. I covered her nipple with my lips, pressing it to the roof of my mouth as I sucked, letting my saliva cascade over her delicious flesh. The coldness emanating from her body chilled my tongue.

Somewhere There's a Love Just For Me

The spray picked up the blood and carried it toward the drain, where it spiraled in warm water before cascading down the pipe. Lovelace let the hot water beat against her skin, warming it to blush, pricking her flesh like needles with every drop. She leaned into it, letting the spray wet her face and hair, rinsing away the blood she had smeared on her cheeks.

Lovelace sang the lyrics of an old Shalamar tune as the warm water washed away bits of flesh from her hair. The water felt good against her skin. It caressed her body the way she imagined Troy's hands would. Or maybe William's. Or Greg's. She had her pick of virile men to sample. A smile crept over her lips as she thought of them.

Lovelace was tired. Preparing Greg had been harder than she expected. His body hadn't accepted the serum as easily as the others had. He clutched to life, even after she cut his throat and hit him over the head with one of the pots from her cabinets. He had lunged at her, grabbed for her throat. His anger was palpable; she could feel it dancing along her skin like electricity. He pressed his thumbs into the hollow at the base of her neck, trying to crush her larynx. But in the end, he fell against her like the others did, nuzzling his face in her bosom before sliding to the floor.

As she lathered, Lovelace remembered all of their attacks. William tried to cut her with a steak knife. Troy tried to push her out of the window. All of them had been feisty, a challenge she relished taking.

Soap bubbles collected at her navel, and she spread them across her stomach. She closed her eyes and anticipated feeling one of her boy's tongues caressing her, delving deeper, pleasuring her. It was only a matter of time.

Lovelace shampooed her hair with thoughts of who would awaken first flooding her mind. Which body would react to the serum best? Who would be strong and sturdy? Who would be stiff and immobile? Her heart beat faster, full of anticipation. She was giddy.

With a last rinse of her hair, Lovelace turned off the water and stepped out of the shower. Her foot sank into a pool of blood. Swearing aloud, she raised her foot off the floor and rinsed it off in the sink. She could see the bloody footprints she created before getting into the shower, leading from the hallway to the shower stall - perfect blots of her feet, as though they had been dipped in ink. Frowning, Lovelace threw a towel on the floor. Using her wet foot, she dragged the towel across the tile while she dried herself, smearing the blood.

The house was quiet. They were waiting for her.

Lovelace left the bathroom, anticipation growing to a heightened pitch inside her. Her bedroom was lit by candlelight, a mood she'd set before getting in the shower. The dim light lit the corners of the room, casting a golden hue on the white walls. William, Greg, and Troy's faces were illuminated by the flickering candle. They were beautiful, works of art in every shade. And they were still. Like stone. Blood was caked on the side of William's head where Lovelace stabbed into his temple. Troy's mouth hung open revealing the tip of his tongue between his darkened lips, discolored from pink to purplish-blue. Greg, her most recent kill, had only been dead for ten minutes, so seeing him rigid and still was no surprise. Their eyes were dilated. The serum hadn't kicked in yet.

Lovelace felt deflated. It was taking longer than she expected. Her father's notes said the serum would kick in within twenty minutes. That's all it had taken for the serum to work on his specimen, the quiet, reserved woman she knew only as Belle, who never seemed to age. Well, it had been exactly that long for the first two, but Troy and William were still dead. Lovelace sighed and started to leave the room when it dawned on her. She chastised herself for not remembering that the serum was based on the height and body weight of a woman, not a man.

Foolish mistake.

It would take a little longer for it to work on her boys.

She almost mistook it for a trick of the eye, imagery created by the dancing flame. But it wasn't the candles, it wasn't the darkness of the room playing tricks on her. Greg had stirred. It was too early, she told herself, but she couldn't deny what she saw. Greg was waking up.

Lovelace sang the bridge low, almost inaudibly, enjoying the staccato rhythm.

Greg's chest remained still, though his shoulders shrugged and twitched. He arched his back, pressing his tailbone against the chair in which he sat before snapping open his bloodshot eyes.

"My love." Lovelace spoke, her voice passing over her lips in a whisper.

Forever

The old, splintering tree bent in the wind. Carly could see it from her window, could almost feel the arch of its brittle frame. It was dying, had been for years. It was hollowed out and ant-infested, broken-limbed and faded. Frail. Sickly. It looked as though it had been bleached; its bark was weathered beyond rejuvenation. The tree wouldn't see the next season.

Unless she did something.

Carly closed the blinds and made her way down the stairs and into the kitchen, thinking all the while of the afternoons she'd wiled away beneath the shade of that tree. That tree which used to have countless branches and lush green foliage. That tree beneath which she had her first kiss; in which she had carved hers and her beau's initials; next to which she had buried her husband and lover of forty years. She glanced at it from the kitchen window before reaching into the microwave. So old. So weary. Much like she felt on that overcast morning. Like she had felt since Gary died.

'C.R. and G.S. Forever', she had carved into the then healthy bark of the tree. Forever.

But Gary was with the tree now. He was letting it die like he had, letting it suffer. Like he had. And Carly was alone in an empty house.

Carly walked barefoot and coatless along the grass toward the tree, ignoring the biting wind and stiff blades as they poked at the bottoms of her feet. She made it to the tree in exactly 12 paces, just like always. She and Gary had counted the footfalls in his last days while she led him out to the aging tree, the friend she'd kept all her life. She set up a chair by the tree and served Gary tea in the waning light of day. He'd fall asleep there, as the sun set and cast shadows over his face. Carly would wake Gary and move him inside once his catheter spilled the contents of his bladder onto the rough bark of the aground roots. She used to smile as they trudged back to the house, Gary as unaware of his unbagged catheter as he was of the sounds the tree made. Sounds of appreciation. Of drinking and slurping.

On that overcast day, Carly heard the cry of frustration the tree emitted as if it were the sound of a baby crying in her arms. As she approached, she could feel the pain, the need, in her stomach as if the hunger were her own. Standing in front of the tree was like standing aside Gary's deathbed, the sour smell of disease emanating from every pore, every orifice. Carly fingered the worn, jagged letters carved in the tree's lackluster bark and inhaled deeply, ignoring the stench of decay.

Forever.

Smiling, Carly uncapped the mug and let the steam mix with the wind. The aroma was pungent, sharp. She swirled the mixture of blood drawn from her wrists and that which had been taken from Gary's body and frozen for a later date. For a time just like that one. She had warmed the cocktail to a palatable temperature before braving the cold to feed her ailing friend. As she poured it into the ground surrounding the withering roots, she could almost feel the blood going down her throat, coating the passage in a velvety stream, as the tree drank.

The Experiment

Papier-mâché and streamers mixed with leather and lace. The party was filled with opposites attracting one another, enticing each other to touch, to taste, to take. The blood on the dance floor paled in comparison to the carnage in the back room, the room where the makeshift bed — a bare mattress stained with the juices of another dead girl — served as his carving table, his laboratory. How they would stare in wonder when they saw her prancing among them, swaying to the music with the elegance of a snake. How they would scream when she puckered her lips to kiss.

Detour

Ten minutes. Cheryl had been sitting in traffic on a side street that was supposed to be a shortcut to the highway for ten minutes. Ten minutes with the sun beaming in her face, heating the cabin of her car. Ten minutes barely creeping along. She was pissed. And she wasn't the only one. People weren't taking it lying down. I mean, it was supposed to be a shortcut after all, right? That it was after 6:30 p.m. in the middle of the workweek and the weather was nice wasn't enough, was it? No, to add insult to injury, the traffic was at a standstill making it impossible for anyone to go home, gather up the family, and enjoy what was left of the evening. That was license enough to lie on your horn these days and flip off the guy in front of you for not moving up the few centimeters of space opened up by the shifting of traffic. You had to keep up, even if keeping up meant moving at a snail's pace.

Cheryl changed radio stations three times in the ten minutes she sat in traffic. She flipped through a long-forgotten novel she found under her seat. She bit her nails, smoothed her skirt. She even tried to call a friend on the cell phone but couldn't get through. By the eleventh minute, she had nothing else to fiddle with.

Sighing, she put her elbow on the door, on top of the rolled down window, and rested her head in her palm. She thought about turning around and going back the way she had come. The same thought had bounced into her mind about five minutes before. She rejected it then because she didn't have enough space to turn around. Not much had changed since then.

Palatial Lane.

Every day she noticed that sign. It was just one of those things that caught her eye, like the way she seemed to always look at the clock at 9:11, both a.m. and p.m., for months after the World Trade Center bombing. Palatial Lane. It sounded regal, rich. As she sat there, stuck, she wondered what the houses on Palatial Lane looked like. Were they the humungous, sprawling estates that seemed to be springing up all over the area? She couldn't image that they would be, nestled in the working-class neighborhood, off the tar-pocked street she was trapped on. Though, when she looked at how the street exited off the road, climbing up a hill, and cresting out of the sight of the street below, she wondered. Cheryl always wanted to turn onto Palatial Lane and check it out. It dumped back into the street she was on and every time she saw the sign signaling the other end of it, she wondered again what was up there. Her mother had always called her nosey. As the desire to turn out of the traffic and onto Palatial Lane mounted, Cheryl conceded that her mother had been right.

She was three car lengths from the entrance to the street. Cheryl rode the bumper of the car in front of her, trying to inch as close as she could to Palatial Lane. After a minute of not moving at all, she decided to drive over the grass. Casting a glance in her rearview mirror, Cheryl drove over the flat land to the asphalt of Palatial Lane. She turned onto the road hurriedly, ignoring the disparaging looks from a driver in one of the cars she passed. She imagined that he gave her the finger, but she suppressed the urge to return the favor.

Cheryl climbed the hill bordered by unkempt woods slowly, taking in the scenery. She crested the hill and cast a glance back at the traffic. The cars seemed so far away. The hill was higher than she thought.

The street was barren. No cars lined the road, no people walked along the overgrown path for an afternoon stroll. As she crept along, Cheryl noticed that the street was abandoned. She encountered an old church first, its paint chipped, its fence broken into jagged pieces. The stained glass had been shattered and boarded up. One of the columns at the entrance had broken in half.

Dilapidated houses lined the street in various degrees of decay. All of the windows were broken, some boarded up, most left as they were. The grass was overgrown and dry, with weeds choking the life out of their roots. It was a ghost town.

So much for Palatial Lane, Cheryl thought as she drove past the empty houses, picking up speed. The street didn't reflect its name in the slightest. Cheryl pressed on the gas, ready to leave the eerily empty street and return to civilization, even if that meant suffering through more traffic. She drove with a purpose, expecting to descend the hill and turn back onto the traffic-laden side street.

But there was no turn.

There wasn't a side street with a similar name connected to Palatial Lane that she could have mistaken to be the same those days she passed it, like Palatial Court or Palatial Road, as Virginia was so fond of doing. Palatial Lane just kept going straight, old houses abandoned for dense forest and dead grass, with no indication of a dip down the hill.

Cheryl stopped the car and threw it into reverse. She was going to turn around and go out the way she came, forgoing the jump on traffic she had anticipated. Something about the street wasn't right. There were no birds chirping, there was no wind blowing. She couldn't even hear the traffic that was only one street away. The way they had been beeping their horns, she should have been able to hear something. Palatial Lane, the desolation of it, made her feel uneasy. She wanted to leave. Immediately.

It was getting dark.

As Cheryl turned the car around, her headlights bounced off of something in the distance. It made her jump; she hadn't noticed anything but trees around her while she was driving. She crept closer to it, inching the car forward to see what it was. A weathered stone jutted out of the ground, partially sunken in the hole beneath it. A tombstone.

A chill came over Cheryl but she didn't know why. She had been in her share of cemeteries—her family visited the graves of dead relatives every year—so she didn't know why seeing the tombstone would bother her. So she had stumbled into a cemetery. So what? Something inside her knew why she was frightened, knew why all she wanted to do was race out of the cemetery and off Palatial Lane as fast as she could. She hadn't overlooked the stone, the stone hadn't been there before.

Cheryl turned back to the road and gunned the car out of the wooded area that she now knew was a cemetery, long forgotten and overgrown. She made for the hill, needing to see the red taillights of the cars stuck in traffic, needing to see another person. A man walking a dog strolled along the path, his step haphazard and sloppy, as though he was drunk. Cheryl's heart calmed at the sight of him, drunk or not. At least there was another person up there. She relaxed, starting to shake the feeling that she was the only other person alive.

As she crept closer to the man and his dog, she began to notice things that her mind didn't want to register, things that her eyes didn't want to see. The man staggering along the walkway did so because his hips were broken. His legs were crushed, the bone depressed and unsteady. His clothing was tattered, his head lolled on his neck. The skin on his face was drooping, falling away with every step he took. His eyes were a sickly yellowish-brown and gelatinous, almost milky. From his mouth dangled the entrails of the dog, still connected to his flailing body.

Screaming within the cabin of the car, Cheryl depressed the gas pedal, jamming it to the floor. She sped past the ghoul and the dog that served as his meal, their images blurring from the speed. She turned the corner and felt her heart race as she anticipated the hill and the traffic below. The woods engulfed her again as they had when she entered the hellish street. She began to calm down. When her headlights reflected the tombstone again, this time illuminating the part of the etching that remained above ground, Cheryl screamed until she felt lightheaded.

When she passed out, her head slammed into her steering wheel and depressed the horn, sending a piercing blare into the darkening night. The traffic a street over responded in kind.

The Proposition

The blade of the knife glistened, kissed by the moonlight that peaked from behind heavy gray clouds. She watched as it came close to her neck, guided by a hand she knew like her own.

"Are you sure?" he asked once more, his voice seeming ethereal in the blackness of night. "Charlene?"

She sighed as the knife cut through the air, sending a breeze that pushed her hair away from her forehead.

Hidden

Legs pass before me, the hustle and bustle of the street oblivious to my cowering. I sit in the shadows, beneath the street, below the world that once fell at my feet: that once adored me like I adored it. Hidden away in the catacombs of this dank, dark place where creatures of the night sing and centuries old spiders dance, I wait. And watch.

Sometimes the men who wander through stumble upon me. They greet me with toothless grins and ply me with cheap liquor. They fall upon me intending to do more than sleep, but never do. I listen to the sounds of their snoring and let it take me to a place far from where I am bound, far away from where I am cursed to remain.

Day turns to night as I watch, then back to day. The people on the street are too busy with their attaché cases and their PDAs, their cell phones and their beepers, to notice me, my eyes peering up from under the dirty grate that seals my hole, my realm, my cave. I smile at them as they go on their way, ignoring the blood, as thick as syrup, dripping from my lips to pool in the cleft of my chin.

The Moment Between

The stumbling wasn't what bothered me. It was the way he fell. The open, face-first dive he took onto the pavement. I could hear his bones crunch as they connected with the unforgiving ground, could almost feel the pain he surely felt in my own body. They said his nose was shattered and his right cheekbone had fragmented, the broken bits sinking into the soft tissue that surrounded his eye sockets. Apparently the glass shards scattered on the sidewalk beneath him punctured his eyes and the flesh on his forehead. But they didn't see what I saw. They couldn't see his smiling face, glowing, alight with resignation, with understanding. They didn't see him step away from his ruined body and walk toward me.

It wasn't the stumbling that bothered me. It was the way he fell as his last living breaths were taken, before taking his first step in Awakening.

By Prescription Only

He pulled a vial from the refrigerator that I was not meant to see. And I wouldn't have seen it if I hadn't just finished rubbing my eyes. I wouldn't have been rubbing my eyes if the reason for why I sat in the doctor's office at 5:45 p.m. on a work night, wondering if the pale little man in the white lab coat was really a doctor at all, hadn't popped into my mind. Again. All day I had been thinking about the visit, dreading the moment when they would call my name and ask me to leave the waiting room and follow them to the private room, or behind a curtain, or wherever they decided to stick me. And it was all her fault.

Some people want to drive cross country and traverse the landscape on their own soil. That's fine, because then you don't have to take immunizations or pills just to be able to go. But not my wife. Sheri wants to see the world, wants to globetrot around like it's a normal thing to do. Like we have the money to do it. Take pills for twenty days? No big deal! Drink this solution and don't eat for 8 hours? Fine! Take a needle fit for a horse's ass? No sweat! Not for her. But it's another story for me.

I once hit a nurse for giving me a tetanus shot. I could feel the medicine burning in my veins, or so I thought. I lashed out without thinking, striking her high on her cheek. She shrieked and pulled away, shaking the needle as she did. My mother said she could hear me screaming from down the hall.

And here I am, about to take a shot that I wouldn't have to take were it not for my wife.

When I tilted my head back I could hear the bones in my neck cracking. The room was quiet – I was the only idiot sitting there waiting to ply themselves with the very disease I was hoping to ward off on the other side of the world. I asked my wife why she would want to visit a country that required you to take a million shots before stepping foot on the soil. She thought I was kidding so she laughed. But I wasn't kidding. And I didn't laugh. Not then and certainly not now.

The woman at the front desk knew my pain. Her eyes were the most sympathetic I had ever seen. She laid them on me from behind thick-rimmed glasses as I filled out every form they could come up with and answered every question about my personal and family health that I could remember. Those same considerate eyes, which seemed covered by a cloudy, murky film, like cataracts, followed me until I found a seat in the dark waiting room. I remarked that they were using mood lighting to disarm the patients. Either she didn't get the joke, or she didn't hear me.

It took her the better part of fifteen minutes to call me into the back, though no one walked in and the phone sat silent. As I walked to the room within which I would take my shot, I noticed that all of the doors were open and the rooms pristine. I tried not to wonder what took so long, but I couldn't. Sheri always says I'm brooding. I guess maybe I am.

The pale, little man in the white lab coat prattled in and glanced at me over his bifocal glasses. Dr. Corning, the nametag on his smock read. MD I hoped. But who knew with a travel clinic?

"You are traveling Europe, you say?" he asked in a nasally voice.

My response was banal – I was too busy obsessing over the shot I was about to take, the foot-long needle that would pierce my skin, the sharp pinch, the burning of the medicine within my veins. I was freaking myself out too much to carry small talk with Dr. Corning.

I shook my head and cleared my throat, trying to snap out of it. The paper covering that they put on the patient table crinkled – I was fidgeting. I pinched the bridge of my nose and closed my eyes, rubbing the lids with my thumb and forefinger, all the while telling myself to relax. It would be over in a minute. I'm a grown man, after all. I need to act like one.

That's when I saw it.

Dr. Corning was pulling it out of the refrigerator when I opened my eyes, shuttling it deftly to the counter and aspirating it into the syringe. The serum, antibody, whatever it was supposed to be was moving.

I bolted upright, putting my feet on the ground and standing, ready to leave. "Dr. Corning, what is that?"

"What?" he asked turning around and squinting in my direction. "The file says you are going overseas-."

"I know what the file says, but whatever is in that vial is… moving."

Dr. Corning's laughter was rich and full, not what you would expect from a man who looked like he did. "Come now, Mr. Wilson. That's ridiculous."

"I saw it." I imagined the thing, some kind of visible amoeba, contorting in the vial of green—was it? —liquid, splitting and reproducing like cells, until there were hundreds, millions of them. I don't remember when I started to sweat, but the arms of my shirt were damp.

Dr. Corning turned to me brandishing the hypodermic needle. "Mr. Wilson, you must relax. Many people are apprehensive about taking needles."

"I saw it, doctor," I said, but I wasn't as sure anymore. The liquid in the needle appeared as clear as water.

Dr. Corning nodded and took a step closer. "Let's get this over with. It won't take but a minute."

I looked at the man, his eyes shining from behind his glasses, his face a mask of sincerity. I thought about Sheri and how badly she wanted to go on this trip. And sat down.

I rolled up my sleeve and pumped my fist as Dr. Corning asked, willing myself to do it for Sheri. The doctor's smile never changed, almost as if it had been frozen on his face. Like a death mask.

I watched as he felt my arm, picking out a suitable vein. I kept telling myself to turn away, to let it happen without watching, but I couldn't. I have never been able to do that. I always have to see what's happening to me. That way the pain is easier to handle. The other way, if I'm surprised by it, hurts all the more.

Dr. Corning lowered the needle and pierced my skin. I clinched up, balling my fist in pain as he guided the needle into my flesh. I tried to relax my fingers, but I couldn't. The shot hurt more than it should have, more than any shot ever had. More than my vivid imagination could ever have concocted. I looked at the doctor, wanting to protest, but I couldn't speak. His face held that same grin, more like a grimace, beneath the film of sweat that coated his brow. His glasses sat low on his nose, pulling at it such that pulsating green veins could be seen beneath his paper-thin skin.

I turned my eyes to the needle, hoping the contents were almost in and the nightmare could be over. The last of the murky green fluid carried a fleshy tail into my vein.

Hindsight

She mourned the burgeoning desire even as it crept up her spine. It was too late to care, too late to change. The tear that fell from her eye to mingle with his that had spilled onto the bedspread was bittersweet.

Eternally Yours

The day was long and tiresome, but Bettie was alert. She waited all day for them to go, to leave her alone to begin her new life. Without him they thought, but she knew better. His playful wink while everyone else cried for him made her sure. Her sister, Norma, thought she was finally letting go of her grief when they lowered him down. The tears that wet her cheeks seemed to indicate as much. But Bettie was laughing. The crying would come later.

Her

Her doting way led him to her door, made him want to stay and take a piece of her with him when he left. When her vengeance reared its head again, for the fifth time since their first meeting, each time more powerful than the last, he wished he'd passed her by.

Sweet Tooth

325

The desire is much like the tickle in your nose at the first sign of pollen, or the insatiable itch beneath the skin after a bug has sauntered over it. The aggravating string on the hem of a skirt that won't lie down, won't be hidden beneath the folds of the material – the one that begs to be pulled, and you want to oblige, but you know you shouldn't. The desire is much like that, some say. Like a craving for sweets, seafood, or pasta. Like an inherent need, quenched only by the feel of fresh blood, like satin over cool skin. Some who kill must kill again to feel whole. Others just like the way it feels. She pondered that as she stood over him, her seventh, as she let his blood engulf her in its warmth.

Aftermath

The turquoise blue rolled over the blade cleaning away the stains Jacqueline made and carrying them away to bubble and roll in the surf. Within his cupped hand Willem brought a handful of salty water to his face after licking what was left of Jacqueline from his lips.

The Joy of Gardening

The soil in the flowerbed that looked into his home office was a rich brown, even in the winter. Every annual that bloomed there was larger than life and in brilliant color. Every day when he left his home his eyes trailed toward the flowerbed, whether blooms sat prettily on their stalks, or if the first of the fall dew settled on the hardening earth, much like they did before he left the house and they landed on his wife's picture. She would be pleased with the way the garden bloomed every year. A smile spread across his face as he considered her view of it.

A Moment in Time

The shadows framed her body, silhouetting her shapely form. She stood basking in the moment, knowing that all too soon her writhing arms would unfold and reach for the one who deemed her beautiful in spite.

The Morning After

The muted singing of the woman on the radio sounded like wailing to her ears. She laughed when she realized how similar she sounded under the blade.

Hangover

Everyone was gone. The clubs were closed and their neon lights were dark. The music that had beat an incessant drum through Charlottesville's corridor was quiet, leaving the space empty somehow. Darren stumbled onto the streets littered with debris—flyers promoting a party the following night at a club in the corridor, take out menus from a restaurant in the vicinity—and looked around. Dead. Like a ghost town.

His head was ringing and a knot had formed on his forehead while he was knocked out. He didn't remember passing out, but he must have. Why else would his tongue be glued to the roof of his mouth by alcohol-laced saliva?

The street was empty, populated only by the remnants of Friday night partygoers and his disheveled, out of sorts self. A movie theater, its lights turned off for the night, loomed ahead and he homed in on it. Stumbling toward it, he tried to remember how he had gotten there.

The club opposite the theater was alive. The doors were open, spilling the party into the courtyard where the under aged "in" crowd got a glimpse of what was to come. He could feel the heat from the club as bodies pressed together and pulled apart, bouncing and jumping, grinding and mashing to the electric guitar. Their heads bounced to the beat like a snaking rainbow; pink and blue coifs spiked and gelled merging together in a dizzying haze. A girl with an earring-laden profile lit a cigarette in front of the door. Her body, pale in the moonlight, glistened with sweat, as did her bald head. With a dramatic puff of smoke sent from her dark-colored lips, she turned to look at him.

And smiled.

He lurched forward, turning away from the movie theatre and lunging toward her, like a man with a purpose. He needed to reach her, needed to touch her, to feel her neck beneath his hands. He needed to feel the stubble on her head scratch his chin. She laughed as he moved, off balance and shaky.

And then she was gone.

In the desolation of the corridor, he turned his head left and right, looking for everything and nothing at the same time.

He awoke on the bench confused. He didn't remember falling asleep, didn't remember sitting down. He craned his neck to get his bearings. The movie theater was behind him, dormant, like a sleeping giant. Before him was the club. It too was closed.

He sighed and let his arms drop to the bench. The cool cement felt like ice to him. He stood wearily, wondering where he had left his car. He remembered that there was a funeral procession when he pulled into the corridor. He remembered thinking how odd that was, a funeral at 10:00 p.m. A man directed traffic, allowing the mourners to turn onto the street unobstructed. He wore the solemn face that all funeral home employees wore, as though they wore a perpetual mask of sorrow. He thought of that man as he made his way toward the parking lot, the way his arm patterned slow circles around, beckoning the mourners toward him, how his face never changed, not even when the wind pushed his hair from his forehead. It was that thought that was pushed out by the girl in front of the club. The girl with the cigarette.

At first he didn't know what it was, that line of darkness that ran from her bottom lip to her chin. It was only when she stepped closer that he knew. It stained her teeth and painted her lips like lipstick.

What he didn't know was whether it was hers or his.

Peculiar

Dotting the water was the most peculiar thing I've seen all day. All year maybe, if I stretched it. They poked out of the murkiness like fingers pointed toward the heavens, cut off at the knuckles by the break. I cast my bait out toward it, wanting to see what might bite. I hit the thing dead on, but it didn't stir. I wadded out a bit further, ignoring the cold water as it sloshed into the top of my boots. What I saw made me think they were fingers, small and delicate, like the ones my Martha had before they bloated up with weight and yellowed from age. But not quite. These were too white and lineless, with no blemishes of any kind. A smile came to my face as I thought of Martha's pretty little fingers and the flat mole that rounded the side of her right index finger. How I used to love kissing that mole as I brought her finger to my mouth. How she used to giggle when I did.

I wanted to turn away and get back to my fishing, but the thing in the water wouldn't let me. I disturbed the water, splashing my arms around in it, trying to shift it so I could see more of the peculiar thing that had caught my eye. When the dark water dipped beneath what must have been the creature's chin, all I could think about was the mole on Martha's finger and how black it was.

All in a Day's Work

Evil. Heinous manifestations from Hell, that's what they are, with their fucking timelines and their condescending glares. I'd like to stick those timelines up their asses and watch them squirm. I wonder if they know? Heather couldn't stop the image from floating into her mind— wads of paper balled up in her hand, overflowing from it, as she crammed them into her boss's ass, laughing as the jagged edges caught the tender flesh of his anus. A smile crept onto her face. It always did when she thought her nasty thoughts.

Fucking prick. Constantly berating her, heaping work on her, weighing her down. She longed to be free, to walk by the ocean on a Tuesday morning without worrying about the office, the due dates, the backstabbing colleagues, the grind. She wished for a day when she didn't have to hear the guy across the hall from her chewing his food, or the girl from the mailroom popping her gum when she dropped off the mail. Every time she thinks about her gray cloth cube and her molded plastic desk, the images of causing pain resurface. And that was almost every day.

Her shoulders were weary, her right hand felt as though it had been clenched tight around a cylindrical shape. She blinked and took in the room for the first time. She was in an office, one just as drab as her cube, but it had four walls and a door instead of three-quarter cube walls. The painting, a lackluster forest scene, faded from years without glass to shield it, hung on the wall lopsidedly. It wasn't noticeable, the raised edge, but she saw it. She always did. Her boss's office.

She was almost happy when she thought about what it could mean. She turned her head to be sure that the office door was closed (it was) and that jackass of a boss wasn't in his chair. Maybe it hadn't been a dream this time. Maybe she had finally taken action. The smile that spread across her face felt feral to her, like an animal baring its teeth.

She began to grind her right hand into her left, wanting to feel his blood squish between her fingers. She pressed and pressed, rolling her knuckles in circles against her palm. When the door opened and her boss stepped inside with three folders in his hand and a smirk on his face, she didn't respond. Instead she raised a finger to her mouth, one that was bloody from where her nails dug into her palm, and touched it with her tongue.

A Glimpse

Reflected in the pool was a girl, her face cherubic beneath the bloody film that tried to mask her beauty. She stared back at me, taunting me with a peculiar gadget she held in her hands—one I'd never seen before, one that might have been from outer space, were I given to such fanciful interpretations. Wallace disliked it when I spoke of such things. Childish, he called them. Fantasies that a woman would never be able to understand. But still I had them, quite frequently in fact; visions that most surely had to be conjured by an unstable mind.

The girl who stared back at me with the contraption lifted to her head, pointed much like a finger to a pensive brow, smiled when she saw me watching, her teeth parting into the most painful grimace I had ever seen. Through the damage the tool caused her, past the membrane of blood and particles that covered her face like a blanket, I could still make out her face. It was pretty, innocent and sorrowful. Much like my own reflection was in the mirror that hung in our home.

Soulmates

From across the room, his eyes bore holes into me as though they looked at my very soul. For one heart-wrenching moment, while I looked back enthralled, seduced, and taken, they did. What they found within was not as beautiful as my outer skin suggested. What they found within held him, captured him in a vice grip from which he could not move. It altered his perceptions and twisted his thoughts, making each of them turn against the other in bloody warfare. I smiled as he slid to the floor shaking, those beautiful eyes of his glassing over and turning cold, watching the horror spread and devour him. I walked toward him slowly, and pressed my lips to his cheek, returning his kiss.

Afterword

"Your mind is off."

"How could such a nice person come up with such terrible thoughts?"

"You would never know she had those horrible ideas in her head."

And my all-time favorite, "You're sick!"

I get my share of, "Where did you come up with that?" and "Your husband must be terrified at night" too. Why? Because I like to write psychological horror. I like it a lot.

I don't fault people for asking those questions or making those comments. On the

contrary, I take them as compliments. If my work didn't spark a tremor or two in a person, if it didn't make them do a double-take behind themselves in a darkened corridor, it would all be for naught. I'll be honest... sometimes when I read my own work, I wonder how I came up with a particular idea, or how I decided to phrase it just right to make the hair on the back of my own neck stand on end. It's invigorating, both writing what I write and reading it. It makes me feel alive.

When I meet people who say they don't like to read horror, I encourage them to try mine anyway. Why? Because my brand is psychological—there's always more beneath the surface meaning, and sometimes, more underneath that. Quiet horror, some might say. I like to write stories that linger with you long after you've put the book down, long after you've settled in for the night. Like watching a movie and discussing the intricacies afterward, I like to write stories that will make you think. So, for the casual horror reader, my work comes off as palatable, "not too bad"... at first. Before long though, something nags at the back of their minds, a minor detail, a concept that was mentioned in the piece but flourished into a full-fledged scenario in the reader's head. It roots itself there, showing itself every time they blink, when they shower, when

they lay their heads down to sleep. Its persistence haunts them, scares them in a way they don't quite understand. It manifests in their restless dreams (yes, I have been told my writing gives people nightmares and that, my friends, is one of the best things a person say to a horror author) and becomes another animal entirely: the one that they have always been afraid of. When they awaken to a new day, they feel off-kilter. As they get their bearings, their eyes fall upon my book lying on the floor next to their bed… and they pick it up to read again, even though they are afraid to.

Yes, I like that.

When people smile, or shudder, or scream (yes, that has happened too) in reaction to one of my stories, I simply smile and say, "Be happy all I do is write it down."

Be happy, indeed.

May 3, 2022
Martinsburg, WV

About the Author

L. Marie Wood creates immersive worlds that defy genre as they intersect horror, romance, mystery, thriller, sci-fi, and fantasy elements to weave harrowing tapestries of speculative fiction. She is the recipient of the Golden Stake Award, a MICO Award-winning screenwriter, a two-time Bram Stoker Award® Finalist, a Rhysling nominated poet, and an accomplished essayist. Wood has won over 50 national and international screenplay and film awards. Wood has penned short fiction that has been published in groundbreaking works, including the anthologies *Sycorax's Daughters* and *Slay: Stories of the Vampire Noire.* She is also part of the 2022 Bookfest Book Award winning poetry anthology, *Under Her Skin.*

Her nonfiction has been published in Nightmare Magazine and academic textbooks such as the cross-curricular, *Conjuring Worlds: An Afrofuturist Textbook.* Her papers are archived as part of University of Pittsburgh's Horror Studies Collection. Wood is the founder of the Speculative Fiction Academy, an English and Creative Writing professor, a horror scholar with a Ph.D. in Creative Writing and an MFA in Speculative Fiction, and a frequent contributor to the conversation around the evolution of genre fiction. Learn more about L. Marie Wood at www.lmariewood.com.

More from L. Marie Wood

A group of friends head out to enjoy a much-deserved night out and paintballing is on the menu. But the team they are playing against has something entirely different in mind. The friends find themselves in a battle for their lives in unfamiliar terrain against well-equipped opponents whose motivations are both irrational and lethal.

Considered, "… a true trip into the darkest depths of what mankind is capable of at its worst," by Midwest Book Review, this story is a classic tale of prey combined with slasher film "edge-of-your seat" vibes with a little modern-day relevance to keep you unsettled.

Blackened Roots is a unique collection and will be a must-have for zombie lovers. Blackened Roots takes the zombie mythos back to its roots. Drawing from a variety of cultural backgrounds, Blackened Roots imagines a world of horror and wonder where Black protagonists take center stage – as zombies, as hunters, as heroes. From a haunting recipe to sibling rivalry, a singing zombie cowboy, a slave ship, and disobedient gods stories, Blackened Roots is a groundbreaking Afrocentric zombie anthology celebrating the rich cultural heritage of the African Diaspora.

Patrick thought he knew what awaited him in the afterlife. He's learning the hard way that he was dead wrong. He is hunted by a race of giant beasts, the likes of which have never been seen by living eyes, and he is surrounded by the newly-dead from worlds beyond knowing. In this Realm, nothing and no one can be trusted.

Patrick's choices will create echoes in the world of the living. He may be the key to salvation in this Hell known as The Realm, but it may come at the cost of his family.

With his legacy on the line, can he make the right choice?

https://www.mochamemoirspress.com

About Mocha Memoirs Press

Established in July 2010, Mocha Memoirs Press's mission is to amplify marginalized voices in speculative fiction genres (science fiction, fantasy, horror). We publish bold, fearless fiction that pushes boundaries and smashes gatekeepers.

We invite you to review our catalog to review the diversity in our stories. You can access the catalog at https://www.mochamemoirspress.com. Join our newsletter here.

You can also find us online:
Instagram - @mochamemoirspress
TikTok-@mochamemoirspress
BlueSky-@mochamemoirspress.com
Twitter (X)- @mochamemoirspress
Facebook facebook.com/MochaMemoirsPress